Charlie Palmer is a 50-year-old voluntary worker who fills his days apologising for a big-boned Labrador. He has previously had a short story published, but *Sitting Down with Evil* is his first novel.

He lives in Colchester with his wife Emma. His two sons, Louis and Oli, have flown the coop for university studies. In his spare time, Charlie follows Formula 1 and travels to satisfy his Epicurean urges. Needless to say, 2020 remains a constant source of disappointment to him.

Emma,

"In all the world, there is no heart for me like yours. In all the world, there is no love for you like mine."

Charlie Palmer

SITTING DOWN WITH EVIL

AUSTIN MACAULEY PUBLISHERS™

LONDON • CAMBRIDGE • NEW YORK • SHARJAH

A CIP catalogue record for this title is available from the British Library.

ISBN 9781398433465 (Paperback)
ISBN 9781398433472 (Hardback)
ISBN 9781398433489 (ePub e-book)

www.austinmacauley.com

First Published 2022
Austin Macauley Publishers Ltd®
1 Canada Square
Canary Wharf
London
E14 5AA

The MPs. You know who you are x

'Hell is empty, and all the devils live here.'
The Tempest,t Act 1, Scene 2

'We are the Pilgrims, master; we shall go
Always a little further; it may be
Beyond that last blue mountain barred with snow
Across that angry or that glimmering sea...'

– Inscription on the clock tower at Stirling Lines

Prologue

In Baghdad, he was Mirin, after the Farsi for death sigh, *mirine mirin*.

He fled through a ventilation shaft in the bathroom stall of a vegetarian restaurant on Sadoon Street and into the night by the banks of the Tigris.

In Belgrade, he went by Bakar, meaning red or copper, after his russet hair. On that occasion, late '93, he stole a fedora and sports jacket from the cloakroom and walked out of the bar into a waiting cab.

In Beirut, he had no name; referenced by a soft whistle and a gentle shake of the head. Just to speak of him was to invoke darkness. That day, an intense, sweaty chase through the souk at Al-Tawileh ended in a dead-end, soon filled with yelling stallholders.

In Belfast, his home town, he was Tam Croall. Or The Technician.

And that was just the Bs.

Book I

1

West Belfast, 1972

The sky darkens quickly. His shift had begun in a crisp twilight softened at the edges with gold but within minutes a bed of bloated clouds, heavy with the promise of rain, rumbles in from the east. There's a low peal of thunder over Milltown Cemetery and the storm breaks with a retina-burning whip of lightning. The rain in the distance falls sideways in blustery sheets and he nuzzles his chin into his jacket. When it finally arrives, it stings like fistfuls of gravel, rattling his teeth and reddening his cheeks. Puddles form swiftly, feeding rivers that run the length of the street, swelling the drains and painting the cobbled street, slick and oily in the sodium glow of the streetlights.

The cleaner leans on his cart. The pavement is wide and loops around the corner but is blocked with a makeshift barricade of rubble, broken bricks and an old fridge. He curses and hefts his cart off the kerb into six inches of black water, soaking his shoes and socks.

'*Fuck's sake.*'

He pulls up the collar of his hi-vis waterproof but the wind is sharp as a paper-cut, whipping up eddies of chip-papers and sweet-wrappers and chilling him to the marrowbone.

'*Fucking fuck's sake.*'

His green-and-white beanie has become a sponge, soaking up the rain and releasing it in rivulets down his face. In some streets, those a stone's throw away, those colours would be enough to earn him a beating, or worse.

But not here. Not in Anderstown.

Glenmachen Street is a canyon of low-slung terraced houses bearing the scars of conflict, silhouetted against the evening sky like a blown fuse box. Broken walls. Gates hanging limply from hinges. Only a few have lights on; the rest look deserted. It's no surprise to the cleaner that he's the only person outside in this squall.

There's a crackle of static in his ear and he brings a hand up to the side of his head.

'Jesus, I might have to put another log on the fire. It's a fuckin' shocker,' says a tinny voice in a thick Belfast accent.

The cleaner glances around, lowers his head and talks into his chest. 'Fuck you, Lucan. If you're cold, get back into bed with LoveSick. He'll warm you up.'

The voice returns with a chuckle. 'Woah. Bit touchy, aren't ya? Nothing a night at "The Plaza" won't cure.'

'It's not just my balls that are blue. It's fucking freezing out here.'

A third voice chimes in. 'Essential talk only, please.'

The cleaner resumes his shuffle into the night.

'Any sign of our man?'

'No. Fuck all. He's got too much sense to be out in this. Run a check on a red Opal, Delta Zulu, Niner Three Three One. Pulled up at the barricade on Tavanagh forty minutes ago, handing out sarnies. Provo meals on wheels.'

A gust of wind catches the cart broadside and nearly upends it. It's a struggle for the cleaner to wrestle it upright. 'Fuck this,' he says to his chest. 'Next job, I want somewhere hot.'

'Ya hated Oman, said all those carpet-kissers wanted to fuck ya or rob ya.'

'Yeah, and for your information, I'd give serious consideration to either option right now. Least there was no chance of trench foot. Little wonder these cunts are always trying to kill each other.'

'Well, take a wee look in the front pouch. Ya might find summat of interest.'

Voice three cuts in again. 'Essential talk only, pl—'

It's drowned out by the Irishman and the cleaner shouting together, '*SHUT UP!*'

The cleaner lowers the cart onto its back legs and comes around the side. Nestled deep in a webbed pouch under a bundle of rags is a half-bottle of non-branded whisky.

'Oh, you fucking beauty!'

'Just don't let Cromer catch ya.'

The cleaner pushes the woollen hat back from his face, takes a long pull, and slips the bottle into his pocket. 'Nae worries, oim jus' gettin' intae character.'

16

'In that case, Mr Robert De fuckin' Niro, I won't keep ya any longer. Check in at twenty-three hundred Zulu; pick up at twenty-four hundred at the yard.'

'Okay, sweetie. Send my love to LoveSick. Tell him to be gentle.'

'You're only jealous,' the Irishman says, and signs off with a click.

The cleaner pulls his hat down to his eyebrows, leans on his cart and sets off down the road. He reaches the end of Glenmachen Street and looks up Donegall Road at the burned-out shell of a bus blocking his path. Someone had painted big white letters on the wall opposite the barricade: EITHER BALLOT OR GUN, OUR *TIME* WILL COME.

'Oh, you're fucking poets now,' he mutters, bending at the waist to pick up a pile of takeaway wrappers that have blown into the gutter.

***

If he hadn't pulled his hat so low he might have seen a Vauxhall Marina—lights off, engine purr carried away on the wind—slow to a halt fifty yards behind him. Or maybe if he'd bent left, and not right, he'd have seen the driver speak into a radio while the passenger leant forward to take something from the glove box.

He also might have called in the registration and been told that the car belonged to a Thomas Croall, South West Belfast Regional Commander, Provisional IRA.

If only.

Owen Twill's life could have turned out very different.

Much later, as blood pooled around his ankles and thick rope cut off the circulation to his wrists, it would dawn on him that he was, for the first time in his life, completely on his own.

2

Basse Desnie, Belgium, 2016

From his vantage point atop a gully overlooking the courtyard of Café Kroegska, Twill lowers his binoculars and shuffles back behind an uprooted trunk. The morning is wide and open, the air sharp. Each intake of breath is an icy stab released in a fist-sized cloud. He stretches out his leg and massages a thigh through his jeans.

It's him, he thinks.

It *has* to be him.

It *could* be him.

Once-red hair is streaked with ash and there's a bald patch the size of an egg that didn't used to be there. He'd gained a few pounds too, the beginnings of a gut over the top of his belt. Add to that the typically Celtic, alabaster complexion and the blood-vessel-cracked nose that must have taken considerable investment, and it *could* be him. But it's the eyes that makes Twill think he's got his man. First seen in a balaclava meant to shield identity, ironically they are the surest marker. Stygian marbles that bely an even blacker soul, Twill would never forget them.

Another look through the binoculars. The courtyard's small and dark in the shade of the café, with stacks of beer crates and broken wood pallets and an overflowing ashtray on an upturned beer barrel. The man stands, side towards Twill and brings a cigarette up to his lips. The tip glows red and a twisting ribbon of grey-blue smoke rises above his head. He drops the butt, grinds it out with his heel and starts for the door. He reaches it, stops and glances over his shoulder. Just for a second. The habit of a professional. But it's not enough for Twill.

He wants it to be Croall. Badly. And he knows the dangers that accompany a desire that's so compelling. He's been here before and won't make the same mistake again. He reaches out for his leg and a long, slow breath comes out in a steady column. He feels himself calm. It's time to let the training take over. He has to confirm it's Croall, but he can't risk being compromised.

Croall isn't the only one who's changed over the years. Glasses are a new addition and he could probably move up a trouser size. What keeps him in a thirty-four-inch waist? Vanity? What next—hair dye and a Harley? But what gives him away—what *always* gives him away—is the limp. You can't un-limp. Twill rubs his leg some more and offers up a curse. The confirmation he needs can't be first-hand.

He lifts his binoculars again. The cobbled streets of Rue Winamplanche are still greasy from the earlier shower but drying under the climbing sun; steam rises from them like spirits. Across the road from Café Kroegska is a bakery and delicatessen, and next to that, a twenty-four-hour convenience store. The previous night he'd pushed his way through a bottleneck of leery youths. One had followed him, aping his limp, and his friends had fallen about laughing. Twill had let it slide. The last thing he wanted was any commotion or attention. He'll go back later and speak to the kids. Kids always need cash. And besides, they don't know it yet, but they already owe him.

Twill lowers himself to his belly, pushes out from behind the tree stump and onto a bed of dead pine needles and twigs. Insects scuttle beneath him and flies buzz around his head.

He can wait, and that's what he'll do. Because *that* is the right thing to do.

***

Twill slows to a stop outside the store and winds down his window. He pushes the peak of his cap back off his face and addresses the tallest boy, a sallow, pinch-faced youth in outsized sportswear.

'You. Come here.'

The boy turns slowly and peers into the car. He dismisses Twill with a 'Fuck off, paedo', and his friends giggle.

Twill sighs and looks across the road at the café. The parasols are down and it's dark inside. He pushes himself up awkwardly, the weight on his bad leg, and launches himself onto the pavement. The cap comes back down. The boys instantly fan out, circling and forcing him against his car. The tall boy spits at his feet and puts on what Twill assumes is his tough face. But it doesn't fool him. He's been here before, a thousand times, in a thousand bars, on a thousand streets. The eyes don't lie. Whoever called them the window to the soul must have had their fair share of bar-room brawls.

Twill spreads out his hands, palms down. 'Take it easy. I got a job for you.'

The kid reaches a hand out behind him and one of his friends hands him a brown paper bag. He takes a long swig, looks over Twill's shoulder into the car and lets rip a shuddering burp. His crew laugh again. He answers in broken English. 'Why dontcha get back into your shitty little car? Your carer must be worried about you.'

Twill pulls himself up straight and takes off the cap, revealing a face scarred like a butcher's block. There's a collective intake of breath from the boys. Some take a step back.

'Didn't you hear me?' the boy says, his voice cracking into a whine. 'Get back in your fucking car.' This time none of his mates laugh.

Twill smiles bleakly as the fight drains from the boy. 'It's simple,' he says, taking a wad of notes from his coat pocket. 'You can't handle simple, then I guess I chose the wrong man for the job.' He turns back to his car.

'Wait,' the boy says.

'You got a phone?'

The tall boy nods.

'Get in.'

***

Fifty euros lighter and five hours later finds Twill back in his hiding place overlooking the café. He's desperate for a cigarette but with the shadows growing longer, won't risk being seen. Instead, he takes a small white container from his pocket and dry swallows a couple of pills. A light comes on and Twill raises his binoculars. Outside the deli, the tall boy flicks his hood over his head and fist bumps a friend. He swaggers across the road and disappears into the bar. Twill frowns. That wasn't in the plan. He wasn't supposed to go alone. Probably didn't want to share his pay out. The instructions had been simple: a face shot of the barman, finish the drink and get out.

The boy had counted his money with wide eyes while Twill spelled it out for him.

'Do. Not. Make. It. Obvious.'

'Yeah, yeah.'

Twill had placed a hand on the boy's forearm and squeezed. The boy had looked up and Twill held his gaze.

'I mean it. Or this ends badly.'

'Alright, alright. I get it.'

'Make like you're taking a photo of your friend. Or the bar. Or anything. But don't make it obvious.'

'What's it to you anyway, old man?' the boy had asked. 'Your boyfriend been cheating on you?'

'Just do as you're told,' Twill had growled, 'and I'll see you back here at nine.'

Twill glances at his watch—8.17 p.m.—leans back against the stump and closes his eyes. A warm glow spreads through his body, starting with a dizzying head reel and reaching all the way down to his toes. For the first time that day, the ache in his leg fades to a more forgiving throb.

***

He wakes with a start sometime after ten. A blue strobe fills the street, lighting the upper branches of his hiding place, and a single, piercing whoop echoes throughout the valley.

'Shit!'

He pulls himself up and stumbles back into the trees. It takes a few seconds to get his bearings. He trips on a root, nearly falling flat on his face, and finds the track down to the road. At the edge of the woods and out of sight, he composes himself and steps onto the road. Two police cars and an ambulance vie for space outside the bar. The first police car must have arrived at speed and was up on the kerb. Twill pulls up the collar of his coat and begins walking, trying to lock his leg at the knee to disguise his limp. The tall boy's friends are gathered outside, talking to a policeman who's scribbling in a notebook. None of them look up as he approaches. There's movement from the front door as a stretcher is wheeled out. A red blanket has been pulled over the boy's head but his trainers poke out at the bottom. One of the gangs looks over and grabs the sleeve of his friend. A thin wail like an animal in pain rings out into the night.

Twill turns on his heels and pivots back towards his car wondering why he feels only a sense of inevitability and irritation and not sadness.

3

Colchester, England

'How was Belgium?'

'Shit.'

The Irishman is big. Double-take big. Broad shoulders and shovel-hands that dwarf a pint glass. A hairline with a V that nearly reaches his brow, set above eyes bright with humour. He lifts his pint but fails to hide a smirk and takes a long draw leaving a foam moustache on his top lip. 'And the leg?'

'Shit.'

This time he laughs and wipes his mouth on his sleeve. He tilts his head, looking Twill up and down, and nods slightly. 'Yer a regular fuckin' ray of sunshine this evening.'

Twill stares back, keeps his expression unreadable, and raises his glass because that's what *he thinks* people do. 'Cheers.'

Lucan slumps back in his chair, two meaty hands raised in surrender and a warm grin replacing feigned shock. 'Cheers to you too, ya miserable fuck.'

Somewhere off to the left, there's a tinny chorus like an ice-cream van and a steady chug of coins, followed by a loud cheer.

'Still taking them pills?'

'Yeah.'

'They help?'

'S'pose.'

'Fuck me, do ya pay by the word or summat?'

'You know me. Strong silent type,' Twill says with a forced smile.

Lucan sighs and shakes his head. 'Never a sentence when a word will do, eh? Well, if I can't rely on the conversation, I'd better ship some beers in.' He rises, tips his head back and drains his glass.

Twill watches his friend walk to the bar. For a man in his sixties, Lucan is still a giant, with a number eight's shoulders and a sunny disposition that contradicts a face that Twill's heard some describe as 'having character'. He's wearing a navy donkey jacket over ripped jeans and thick-soled boots. This is no fashion statement, Twill thinks, not doubting the jeans had been torn through misadventure. Lucan approaches the bar and the drinkers part like the Red Sea. He's *that* big.

He returns a few minutes later and places a pint in front of Twill, taking the seat opposite and fixing him with an amused look. 'So, let's see if ya can string together a few of those words you seem to hoard so preciously. Belgium. Speak to me.'

Twill shrugs. 'Same ol' shit. You know the drill. It's like he knows I'm coming.'

Lucan leans forward on his elbows and his eyes flicker with the merest hint of irritation. 'What are ya trying to say?'

'I'm not *trying* to say anything,' Twill says, and takes a sip. 'I'm just saying, it's like he knows I'm watching.'

'It's not like you two don't have history.'

'What does that mean?'

'Jesus Twill, it means you've been chasing him round the planet for the last decade. He'd have to be some kind of special fuckin' eejit not to assume ya still were.'

Twill holds his gaze, then looks down at his nails.

'But it was him?'

'Yes. It was him.'

'And given you've a face like a smacked arse, he got away?'

'Yes,' Twill says, exhaling heavily. 'He got away. Now, can we talk about something else?'

Lucan's eyes sparkle for a second. 'Who's going to win *Strictly* this year?'

'Oh, do fuck off.' Then adds, '*Please.*'

Lucan reaches over and ruffles his hair. 'There ya go. Nearly a smile, ya little rascal.' They sit in silence for a minute, then Lucan puts his pint down with a start. 'Nearly forgot. Ya get one of these?'

'One of what?'

'Hang on.' Lucan checks the inside pocket of his jacket, frowns, and tries the other side. He pulls out an envelope and throws it on the table.

Twill picks it up and holds it at arm's length, noting the regimental post mark. He steals a glance at Lucan, who nods at him to go on. The letter's on formal paper addressed to R. Puller, and begins *We regret to inform you…*He folds the letter and puts it back in the envelope without finishing. 'Here,' he says, holding it out to Lucan.

'Don't ya want to know *who?*'

'You can tell me. That's what friends are for.'

'Tumble.'

Twill chews on his thumbnail and gives a small shake of the head. 'Fuck.'

Lucan lifts his glass in a toast. 'Tumble. One of the hardest, most loyal friend a man could ever have.'

Twill does the same and they drink heavily, Lucan finishes his with a hearty smack of his lips.

'How?' Twill asks.

'Who fuckin' knows?'

'What does that mean?'

'It means they say he'd struggled since he came back from Northern Ireland.' Lucan gives a little wiggle of his eyebrows. 'Like who fuckin' hasn't?'

Twill draws his head back. 'He offed himself?'

'What a beautiful turn of phrase ya have there, Mr Twill. Have you ever considered a career in the Samaritans? But yes, as you so succinctly put it, the language employed by the MOD would suggest our dear old friend Tumble has, indeed, *offed himself.*'

'Fuck. How many's that then?'

'If true, that would make him the third, after Mincer and JR.'

The hush is broken by the tinkle of breaking glass and a cackle from the table behind. Lucan is quick to swivel around.

Twill stares down at the table and raises his pint… 'Early fifties. Sequin top. Blonde hair. Too much lipstick…and too much white wine.'

Lucan turns back and beams. 'I fuckin' love this game.'

'Shoot.'

'Okay, now then…' Lucan clucks his tongue against the roof of his mouth and scans the room. 'Three at the bar. Middle one. Go.'

Twill sighs. The idea bores him but he plays along and puts his hands over his eyes. 'Male. Six foot. Grey suit. Double-breasted. Nursing a half of ale. Dark hair parted on the left. Needs to use a dandruff shampoo. Say, mid-forties.'

Lucan giggles. 'And next to him?'

'Male. Tracksuit. Fat. Really fat. Bald.' Twill pauses. 'No...not bald, shaved head. Snakebite and black. Late thirties.'

Lucan leans forward, his eyes shining with mischief. 'No. The other side.'

'Tall, six three or four. Brown leather jacket. Hair gelled up. Jeans. *Fucking skinny jeans.* What was he thinking?'

Lucan looks over at the bar then back at Twill who still wants an answer to his question. He shakes his head and spins around. The three men standing at the bar are exactly as described. He turns back and Lucan is chuckling.

'Fuck off.'

Lucan puts an empty glass back on the table. 'Perhaps if ya spent a bit more time at the bar, instead of just talking about it...'

Twill gets up, stretches his leg and hobbles to the bar, glancing around. Top left, up by the optics, closed-circuit camera. Not wired. No LED. Possibly fake. Double doors off to the right, twenty metres away, patterned glass, impossible to see through. Four, maybe five seconds' sprint. Bay windows opposite the bar. Locks have been painted over in thick matt, same as the frame. Probably not been opened in years. Couldn't be opened now. Back door leads to a walled beer garden. Thirty metres, say six to seven seconds. Double doors the only exit...

'What can I get you?'

Twill orders two pints and eyes the jeans on the man next to him while he waits. *Ridiculous.* He goes back to the table. Lucan has spread the letter open.

'Cheers.'

Twill nods and lowers himself back into his seat.

'So then, ya going?'

'Where?'

'The funeral, Captain Autismo.'

'I don't think so.'

'Why the fuck not? There'll be a few of the boys there. Turn it into a reunion. What do ya say?'

'I don't know. If they wanted me there, they'd have invited me.'

'Aww,' Lucan says, and sniggers. 'Did they hurt yer feels?'

'You have to believe me when I say I couldn't give less of a shit.'

Lucan cocks his head. 'When ya moved back into yer ma's, did ya let the regiment know?'

Twill shakes his head.

'There ya go then? Went to the wrong address. It's settled. Be good to get the boys all together again.'

'If there's any left…When is it?'

Lucan rereads the letter. 'Two weeks tomorrow. Thirteenth.'

Twill shrugs.

'Oh, sorry. Ya got one of them there calendar conflicts? What ya got planned, a visit to Tate Modern? Spot of dressage? The opera maybe?'

'Okay, okay. Jesus H. I'll go if you shut the fuck up for one minute.'

'Cromer's going to be there.'

That fucker.

'Christ, man, look at the face on ya. Uh huh. Got his scribble at the bottom,' Lucan says, sliding the letter across the table. 'Besides, why wouldn't the commanding officer be there?'

'Dunno,' Twill mumbles, thinks for a moment, then adds, 'Isn't he some kind of big deal now?'

'Yeah.' Lucan puts on a posh voice. 'Government minister, don't ya know?'

'Ooh,' Twill says and they both laugh.

'Ya all settled into your ma's?'

'S'okay.'

'Gonna stay there?'

Twill blinks. 'Maybe. Lots of memories.'

'How long's it been?'

'Couple of years.'

Lucan gawps ridiculously and rubs his forefinger and thumb together. 'Ya worked out how to spend all that inheritance yet, apart from Project Croall?'

Twill takes another drink and doesn't answer.

'Well, just a suggestion,' Lucan says, holding his empty glass upside down, 'but you could make a start by getting some fuckin' beers in.'

***

Two hours and five pints later, Twill returns from the bathroom to find the table empty.

'Fucking Lucan.'

It's a relief to leave the pub and the cacophony behind. Public spaces make him queasy; too many voices wrapped up in a wall of noise make it difficult to keep track of individual ones. Giving up control doesn't come easy. He lets the doors close behind him and stands still for a moment drinking in the quiet. The night air is crisp and cool. An owl calls out into the dark and a distant babble of laughter comes from behind. A fat moon pokes out from behind a fleecy cloud and casts everything in a silvery wash. Twill sets off home, the evening's drinks numbing the pain in his leg.

At the end of the road he turns right into the woods. A short cut not for the faint-hearted, but he doesn't scare easily. The walk is uneventful apart from a stumble into some bracken and by the time he reaches his front gate, his bladder is fit to burst. A quick inspection reveals a short length of clear tape still connecting the gate to the frame. He steps into his front garden, closes the gate behind him, drops to his haunches and puts the tape back in place. A short fumble with the key and the front door swings open. Twill falls into his hallway engulfed by familiar smells. A quick tap on a keypad on the wall stops the alarm beeping. He checks all the doors off the hall and upstairs landing and satisfied there have been no visitors, takes a piss that seems to last forever. Back at the front door, he waits. There is a rustle in the hedge separating him from next door. Then still. He makes a clicking sound with his teeth and two green eyes appear.

'C'mon, Graham, you dopey bastard. S'only me.'

A grey striped cat emerges and pads past pausing only to wrap its tail around Twill's leg.

'In your own time.'

In the kitchen, Twill washes down two pills with a glass of water and wanders into the front room. He collapses into a lumpen floral armchair opposite a fireplace glowing orange with plastic coals. The curtains are a thick serge, heavy enough to blot out light and sound and stop shrapnel. The chair is the only furniture in the room. All framed photographs, vases, plates and his mum's prized porcelain shire horses have been packed away in the loft. Even the ducks on the wall came down. He'd seen first-hand how bombs turn trinkets into deadly buckshot. A clear room saves lives.

The pills kick in and his eyelids grow heavy. He shuffles in his chair and reaches beneath him. The cat waits until he's settled then curls at his feet in front of the fire. Twill slips a cushion behind his neck and lets the darkness in…

The pond's in a wooded glen and he's up to his knees in dark, brackish water. He's staring at a bed of reeds that border the pond's edge opposite. Occasionally, a golden spire of light breaks through the trees and glints and dances on the surface temporarily blinding him. Small clouds of midges' blur and disturb the air. From somewhere far off beyond the tree line and into the distance, Gaelic music plays. But the mood at the pond is far from cheery. A stiff, northerly breeze ripples across the water whispering into his ear and sending his heartbeat racing. He wants to step backwards but his legs won't obey him.

The reeds opposite bow and rustle, and something stirs behind them.

His right leg is throbbing like an infected tooth. He looks down. The flesh just above the knee is a deep gash, grainy and plum-coloured. He applies pressure, pinching the sides together but the tear widens and splits until he can see chalky bone within.

'*FUCK.*'

He tries to lift his legs but he's stuck firm and every attempt pushes him further into the mud. He bumps his hips but only sinks deeper. Fetid, black water laps mockingly at his waist.

There's a swish and the rushes quiver, then fall still again.

He remembers his training and lowers himself backwards into a horizontal position. The water is so cold it steals the breath from his lungs. Still, his legs refuse to budge and onyx, stagnant liquid stings his eyes and fills his mouth. It takes every ounce of strength to straighten up; the effort leaves him spluttering and gasping for breath.

The reeds shake again, this time without a sound. Twill knows he's being watched. Whatever's there is anticipating him to weaken. Biding its time.

It won't have long to wait.

Pain slices through his leg and a mass of shiny black insects swarms from the open wound. Twill screams and bats them away as they take to the air. They twist and turn as one, a murmuration of clacking, winged beetles. They rise high then swoop down, enveloping his head. He opens his mouth to scream and it fills with the piceous scarabs. They land on his face, his hair and his screwed-up eyes, the air around him thick as a cloak. He roars and splashes water over his face. The buzzing black cloud disperses, leaving him coughing and gasping for air.

The pond falls silent again. His gaze is drawn back to the clumps of reeds opposite. The grasses part and a vast swan, tall as a man and white as snow, glides gracefully out onto the water towards him. The bird arcs wide and Twill has to twist at the waist to follow its path. For a moment, he forgets the pain in his leg, the horror of the beetles, and is struck dumb by the creature's beauty. It sashays to a halt in front of him. The plumage is a brilliant white, large wings are folded against its body and a loose neck loops up to a small black head with an orange, patterned beak. Twill stares at the bird. His breathing slows and his anxiety drains away. The fear has dissolved. The swan gives a kick and glides closer, stopping two feet away.

Twill smiles and reaches out.

The bird rears back and opens its wings, swallowing Twill in its shadow. Charcoal eyes flare red and its beak opens exposing a row of sharp teeth. The air shakes with a shrill howl. A scream rises in his own throat but no sound comes out. The beast lurches forward and Twill feels the white-hot agony of teeth tearing at his flesh.

***

Twill wakes like he's bursting through the surface of a swimming pool, and it's a few seconds before he realises the high-pitched wail is his. He pushes himself up on shaky legs and wipes sweat out of his eyes.

'Fuck that,' he mutters. He leaves the room and climbs the stairs to his bedroom.

4

Kings Cross, London

Even with his bad leg, Twill moves like quicksilver. Short, liquid movements from doorway to doorway, ducking under canopies, tucking in behind shoppers with raised umbrellas. Anyone watching on CCTV would be hard put to pick him out from the crowd, which is no accident as every camera's position has been noted, and avoided.

He's decked out in neutral colours, grey to match the wet pavement and granite sky. Hood up, head low, chin tucked. He makes as if to join the queue at a bus stop, then darts to the other side of the street, doubles back and crosses over again, narrowly avoiding a black cab. He continues in his original direction. A sideways lurch brings him into the grand portico of a Georgian townhouse. A brass plaque on the wall reads *The Wellington Centre* and underneath, on a smaller sign, next to a row of buzzers, *Dr Emily Walsh, MD, PsyD, LCSW.*

***

'You look tired.'

'I am.'

The doctor crosses her legs and inclines her head. 'Was it the dream again?' Twill dismisses her with a wave of his hand.

'Was it the same as the usual ones?'

He doesn't answer, preferring to stare at his feet.

'What do you think it means?'

'What do *I* think it means?'

'Yes. What do you take from it?'

He shakes his head, glances at the window. 'Some fucking racket this is. How much are you getting paid to ask me what *I* think?'

The doctor brushes lint from her trousers and looks up. 'I think we've had enough sessions to be candid with each other. You don't like coming here, do you?' When he doesn't reply, she adds, 'You think this is all a waste of your time?'

'I do.' He grins. 'What do *you* think *that* means?'

Walsh taps a pen on her teeth. 'I think you're embarrassed about how the dream makes you feel.'

Twill pushes himself up with a grunt and grips the edge of his armchair, stretching his leg out.

'Is the leg still bad?'

He shoots her a look. *Unbelievable.* 'Only when I sit in one place for too long.'

Walsh scribbles something in her notes and clears her throat. 'Do the pills help?'

'Huh. They knock me out. I s'pose it stops me thinking about my leg.'

'Is that a bad thing?'

Twill thinks back to a wood in Belgium and a young man in sportswear with his head twisted at an impossible angle. 'It has its…downsides.'

'Like what?'

Twill switches legs and leans forward. 'I like to be in control.'

'Why do you think that—'

Twill raises his index finger. 'Uh-uh. There doesn't have to be an answer for everything. Let's leave the questions for today, eh?'

Walsh flushes, maybe with anger, maybe embarrassment, and straightens her glasses. 'Do I have to remind you that these sessions are mandated by the MOD?'

'No, you fucking don't. If they weren't, I wouldn't be here.'

'And what if I were to tell you I've had significant success treating PTSD in other patients?'

'And what if I was to tell you'—he waves an arm across the room—'that these certificates, these leather fucking books…*you*…it's all bullshit. You don't live in my world. I can't think of a single fucking thing that makes you qualified to tell me how to live my life. You and your fixed-rate mortgage, new car every three years, Chardonnay in the fridge. Bet you've got a fucking dog.'

Walsh takes off her glasses and smiles warmly. 'Two actually. And I prefer a New World Sauvignon Blanc. Also, what qualifies me is eight years of post-graduate study and twenty years in practice.' She leans forward on her elbows.

31

'It doesn't have to be like this, Owen. Take a seat, please. Even if you think you're just ticking a box, you know a failure to comply has consequences. Neither of us want that. Plus, you never know, I might surprise you.'

Twill mumbles and flops back into his chair with a sigh.

'Good. Thank you.' Walsh puts her glasses back on and flicks back a couple of pages of her notes. 'What,' she asks without looking up, 'is it about the swan that you don't like?'

'What don't I like about an animal tearing me apart? Why don't you take a stab in the dark?'

'Animal?'

'Swan. Whatever.'

'But it's not whatever. It *is* a swan. A beautiful, proud creature. And maybe *that's* why you're scared of it.'

Twill coughs into his hand. 'I didn't say I was scared of *anything*. Your words. Not mine.'

'Perhaps the swan is Caitlyn.'

'Oh, here we fucking go. What do you fucking know about Caitlyn?'

'As your therapist, I have full access to your service records. Would you like to talk about her?'

'No, I fucking wouldn't.'

Walsh nods and writes something down. 'You mentioned downsides to the pills. Tell me what you mean.'

Twill rubs his jaw. 'They help with the leg…but they're like knockout drops.'

'How bad is it? Do you want to try something new?'

Twill waves her away again. 'Nothing I can't live with.'

Walsh continues to stare. He doesn't speak. A moment later, she breaks the silence.

'You're immobile in the dream. The wound in your leg. The attack, swan or otherwise. I think we both know what this is all about. Are you ready to talk about the night it all happened?'

'What night what happened?'

Walsh pops the button on the end of her pen and attaches it to her clipboard. '*The* night—the *nights* it happened,' she says, looking deep into his eyes. 'The reason why you're here.'

32

5

Colchester, England

The number twenty-three bus is scheduled to leave Prettygate at 2.23pm, head down Straight Road and arrive seventeen minutes later at its destination in the town centre outside the Odeon. From there it's a two-minute walk to the Fox and Fiddler. Twill takes a seat at the back of the top deck, giving him a clear view of who gets on and off. He's dressed in full regimental uniform with blue striped trousers that bite into his waist and a matching stable belt. But instead of pride, he feels self-conscious. After a lifetime of trying to blend into the background, dressing up like a toy soldier doesn't feel right.

But today isn't about him.

Much to his irritation, the traffic is backed up, but he still arrives with time in hand. The bus stops on Head Street and announces its arrival with a hydraulic hiss. The pub is visible from the top deck. He knows the bus won't leave for five minutes so uses that time to scan the area. There's the usual beggars outside the cashpoint. Kids waiting for dates by the Odeon, immersed in their phones. Further down, the traffic lights are green. If he gets up the second they go amber, he can be out and across the road without having to wait for them to change.

He knows because he's practised.

As he prepares to leave the bus, a crowd outside the pub catches his eye. It's too far away to pick out faces but he gets a tingling sensation in the pit of his stomach. He pushes himself up, cursing when he scuffs his boot on the seat in front, and takes the spiral steps, holding on to the rail for support.

The lights turn red just as he reaches them and he crosses the road without a break in step, head down, ignoring the looks he gets. The mob he's seen from the bus is a group of heavily tattooed men with pot bellies and shaved heads, some waving home-made banners. He glances at his scraped boot, swears, turns his attention to the crowd. They're circled around two men in uniform—nose to nose—one black in his mid-sixties, the other white and half his age.

Twill shoves his way through to the centre of the throng. 'Alright, Cilla.'

The black man turns and greets him with a grin. 'Twilly, you ol' bastard!'

'You got a hanky?' Twill asks, looking down at his scuffed boot.

Cilla looks from Twill to the man in his face and back again. 'Erm, I'm a bit busy at the moment, mate.'

Twill looks at the man squaring up to his friend. Mid to late thirties. Six foot three. Non-regulation boots. Trousers too tight and too short, stopping just above the ankles, exposing white socks. Sleeves of his jacket too long, as is the hair that's poking out from the side of a loose-fitting, peaked green cap. Row of five brightly ribboned medals.

Twill turns back to Cilla. 'How ya been?'

Cilla shakes his head and chuckles. 'Really, Twill? You wanna do this now?'

The tall man shifts his weight from one foot to the other and takes a step forward. 'What's this? Dad's Fucking Army?'

'No,' Twill replies in a measured, almost mechanical voice, turning to face him. '*Her Majesty's* Army.'

The tall man blinks.

Twill turns to Cilla. 'Who's your mate?'

'No mate of mine. Britain First, apparently.'

Twill frowns and looks back at the tall man. 'And *who* or *what* the fuck are Britain First when they're at home?'

'Think of them as a two-bob, rent-a-Nazi outfit. Sergeant Bilko here thought it was funny to make monkey noises at me.'

Twill plucks a medal from the tall man's jacket, not taking his eyes off him. Nothing gives him any reason to believe violence is imminent. In fact, all indications are to the contrary. Squirrelly eyes, dry mouth. He's showing all the symptoms of being more concerned with how to *avoid* violence right now.

Twill dangles the medal—silver with a blue-edged ribbon that fades to white over a green central strip—under the man's nose, and when he speaks, the words come out in a low growl. 'The South Atlantic Medal. Even if you'd crawled out of your mum's cunt by '82, I very much doubt you were eight thousand miles away fighting the Argies.' His voice lightens. 'Or were you?'

The tall man drags his palms down the side of his trousers and looks around at his mates.

'Where did you get it?'

Cilla steps forward and spits at his feet. *'Fucking Walt.'*

Twill continues. 'I asked you a fucking question. *Where did you get it?'*

'Give…give it back,' the man croaks.

Twill sneers and slowly raises his hand. The tall man flinches and pulls away. Twill points to his sand-coloured beret. Central is a pin of a downward-pointing dagger, wreathed in flames. The tall man's eyes widen and his breath catches.

Twill relaxes his face. Impassive. Still as a millpond. His voice drops an octave. 'Take it off.'

'W-w-what?'

'Take it off. Every. Last. Fucking. Thing.'

'But—'

Twill plants his feet in a wide stance, legs slightly spread, arms locked behind his back. All the while, scanning the man's face.

The man starts undressing, only pausing when topless. He looks at Twill, who nods curtly. He unbuckles his trousers and continues until he's shivering before them in a pair of Spiderman Y-fronts. He hooks his thumbs into the top of his underwear and shoots the older man a plaintive look.

Twill shakes his head. 'Now, be a love and fuck off.'

Twill hasn't finished speaking before the man's on his heels, sprinting down St John's Walk, boots clacking on the pavement.

A cheer goes up behind him and Twill turns. A group of men in uniform are standing outside the pub, pints in hand. Beast, LoveSick and Ghost. Next to them and at least a head taller than the rest, is Lucan, laughing so hard tears are streaming down his face.

Twill looks down at his boot then back up at his friends. 'Anyone got a hanky?'

***

'And a coke for the lady,' Ghost says, handing LoveSick a drink.

'Fuck off,' he replies in a heavy Scouse accent.

'You want some ice, sweetheart?' Beast chips in.

'Maybe one of them ickle umbrellas?' Lucan adds.

There's more laughter.

35

'The both of youse can fuck off,' LoveSick says, shaking his head. 'To think I was actually looking forward to seeing you cunts again.'

'Aw, don't be like that,' Lucan says, punching his arm and spilling his drink. 'Cunts.'

Twill lifts his pint and looks around the table. Beast is fatter, LoveSick thinner and Ghost still so pale as to be almost translucent. Cilla's head's topped with a crop of curly white hair, like candy floss. He'd recognise these oldest of friends anywhere but it's been so long since he's seen them, the changes are all the more marked. They look how he always imagined their dads looked.

Lucan pitches his glass skywards, shouts, 'Tumble,' and the rest of the soldiers chime in.

The toast over, Twill says, 'Why the coke, LoveSick?'

Lucan wiggles his fingers in the air. 'Ooh, it speaks!'

'Careful,' Beast says, then adds in a camp voice, 'or he'll strip you down to your pants!'

Twill shakes his head and takes a deep draw on his pint. 'You're safe, you fat prick.'

They all laugh apart from LoveSick. 'Dunno. Guess it was becoming a problem.'

'A problem for who?'

LoveSick looks up from a table loaded with glasses. His skin is grey and blotchy. Dark eyes are set deeply into bruised folds of skin. He looks tired. Maybe sick.

'The police. Got picked up a few times. You know, usual stuff. Coupla scraps. Nothing serious. Then one-night things got out of hand. Chinned a copper by mistake, like. Spent a few nights inside.'

'Fuck,' Beast says.

LoveSick shrugs. 'I never thieved or nothing like that.'

He splutters with such an earnest expression that Twill feels a twinge that lies somewhere between embarrassment and irritation.

'It's just the booze made me angry all the time. I gave them Cromer's name and he got me out. He were brilliant. They got me seeing some quack…'

'You too,' Ghost says. It's barely a whisper.

'…and she says if it happens again I lose my pension.'

An uneasy quiet descends and they sip their pints in silence.

'Why didn't ya come to the service?' Lucan says to Twill.

Twill runs a finger around the edge of his glass. 'No point. Don't believe in all that stuff. That wasn't Tumble they put in the ground.'

'S'pose so,' Lucan says, taking another drink.

'Was Cromer there?' Twill asks.

'Oh, yes,' Lucan says, slapping his knees with both hands, 'and didn't he look the part!'

Twill nods and drains his glass. 'Anyone?' he asks, holding it up.

There's a round of murmured consent.

'C'mon,' says Lucan. 'I'll give ya a hand.'

At the bar, Lucan pulls him in tight. Twill tenses, keeps his arms by his side.

'You okay, mate? Ya look tired.'

'All good,' Twill replies, trying to catch the barman's eye.

'Listen,' Lucan says, laying a hand on Twill's shoulder. 'Cromer said he's coming down. We're not going to have a problem, are we?'

'Six pints of IPA and a coke,' Twill says to the barman, and then to Lucan, 'Not with me, you won't.'

'Good.' Lucan grins and digs an elbow into Twill's ribs.

Twill leans forwards and whispers into Lucan's ear, 'Any word on you-know-who?'

Lucan shouts to the barman, 'And give us some crisps and peanuts,' then to Twill without looking at him, 'You know the drill. He'll go to ground for a few months. When there's anything to say, you'll be the first to hear it.'

Back at the table, the mood lightens, and Lucan leads them in another toast. "The Eagles!"

Twill strikes up a conversation with LoveSick. On the other side of the table, Cilla is busy explaining his marital arrangements to Ghost; there is much shaking of heads and clucking of tongues. Beast sits at the far end, on his own, fast emptying a packet of peanuts.

The door opens and Cilla leaps up, straightening his back and shoulders. Ghost and Beast stand too. Lucan exchanges a nervous look with Twill and follows suit. Twill takes his time, finishes his drink, wipes his mouth with the back of his hand and pushes himself up.

'Gentlemen,' Lieutenant-Colonel Ellis Cromer says, with a cut-glass accent and a politician's polished smile. 'At ease.'

Twill spends the next thirty minutes avoiding his commanding officer. His colleagues' breathless efforts to have their five minutes irks but make it easier for him to remain invisible. He inserts himself in a conversation with Ghost, his back to Cromer, hoping he'll take the hint. But he can feel his old boss's eyes on him.

He keeps one ear on the group behind. With the conversation winding up, he takes this as his cue.

He makes his excuses and hobbles to the bathroom, passing a mirror on the wall that shows Cromer staring after him. The door closes. He splashes water on his face and examines himself in the mirror. Salt-and-pepper hair is thinning and his forehead's heavily creased with worry lines. His eyes are small and beady and a small tuft of hair sprouts from a patch on his cheek he missed shaving. Not wanting to dwell on the old man staring back at him, he smooths his hair into place and turns. Wedging the door open with his foot gives him a view of the table. All his friends are there but Cromer's chair is empty. He grunts, satisfied, and steps out into the saloon.

A small but firm voice halts him in his tracks.

'Anyone would think you were trying to avoid me.'

Twill straightens his back in an act of muscle memory, 'No, sir.'

'Oh, come on, Twill. I think we can drop the formalities.'

Twill turns and looks into his boss's face. Chestnut hair has faded to oatmeal, and is combed into a side parting. Moist eyes are framed by laughter lines and pouches of sagging skin but his jaw is square enough. And in a tailored, double-breasted suit offset with regimental tie, he could still pass for handsome.

Cromer's face softens and he gestures to a small table away from the others, already laid with two pints. 'C'mon. You can give me five minutes.'

Twill lets himself be led by the elbow and eases himself into the chair opposite. Few people in the world could get away with this. Perhaps only the one.

'So,' Cromer begins, rubbing his hands together, 'what have you been up to?'

A narrowing of the eyes suggests he's in the habit of asking questions he already knows the answers to.

Twill shrugs and avoids contact by sipping from his pint.

'I'm reliably informed that Belgium's pretty grim this time of year,' Cromer says, his words hanging in the air.

Twill takes a sharp intake of breath and lets it out between his teeth. 'If you already know, why fucking ask?'

Cromer's lips curl into a half smile. 'Now, now, Twill. Let's not forget we're all on the same side here.'

Twill looks at his old boss and feels nothing. He can't even be bothered to fake a response, which is his usual reaction.

'Listen,' Cromer says, leaning in, 'I know because it's my business to know.'

Twill looks at his watch and back at Cromer, a familiar tickle growing at the back of his throat. 'What do you want, a round of applause?'

'You know what I want, Twill.'

Twill fusses with his tie, blanks his expression, and looks back up. 'It looks to me like you've got everything you want.'

Cromer chuckles and drinks deeply from his pint. 'Where in the merry fuck do you think Lucan gets his intel?'

Twill stiffens. His focus intensifies on Cromer but he stays mute.

'Don't you ever wonder where it all went wrong?'

'Try every fucking day.'

'Yes, well, we've got that in common. You may not like it Twill, but we're linked. We've got the same DNA. Me, you, LoveSick, Lucan…everyone— there's a shared history that binds us together. And we all want the same thing here.'

'I guess some just want it more, eh?'

Cromer's eyes flash for a moment and he slams a fist down, sloshing beer from their glasses. '*Don't you fucking tell me what I want.*'

The surrounding tables go quiet.

He leans in and lowers his voice. 'I get that you think you've earned the right to be angrier than us, but you're wrong if you think that means we don't care.'

'Look.' Twill puts his glass down and speaks slowly and clearly. 'If you want to feel outrage on my behalf, that's fine. I hope it makes you feel better about what happened. But until you've got something of interest to say, why don't we drop the long-lost pal routine, eh?'

Cromer tips his head back. He drains his pint, his eyes on Twill all the while. He scrapes his chair and stands, pulling on his sleeves and straightening his tie. The smile is one of a consummate professional, cheesy and spread across his face like a game-show host's.

'I'm not in the habit of asking questions twice, Twill. There won't be a third. *Don't you ever wonder where it went wrong?* Where the weak link was?' He turns to the table of old soldiers laughing and chatting amongst themselves, then back to Twill.

'One of them? Fuck off.'

'I didn't say that. Sometimes it pays to listen to what *isn't* said.'

Twill puts his hands under the table to stop Cromer seeing his balled fists.

'Sometimes,' Cromer continues, 'it's who *isn't* there that's important.' He stands and pats down his pockets. 'Come see me at my office. I believe I may have something that could be of interest to you.'

With that, he turns and walks back to the others, leaving a waft of expensive cologne in his wake.

'Fucking joke,' Twill grumbles and reaches for his pint.

It's only then that he spots the business card on the table.

6

Cornwall, England

Eagle's Croft is a modernised Jacobean house with panoramic views over Crantock Beach. A contemporary hillside monolith on one side, red-brick manor house on the other, it has the unique characteristic of overlooking both the Celtic Sea and Gannel Estuary. A small fortune has been spent bringing the original building into the twenty first century but it's the glass-fronted extension where Lewis Bridges spends most of his time. From there he can see the boats bobbing on the waves in their hunt for sardines, and the tourist boats approaching directly behind on the Gannel. A mossy slope from the double glass doors leads to a winding path down to a boathouse on the beach with a heavy iron gate. The whole property is encircled by a six-foot perimeter fence with motion-sensor floodlights at regular intervals. The CCTV cameras are placed so as to be visible to the trained eye, but not obvious.

Bridges asks for, and receives, no visitors.

The single-room extension is German designed: minimalist open plan; three tall, white walls with bright splashes of modern art lit by down-lighters; polished marble floor. The fourth wall, overlooking the bay, is double-height glass and runs floor to ceiling. Furniture is sparse. There's a white gloss kitchen that looks like it's never been used, a few bits of gym equipment, a table with a bank of monitors, and a black leather Barcelona chair and stool overlooking the beach.

This is where Bridges sits, nursing his third coffee of the day, skim-reading the news on his iPad while Owen Twill is fingering a business card in a pub with sticky carpets three hundred miles away.

Nothing in the news interests him. Another war. Another political scandal. He swipes from one page to the next, paying scant attention beyond the headlines. An alert buzzes from the panel of monitors and he puts down his coffee and saunters over. He pushes a button and an LED stops flashing above one of the screens. It shows a postal van trundling past.

He walks back to the glass wall that separates him from the elements, picking up his coffee on the way. A glance at his watch confirms it's after three and he swears under his breath. To kill time, he climbs onto an exercise bike and begins pedalling. He might be closer to seventy than sixty but he retains a sinewy athleticism—the result of a lifetime of training.

Just when he's picked up speed the pealing bells of his phone ricochet off the high ceiling. He hops off the bike, takes glasses from his cardigan pocket and slips them on the end of his nose. He clears his throat and picks up the phone.

There's background noise. Chatter and some laughter.

'Yes?'

'It's on.'

'When?'

'Not yet. I'll let you know.'

There's a click. The line goes dead.

Lewis Bridges puts the phone down on the kitchen counter and looks out to sea.

7

London, England

Twill arrives at the Cromwell Green visitor entrance fifteen minutes early. He flashes his service card to the soldier and nods awkwardly at the salute he gets in return. By the time he clears the walk-through scanner, it's eleven a.m.

He's led across New Palace Yard to the Member's Entrance. The squaddie whispers in the ear of the plain-clothed officer on duty and he clicks his heels and salutes Twill too. This time, Twill sees the dagger tie-pin and salutes back. The officer checks his clipboard and asks him to wait in Westminster Hall.

The vast hall makes him feel exposed and he experiences the closest thing to fear he's capable of. It's a cavern as long as four cricket pitches with arched wooden beams stretching up to the ceiling like a prehistoric rib cage. Every step echoes around the hall and he regrets not wearing soft soles. When the sense of exposure becomes too much, he feigns interest in a display backing on to the main entrance. It's from there that he sees Cromer skipping down the stone steps from St Stephen's Porch with long, confident strides, wearing the same dark suit and tie from Tumble's wake.

All dressed up. More power plays.

Cromer scans the hall and registers what must be mock surprise when he spots Twill flush to the wall by the entrance. He crosses the hall, brogues clipping the stone floor with the brashness of an estate agent, stops a foot away holding out a lanyard.

He grins. 'Corporal Twill, glad you could make it.'

Twill nods and hooks the ribbon around his neck.

'Follow me,' Cromer booms and turns on his heels.

Twill takes off after him grimacing at the pace. He considers asking Cromer to slow down but the thought of the man's smug face chalking up another victory stops him.

'Oh, sorry.' Cromer says, pulling up. 'The leg. I forgot.'

No, you fucking didn't, Twill thinks.

Cromer waves an arm in the air. 'Westminster Hall is the oldest—'

'I didn't come all this way for a history lesson.'

Cromer beams back at him and the rest of the walk is conducted in silence, but this time at an excruciatingly slow speed. They turn into a narrow corridor and stop outside an office. While Cromer fishes around for the key, Twill eyes a raised plate bearing the words *Ellis Cromer, MP, OBE.* And underneath, *Parliamentary Private Secretary to the Secretary of State for Defence.*

Cromer sweeps into his office talking over his shoulder. 'Come in, come in.'

Twill follows and takes the chair Cromer pulls out for him. He sits, realising the seat has been dropped to its lowest setting. Another cheap shot. He can file that along with being kept waiting and Cromer's fast/slow walk. He's no stranger to subliminal subjugation and is surprised how insulted he feels to be on the receiving end for once.

'I trust you had a good journey here.'

Twill shrugs and looks around the room. Dark wood panelling, a low ceiling, and rows of books along one wall—a mixture of military-history journals and leather-bound *Hansard*s. It smells of musty carpet. Opposite the shelves is a curved bay window strewn with velvet cushions, letting in the only light in the room. The windows appear to be secondary double glazed, alarmed and locked. The only sound is a ticking grandfather clock. Hanging on the wall is a collection of framed photographs and certificates. Twill hasn't met any of Cromer's family but a toothy young man in army fatigues stands out. Has to be his son. Pride of place is an A3 canvas of Cromer in full uniform, saluting Prince Charles. Twill recognises the long red-brick building with a pitched green roof in the background.

'Stirling Lines,' he says.

'What do you think?' Cromer asks, reclining in his seat.

Twill turns back, glad of the desk between them. He reaches down and raises his chair until he's level with his old boss. 'Not bad for a secretary.'

Cromer laughs. Too loud. And for too long. 'Oh, there's a bit more to it than that.'

'Yeah,' Twill replies, deadpan. 'You're a secretary to a secretary.'

Cromer rises, still chuckling, and moves across to a drinks cabinet. He returns to his desk, cradling a bottle of Dalmore and two glasses. He pours generous measures; flips open a globe and drops ice into the glasses. A quick glance—no doubt to see if Twill is impressed—goes unrewarded. 'Here. Good health.'

Twill takes the glass.

'I've always liked you, Twill. You're a special guy, you know that?'

Twill takes a deep slug and pulls a face. 'If you wanted to ask me out, you could have done it on the phone.'

'You, the gang. All eight of you. Special. You ever stop to wonder about that?' Cromer says.

Twill can hear the relish in every word. He leans forward. 'You do know that "special" means something completely different these days?'

'And *you* know I don't mean that.' Cromer's chair groans as he leans back. 'I'm glad you're here. This place. This is where it all happens, you know. The crucible of British democracy.'

Twill tries to appear nonplussed, fishing around his glass and hooking out an ice cube.

'Everything we did, everything *our* people still do, is decided here. Wars are started and wars are finished in these corridors.'

'Wars end on the battlefield, not when some twit in a suit gets sleepless nights over his poll numbers,' Twill says, and yawns into the back of his hand.

Cromer chuckles. 'Now who's being naïve? The last little jolly we worked on ended diplomatically.'

Twill scoffs, and pops the ice cube into his mouth. 'Amazing what people will do when their balls are in a vice.'

'You are, of course, absolutely correct. The Eagles played a very important role in getting everybody around the negotiating table. The country owes you and the lads a sincere debt of gratitude.'

A phone on Cromer's desk rings and his eyes move to it. He looks back at Twill and gives a little shake of the head. They sit in silence until it stops.

'This is all very nice, but did I come all this way for you to put your hand up my jumper and squeeze my tits?' Twill says, crunching down on the ice cube.

'As you wish.' Cromer tops up their glasses. 'Tell me about Tam Croall.'

Twill bristles and pulls himself upright. 'Me and him have some unresolved issues. You got a problem with that?'

'On the contrary, Twill.' Cromer puts down his glass, his smile gone. 'I think your enthusiasm for settling outstanding grievances is highly commendable. All

45

this'—he motions around him—'means nothing to me. If I had to choose between soldier and politician, I wouldn't hesitate to drop it for one fucking second.' There's a pause, then he adds, 'I'm a soldier first and foremost. The Eagles. The two-two.' He raises his glass.

'The two-two,' Twill says. 'And Tumble.'

Cromer bows his head.

Twill says, 'Did you see him after Belfast?'

Cromer shakes his head. A little too enthusiastically. The moment, and the ensuing pause, is not lost on Twill.

They sip their drinks in pin-drop silence until Cromer starts up again.

'Revenge, call it what you will—'

'Fucking justice is what I call it,' Twill says, gripping the glass with white knuckles. 'Don't forget, you lot let me down. You let us all down when you signed that piece of shit surrender.'

'I get that you're unhappy, but there are people walking around today who wouldn't be if it weren't for the Good Friday Agreement.'

'Too fucking right.' Twill spits out the words. 'Most of those cunts walked scot-free because it gave them a pass. If you'd let us finish our job—'

'Compromises had to be made and look where we are now. The ends justify the means.'

Twill laughs without joy. 'I remember you using the same line forty years ago. The ends justify the means. But the context was *very* different.'

'And what a waste of breath that was. Like I ever had to justify anything you were asked to do.'

'We never asked why. We had a job to do and we got on and did it.'

'I know, I know. The two-two. The best, most ambitious and motivated team I ever had the privilege of working with. But you're not here today to talk about the past. I want to talk about the future. About righting wrongs. You say you were let down. *I* feel let down. Every time one of my boys got hurt, I took it personally. It hurt then and it hurts now.' Cromer attempts a sympathetic face but can't quite pull it off, looking more like he has trapped wind.

'That might be true but don't tell me giving Croall a pink slip meant anything other than more bodies. If I'd been allowed to get on and finish my job—'

'This is my point, Twill. I agree one hundred per cent. Who do you think's been giving Lucan intel, knowing it goes straight back to you? Me. Because your blind refusal to accept the truth means I have to tiptoe around you like I'm on eggshells. Do you realise what a risk this is for me?'

Twill shakes his head and rubs his leg. 'Are you really going to sit there and lecture me on risk?'

'I want to talk man to man with you, Corporal Twill, without being fucking interrupted every two fucking minutes by your pity parade. I can't change what happened all those years ago, no matter how much I'd like to. What I can do—what *we* can do—is stand up and be counted. Live up to the pledge of loyalty we took to each other and right the fucking wrongs. Tam Croall is an abomination. An enemy of our regiment, an enemy of the state and enemy of every decent human being on this planet. And you've been running around town doing a half-arsed job of holding him to account. Am I right?'

Twill puts down his drink, takes a deep breath and lets it seep out between his teeth. 'If you say so.'

Cromer gets up and leans forward on his knuckles, eyes shining like an evangelist's. 'I asked, am I right, *Corporal Twill*?'

'*Yes!*' Twill says, pushing himself upright.

'Good man!' Cromer booms and flops back into his seat and repeats the words, quieter this time. He tops up their glasses. 'We'll get Croall. Together. But from now you'll be reporting to me, okay?'

Twill nods. 'Sir.' The word grates as it passes his lips.

'After Belgium he went underground which fits a pattern. I'll let you know when I hear something. Anything. But you're not here so we can talk about just Croall, as important as he is.'

Twill perks up. He hasn't seen this coming although it's typical of Cromer to go around the houses. Cromer climbs out of his chair and walks over to a metal filing cabinet. He removes a bunch of keys on an elastic key ring and selects one. Within seconds, he's back at his seat, slapping a tan folder on the desk. Twill doesn't have time to read the cover; Cromer's already opened the file.

'After the Good Friday Agreement, there were a series of disclosures on both sides. Not everything, you understand, just enough to let them think we were complying fully. Naturally, they were equally suspicious and probably held back as much intelligence as we did. Both us and the Provos were cautious about slipping back into hostilities. But after a few months, new info started coming in dribs and drabs. They'd become comfortable in their new lives; maybe they wanted a bit of cash to fund a business, or fancied a new car. You'd be surprised how many used this newfound trust to bury enemies and settle scores. We didn't care why or who. We didn't give a shit as long as they kept on chucking each other under the bus. Mick owes Pat a few quid? One call and Pat's no longer an issue and Mick's one happy terrorist. You see, they're just people at the end of the day. And that's our greatest advantage. *This* is where they play into our hands. They're just people. Weak, undisciplined people with lust and debts and grudges…their own agenda. And take away the only thing they ever had in common,'—Cromer stabs a finger at his chest—'an intense dislike of us, and the whole thing collapses like a house of cards.'

'If we're no longer at war, why do we give a shit?'

'Because we're men,' Cromer shouts back. 'And we stand shoulder to shoulder. Wrongs must be righted. Pride must be upheld. We have to stick up for each other. What else is there? Think back, Corporal Twill. Think back to that night it all went wrong. Don't tell me you never wondered how they knew who you were and where you were going to be.'

Every muscle in Twill's body tenses. He puts his hands under the desk and grips his knees.

'Does the name Padraig Fealty mean anything to you?'

Twill comes up blank. 'Should it?'

'Provo commander, West Belfast Brigade. Died last week after a long battle with cancer.'

'Cry me a river. So what?'

'Hospice. Long days and lonely nights. Get the right man in the room, with the right drugs, even a hardliner like Fealty talks.'

Twill shuffles forward in his seat. The words tumble from him. 'Who was it?'

'Who wasn't there last week? Who has never turned up to a single fucking funeral or get-together since we disbanded?'

'If you're saying it was one of us, you've got to be certain. There can't be mistakes.'

'I know I'm right, Twill. We don't throw accusations like this around lightly. Checked, double checked and cross-referenced by three individual sources.'

'You know what this means.'

Cromer takes a pair of reading glasses from his jacket pocket, licks a finger and flicks through the file. He finds what he's after and rips it out, removes his glasses and stares deep into Twill's eyes with a look so dark it reaches deep into the pit of his stomach. A look that would make most men crumble. Most men, but not Twill.

'We are men, Corporal Twill,' Cromer says in a low voice. 'We stand together. And we look after each other.' He slides a sheet of A4 across the desk.

Twill reaches for it and Cromer slaps his palm down, pinning the paper to the table.

'This stays between us. Got it? Just us. No one else.'

Twill nods and Cromer removes his hand. Twill picks it up and reads the top line: *Confidential Sig Int Summary—Lewis Bridges*, and looks at his CO.

'I know you'll do the right thing,' Cromer says, slipping his glasses into his jacket.

***

Twill makes the 17:30 from Liverpool Street and settles into his seat, closes his eyes, clears his mind and lets his thoughts churn and take shape. He needs a plan. And planning comes as natural to him as choosing an outfit is to others. It has to suit the situation, play to strengths, mitigate weaknesses.

He knows his strengths. And his weaknesses.

The irony is, what most consider a weakness, he considers a strength. Emotions—melancholy to joy and everything in-between—are not experienced, only observed in others. Over the years, he's learned to mimic. A social minor-bird. He spares Lucan the whole act—they're too close—but even then he's sure his friend never gets to see the true extent of his apathy. Some people, such as Cromer, simply aren't worth the effort. The only person who gets the full Oscar-winning performance is Walsh. And that's only because the thought of her poking around his head presents a risk. It doesn't anger or scare him. If anything, it bores him. But if she knew what really went on between his ears, she might suggest all kinds of treatment. And that's not happening.

His indifference to the human condition is a benign inconvenience but one that can occasionally be an asset. The suggestion that he's been betrayed by one of his own doesn't light a fire of rage under him or trigger some primal thirst for blood. It's more a slow, burning hunger. An itch that needs to be scratched.

Whatever made him like this, whatever the name for *it* is, it has spared him hours of naval-gazing. The *whys* aren't important. There is no soul searching, wailing and gnashing of teeth. It is simple. He's been presented with some new information, and he needs to plan his next move. Logically and without emotive, knee jerk responses. Whether he's up against a close friend or a complete stranger matters only in the nuance of his response. A friend would make it easy to get close. A stranger would be wary, more difficult to read. Easier for them to hide their guilt.

Strengths. Weaknesses. And how to apply them.

Bridges—although Twill hasn't seen him in decades—is no stranger. He's been through the same training, therefore runs on the same operating system. And that makes him predictable.

Twice Twill stops to think back to what Bridges was like in the days leading up to his abduction, and twice he comes up blank. Looking out the window at the blur of the Essex countryside, he picks apart his own arguments and blueprints for revenge, searching for some competitive edge. The answer's there. It always is. He just has to find it.

Bridges received the same training but wasn't a front-line operator. Good backup, solid administrator, disciplined and well-schooled but no triggerman. Not like Twill. Even if it's only psychological, *that's* an advantage. Removing fear from the decision-making process shaves seconds off the response time. And fear is an emotion Twill has never experienced. Even as a boy he would climb trees taller than anyone else. Always first to wade in, whether in a pub car park or on the rugby pitch. Remove self-preservation from the equation, you become the ultimate soldier. Not that he's reckless—every decision still has an evaluation process but it's measured in terms of chance of success, not exposure to harm. A situation like this, up against a well-trained enemy, is a game of 3D chess. Every angle has to be analysed, moves assessed two or three steps in advance.

In Twill's favour:

Bridges doesn't know he's coming.

He doesn't know that Twill knows.

He could be complacent after so many years.

Against:

Twill's leg.

He arrives home tired but buzzing. A brutal head spin rules out sleep. He takes his seat in the front room and props a pillow under his thigh.

Then there's Cromer. Can he trust him? That's a clear no. One of Twill's golden rules is to *always* work out what someone has to gain, in *every* scenario.

Question each and every motive. Do they have skin in the game? If it plays out, who are the winners and who are the losers?

If Lewis Bridges is guilty as charged, there can only be one penalty. But Twill won't know until he looks him in the eye. Certainly, Cromer's word isn't enough.

With the outline of a plan beginning to take shape, he heads for bed.

Sleep, when it comes, brings with it a screaming swan.

8

Cornwall, England

He watches from the car, a kilometre away. At first, it's no more than a dot on the beach. But as the dot gets closer, it takes the shape of a man. Long green coat, the hood pulled up over his face. A gusting headwind whips across the water and dot-man lowers his head, buries his hands in his pockets and leans into it. Overhead, a crop of chubby clouds chase each other.

Closer still. Dot-man is dragging his right leg, leaving a trail in the sand. Footprints like Morse code. He briefly disappears from view as he pulls level with his observer.

The watcher shuffles in his seat and dot-man appears again, twenty yards down the beach, stepping over a chunk of driftwood tangled with seaweed and fishing line.

Dot-man disappears behind a dune topped with a clump of swaying grass. The observer puts down his binoculars, turns the key in the ignition, and sets off after him.

***

Lewis Bridges dips his head and pumps his legs in time to the music. His face is crimson and blotchy, and a single bead of sweat hangs off the end of his nose. There's a beep from his watch and he slows his pace and straightens up, gasping for air.

'Fucking hell.'

He leans over and checks the exercise bike's control panel. Shakes his head and clicks a small remote over his shoulder. The music fades.

He takes a bottle of water from the fridge and crosses to the glass wall overlooking the bay, drinks deeply and wipes his face on a towel. Now the music's muted, he can hear the distant crash of white-capped waves rolling inland dissolving into foam on the shoreline and the cawing of seagulls overhead. But the stillness in the house unnerves him. He clucks his tongue against the roof of his mouth and returns to the kitchen.

Everything is set. Worrying is illogical because he holds all the cards. He pats the waistband of his tracksuit bottoms for the fifth time in as many minutes, like a nervous traveller checking his passport, and feels the weight of his gun. There are two more in the house. Just in case. One in a never-used kettle on the kitchen worktop, and one stuck with gaffer tape to the underside of the dining table. There can be no short cuts, not when dealing with professionals.

The worst thing is the waiting. It's a strange way to live, bizarre to invite violence into your life, but once you know it's coming, it's better to get it out the way.

He checks the bank of monitors on the wall but there's nothing to see. Maybe Twill won't come after all.

He berates himself for complacency. He *wants* Twill to come so it can all be over.

A scalding shower invigorates. He steps out of the cubicle and stands for a few moments admiring his reflection. His skin is pink from the burning water but he's in good condition for a man his age. He turns side on, sucks in his stomach and flexes his biceps, then towels himself dry. Slips the gun into the pocket of his bathrobe.

Back downstairs, he takes another kettle from a cupboard above the sink and makes himself a coffee, which he sips from the armchair overlooking the bay. When that's finished he contemplates another cup, out of boredom.

The figure on the beach makes him think twice. Distant. On their own; no dog. Bridges cups his hands around the side of his head and presses his face to the glass. The figure comes closer. It walks with a limp. Bridges gets a hollow feeling in the pit of his stomach.

'Okay,' he says, fingers beginning to tingle. 'Showtime.'

He waits, watching. Hands on hips.

The figure walks the length of the beach and stops at the bottom of the steps by the boathouse.

A buzz over his shoulder startles him. An LED blinks above one of the monitors which shows a red van stopping outside the front gates. The driver gets out and holds up a parcel to the camera.

Bridges presses a button and speaks into the intercom. 'Leave it there.'

There's a crackle and an indifferent voice says, 'Registered post, mate. Needs an autograph.' The driver waves the parcel with one hand, and writes in the air with the other.

Bridges crosses the room. The figure by the boathouse is circling in faltering steps. Fucking bottle-job.

The intercom crackles again. *'Hull-oo?'*

Even if the man on the beach is Twill, and *even* if he runs up the stairs—which Bridges knows he can't—it would be three minutes before he reaches the house. Maybe. Three minutes for a fit young man with two functional legs.

Bridges buzzes the gates and returns to his lookout. He hears a knock and runs the short distance to the front door. Presses a button on a wall monitor and scrolls through the CCTV cameras until he sees the man on the beach. He's still hovering by the back gate. Bridges unlatches the door without taking his eyes off the screen. The man on the beach stops, raises a hand to his ear and waves at the camera.

The door behind Bridges swings open.

Twill. Red-shirted uniform, arm stretched out in front of him.

'Hello, Lewis.'

Bridges fumbles for the gun in his pocket. Too slow. The last thing he sees is the blue spark of a taser.

***

Bridges groans and stirs. Twill turns to look at him from the dining table a few feet away. Lucan sits opposite, talking.

'Have ya ever noticed I always get the shitty end of the stick in all yer plans? Walk down a beach, ya said. Sounds fuckin' great but let's face it,'—he waves an arm in the air—'it's hardly the Caribbean out there.'

'Are you still going on?' Twill says. 'Worked, didn't it?'

'Oh, yeah, fuckin' perfect.' He stands and grabs his groin. 'If these bastards ever defrost, that is. Fuckin' frozen meatballs is what I got—'

Twill flaps a hand and stage-whispers to Bridges, 'Ignore him. He's always moaning.' He takes a noisy slurp from a mug. 'How're you doing, Lewis? Long-time no see.'

Bridges pulls himself upright and grimaces.

'Still gonna need that signature,' Lucan says, sticking the postman's hat on at a jaunty angle.

Bridges rubs his chest where the taser hit. 'W-what's going on?'

'Where are my manners?' Lucan says, gawping at his mug. 'Let me get ya a cuppa. After all, it must-a been *hell of a shock.*'

Bridges stands quickly and stumbles. 'I'll get it.' The kitchen counter breaks his fall.

Lucan is talking to Twill again. 'Get it? *Hell of a shock.*'

Bridges grabs the kettle and reaches inside. Pulls his hand out. Empty. He turns and looks across the room.

Lucan waves the gun in the air. 'Honestly,' he says, shaking his head, 'I'm wasted on you lot.'

'Sit,' Twill says.

Bridges slumps back down.

'I don't understand,' he says in a nasal whine. His arms hang at his side and he refuses to meet their gaze.

Twill. 'Don't do that.'

'Be a man,' Lucan snaps, baring his teeth. His nostrils flare for a moment, then his face relaxes. He shrugs off the green overcoat and pulls off his shoes. Shows Bridges the right one. 'The old stone-taped-inside-yer-shoe trick. Works every time. Instant limp.'

Bridges looks from Lucan to Twill. 'I—I can explain.'

'You see,' Twill says, drumming his fingers on the table top, 'I was kind of counting on that.'

Lucan puts his hands on his hips and whistles between his teeth. 'Helluva place ya got here, Lewis, old son. Business must be good. Remind me again, what *is* yer business?'

Bridges clears his throat and a flush creeps across his neck. 'Intelligence. Intelligence and security.'

Lucan slaps his hands on his knees and says to Twill, 'Ya see? I fuckin' told you we were mugs. We got this shit *down pat*, and we've nothing to show for it.'

Bridges raises a hand and his words spill out. 'I've got money—'

'We don't want your fucking money,' Twill says. He takes a sip from his mug and tips his head towards Bridges. 'I don't suppose this business of yours gets much work from the private secretary to the MOD now, does it?'

'I can't talk about—'

Lucan snorts and raises his voice. 'We're well past that stage, Bridges. You're gonna tell us what we want to know or this ends badly.'

Twill pushes himself up, rubs his leg and ambles into the kitchen. He tries a few drawers then returns to his seat, brandishing a wood-handled carving knife, flipping it this way and that. He inspects his nails, scrapes them with the tip of the blade. 'Talk.'

Bridges scratches at his neck. 'I have done some work for Ellis.'

Lucan throws his head back and laughs. '*Ellis?* Get you. It's fuckin' Cromer.'

'What kind of work,' Twill says.

Bridges pauses. 'Wet work. Amongst other stuff.'

'Where and who?'

Bridges sighs and offers a half-hearted shrug. 'All over. Enemies of the state is how Ell—' He steals a glance at Lucan. '…Cromer likes to put it.' He leans his elbows on his knees. 'Listen, you know what we do. I just monetised it. You say business is good, I say its fucking booming! The world's gone mad—our enemies still live in the shadows but it's not so easy to get away with shit like we used to. There's still a hundred ways of doing it but *only* if you blur the lines of engagement. What do you think politicians can do? Ask someone nicely to stop funding terrorism? Trot out some toothless sanctions? Do you honestly think they give two flying fucks if there's the occasional "accident" that helps their cause? Of course they don't. There ain't a government out there that will turn its back on clean solutions. And they don't waste *any fucking time* asking questions or have *any fucking sleepless nights* either. Banker in Zurich? Drowns in the bath. Forger in Dubai? Hangs himself after a row with his girlfriend. Arms dealer in St Petersburg? Heart attack. I *make* problems go away.'

Twill puts the knife down and rubs his leg. 'Was I one of the problems Cromer asked you to make go away?'

Bridges runs a hand through his hair and laughs nervously. 'Don't be stupid.'

Twill clenches his jaw and speaks in a steady, lower-pitched voice. 'If you lie to me again, I'll open up your throat.'

Bridges swallows and answers quickly. 'He tipped me off, said you were coming…And I suppose he told you where to find me.'

Twill nods.

'Fucking Cromer.' Bridges laughs bitterly. 'Tying up loose ends—'

'What he actually said was, it was you that ratted me out to the Provos, way back when.'

'*Bullshit.*' Bridges leaps up.

Twill doesn't move but feels Lucan's eyes on him. The room falls silent but for the distant crash of the surf.

Bridges crumbles back into his seat and folds his arms across his chest. He wears a grave expression and when he speaks his voice is thick. 'Where are you going with this?'

'What, that's it?' Lucan says. 'No impassioned defence? No begging for forgiveness?'

'Fuck your forgiveness,' Bridges roars, his face now taut. 'You've already made your mind up.'

Lucan chuckles. 'I gotta say, you should really work on the whole I-didn't-do-it thing.'

Bridges addresses Twill. 'What you should be doing is asking: Why now?'

Lucan stands and makes to approach Bridges but Twill stops him with a raised finger.

'What do you mean?'

'Belfast was four decades ago. I haven't heard or seen or even thought about you lot since then. Why now? Why has Cromer suddenly got a pickle up his arse *now*?'

Lucan shakes his head. 'This is stupid. He's yanking our chain.'

'No, wait,' Bridges says. 'Have either of you spoken to the American woman?'

'Oh, yeah,' Lucan says. 'I can't get that Hilary Clinton off the phone.'

Twill turns to Lucan. 'Shut the fuck up for one minute, will you?' And then to Bridges 'What American woman?'

Colour rises in Bridges' cheeks. 'Animus. That mean anything to you?'

Twill thinks back to the folder in Cromer's office. Shakes his head.

'What about Blaggard?' Bridges continues.

'What is this?' Lucan shouts, his hands imploring the air. 'A fuckin' game of scrabble?'

'Go on,' Twill says, keeping his voice calm.

Bridges leans back in his chair, spreads his legs wide and sneers. 'You stupid old fucks. And I suppose you think JR and Mincer killed themselves?'

Twill exchanges glances with Lucan, then looks back at Bridges.

'You know nothing. Cromer shouts 'jump' and you ask 'how high?' A fucking pair of lap dogs.'

Lucan storms across the room and lifts Bridges out of his seat by the neck. Bridges' eyes bulge, his face turns crimson and his throat rasps.

'Put him down,' Twill says with the tone of a bored teacher.

Lucan looks from Bridges to Twill, and back again. He grits his teeth and his knuckles go white. Bridges' lips are turning blue and there's foam at the corner of his mouth. He scrabbles under Lucan's grip, legs kicking wildly.

Lucan howls and throws Bridges at Twill's feet. Bridges pushes himself to his knees and gulps for air.

'Which American woman, and what is Animus?' Twill asks.

Bridges leans on the table. His right hand drops then rears back. He's holding a gun, duct tape flapping from the stock. He turns, aims at Lucan. The gun clicks three times.

His arm falls to his side and the blood drains from his face.

Lucan laughs and puts his hand in his pocket. The bullets inside rattle and he apes Bridges in a yokel voice. '*Stupid old fucks.*'

Twill grabs Bridges by the collar of his dressing gown and gets in his face. '*WHAT WOMAN?*'

Bridges ducks under his arm and lunges for the knife on the table. Twill pivots, blocks Bridges with his shoulder and snatches up the knife. He flips it into his backhand, twists his torso and slams it into Bridge's side. Bridges makes a whistling sound and staggers backwards.

Twill grabs the top of his arms and pulls him in close. '*What American?*'

Bridges gasps and expels a lungful of hot air. A blood bubble emerges from his lips and bursts on his chin.

'She'll find you,' he says. He blinks rapidly, then the light behind his eyes dims and his head flops onto his chest.

Twill gives him a shake and shouts his name.

Bridges lifts his head and smiles grimly. '*Blaggard.*'

His body goes limp. Twill lets it fall to the ground.

Lucan comes around the table and lays a hand on Twill's shoulder. 'I'll tell ya one thing…'

Twill wipes the knife on his sleeve, first one side, then the other. Slow, deliberate. 'And what would that be?'

Lucan flips a thumb over his shoulder at the storm raging outside. 'I'm not walking back in that.'

***

They move quickly. Bridges is bagged and zipped. Lucan raids the fridge while Twill wipes down the surfaces and door handles with alcohol. He cleans the floor with towels and puts them into a duffel bag along with the cups they used. Lucan drops into the recliner, clutching a hastily made sandwich, and says something through a mouthful of bread.

Twill shoots him a look of distaste. 'Can you not fucking do that?'

Lucan swallows. 'What about the CCTV?'

'It's digital. Only keeps the data for seven days.'

Lucan sits up. 'Still though, seven days?'

'There's no neighbours and no numbers stored in his phone. Last incoming call was a month ago.' Twill zips up the bag and rests on his knee. 'Our man Lewis was not one for visitors.'

'Can't we take the tape?'

'Tape? Fucking luddite. Hard drive's in my bag.'

Lucan grins and takes another bite. 'So, the plan is to hope no one notices he's missing?'

'*Hope*? Hope isn't a plan,' Twill says, taking the bag to the front door. 'He travels regularly and there's no family. No one will miss him. And maybe,' he says, coming back into the room, 'you could get off your fat arse and find his passport. Try the bedside table. That way, if someone does come looking for him, they'll think he's away.'

Lucan doesn't move, treats Twill to a sandwich-spilling smile.

Twill sighs and snatches the plate from him, dropping it in the bag at his side. 'C'mon,' he says, checking his watch. 'We should move out.'

***

They drive east on the A392 for an hour. The sun is sinking below the treetops as they arrive at Goss Moor Nature Reserve and pull up in a deserted car park next to Lucan's Fiesta. A short trek through woodland with their cargo brings them to a hole dug the previous day, far from the footpath. The body is tossed into the ground and drenched in quicklime from a bag under a nearby bush. They slake Bridges with water and cover him with leaves and soil. Then it's back to the van for the duffel bag and another plastic bag full of clothes. They follow a sign to the fishing lake and find a decent-size rock. Twill strips down to his pants and dresses in his own clothes while Lucan untethers a wooden rowing boat. The uniform is added to the duffel bag along with the rock, and dumped in the middle of the lake. They wait until the bubbles stop, then return to the van.

Lucan follows Twill south for another twenty minutes. They turn off Brewer's Hill at Whitemoor, and stop at a dead end surrounded by hedgerows and fields. Twill takes a can of paraffin from the back of the van and walks clockwise, sloshing the vehicle. There's a flash, then a *whoomph* as the van ignites. He climbs into Lucan's car and they pull away, the soft glow of the van lighting up the night sky behind them.

9

Colchester

Lucan walks in a straight line from the bar to the table, brushing past three drinkers and crashing through a circle of friends. He leaves a trail of angry faces in his wake but their protests never rise above a shared murmur.

'You're showing some skills there,' Twill says, as his friend places a beer down in front of him.

'Eh?' Lucan rubs his hands and pulls up a chair with a scrape.

Twill shakes his head and they chink glasses.

'Thanks for letting me stay,' Lucan adds.

'I wasn't aware I had.'

Lucan sashays his hands and sings, '*Gonna make this a night to re-mem-ber.*'

Twill pulls a face.

Lucan, 'I feel fuckin' great!'

Twill rubs his hands through his hair. They'd reached Colchester just after nine p.m. Too late—apparently—for Lucan to make his way home.

'How come?'

'Ah, c'mon. Don't tell me ya don't feel it.'

'Feel what?'

'This!' Lucan says, throwing his hands up in the air. 'We're back in the game.'

'I didn't realise it was a game.'

'Oh, yes it is, and ya fuckin' know it. I can't remember the last time I felt so...alive!'

'That'll be the shock of getting a round in,' Twill says over the top of his pint. 'You should try it more often.'

Lucan folds his hands in his lap and his expression settles on grave. 'Don't ya see now? We struggled for years with what happened in Belfast. This feels like closure.'

Twill sticks his bottom lip out. 'Speak for yourself. Until they invent a time machine, there's no point in giving two fucks about things you can't change.'

'Yes! You're making my point for me. We found out what happened, and we did something about it…and it feels fuckin' great!'

'Before you piss your knickers over there, I'm not convinced we know more than we did this morning.'

Lucan frowns and his hand drops. 'What are ya talkin' about?'

Twill sighs and puts his pint on the table. 'I'm just saying, I think today raises more questions than it answers.'

'Well, this is a record. Yer talking shite after less than two pints,' Lucan says with a smile, sliding Twill's beer away from him.

Twill snatches it back and drinks deeply. 'Fewer.'

'Eh?'

'It's fewer, not less. When it's countable, you use fewer. You're talking shite after *fewer* than two pints'

'Well perhaps you could be fewer of a cunt then, Carole Fuckin' Vordeman.'

Twill wipes his face on the back of his sleeve and fixes Lucan with a stare. 'I meant what I said about today.'

'Fuck, yer being serious, aren't ya?'

'This isn't over by a long chalk. I think there's a good chance we've only scratched the surface.'

'I don't understand. The unit had a rat, and we got him.'

Twill waves him off. 'We don't know for sure Bridges did any of those things.'

'Balls. Ya saw with yer own eyes—he was ready to kill ya alright.'

Twill raises his voice and jabs a finger at Lucan's chest. 'I know what I saw and it was you going in with a prejudged conclusion. Bridges was right—we'd already made our minds up.'

Lucan leans in and whispers, 'Well, why did ya stick him like a pig then? Or maybe ya weren't looking when he pointed that gun at me and pulled the fuckin' trigger.'

'He was scared. And scared people do silly things.'

'*Silly?* Putting red socks in a white wash is silly. Pulling a gun on someone you've known for forty years is hardly fuckin' *silly*…Did ya not see the wee bastard's face? He was sweating like a whore in church.'

'Precisely. Ask yourself: why was he so scared?'

There's a commotion and a loud cheer from the other side of the bar. Lucan spins around. A group of men circle a TV fixed to the wall, watching a slow-motion replay of a team in red scoring from several different angles. Half the group are hugging each other; the other half are shaking their heads. He turns back to Twill.

'Now you're making *my* point. He *knew* I was coming.'

Lucan leans back and rubs his neck. 'You don't know that. Ya don't do a job like Bridges' without making a few enemies.'

'I knew the moment he opened the door. It was written all over his face.'

'Okay, let's say he did know you were coming. What does that even mean?'

'Who told me Bridges was the rat?'

'Cromer.'

'Who made me swear not to tell anyone?'

'Cromer.'

'Who tipped Bridges off I was coming for him?'

'Aww, c'mon. You can't be thinking that. Ya said yerself, scared people do silly things. We caught Bridges red-handed and you know better than anyone that if ya put someone up against the wall, they'll say *anything* to save their arse.'

'I'm more interested,' Twill says, holding Lucan's gaze, 'in why you're so keen to defend Cromer.'

'Fuck Cromer.'

His voice is raised. People on the next table break off their conversation to look over.

'What?' he barks, and they return to their drinks. He turns back to Twill. 'Listen, I don't owe Cromer nothing. I just don't think ya should get yerself all worked up looking for the bogeyman under the bed. Granted, it may look…odd, but where's the fuckin' evidence?'

'Absence of evidence is not evidence of absence.'

'Get to fuck, fuckin' Confucius. Coincidences, mate. That's all. And coincidences do not equal conspiracies.'

'I don't believe in coincidences. I've been involved in a fair few myself. They take a lot of setting up. Look…' Twill spreads his palms out in front of him. 'All I'm saying is, there's a conversation to be had.'

Lucan's mouth drops open and his hand flies to his face. 'Ya…ya saying Shergar shot JFK?' He dissolves into a fit of giggles.

Twill ignores him and counts off points on his fingers. 'One. Cromer told me Bridges was the rat, without evidence, and we just blindly went along with it. It's stupid to think that was a given. Two. He told me to go alone and not mention it to anyone. If I'd followed his instructions, it would be me feeding the worms on Goss Moor right now.'

Lucan nods. 'I'll give ya that.'

'Three. What did Bridges have to gain by ratting me out? Nothing, but everything to lose. Four. He knew he'd seen his last sunrise, so why didn't he confess? We gave him plenty of opportunities to come clean. You know as well as I do, people sing before they go. Five. He's had more dealings with Cromer over the years than us. And who had most to gain by getting Bridges out of the picture? Cromer's some kind of big cheese now. Does he really want all this history catching up with him?'

Lucan slumps in his chair and takes a drink. 'Unbelievable.'

'What's unbelievable? Name one thing I've said that's not true.'

'Not that,' Lucan replies. 'It's just I don't think I've ever heard ya say so many words in one go.'

'In that case, as a little treat because you like them so much, here's two more. Fuck off.'

Lucan leans over and ruffles Twill's hair. 'Aw, I can never stay angry with you for long.'

Twill shakes him off and smooths his hair back into place.

Lucan traces a finger around the stain of a glass rim on the table. 'So, what do we do next? We can't just bowl up to Cromer and ask him outright.'

'We don't have to. He'll come to us. If I'm right, he's heavily invested in what happened today.'

'And how do we find out the truth?'

Twill drains his glass and places it on the table. 'We roll the log over and see what crawls out.'

***

Twill is floating around the ceiling, looking down on himself. He's tied to a sturdy wooden chair with thick legs. It's old, maybe a school chair, and wears the scars of a hundred scratches and scribbles. Someone has carved *LH 4 ever* into the arm rest. A single act of love, born of innocence, now witness to a horror. The room is dark, the sole window blocked with thick drapes nailed into place. Where the two curtains meet there's a slight billow, enough to project a thin bar of light at his feet that will serve as an oche for his tormentor. Twill closes his eyes and breathes deep from the stomach. He holds the breath, counts to three then releases it and opens his eyes. There's a wall vent above the door but it's so furred with dust as to be useless. The air lies heavy and dank, somewhere between the sulphur of a teenager's bedroom and the fungal must of mildew.

It's warm, approaching hot. A single radiator on the far wall blasts out heat, night and day. There are scrapes on the pipe, like something or someone's been chained to it, and a claret stain by the side that's bled onto the floorboards. A memory. A shroud of Turin. Like the shadows of Hiroshima or Pompei.

Floral wallpaper is coming away from the wall in ragged patches, curling at the edges, exposing the room's lathe-and-plaster rib cage. The skirting boards are stained and scuffed with crusty, peeling paint. There's a hole, no bigger than a match box, from which something skitters and scurries behind him. The floor is strewn with litter, empty beer cans, pages of faded newspapers, a pile of rags and several cigarette butts. The window sill is dotted with rat droppings and dead flies.

His cell is wretched and filthy but that on its own doesn't explain the malevolence that seeps from the walls or the flickering shadows that whisper from every corner or the evil that cloys the air, fed by the dark heart of his tormentor. The room's alive. It *breathes*. Pipes buried behind the wall rasp and sigh like the rise and fall of an old man's chest.

Twill shuts his eyes again and focuses on what he knows. Twice a day there's the distant, tinkling refrain of children's laughter. A school? Mid-morning break and lunchtime? With the first, the narrow strip of light from the curtains is further across the room suggesting the sun is lower in the sky. There's little traffic, and what there is, is cars spluttering into life or being shut down, not passing through. A dead end? A cul-de-sac? Birdsong is loudest in the morning, picking up again in the evening, meaning the possibility of a tree outside the window. There are scratching sounds. Could be branches against the glass but sometimes they come from inside the walls. At night—no light from the split in the curtains, soft light under the door—comes the far-off cries of a baby. Two, sometimes three full-throated rages before dawn's silvered fingers poke through the drapes.

Such speculation keeps Twill busy. It would be easy to sit with caged breath, waiting for footsteps on the stairs. And when they do come, they are muted, not a hard click on bare floorboards. Thick carpet? The third step always groans and he knows atrocity is near. He counts. One, two, three, four, five, six. A pause then the door creaks open and a tea-stained light from the stairwell floods the room…

Twill's eyes snap open. It's not the stairs, just a car door slamming. He tries to wriggle his fingers but his hands, bound tightly behind him, remain numb. Numb, yet tingly at the same time. He imagines his fingers…bloated and purple like black puddings. The rope that anchors him to the chair secures his hands and loops around and under to his legs. It's so tight that his wrists feel like they're swallowing the binding.

Another bang. Footstep or car door? The gap between the first and second step is the longest. Time stops. His breath burns in his lungs, waiting for the second thump, which doesn't come. This time.

Ten days he's been here. The first day, nothing. The second day his tormentor steals into the room and stands spread-legged before him. Twill takes comfort from the balaclava. If the tormentor doesn't want to be recognised, there's a chance Twill will be allowed to live.

Twill tries to speak but after two days without water, the words catch, part formed. The tormentor stares at him for five minutes, then leaves. When Twill stirs the next morning, there's someone different in the room. They lift a bottle of water to his lips and feed him a sandwich. The act is almost tender. Twill remembers his training, asks, 'Why are you doing this to me?', 'What have I ever done to you?' Psychology 101. Create a bridge between you and your captor. Appeal to their humanity.

Not so much a mistake as a waste of breath.

On the fourth day the tormentor walks up to Twill and jams a sock into his mouth. If the intention is to get him to speak, it's not been well thought out. The host pulls a small, sharp knife with a tapered tip—what Twill will later find out is an oyster shuck—from his waistband with his left hand, and leans on Twill's shoulder with his right. The blade catches the light from the gap in the curtains as it falls. A synaptic flash of mercury, and then what feels like a series of icy punches as the blade repeatedly plunges into him. It's over in seconds. The tormentor doesn't even hang around to view his handiwork. After the final stab, he turns and leaves the room, closing the door after him.

It feels like a cold wind is blowing over him. Then a thin arterial spray of blood shoots a metre into the air. And then another and another and another until Twill's leaking like a colander. He tries screaming but the sock absorbs his howls. And then the heat comes. A raging bushfire from his midriff enveloping his whole body. It dawns on Twill that he's dying, and a torrent of scalding puke erupts from his gullet and out of his nose. He struggles for breath. Grey closes in at the edges of his vision. Then darkness, and with it, respite.

Twill wakes. He's naked. His clothes have been cut from him and used to mop up the blood at his feet. His body's covered in eight or nine surgical dressings and the surrounding skin is iodine yellow. A tube loops from his arm to a clear IV bag supported by a metal frame at his side. He passes out again.

The next morning, the feeder comes back, changes his dressings and brings him a drink and another cardboard sandwich. The sock goes back in afterwards, over his protests.

It continues for days five, six and seven. Day eight finds him stronger and more resolute. The pain is manageable. For all the blood, the cuts have been engineered for maximum psychological effect but minimum physical damage. Twill passes the time by dreaming up cruel and unusual punishments for his captors.

Day nine, the feeder doesn't come and Twill sees no one all day.

Day ten. Twill hears the first thump. He strains against his bindings, every pore in his body listening, waiting. And then it comes. The next thump, followed by a creak. Six more steps and the door swings open. The tormentor stands silhouetted in the door frame, like he's wondering what to do next. Twill shouts obscenities into the sock and wrestles with his restraints. The tormentor crosses to Twill and drops to his haunches. He's holding something in his left hand, down by his side and out of sight. A clump of auburn hair pokes out the back of his balaclava. His eyes are cold and flinty and empty of emotion. The eyes of a predator. He levels his hand with Twill's face and twists a large hunting knife in the air. It has a worn wooden handle and a long blade with a scalloped edge and serrated teeth. He pushes himself up and Twill flinches. The sock is pulled out of his mouth and thrown to the floor. Twill hears a panting sound and realises it's coming from him. The tormentor tilts his head and brings his arm down, pushing the first inch of the blade into Twill's right leg above the knee.

Twill holds his breath and looks into the tormentor's eyes. What is that? Amusement? The knife is pulled out half an inch, then pushed in three—a slow, sawing motion. Bile rises in Twill's throat but he doesn't make a noise or look away. The tormentor's eyes flash with annoyance and the blade is pushed in up to the handle, slicing through muscle and sinew and scraping against bone. Twill's leg burns with the intensity of molten lava. Sparks shower in the corner of his vision but he won't give his tormentor the reaction he craves. It's a funny thing, but he will later remember how the teeth of the knife tear and rip at his flesh, unlike the glacial kiss of the shuck.

Twill's persecutor takes two steps back, pulls off his balaclava and smiles. His expression is one of unspeakable darkness. So bleak is it that Twill is swamped by despair. His tormentor has wavy red hair and twin pebble eyes that sit too close together. An upturned, porcine nose sits atop thick, cherry lips. It's a face Twill knows well. And that's when he knows he's completely fucked.

Tam Croall starts back towards him, twirling the knife.

***

Twill shoots upright. A hoarse sound rises from his belly, scraping his throat raw. It takes him a few seconds to realise he's not tied to a chair in a back room in Belfast. The bedroom is dark and the clock on his nightstand glows green: 3.02 a.m. His throat is sore, his leg is throbbing and his sheets are drenched with sweat. He switches on the bedside lamp, slips off his T-shirt, wipes his face on it and throws it on the floor.

'Fuck this,' he says, opening the window and leaning on the sill, gulping lungfuls of cool air.

'I'm not staying here again. Fuckin' noise is off the scale. When you're not screaming yer tits off, you're snoring like a fuckin' wounded hippo. How's a fella s'posed to get any sleep?'

Twill turns. Lucan is hovering in the doorway. Twill looks back out the window.

'You okay?'

Twill nods and puts his head back in the bedroom.

Lucan's eyes move to his scars. 'Fuckin' swan again?'

Twill shakes his head, no. 'How do you know about the swan?'

Lucan squirms, only for a fraction of a second, but it's enough. 'Ya told me about it yerself, silly old fuck.'

Twill rubs his eyes and lets it go.

'Besides,' Lucan continues, 'when ya said you were getting noshed on by a bird, I did *not* think that was what ya meant.'

'Go to bed,' Twill says with a snarl, and climbs back into his own.

'Okay.' Lucan stabs his finger in Twill's direction. 'But I'm telling you this for nothing, all of this is going on TripAdvisor.'

'Fuck off.'

'EVERYTHING.'

Twill turns off the light and waits for the door to shut. He stares at the ceiling for a few minutes, then sighs and takes a small bottle of pills from his bedside table.

10

Newbury Park, East London

Twill drives in a circle for twenty minutes and regrets not taking the bus. The roads are packed tightly with near-identical terraced houses. Row after row of small gardens and lean-to porches, very few with house numbers. This is a community that expects people to know where they're going. He pulls to the side of the road and examines a scrap of paper as if the hand-written address holds further clues. Cursing under his breath, he eases his foot on the accelerator past a parade of shops topped with flats, almost missing the sign for Glenham Close, high up on the wall of a thin street branching off to his right. He stamps on the brake and the Rover squeals to a halt. Looks over his shoulder and slips the car into reverse, backing up just enough to turn in.

He doesn't need the house number in the end—72 Glenham Close has a wreath of roses in the front window that spell *Tumble*. Twill finds a space a few doors down, wriggles out of his car and leans against the side, stretching his leg out straight. Tumble's home is a neglected two-up two-down, in a cul de sac. Twill pushes past a gate half off its hinges, down an uneven path with weeds sprouting from the cracks. There's a dark stain down the front of the house. Creepers coil from a length of broken guttering held up with string. He can't find a doorbell so knocks and smooths down his hair while he waits.

A middle-aged woman in a blue housecoat answers. Grey-streaked hair is pinned up and she wears a slash of scarlet lipstick. Maybe early fifties. Or forties with a tough life under her belt. Her face is puffy and her eyes are red.

Twill pulls what he hopes is a warm smile and extends a hand. 'Mrs Dwyer?'

The woman folds her arms across her stomach and leans on the doorway. She brings a cigarette up to her mouth and takes a long draw; the tip glows red and she blows a cloud of grey-blue smoke above his head. 'Once upon a time.'

Twill starts to speak. 'I'm—'

'Oh, I know who you are,' she says with a withering glare. 'I grew up looking at you and your mate's ugly mugs.'

Twill's smile fades and his hand drops.

The woman takes another drag on her cigarette and looks him up and down. 'C'mon. You'd better come in.'

Twill follows her into a narrow hallway with peeling wallpaper. It's oppressively hot with sticky carpets and an odour of fried food and fags. The woman pushes on the lounge door and nods. Twill enters and she closes the front door behind him. She motions to one of two armchairs with white lace headrests, facing each other in front of a glowing three-bar heater. He slips off his jacket and lowers himself into the chair. She sits opposite, stubs out the cigarette in an already overflowing ashtray teetering on the arm of her chair. Without taking her eyes off him she picks up a crumpled packet and lighter from a side table and lights another. She sucks on it, then jabs it towards the wall, tendrils of smoke snaking out from her nose. Twill turns. There's an old regimental photo in a cheap gold frame on the mantelpiece.

'May I?'

She nods.

He winces as he leans forward, putting weight on his bad leg. The picture is black and white. The team are lined up in two rows in front of what looks like an Anderson shelter. Cilla, Tumble, JR, Max and him at the front on their knees, and behind them, Beast, Ghost, LoveSick, Mincer and Lucan. They look like a glam-rock band, all long hair and bell-bottom jeans. He lingers on the figure at the end. Bridges. *The Eagles. Hereford, 1972* is a shaky scribble at the bottom.

'So, I finally get to meet the famous Owen Twill,' the woman says, her voice flat.

Twill tries another smile even though his jaw's beginning to ache. 'You recognise me from the photo?'

'Well, it wouldn't be from the funeral would it?'

Twill glances down. 'No. Sorry. Funerals aren't my thing.'

'That's okay. Not my bag either,' she says. 'And, no. It's the leg that gave you away. I'm Terri.'

Twill nods and smiles thinly. 'How long were you married?'

Terri laughs which is soon a hacking cough. 'I'm not his wife, you daft bugger. He was my dad.'

Twill pulls his knees together. 'Oh. Sorry.'

'You do that a lot.'

Twill raises his eyebrows.

'Say sorry, I mean. You've nothing to be sorry for…as far as I know.'

'I see. I didn't want to go to the funeral because it seems like they're the only invites I get these days. But I wanted to say how sorry—'

Terri rolls her eyes and takes another pull on her cigarette.

'Okay, not sorry…how sad I was to hear about Tumble.'

Smoke billows from her mouth. 'Don't call him that. His name was Jim. I always hated that nickname. Tumble Dwyer. Ha bloody ha. Which comic genius came up with that one?'

Twill blinks but doesn't look away.

Terri flicks a length of smouldering embers into the ashtray. 'How come you never got a nickname?'

'Dunno. Maybe that was the joke. I'm not funny enough to get one.'

She sniffs, digs out a tissue from under her sleeve and wipes her nose. 'What do you want, Mr Twill?'

'Owen, please.'

She rubs the heel of her hand against her chest.

'I don't want anything—'

'Oh, don't piss in my pocket and tell me it's raining. You've not seen my dad in what, decades, and all of a sudden he's Mr fucking Popular.'

Twill shifts forward in his seat. 'Popular?'

Terri snorts and her shoulders drop. 'My dad was a good man. None of you lot gave a shit when he was alive.'

'What do you mean by popular?'

She takes another drag and flicks ash onto the carpet. A cloud of smoke rolls in the air and she gets up. 'I s'pose you want a cup of tea.'

'Wouldn't say no.'

'Right,' she says, and leaves.

Twill undoes his top button and loosens his tie. He's drawn back to the mantelpiece. There's something about the picture that isn't right. Then it comes to him—everyone in the shot is off centre. He picks up the frame, turns it over and unclips the back. The glass slides out easily. One third of the photo is folded back on itself. It springs up and he flattens it. There's Cromer looking pleased with himself, and a tall man with a buzz cut and square jaw in a tan uniform Twill doesn't recognise. Neurons fire in his limbic system. He feels he should know the face, but it's out of reach. A hoarse cough erupts from the kitchen. He snaps the picture on his phone and puts it back in the frame. By the time Terri shuffles back into the room with two cups and a cigarette—more ash than filter—hanging from her bottom lip, he's already in his seat.

'Thanks,' he says.

Terri settles herself and sips her tea. 'So then, you gonna tell me what this is all about?'

Twill searches her face. 'I want to know how…Jim died.'

'He didn't fucking kill himself; I can tell you that for nothing,' Terri says, jabbing her cigarette toward him.

'That's what I was told.'

'You was told wrong then.'

'What did the coroner say?'

Terri drains her cup and lights another cigarette. 'You people. You think you know everything.'

Twill stretches his hands out in front of him, palms down. 'I don't know *anything*. That's why I'm here.'

She stares back.

'What makes you think he didn't kill himself?' he says. 'Did he leave a note?'

Terri straightens and pulls her shoulders back. 'Dad was doing well. *Really* well. I was so proud of him. And, no, there was no note because there was no suicide.'

'He had…problems?'

'Had problems?' Her voice is high. 'That don't come close to covering it.'

'Go on.'

'Listen, Mr Twill, he was doing great. The therapy was working and he was the happiest I can remember—'

'Wait, he was in therapy?'

'Yeah, so what? Nothing wrong with it. Only thing that bloody worked if you ask me.'

'Where?'

'Kings Cross.'

'Why?'

Terri studies him. 'PTSD they call it. He got it in spades. Nightmares, the lot. His doctor gave him some magic pills. She said—'

'She?'

'Yeah,' Terri replies. 'They got women doctors and everything now.'

'I didn't…never mind. Go on.'

'I don't know what you want me to say. I know my dad. He was doing okay. No way he jumped off some bloody cliff. He was terrified, and I mean shit scared of heights.'

Twill shuffles back into his seat. 'Where?'

Terri sighs heavily and looks down at her feet. She crumples and clasps her hands in her lap. 'They found his car near Eastbourne.'

'Beachy Head?'

She begins to sob. Twill thinks about reaching out but changes his mind. A few moments pass, then she sniffs and looks up at Twill with a slack expression and dull, wet eyes.

'He wouldn't do that. Leave me alone, I mean.'

Twill nods. 'What did he drive?'

Terri frowns and points at the window. 'Blue Renault. Outside.' Her face darkens then she stands and clears her throat. 'I had to go and collect it myself.'

'When was all this?'

'Friday, March 23rd. He was there…here, exactly where you're sitting actually, when I nipped out to the shops. Half an hour later. Gone.'

'What time?'

'We'd just listened to *Desert Island Discs*, so must have been ten o'clock. I went straight out.'

'And how was he that morning?'

Her hand, still clutching a cigarette between two fingers, rubs at a temple. 'I can't deal with all these questions. I know he didn't kill himself, okay?'

'Did you tell the police this?'

'Of course, I bloody did. Did they give a shit? No!'

Twill gives her a second and starts to speak but she talks over the top of him.

'I think you should go now, Mr Twill. It does me no good raking up all this shit.'

He rises slowly and hands her a cup of cold tea. She puts the cup on the table and ushers him to the front door.

'One last question. Why did you say he was popular?'

Terri shakes her head. 'What does it matter? He's gone now.' She dabs at her eyes with the same tissue she'd been blowing her nose on.

'It matters,' Twill says, voice dropping. 'Tell me.'

'First there was his CO, Cromer. He came to see Dad about a month before he…before he died.'

'First?'

'Then there was some bloke, Mason or summat.'

Twill shakes his head. 'Who's that?'

'Old friend from the army, Dad said. You don't know him?'

Twill feigns a benign smile and throws his hand up. 'There's a lot I don't remember. I'm not getting any younger. Describe him?'

Terri rubs her face. 'Dunno really. Typical old squaddie. About your age, I s'pose.'

'And this was before he died?'

'Yeah, day before.'

'Anyone else?'

'No, but you got to remember, Dad went years without getting a single visitor. Then two old faces from his past turn up and he…' Her shoulders start to shake again.

'It's okay. I'm sorry.'

Terri cracks a grin through tear-filled eyes. 'There you go again.'

Twill shrugs.

'Look, I'm sorry I can't be of more help, Mr Twill, but I promise you, I swear to you, Dad never took his own life. I know that.'

'I believe you,' Twill says and turns away.

He's almost at the gate when she calls after him.

'Oh, there was a phone call too.'

Twill halts and turns. 'Phone call?'

'Yes. Just before Cromer's visit.'

'Who was it?'

'Some woman. Foreign accent. I took the call and put Dad on. He didn't say much. Went white as a sheet though.'

'What kind of accent?'

'American,' she says. 'Just like off the telly.'

***

Twill gives his number to Tumble's daughter and leaves Glenham Close, his head buzzing with questions and a jumble of half-formed theories.

Tumble didn't leave a note.

Cromer lied when said he hadn't seen Tumble since Belfast.

Bridges. Everything about Bridges.

The mystery phone calls from America.

Who are Mason and the gate-crasher in the photograph?

He drives past the blue Renault, committing Bravo Yankee Ten, Yankee Zulu Oscar to memory, hangs a left at the junction, and slows outside the parade of shops. There's a chip shop and a dry cleaner's but it's the newsagent that interests him. Sitting atop a red striped awning is a CCTV camera, angled to take in the entrance but also catching the corner of Glenham Close.

A car pulls out forcing him to brake heavily. He breaks into an instant sweat and the car windows begin to steam up. A knot of compulsion appears in the pit of his stomach and tendrils of white-hot anger lick at the back of his throat. He leans on the horn and gets a finger out of the window in return. It takes every ounce of self-control not to floor the accelerator and ram the car. He imagines dragging the protesting driver out of his seat and slamming his face against the tarmac until it's a bloody mess and the pleading stops…

He pulls into the vacated space and switches off the ignition. Closes his eyes and sucks his breath in—one, two, three. Hold. Repeat. He taps the steering wheel, gear stick, heater nob and radio switch, then recites the alphabet backwards.

The fizzing in his temples subsides and he undoes his seatbelt and climbs out.

The door to the newsagent opens with a tinkle. The man behind the counter is barely visible beyond a stack of chocolate bars and racks of brightly coloured sweets. He looks up briefly, then returns to his crossword. Twill picks a packet of gum at random and rattles his pocket for change. Without looking up, the newsagent scans the gum and holds out his hand. He speaks with an Asian accent. 'Forty-five pees.'

Twill examines the contents of his pockets, takes his wallet from his jacket and slaps a twenty-pound note on the counter.

The newsagent looks from the note to Twill then back to his crossword. 'No.'

Twill clenches and unclenches a fist. 'What do you mean, no?'

A look of irritation crosses the newsagents face, and he gives Twill a hard smile. 'No.' He picks up the gum, places it back in the rack and looks down at the crossword.

'What if I was to say keep the change?'

The newsagent jolts his head up and studies Twill. He frowns and tugs on his ear. 'I'd wonder what you wanted. Other than chewing gum.'

'Your CCTV.'

The newsagent follows Twill's eyes to the front of the shop.

'You're going to do something for me,' Twill says, picking up and opening the gum packet. He pops a strip into his mouth and glares at the storekeeper. 'Okay?'

The newsagent shifts his weight from one foot to another. 'That depends…'

Twill scowls and spits the gum onto the floor. He reads the packet. 'Fucking blueberry?' He turns back to the newsagent. 'Get a pen.'

'What are—'

'*Get a pen.*'

The newsagent scrabbles around, finds one, and folds the newspaper in half.

'Write this down: Friday 23rd March, sometime between 10 a.m. and 10.30 a.m., a blue Renault, registration Bravo Yankee Ten, Yankee Zulu Oscar, exited Glenham Close. You are going to send your clearest image to this email address.' Twill grabs the newspaper and pen from the startled newsagent and scribbles something in the margin. He slides the paper back across the counter. 'Are we clear?'

The shopkeeper nods and bites his lip. Eyes the note. 'This is going to take a long time…' he says, and looks up at Twill optimistically.

Twill leans on the counter and puts his face an inch away from the shopkeeper's. 'If I don't hear from you by close of business tomorrow, I'm going to come back and burn your shitty little shop to the ground. With you inside.'

***

Twill gets back into his car. The return journey takes just over an hour. There are two emails waiting for him when he arrives home. The first is from Cromer and reads: *Call me.* The second is from an address he doesn't recognise but includes an attachment, a series of JPEGs with the view outside the newsagent. One of the images shows the blue Renault. Tumble is clearly visible, looking straight ahead from the passenger seat. The driver is a blur but too big to be his daughter.

It seems every time he finds an answer to a question, another five pop up. His head starts to spin again so he knocks back two pills and pours himself a Scotch. He sinks into his armchair and shuts his eyes. The seed of a plan starts to germinate.

It's time to start laying some breadcrumbs.

11

Kings Cross, London

The room is beige and bland, carpet, furniture, curtains—all of it. A masterclass in banal. Nothing to distract.

A glance at the doctor. She's cross-legged, head tilted, staring at him with that awful, cloying expression based in arrogance, but flirting with amusement. Fawn hair parted in the middle. Cream cardigan. Pearls. Does she dress to be sexless? Maybe she's gunning for the mumsy look. Perhaps it's supposed to encourage him to open up.

Talk to mummy…

She can fuck off, Twill thinks. Straight on the bland list, in at number one.

Did Tumble sit in this same uncomfortable chair, feeling the same resentment and facing the same barrage of well-rehearsed lines? All these patronising little sneers, tricks and traps? It's been four decades since he left the regiment and the grip around his neck is as tight as ever. Still beholden. How the fuck does that work? Turn up for these appointments or you lose your pension. What kind of a choice is that? Him and his mates changed the world. And this is their reward.

Twill switches his weight from one buttock to the other and sighs loudly.

How many of his mates still come to this bullshit? What about JR and Mincer? Did they come too? No point in asking Lucan. He'd just laugh it off, make some stupid joke or cuckoo noise, and that would be that. His mates don't do weakness. Back in the pub, LoveSick had mentioned meetings. Was that here? And is he so low that he doesn't care anymore? How low do you have to be? It's not as…

Walsh clears her throat. 'Don't you think we should continue?'

Twill makes a point of looking at the clock on the wall behind her. 'Seven minutes. Not bad. Probably the most productive seven minutes I've had in here.'

She smirks and scribbles on her notepad.

'See, that annoys me. What are you even doing there? Playing noughts and crosses? The *Telegraph* crossword?' He purses his lips. 'You sunk my battleship?'

'It's interesting that you feel the need to push back against everyone who tries to help you, Owen.'

'Oh, yes. Very interesting,' Twill mimics, rubbing his chin. 'Truly fascinating, one might say.'

Walsh laughs politely and writes something down, then taps the pen against her teeth and looks over at him. 'You're positively verbose this morning. I think that little outburst is the most words you've ever said in one go.' A warm smile spreads across her face. 'You must be exhausted.'

'Oh, we can go back to the silence if you want,' Twill says. 'After all, you just got paid for a seven-minute game of Statues.'

'I think we'll continue,' Walsh says, winking. 'Let's see if we can channel some of this new found…loquaciousness. Strike while the iron's hot, as it were. Are you still having the dreams?'

Twill waves her away and grunts.

'The swan or…' She studies him.

A red-hot anger flares briefly in his gut.

'…the period you don't want to talk about?'

'Which fucking period would that be then?' Twill snaps, struggling out of his seat. He walks around the back and grabs the backrest with both hands, stretching his leg out behind him.

'We both know why we're here. And we'd both benefit if you'd extend me a little trust—'

'Trust has to be earned,' Twill says, calm once more.

Walsh pushes her glasses back up the bridge of her nose.

Twill switches legs and says, 'Did Tumble trust you?'

Walsh lowers her chin to her chest and her neck flushes.

'Who is Tumble?' she asks in a high-voice.

She's pretending to read her notes but he's not fooled.

Twill straightens and folds his arms on the backrest. 'In fact, you could say your track record looks a bit shit. What about Mincer and JR? Fuck all use to them, weren't you?'

Walsh coughs into her hand. 'Even if I knew who you were talking about, I couldn't possibly discuss the work I do with other patients.'

'What about LoveSick? Does he sit here and cry his little heart out?'

'Owen, these are names I don't know and I refuse to engage you in what is nothing more than a distraction technique.' She shuffles her papers and removes a page from her clipboard. 'Let me see…you were snatched off the street in Anderstown, West Belfast, on the twenty sixth of October, 1972. You were held, tortured and dumped near your barracks ten days later.' Walsh licks a finger and flicks through some pages. 'Part of some prisoner exchange.' She lets the pages fall back into place and returns to the sheet in her hand. 'The surgeon saved your leg but you subsequently displayed symptoms of post-traumatic stress…you eventually returned to the regiment having been awarded the Conspicuous Gallantry Cross but you became unstable. And, although sympathetic to your plight, your commanding officer deemed your decision-making abilities compromised. All of which led to your honourable discharge with full pension in August 1978.'

'Aha. Full pension *if* I dance like a monkey on a piece of string.'

'So, all this latent anger—against me, your commanding officer, your injuries—all these…consequences can be traced back to what happened in those ten days. And yet here we are. Four decades on and you refuse to talk about it.'

Twill looks down at his fingers and nibbles at a hangnail.

'What happened, Owen? Talk to me.'

Twill shrugs.

Walsh leans forward. 'Everyone understands. They were exceptional circumstances and you were under tremendous pressure. If you told them—'

Twill is out of his seat, face burning, teeth bared. '*I told them nothing.*'

Walsh lifts her palms, face out. 'It's okay. No one would blame you if you did. What you—'

'NOT A FUCKING WORD. YOU HEAR ME?'

'Fine. Okay.' Walsh, ashen-faced and blinking hard, pushes herself back in her seat. 'Please, sit down, Owen.'

'Fucking joke this is,' he mutters, but sits down all the same. He turns side on to the doctor and starts counting his breaths. She'll let him finish. She always does. The fury subsides and he mumbles a barely audible apology.

'Can I get you a drink of water?' she asks softly.

Twill shakes his head.

'You seem more…animated today. Have you been taking your pills?'

He turns back to her. 'Yes. One a day, plus a little Brucie bonus when the leg plays up.'

'What about alcohol? Are you drinking more than usual?'

'I don't touch the stuff. Gave up ages ago.'

More scribbling. 'Any other external stimuli you can think of?'

'No…it's…' Twill puts his head in his hands. 'It's the dreams.'

'We can always try some new medication.'

'No, no more pills.' Twill attempts a smile and says in a soft voice, 'I'm sorry about the…you know.'

Walsh looks at him expectantly but a buzzer sounds and a flash of relief crosses his face. Without waiting to be asked, he stands and leaves the room.

Outside in the corridor, he pulls the door closed with a heavy click. It's always the same. The people who think they're the smartest are the easiest to fool.

***

The journey home is uneventful. A bus to Liverpool Street, a train to Ashford but getting off at Stratford and jumping last minute through closing doors on a fast train to Colchester.

His leg is throbbing like an infected tooth so he pops a tablet and gets a cab instead of walking the rest of the way. The taxi drops him a street away and he takes up position at the bus stop opposite his house. He waits five minutes but no traffic passes twice or slows down. He crosses the road feeling suddenly very tired and very old. He slows as he approaches the gate. It's ajar and the length of tape is flapping in the wind. His pulse quickens and the fatigue leaves him. He reaches into his coat and flicks his wrist. A thick metal baton is extended.

An ear pressed to the front door gives no clues. The key slides in silently and smoothly. He turns it. The door clicks and Twill tenses every muscle, like an athlete waiting for the starter pistol. He counts to five and nudges the door. It glides open without a sound. A glance at the wall—the alarm has been deactivated. He takes a deep breath, holds it and steps into the hallway.

Muted voices drift from the lounge. One deep and low. Then another. He waits. There's two of them, but they're too quiet to identify. He lets the breath out in a controlled whoosh and pants until he feels energised, a little dizzy even. He tightens his grip on the baton, leans back and kicks the lounge door. He's in the room swinging before it can bounce back at him.

'*Jesus Christ!*' Lucan screams, leaping up from the floor and scrabbling away from the mill of twirling metal. 'Are ya trying to fuckin' kill us?'

'Fuck's sake,' Twill says.

LoveSick is slumped in his armchair, shoulders hunched, arms crossed in his lap. His eyes are lined with red and dull like frosted glass. Even from the other side of the room Twill can smell the fumes radiating from him.

'You look like shit.'

'Of course, he looks like shit. There's no food or booze—nothing—in the fridge. What kinda joint ya running here?' Lucan says, straightening his donkey jacket, and then quieter, 'Scared the shit outta me, Bruce fuckin' Lee.'

Twill lowers the baton and turns to him. 'What the fuck are you doing here?'

'Oh, nice,' Lucan replies. 'Charming. Pleased to see ya too, mate.' He spits out the last word. 'Ya gave me a key, ya fuckin' spaz, remember?'

Twill flicks his wrist and the baton retreats into the handle. He puts it back in his coat and pats his hair into place. 'I didn't give you any key.'

'But. still, there it was, hanging up on the hook yesterday morning, calling to me…'

'How's that giving you a fucking key?' Twill says, voice rising.

Lucan screws up his face and dismisses Twill with a wave of his hand. 'Let's not get bogged down with who did what.'

Twill folds his arms and raises his eyebrows. 'And the alarm?'

'What *now*? 9-7-2-8-4. If ya didn't want me to see it, ya shouldn't let me stand so close.'

Twill clicks his fingers and extends a hand, palm up.

'You can be very hurtful sometimes, ya know that?' Lucan tuts and takes a key from his jacket.

Twill pockets the key and is about to speak when Lucan butts in. 'And what's the deal with the single chair, eh? Hardly cosy now, is it?'

Twill looks across at LoveSick, who gives him a forced smile.

'C'mon,' he says. 'The Prettygate.'

Lucan slaps Twill on the back and winks at LoveSick. 'Let's go. Last one there gets 'em in.'

***

LoveSick sinks half his pint in one gulp. His eyes soften and lose some of their hardness.

'Cheers,' he says, wiping his mouth on the back of his sleeve.

'Cheers, mate.' Lucan raises his glass. 'The two-two.'

'Aye,' LoveSick replies. 'The two-two.' He takes another deep draw on his drink—nearly finished after two swigs—and adds, 'To absent friends.'

'You want to tell me what this is all about?' Twill says, prompting a dig in the ribs from Lucan. 'I mean, nice to see you and all, but what the fuck's going on?'

'It's okay. I always liked you, Twill,' LoveSick says. 'You speak your mind. Makes it easier to know where you stand.'

'We need to go back a bit,' Lucan says. 'LoveSick turned up on my doorstep last night. This morning. Whatever. He was there when I opened the door anyways. Fallen off the wagon and in quite an impressive way.'

Twill weighs up his friend. He's rubbing his wrists, and his lips are on the move, mouthing words that die in his throat. Lank hair falls in greasy locks over a pallid, pitted face. Skin is bunched up around bruised eyes, and his stare is pained and unfocused.

LoveSick looks at Twill then back at his empty glass. Twill puts a twenty on the table and says to Lucan, 'Get them in.'

'Do ya think that's—'

'The man wants a fucking drink,' Twill snaps. 'We're not children here.'

Lucan rolls his eyes, says, 'Yass, bawss,' and snatches up the note.

Twill waits until Lucan is some feet away before turning back to LoveSick. 'What's going on?'

'I'm a fucking mess, mate.' He sucks his cheeks in.

'You don't say?'

'I can't sleep. I can't concentrate. I can't do anything.'

'Why not?'

LoveSick snorts. 'Go on. Take a wild stab in the dark.'

Twill takes a sip and sets his glass down, shuffles it so it fits a ring stain on the table. 'What happened back then…it was important work.'

There's a desperation on LoveSick's face that surprises Twill.

'It never bothered you what we did?'

Twill shakes his head. 'Just a job. That's all.'

'You don't ever think about Caitlyn?'

The words sting. LoveSick reaches for him and he leans back.

'You know if you hadn't done what you did, there would have been four funerals instead of three?'

'Never do, never has. Bothered me, I mean. Just the way I am.'

'You're special, that's for sure.'

Twill makes to speak but LoveSick talks over the top of him. 'I don't mean that as an insult. We were all special.'

Cromer's words ring in Twill's mind—*You, the gang. All eight of you. Special. You ever stop to wonder about that?*

'What is it?' LoveSick says.

'Someone else said the same thing recently.'

LoveSick scratches his wrist. 'It would take someone special to do what we did and not crack.'

'Is that what this is? Are you cracking?'

'*Cracking?*' LoveSick laughs scornfully. 'Try fucking cracked, mate. Broken. As. Fuck.'

Twill grabs LoveSick's arm with one hand and rips up his sleeve with the other, exposing a row of purple scars running from wrist to elbow.

'Jesus fucking Christ, LoveSick.'

LoveSick yanks his sleeve down and cradles his empty glass.

'So,' Twill says. He looks over at the bar. Lucan still in line. 'You mentioned you were seeing someone…to help?'

'Aye,' LoveSick replies, still looking down at the table. 'Some bird.'

'Walsh?'

LoveSick looks up, startled. 'You know her?'

'Oh, yeah. I know her alright.' A flush of adrenalin makes him tingle. 'You think she's helping?'

'What do you fucking think?'

'I don't know. That's why I asked.' Twill glances over his shoulder. Some guy in an England shirt is jabbing Lucan in the chest; his friend looks amused.

'She talks a lot about…suicide. Keeps asking if I feel like hurting myself.'

'Does she know about—' Twill gestures at LoveSick's arm.

'No.' LoveSick looks up. His eyes are full of tears. 'She keeps banging on and on about it. Won't fucking shut up.'

Twill rests a hand on his shoulder. 'It's okay.' Raised voices come from the bar but he doesn't look round. 'Does she give you pills?'

LoveSick wipes his face on his sleeve, sniffs, and rummages around in his jacket. He produces a plastic container. Twill takes it from him and holds it at arm's length. Thorazine.

'They help?' Twill asks, holding them under LoveSick's nose and giving them a rattle.

LoveSick scratches his cheek. 'Dunno. Been having some right 'orrible nightmares. Real shockers. They started about the same time as the pills. Dr Walsh says it's a coincidence.'

Twill drains his pint. A hush has fallen behind him at the bar, and he resists the urge to look over.

'Coincidence is the word we use when we can't see the levers and pulleys.'

'Eh?'

'I read that once. Stayed with me.'

'But what does it mean?'

'It means I'm keeping these.'

There's movement in the corner of his eye and the pills go into his pocket. He and LoveSick turn at the same time. A fat man is hovering next to them. Mid-thirties, England shirt two sizes too small, stretched over a third-trimester stomach, rosy cheeks and fidgety eyes. He's clutching three pints. Lucan's round face pops up over his shoulder, split from ear to ear in a grin.

He tips his head forward and whispers theatrically into the man's ear. 'Go on, then. As we discussed, Gary.'

The man steps forward, clears his throat. 'Gentlemen, here are your beverages.'

Lucan claps with his fingertips and squeals, 'Twill, LoveSick, this is my new friend Gary.' He turns to the man's ear again. 'Go on, don't be rude. Say hello, Gary.'

Gary sets the drinks down with trembling hands and smiles awkwardly.

'Thanks for the drinks, Gazza,' Lucan says in an exaggerated cockney accent, his smile fading. 'You can be on ya way now.'

Gary turns, trips over his own feet and runs back to the bar.

'You're a fucking lunatic.' Twill sighs and shakes his head.

LoveSick dissolves into giggles. When he stops his eyes are bright and shining. 'I fucking miss you guys,' he says and drinks greedily from his pint.

Lucan pulls up his chair. 'So, what are you girls talking about?'

Twill looks from LoveSick to Lucan. 'Stuff.'

'What kind of stuff?'

LoveSick shoves his hands in his pockets and looks up to the ceiling. '*FUCK.* This is so embarrassing. I'm sorry. I shouldn't have come.'

'Hey,' Lucan says. 'Bullshit. We're brothers. Ya did the right thing.'

'He's right,' adds Twill. 'Bring Lucan up to speed.'

LoveSick lays his palms on the table. 'I'm a fucking mess, mate. I don't sleep, and when I do, I see things. Things you don't want to see.'

Lucan leans forward on his elbows. 'Go on.'

'And it hurts. It fucking shouldn't but it hurts. I drink, I fight and they go away, *but they always come back.* The voices. Pleading. Begging. *I see their faces…*'

Twill looks Lucan in the eye and waits for a reaction. 'LoveSick's got a therapist.'

Lucan's pupils dilate for a fraction of a second. He throws his hands up. 'So what?'

Twill says, 'So do I.'

Lucan clicks his fingers and looks sideways. 'Is this that mandated therapy crap they sent letters about?'

'Yes! Some bird, Dr Walsh.'

Lucan blasts out a sigh that rattles his lips. 'Fuck that. I told them to poke it.'

'Did that work?'

'Course. They're only covering their arses. They don't give a shit about us.'

'LoveSick, look at me,' Twill says, lowering his head. 'I don't think you should go anymore. I mean that.'

'I don't *want* to go…They threatened to stop my pension.'

'They ain't gonna do shit,' Lucan says. 'Leave it with me. I'll speak to Cromer.'

LoveSick looks wistful for a moment. 'Isn't it supposed to help?'

Twill snorts. 'Didn't help JR or Mincer. And it's not helping you now, is it?'

'Or Tumble,' Lucan adds.

Twill takes a deep breath. 'Tumble didn't kill himself.'

'Whaaat?' Lucan squeals.

'I went to see his daughter. It was the therapist that said he was suicidal. His daughter admitted he was troubled, but he wouldn't have topped himself.' Twill thinks about sharing the CCTV image of Tumble being driven to a windswept clifftop by a mystery driver but instinct stops him.

LoveSick drains the last few drops from his glass. 'If I wasn't confused before, I am now.'

Lucan presses his lips together and whispers, 'What about JR and Mincer?'

Twill shrugs.

Lucan continues. 'So, if Tumble didn't top himself, what happened?'

'Look,' Twill says, 'I don't know. But I don't trust the therapy we've been roped into, and I certainly don't trust Cromer.'

He can almost see the cogs turning behind LoveSick's eyes.

'Cromer again.' Lucan huffs. 'Ya gotta drop all this conspiracy bullshit.'

'Twill, are you saying Tumble was killed?' LoveSick says.

'I'm not saying anything. And I don't know about the others but I'm not going to sit back and wait for a "coincidence" to throw me off a fucking cliff.'

'Have you spoken to anyone else?'

An image flashes through Twill's mind—Lewis Bridges, eyes cloudy and frozen over, mouth wide in a silent scream. Bloody hands scrabbling at a knife handle buried in his chest. He looks at Lucan. 'No. And I think it's best we keep it that way until we've done some digging. You?'

LoveSick wrinkles his brow. 'Got a few letters from Max, but they stopped about a year ago.'

'Fuck, Max,' Lucan says. 'Forgotten about him. Never came to any of the funerals.'

'Said he wouldn't. Said he couldn't look you guys in the eye.'

'What does that mean?'

'Dunno. In his last letter he asked after you. I'd already said we should organise a get-together. You know, one of those regimental reunions. He said he wouldn't come.'

'And the letters stopped a year ago?' Twill says.

'What…you don't think—'

'I don't think anything. What did they say, the letters?'

'Nothing really. You know we was always close. Not in regular contact, like. Just Christmas cards and the occasional updates. Always asked about you lot. It's like he wanted to be kept in touch, but at arm's length.'

'How was he doing?' Lucan asks.

'Fine. Really well, actually. He had some firm; he was his own boss. Life sounded good.' LoveSick smiles. 'He even offered me work.'

'What line of work?'

'Security or summat.'

Lucan looks at Twill then back to LoveSick. 'What kind of security? Door work? Security guard?'

LoveSick squints and shakes his head. 'Dunno. Never got that far. I…wasn't ready.'

'What was his real name?' Lucan asks, pulling his phone from his pocket.

'Darren Mackie.'

'Let's see what good old Google has to say on the matter.' Lucan taps on his phone, his face lit up by the small screen. He pauses and frowns. 'What's fuckin' LinkedIn when it's at home?'

More tapping. He waits. His face darkens. He tosses the phone to Twill. Twill holds it at arm's length and squints. There, on the screen, is Max. He's laughing and has his arm around Lewis Bridges. Above them, a banner reads *Animus Security Services*. And underneath, in a smaller font, *Bespoke Solutions for Governments and the Corporate Sector*.

'Do you think he's alright?' LoveSick asks in a high voice, rubbing his arm again.

'I think we should pay him a visit,' Lucan replies. 'Check in on him, like.'

Twill gives a single nod.

Lucan smiles mischievously. 'I fuckin' love a road trip.'

LoveSick upends his empty glass over his mouth. 'Fuck it. I'm in.'

12

Burley, New Forest

The next day brings an expanse of blue sky blotted with ribbons of wispy cloud. The temperature has tipped into the low teens for the first time, and the birds are out en masse, voicing their approval. Lucan sits up front with Twill, while LoveSick stretches out on the back seat.

A couple of times, Twill catches him in the rear-view mirror, nipping from a pocket-sized bottle. At one point, their eyes meet and LoveSick looks away, face heavy with shame.

As the sun climbs, the mood brightens. Lucan turns up the radio and leads them in a chorus of 'Going Underground'. Twill's contribution is limited to a shallow nod. Twice his phone rings and twice he lets it ring out. Both times he feels Lucan's eyes on him. The emails, texts and voicemails from Cromer are piling up. There'll be time for him later. When he has some answers.

As the house-lined streets become a tangle of wooded back roads, a firm determination hardens in his gut. He will allow Lucan's attempt to rally spirits and look the other way as LoveSick drinks himself into a fog, but he cannot let it get in the way of their primary target. They're here for answers and he's not leaving without them.

The Animus website had given a contact number that went straight to voicemail, and an email address that bounced back with *Out of office*. The website domain is registered to an address on a nondescript industrial park on the edge of the New Forest. And that's where they're headed.

Twill's car picks its way through a series of seemingly identical picture-postcard villages, each with rows of cottages, neat, striped lawns and freshly trimmed hedges. They pass a pub on a village green and LoveSick sits up for the first time. Twill keeps his foot to the floor. If things go tits up with Max, the last thing they need is to be remembered in the local. Lucan and LoveSick are friends, and good ones, but inconspicuous they're not.

They eat up the miles and Twill's mind works overtime on a playbook. If Bridges was a partner, how much does Max know? Is he in contact with Cromer? Has he worked out what happened to Bridges? With three of them they had numbers on their side, although it's anyone's guess how much fight LoveSick has left in him. He talks the talk but Twill suspects any mental or physical fortitude has long been left at the bottom of a bottle. The element of surprise helps, but only goes so far. Once you're over the initial surprise, it's easy to slip into a role. Anyone who's been undercover is a better actor than most. What matters is those first few seconds before they realise a storm's about to hit.

'Slow down,' Lucan says, wrestling with the map. 'Ya want the next left.'

LoveSick pokes his head between the front seats. Twill doesn't mean to but recoils from the smell.

'It's okay,' LoveSick says in a quiet, determined voice. 'I know you think I'm a joke, but I'm up for this.'

Lucan glances at him. 'No one said—'

LoveSick shushes him. 'It's good...I'm good.'

Twill half turns and raises an eyebrow. 'You sure you don't want to sit this out?'

'Nah,' LoveSick replies. 'Fuck that.' He hands the bottle to Lucan, who puts it in the side pocket of the door. 'Just a little sharpener to stop the shakes.'

'Fine by me,' Lucan adds.

Twill just shrugs.

They drive for another five minutes through a windy lane skirted by woodland, and turn into a modern industrial park with rows of prefab offices with corrugated iron roofs.

'Plot number?' Twill asks.

'Er...27A.'

'Glovebox,' Twill says, clicking his fingers. 'Sunglasses and cap.'

Lucan pushes the map down into his lap and passes the gear to Twill.

'Right, LoveSick, get down and stay down. Lucan, look straight ahead and hold the map up to cover your face, don't be tempted to look. We'll drive past twice like we're lost, then we'll loop around and park in the next row along.'

LoveSick and Lucan nod. Twill puts on the glasses—green-lensed aviators—and pulls the peak of the cap down over his face.

'Oh,' Lucan says holding his phone to his ear, 'the 1970s called. Village People want their singer back.'

Twill sighs. 'Fuck off. And when you've finished fucking off, some focus please.'

They crawl past 27A and Twill shoots side-eyes from behind his glasses, and again on the return. He guides the car around the corner and pulls up a few doors from the back of the unit.

Lucan lowers the map. 'And?'

'No sign of life, shutters down. Single CCTV camera. Fixed mounting, possibly just for show. No signage either. You sure it's 27A?'

Lucan nods. 'Yep. Double checked domain registration and cross-referenced with filing at Companies House.'

Twill releases his seatbelt and makes to get up but a hand from behind pulls him back.

'I've got this,' LoveSick says. 'I'll be a surprise but he'll shit the bed if he sees you two. If he's there, it's better I'm first contact.'

The door slams and he appears at the driver's-side window. His face is grey but his eyes are clear. Twill presses a button and the glass slides into the door.

'Wait for my lead.'

Twill turns to Lucan, who nods. By the time he turns back, LoveSick is gone.

Twill reclines his seat and leans back. Time to kill. Lucan plays with his phone and whistles an irritating ditty. After just a few minutes, when Twill is close to saying something he might regret, LoveSick returns.

'No sign of him. Doors shuttered and padlocked. Cobwebs on the handle. Nobody been here for weeks, if not months.'

'Next door?' Twill asks, pulling his seat upright.

'Empty to the left, framing business on the right. Lights on and door open.'

'Okay,' Twill says, opening his door. 'Let's go meet the neighbours, shall we?'

They walk past 27A. Lucan rattles the shutters and Twill checks the post-box on the wall. LoveSick steps back into the road and looks up at the first floor, shielding his eyes from the sun.

'There's more life in Twill's dick,' Lucan shouts across to LoveSick. 'And that's saying something.'

Twill enters the store next door.

"You've Been Framed" has a showroom up front, with a desk and door through which Twill can see a workshop out back. There's not a clear inch on the walls; posters, prints and sport memorabilia from floor to ceiling. Twill marches past a hat stand made from antlers and up to the desk. A middle-aged man with a shiny pate stands. He's tall, angular and bubble-eyed and carries a permanent air of startled.

'Good morning.'

Twill grunts and takes his hat and glasses off.

'How can I help you today?'

'You are?' Twill asks.

The shopkeeper extends his hand. 'Gareth. Gareth Walker.'

'Pay attention, Gareth Walker. Next door. Animus.'

'Yes,' the man says, putting his hands on his hips. 'All gone quiet there.' He chuckles nervously.

Twill clenches a fist by his side. 'When did that happen?'

'Let me see…maybe twelve, fifteen months ago? It was never a hive of activity to be honest. The owner was nice enough…Darren something?'

'Mackie.'

'Yes, that's it. Mackie. I remember that because my mother-in-law comes from Macau.' He tilts his head. 'You know. Macau. In China.'

Twill's eyes bore into the shopkeeper and he growls.

'Kept himself to himself, really. I got the feeling this was just the registered office—you know, somewhere to get mail delivered to. Not as if you get much passing trade in that line of work. I was just saying to Carol from Paws For Thought at number thirty-two—'

'Have they shut down?'

The shopkeeper's face drop, and he sits back down and flicks through paperwork. When he speaks again, his voice is clipped. 'No. He popped around; said he was going away. That's all I know.'

'But the business is still open?'

Walker doesn't look up, just replies haughtily, 'I suppose it is.'

Lucan leans his knuckles on the desk, his face inches from the shopkeeper's. 'And what makes you *suppose* that, then?'

Walker takes his glasses off and pushes his chair back until it hits the wall. 'I…uh…'

'It's okay,' Twill says, laying a hand on Lucan's shoulder. 'We're old friends, trying to track him down.'

The shopkeeper remains pressed against the wall. 'Are you...are you bailiffs?'

Lucan turns to Twill. 'Did he not fuckin' hear ya?' And then to the man behind the desk. 'We're old friends, in town for a couple of days. Thought we'd look him up.'

'I'm sorry,' Walker says, returning to his paperwork. 'I really can't help you.'

Twill looks over his shoulder. LoveSick is leaning against the door frame, arms crossed. He turns back to the desk. 'I've got this pet hate, Gareth Walker, and it really doesn't bring out the best in me. Call me old-fashioned, but I have a big problem with people lying to me.'

Walker splutters and turns puce.

'His post.'

'Eh?'

Twill sighs and looks down at the pile of mail on the desk. 'Mackie's post-box is empty. These his?'

'No,' Walker says quickly, laying a hand on the pile.

'May I?' Lucan peels one of Walker's fingers back and the storekeeper man pulls his hand away sharply. 'Nah.' Drops a letter on the floor. 'Nah.' Same again. He waves a pizza voucher at Twill. 'This is making me hungry.'

'Wait,' Walker says.

Lucan pauses.

'I don't get his mail.'

'Who does then?'

'I-I suppose it's redirected.'

Twill crosses the room, takes the framed pictures off the wall and drops them on the floor. Walker shoots up but Lucan pushes him back down. His shoulders bunch up and flinch with every crash.

'It might be an idea to stop fuckin' *supposing* and start telling us the truth,' Lucan says. 'Maybe, and it's been said it's a fault of mine, I've been too subtle. So let me spell it out for ya. The truth, or by God I'll fuckin' beat ya like a rented mule.'

Twill returns to the desk. 'Junk mail and pizza vouchers wouldn't get redirected, would they? His post-box has been cleared out today. Completely empty. No vouchers, nothing.' Twill motions to the shopkeeper's pile of mail. 'And you're going to tell me by who.'

'But—I—look, if I say anything I might get hurt.'

'And if ya don't, you'll definitely get hurt.' Lucan adds in an American accent, 'Kinda sucks, huh?'

Walker scratches his neck and shakes his head. 'This is really not on. I don't know who—'

Lucan brings a finger to his lips. 'Don't make the mistake of thinking we give a flying fuck about you and ya precious sensibilities. Ya can give us what we want, and we're gone, or I can make the next fifteen minutes the longest of yer miserable fuckin' life. So, really, it's up to you. I'll end up getting what I need one way or the other. But don't think I care how, cos I don't.'

Walker's shoulders sag and he sucks in his cheeks. He reaches into a drawer, removes a pile of mail and drops it on his desk.

'And what do you do with it?' Twill asks.

'There's a kid,' Walker replies. 'Comes after school on his bike. I don't know what happens next.'

'How often and what time?'

'Every Wednesday. He'll be here later, after four.'

'In that case, so will we.' Lucan grins at him. 'And in the event you should feel tempted to tip him off—either the delivery boy or Darren—I would recommend having a long, hard word with yerself.'

'That would be foolish,' Twill says in a dark voice.

Walker nods quickly.

Twill calls for LoveSick over his shoulder, and says to Walker, 'My friend will stay and keep you company. You know, to discourage you from doing anything stupid.' He looks at his watch. 'Right. We're going to get pick up some lunch. LoveSick, we'll bring you back something.'

***

They're back within the hour. LoveSick demolishes a burger at the desk. When he's finished, Walker leaves the room, and returns with a fistful of tissues and a packet of wet wipes.

Twill explains he'll take up position at the end of the road in the car. LoveSick will stay in the store and Lucan will wait around the corner. At first sight of the boy, Twill will flash his headlights once. That's Lucan's cue to follow the boy into the store and secure the premises. Twill stays in the car until he sees Lucan at the front door, in case the boy makes a break for it.

***

At 4.12 p.m., a boy on an orange mountain bike whistles by the car, rucksack flailing in the air behind him. He skids to a halt outside the store, laying down a crescent of rubber, kicks out the bike's stand and rearranges his hair in the reflection of the shop window. Early teens, dyed claret hair and the anaemic colouring and dark eyes of a gamer that doesn't stray too far from his bedroom. Pipe-cleaner legs poke from the bottom of khaki shorts. He barges into the store, bag slung over one shoulder.

Twill flashes the headlights and Lucan appears from the shadows. He gives Twill the thumbs-up and follows the boy into the shop. The door closes behind him. Twill edges the car up to the storefront and nudges the bike with his bumper.

He goes inside the store. LoveSick stands between the boy—wide-eyed and close to tears—and Lucan. Walker is slumped in his chair, ashen faced.

The boy keeps repeating, 'I don't understand.'

'It's okay,' Twill says, and Lucan backs down. To the boy, 'Listen to me. You're not in any trouble but it's very important that you answer our questions, okay?'

The boy covers his mouth with his hand and nods.

'Right. We know you take this mail.' Twill gestures at a pile of letters on the desk. 'All we need to know is what you do with it.' He spreads his hands out in front, palms up. 'That's all.' Then adds with a smile, 'Then you're free to go. Got it?'

The boy sighs and sinks his hands into his pockets. 'I leave it for the man in the woods.'

Walker frowns.

'Who the fuck is the man in the woods?' Lucan asks.

The boy takes a half step back. Walker screws up his face and squishes his eyebrows. He's either extremely confused or an exceptional actor. No, the man's no actor.

'It…he's a homeless guy, lives in the woods. The local kids give him some stick but he's harmless enough.' Then to the boy, 'You give the post to him?'

96

The boy nods furiously.

Twill says to Walker, 'Is the man in the woods Darren Mackie?'

'I-I don't know.'

Twill holds his gaze for a second then turns back to the boy and softens his tone. 'Last question. How do you get the mail to him?'

The boy's eyes flit between Twill and Lucan. Saucers with pinpricks for pupils. 'The Owl House.'

'What's that?'

Walker says, 'It's a wooden bird box—'

Twill shoots him a look that freezes the words in his throat. Looks back at the boy.

'Go on.'

'He's right. It's a bird box at the entrance to the woods, by the car park. I can reach it by standing on my bike. He leaves a tenner for me, and I leave any mail in there. Then I wait.'

'For what?'

'Him. The man in the woods. He's usually already there, watching me, but sometimes he makes me wait, in case there's something needs posting. I leave the bike against the tree and sit on the bench. He gets his mail and if there's nothing for me to post, he disappears. We hardly ever speak.'

'Good lad,' Twill says, peeling a twenty from a wad of notes. 'Here. Tell me, is this your man in the woods?'

He holds up his phone and the boy narrows his eyes.

'It might be. He's got a beard and his face is covered in mud and stuff. His hair's longer too…but I think so.'

'He got one of these?' Twill rolls up his sleeve, exposing a tattoo of an eagle.

'Yes!' the boy replies. 'I've seen it.'

'Okay. Now, this is what you're going to do. I want you to carry on as usual, but don't make the drop until you see us. We'll be in the car park. And'—he leans forward so close he can feel the boy's breath on his face—'no matter what happens, no matter what you hear or read, no matter who asks today, tomorrow or in five years' time, this afternoon never happened. You've never seen us before. Right?'

The boy makes a move for the note but Twill pulls it back out of reach. 'Right?'

'Right,' the boy says, stuffing the money into his back pocket.

'Same goes for you,' Twill says to Walker, and the man nods.

Twill stands aside and the boy snatches the mail off the desk and runs past him and out the door.

Twill says to Lucan over his shoulder, 'Get the map from the car.' Then to the shopkeeper, 'You're going to show us where this Owl House is, Gareth Walker. Then we'll be out of your hair.' He twists his mouth into the ugliest smile he can manage. 'Unless you decide to break our little agreement.'

'I won't, I won't,' Walker says.

His voice is weak, his skin grey.

Twill believes him.

***

It's shortly after five and the sun is sinking below a skeletal tree line, stretching shadows and casting everything in an ochre blush. The boy weaves through the car park, his bike leaning with each downward pedal, and skids to a halt under a large oak at the start of the footpath. He glances over his shoulder at the car then leans the bike against the tree and clambers up. He reaches into the owl box and the door swings open. He takes something out and drops the mail in. He looks around at the car again and nearly loses his balance.

'Don't keep fucking looking,' Twill mutters.

The boy hops down, brushes his shorts and wanders over to a bench some twenty feet away. He busies himself on his phone.

Minutes pass. Visibility is fading fast. A figure emerges from behind a billowing rhododendron. He's almost a trick of the light—a long shadow in a dark coloured parka. If the boy notices or is bothered by his appearance, he shows no sign of it. The shadow is tentative at first. One foot onto the path then another. He pauses, framed against a leafy backdrop. Another minute passes, then he darts to the bike, hops up and rummages in the owl box.

Twill cranes his neck. 'Is that him?'

LoveSick, who hasn't had a drink in several hours and has fallen into a sulky trance, shrugs.

The shadow drops to his feet and looks around. He says something and the boy looks up from his phone and raises a hand.

Twill's still not convinced LoveSick's up to it but options are thin on the ground. 'Okay. Go now.'

The car door opens and the shadow freezes. LoveSick takes a few steps towards him. His voice, high and wavering, pierces the evening gloom. 'Darren…Max…It's LoveSick.'

The man backs up against the trees.

'Mate…I only want to talk.'

The shadow pauses then flicks the hood of his parka off his face. He stuffs the post into his jacket and moves his hand behind his back. The whites of his eyes are striking against his grimy face.

'LoveSick?'

'Yes, mate. It's me.'

Twill whispers, 'Go to him, but watch his right hand.'

LoveSick turns and looks at Twill.

'Who the fuck is that?' the man shouts.

Twill groans, gets out and stands beside LoveSick. 'Max. It's Twill.'

'*TWILL?* What the fuck are you doing here?'

'Nice,' Twill mumbles.

'I'm sorry,' LoveSick says.

Max glances around, the movement jerky, bird-like.

'Just talk, LoveSick. We're losing him.'

'Mate…we're worried about you,' LoveSick calls out.

The car park is silent except for the caws of a crow in a distant tree top. A streetlight flickers on, bathing Max in an orange glow, and he flinches. Other lights come on, one by one.

'It's him. It's Max,' LoveSick murmurs.

Max bends and sprints down the path. Three steps from the woods, Lucan shoots out from behind a tree and drops his shoulder. They both crash to the floor. A knife clatters from Max's hand and skitters across the path. Lucan is first up. He tucks the blade into his belt.

'Jesus, Max. What're ya fuckin' playin' at?'

Max tucks his knees up against his chest, gulping like a grounded fish.

Lucan bends and rests his hands on his knees. 'I'm getting too old for this shit.'

LoveSick runs over. Twill limps behind.

'Darren, you okay?'

Lucan laughs with an edge. 'I'm fuckin' grand, thanks for askin'.'

'This is it, then. My turn,' Max says.

'Darren, what're you talking about?' LoveSick says, lowering himself to his haunches.

Twill steps forward and extends a hand. Max shakes his head, takes it. Twill pulls him up. Max shoots Lucan a sideways glance and brushes down his trousers.

'Ya missed a bit,' Lucan says, pointing.

'Fuck off,' Max replies, squaring up.

Lucan grits his teeth. 'Ya not had enough, Worzel Gummidge?'

'Okay, Lucan. Stand down,' Twill says. 'Darren, we just want to talk. We're not here to hurt you.'

'Why would you think that?' LoveSick asks.

Max screws his face up. '*Why would I think that?*'

'Yes,' Twill says. 'Why?'

'You're either as clueless as Lucan looks or you know what's going on. You showing up after all this time kinda rules out the first.'

'You need to calm down, Darren. You're with friends. Come with us.' Twill hooks a thumb over his shoulder towards the car park.

'I'm not getting in any fucking car with you,' Max says. 'I doubt you've forgotten what we used to do to people who got into cars with us.'

Twill sticks his hands in his pockets and looks over Max's shoulder. The boy is watching, mouth agape. 'Fuck off home,' he calls, but the boy doesn't move. 'Okay,' he says to Max with a sigh. 'If you feel safer, we can do it here.'

'Why don't *you* tell us, if ya know so much. What *is* going on?' Lucan asks.

Max snorts. 'Someone's going around, taking us out, one by one. The two-two. Mincer, JR, Tumble.' He swallows hard. 'And I can't get hold of Bridges.'

'And you think it's *us*?'

'*Us*? No, Twill,' Max says. 'I think it's *you*.'

Twill throws his head back and laughs. 'Me? You crazy cunt. You've been eating hedgehogs and fucking badgers too long.'

'Yeah, I think it's you.' Max's eyes soften and he speaks quietly. 'And I don't blame you, after what we did.'

'And what *did* you do?' Twill asks, his hand moving to his leg.

Max looks down. 'The briefing.'

'What briefing?'

'That last briefing. I was told to do it.'

'Jesus, you're talking in riddles. *What* briefing and *told to do what?*'

Lucan spits blood at his feet and wipes his mouth on the back of his hand. 'I think living on berries has turned him soft.'

'I'm sorry,' Max mutters.

'What's he talking about?' LoveSick says.

'Sorry for what?' Twill says.

Max looks back up, hands limp by his side. Tears have cleaved tracks down his face. His eyes are puffy and red. He sniffs and wipes his nose on his sleeve. 'It's taken forty years, but I always knew Blaggard would come.'

'It's okay,' Twill says, laying a hand on Max's shoulder. 'Let's get you cleaned up and go somewhere warm, yeah?'

Max threads his arm under Twill's, grabs the top of his shoulder and twists. Twill is thrust forward and speared onto Max's knee. His lungs empty with a hiss. Lucan reaches forward and Max chops him in the throat. Lucan's eyes widen and he falls to his knees, clutching his neck. LoveSick stares back, open mouthed. Max says something Twill can't hear, and breaks off. Three short strides and he's swallowed up in the darkness of the woods.

'*Shit shit shit,*' LoveSick yells, and sets off after him.

Twill grimaces and clambers up. 'You okay?'

A fat blue vein is pulsing on Lucan's temple. '*JUST FUCKIN' GET HIM.*'

'Fuck this.' Twill launches himself onto the bike and pumps his legs. The boy's high-pitched protests ring in his ears as he heads into the toothless yawn in the trees.

Sun-dappled leaves create flickering shadows on a carpet of dead leaves and pine needles. Moss-covered branches claw and scrape at his face and cobwebs catch in his hair. More than once, he leaves the path, bumping and skidding over pine cones and rotten logs that threaten to derail him. A thousand white hot needles cauterise his thigh. There's a tightness in his chest, but the pain is dampened by adrenaline. He turns a corner. LoveSick is bent double in the middle of the path. Twill throws himself off the bike to avoid hitting him and lands on a bed of spongy moss and brambles that tear at his skin. He half-rolls and comes to his feet.

'You okay?'

LoveSick's mouth yawns. A torrent of puke erupts and his body is wracked by convulsions. He stabs a finger towards the path. Twill gets back on the bike and pedals hard.

Ahead, he hears a crashing through the undergrowth. The path forks and Twill slides to a halt, scrunching his eyes shut and steadying his breathing. All his energy is diverted to his ears—the leaves rustling in the wind, birds calling to each other, a squirrel chattering in the branches high above. But no Max.

'*Fuck.*'

He guesses left and sets off down the path. Off to the side, a wisp of grey smoke rises above the tree tops and the aroma of wood-smoke drifts under his nose. He dismounts and takes measured but quick steps through a line of berry bushes. Dead twigs crunch underfoot. A flame flares and flickers through the trees ahead like a zoetrope. Twill gets close, puts his back against a tree that leans drunkenly against its neighbour. The fire crackles and spits, and the branches above him groan and creak in the evening breeze. He takes a lungful of air and holds it, then pokes his head around the mossy trunk. Max is crouched low, feeding stacks of envelopes into a blazing fire. A bivouac stretches between two trees behind him. Twill picks up a thick branch at his feet. He weighs it in his hand and steps into the clearing.

A twig snaps. Max looks up and Twill throws himself the last few feet, his arm swinging overhead. Max shoots up and side-steps, grabs Twill's arm and twists it behind him. Twill lands on his side, the wind knocked out of him. Max is on top of him, full weight in the small of Twill's back, an arm wrapped around his neck. His head is jerked back and he feels a sharp point under his chin.

Max's breath is hot on his neck and his words are short and snatched. 'I didn't want to, understand me. Cromer said you were in on it. Just read the briefing like a script, he said. It wasn't till we found out what happened that we realised you didn't have a fucking clue. By then it was too late.'

Twill gasps. 'Get off me and we'll talk.'

Max chuckles, increases the pressure. The sting on Twill's neck intensifies.

'They said Blaggard would come for me. And here you are, like a thief in the night.'

Twill starts to feel light-headed. A greyness creeps into the edges of his vision. Stars whizz and pop. A weightless calm comes over him, and the world goes quiet apart from a high-pitched whine, like a phone off the hook. Twill closes his eyes and waits for it to be over.

***

Twill opens his eyes to a sideways view of the blaze. He chokes down smoky air and tries to focus. Rising unsteadily, he kicks out at the fire, stamps on the smouldering letters and places the least charred ones in his coat pocket.

Where's Max?

He's still woozy but he mounts the bike and rides deeper into the woods. The buzz in his ears recedes and a fresh determination takes hold. Max could have killed him back there but didn't. He needs to catch him, if only to find out what he meant. *They said Blaggard would come for me.*

He bellows Max's name into the night sky, his frustration swelling. 'I only want to talk.'

The woods close in around him, and a light rain begins to patter on the dirt floor.

Twill stops peddling and free wheels to a halt. 'Fuck!' He thumps the handle bars. '*Fuck!*'

The woods are silent apart but for the wheeze in his chest and the soft beat of the rain on his face. A screech—an animal?—rings out in the distance. For a moment, Twill is transported to a back room in Belfast. Maybe Cromer was right. He had done a half-arsed job of taking Croall down and let Max put him on the floor twice in one night. And now he's gone, off in the wind with the answers Twill needs.

Twill climbs off the bike, wheels it around and walks it back to the car park. Max's words echo in his head. Cromer had set him up with a false briefing the day before he was snatched. Was that the plan—plant misinformation and feed him to the Provo torture squad? And who is Blaggard? Why would he come for Max?

He reaches the fork in the path and for reasons he can't explain, takes the right-hand trail instead of heading to the car. A cooling breeze ruffles his hair. The rain has dried up. Two rows of trees heavy with leaves lead him to a pond glowing silver in the light of a waning moon.

He dry swallows, lowers the bike to the ground and walks towards the water's edge. Every cell in his body begs him to stop but he's driven by some primal instinct. He stops at the bank. A bead of sweat rolls from his hairline down the side of his face. His leg begins to throb. The image of a swan with fangs and blood-red eyes flashes behind his eyes and an icy shudder goes down his spine all the way to his boots. He shakes the spectre from his head. A coot or moorhen scuttles from behind a bed of reeds and runs across the water towards him, then veers away. Twill feels light-headed and realises he's been holding his breath. He lets it out in a rush and jams his hands into his pockets.

On the other side of the orchard, birds flock to the sky as if disturbed. He limps back to the bike and threads his way through the trees.

He leans on one leg and waits.

Not for long. A lone figure crashes through the thicket fifteen feet away and sprints past him. He swings his leg over the saddle.

Lucan appears at the tree line, face tight, arms and legs pumping furiously. Twill pedals after him, ducking below a low hanging branch, and catches up within seconds. Lucan shoots him a relieved look and slows.

'Fuckin' Max…' Lucan says between ragged breaths. 'Looped round and was watching from the car park.'

'I've got this,' Twill says and pulls away.

Max is not far up ahead, darting under branches and leaping over logs, running parallel to the path. Twill takes a gamble and re-joins the paved trail. It gives him the speed he needs.

He hears Max and steers hard left, narrowly missing him. He skids the bike around and continues the chase. Max glances back, pale-faced and wild-eyed in the moonlight. Twill makes ground on him. Soon he's so close he can almost reach over and grab him. Just a few more strokes…

They crash out of the tree line, nose to tail. Max gasps over his shoulder, his face etched with panic. Twill pulls on the brakes and his back-wheel slides around but Max continues into the road. A horn blasts and Twill's warning is drowned out by the squeal of rubber on tarmac. A puff of smoke comes from the truck's wheels as they lock and auto-rotate. The trailer pivots and slides across the carriageway.

Max stares back at Twill with a sorrowful expression, and disappears under the lorry.

Lucan bursts out of the trees, red-faced and panting. '*What the fuck?*'

'C'mon.' Twill says, wheeling his bike around to face the trees. 'Let's get out of here.'

***

They find LoveSick back at the car, strung out, pacing and muttering to himself. He runs over and a torrent of questions merge into one long babble. The boy takes his bike and rides off.

'Get in the car,' Twill says. His leg hurts like hell and his chest still feels tight.

LoveSick puts his hands on his hips and blocks the way to the car. 'Not till you tell me what happened. Did you lose him?'

Lucan grimaces. 'Sort of.'

'Fuck off, Lucan. This ain't no fucking joke.'

Twill places a hand on LoveSick's shoulder. 'He's gone, mate.'

'What do you mean, gone? He got away?'

'No. He ran out into the road. He's dead, mate.'

'What?' LoveSick laughs but it dies in his throat. 'Are you sure? I mean, did you check?'

Lucan tuts. 'Those artics don't fuck about...'

LoveSick takes a step towards him.

'It was an accident, LoveSick. Get in the car,' Twill says.

LoveSick pauses, then edges in and says over his shoulder, 'It ain't fucking funny.'

Twill looks at Lucan.

'*What*?' Lucan says, shrugging, and climbing into the car. 'Let's swing by the framing store. It's just become very important we don't get linked to what happened here tonight.'

***

The lights are still on in the store, and when Lucan jogs back to the car, no one mentions the blood spot on his shirt.

13

The booth overlooks the car park and is surrounded by empty tables. Lucan is examining a laminated menu and LoveSick is playing with the salt cellar, making little white piles on the scratched table top. Apart from low chatter from a bunch of truckers sitting near the door and a clink of someone stirring their drink, the diner is quiet.

A hard-faced waitress in a tight uniform wanders over and takes their order in a bored voice. Twill and LoveSick order coffees; Lucan opts for the full English. She walks away from their table and Lucan nudges Twill.

'Ya don't get many of those in a bucket without putting your foot on top, eh?'

'Shut the fuck up,' Twill snaps.

'Okay, okay.' It's the first time LoveSick's spoken since the car park. 'Christ, I wish you could tab up in these places.'

The drinks arrive. LoveSick says, 'I don't understand it. Any of it. It's time you guys told me what's going on. And I mean everything.'

Twill lifts his cup and blows on it. 'We don't know much more than you.'

LoveSick chews a nail. 'What happened to the others? Is there someone going round taking us out, like Max said?'

'Don't be fuckin' soft,' Lucan says.

'We don't know that,' Twill says. 'But we also don't know that *isn't* true. On that basis, we have to prepare ourselves.'

'What happened to Mincer, JR and Tumble?'

'Tumble was murdered. Could be coincidence, a business deal gone wrong, a feud, anything. Until we fill in the blanks, we have to assume it was the same with Mincer and JR. I think I speak for us all when I say killing yourself is…not our way.'

Lucan nods. LoveSick looks less sure.

'All we know is, it looks like'—Twill shoots a glance at Lucan—'bad things are happening to the two-two.'

'If we're going to war, I'm going to need more than looks like,' Lucan says.

'What we don't know is who or why. What motive could there be after all these years? Who gains from knocking off a bunch of old men?'

'Revenge?' LoveSick says.

'Not necessarily. Yes, it's possible, but more likely someone wants to silence us.'

'*Silence us*?' Lucan says. 'It's not like we're writing books or going on talk shows. Jesus, I've spent the past forty years trying to forget what we did.'

LoveSick tips his head and they fall silent as the waitress arrives with Lucan's breakfast.

'Thanks, love,' he says with a grin.

The waitress appears unmoved. She sets down the plate and removes a bottle of ketchup from her apron. 'Anything else?'

Lucan looks her up and down and leers. She rolls her eyes and walks away.

'Have you spoken to Cromer? What does he think?' LoveSick asks.

'There's something else,' Twill says.

LoveSick and Lucan look up together.

'Max fed me a fake briefing. Misinformation. The day before—'

'The day before what?' Lucan asks.

'The day before I was taken.'

The mood darkens, and Lucan puts his knife and fork down and pushes his plate away.

'Nah. I don't buy it. Not Max,' LoveSick says.

'He was following Cromer's orders. He thought I was in on it.'

Lucan tuts and looks out of the window. 'Here we fuckin' go.'

'Look,' Twill says, leaning in. 'It makes sense. It's why Max shit himself when he saw me.'

'And why would he give you a bullshit briefing? You honestly trying to tell me you were served up on a platter to the Provos? Not one of us thought you would sing.'

'It explains why Max was so scared. He thinks…he thought I was coming for him.'

LoveSick looks down at his hands. 'And you weren't?'

'No. It's not like that. He'd been told I was coming.'

'By who?'

'I have no fucking idea.'

'And who or what, in the name of all that is holy is Blaggard?' Lucan says.

'He thought it was me,' Twill says.

'I can see how he got the two confused…I mean, Blaggard *does* sound like a right cunt.'

Twill ignores him and sips his coffee.

'If it's revenge,' LoveSick says, 'what about Croall?'

'No.'

'Why not?'

'I've been keeping an eye on him. He was in Belgium when Tumble was killed. Besides, I would be top of Croall's wish list. He wouldn't fuck around with Tumble and the others first.' Twill puts his cup down and runs a finger around the rim. 'So Max was tipped off by someone we don't know, and accused me of being someone we don't know. It's safe to say we don't know shit from Shinola.'

'An unprincipled, contemptible man,' LoveSick whispers.

'Eh?'

'Blaggard. That's what it means. An unprincipled, contemptible man.'

'You swallow a fuckin' dictionary?'

'How do you know that?' Twill asks.

LoveSick shrugs. 'I like crosswords. Thought everyone knew that.'

'Yeah,' Lucan says, the corners of his mouth curling into a smile. 'Everyone knows that Twill, ya thick twat.'

'So, what's next?' LoveSick asks. 'What about Bridges? He was close to Max. He might be able to fill in a few blanks.'

Twill looks down.

'Well, this is awkward,' Lucan says, drumming his fingers on the table.

'What do you mean?' LoveSick says.

When there's no answer, he stands, knocking his cup and spilling coffee on the table. '*Jesus fucking Christ.* He's dead, isn't he?'

The waitress, three tables away, stops and looks over her shoulder.

'Sit down,' Twill hisses.

'Before I do, I want you to promise you're telling me everything.'

Twill nods.

Lucan holds up three fingers on his right hand. 'Scout's honour.'

LoveSick slumps into the seat with a sigh, plucks a sausage from Lucan's plate and dips it in his beans. 'Come on then. Let's have it.'

Lucan scowls and pulls the plate away.

'Cromer told me Bridges knew what happened that night. Even suggested he played a part in it. We paid him a visit but he was expecting us. Things turned nasty. He lost his shit, went crazy. It was self-defence.'

'So, to confirm, there are five dead…so far.'

'That we know of.'

'That we know of. And youse are responsible for two of them.'

Lucan grins sheepishly.

'We didn't kill Max,' Twill says.

LoveSick scratches his wrists. 'I'm confused. Who told Bridges you were coming?'

'Can only be Cromer,' Twill says.

'Again, with the Cromer,' Lucan says.

'No. He's right,' LoveSick says. 'Cromer is the only name that keeps cropping up in all this. If he tipped off Bridges, while sending you after him, he's up to his neck in whatever shit this is.'

'That's not all,' Twill says, staring at Lucan. 'He visited Tumble a month before he died, but he told me he hadn't seen him since Belfast.'

Lucan chews his lip.

'I think it's high time I had a little meeting with our CO, don't you?' Twill asks.

LoveSick nods. Lucan shakes his head and picks up his knife and fork. 'Do what ya fuckin' want. But if you're going to waste ya time chasing shadows and hearsay, count me out. Bring me proof about JR and Mincer and I'm in. Until then—'

'We can't afford to be passive. We could be next.'

'Lucan's right,' LoveSick says. 'We need to find out what happened to JR and Mincer.'

'How?'

'I spoke to Mincer's other half at the funeral. I could ask around, get his number. Give him a buzz.'

'You do that. I'll do some digging about JR. That okay?'

Lucan avoids Twill's gaze. Twill takes the wad of charred envelopes from his pocket and drops them on the table.

'Max was trying to burn these in the woods.'

LoveSick pops the last bit of sausage into his mouth and starts ripping them open. Lucan and Twill join in.

'Anything?' Twill asks.

'Got a utility bill for a Burnt House Farm. That's about it.'

Lucan throws a letter down on the pile. 'Same. Burnt House Farm, near Brockenhurst.'

'We should take a look. Before the police ID the body.'

Lucan pushes his plate away again. 'Fuck it. Wasn't hungry anyway.'

***

They sleep in the service station car park and hit the road shortly after dawn. Brockenhurst is a thirty-minute drive but it takes an hour to find the lane that runs along the ridge of the valley. Burnt House Farm is nestled at the bottom. They hide the car in bushes and trek the last fifteen minutes on foot. A light drizzle starts to fall and a chill settles into Twill's bones.

Burnt House Farm is more modern ranch style than traditional stone farmhouse. A wide covered deck with a screened porch runs along the front and faces a meadow of wild grass. Its roof droops and sags under the weight of dead leaves. A light above the front door burns through the morning mist. Chickens wander the enclosed yard behind the farm, pecking at bugs in the dirt. The smell of diesel hangs heavy in the air.

They sit and wait for an hour.

The deck light blinks off and Twill checks his watch. 'Eight a.m. to the second. The light's on a timer.' He walks down to the farm, calling over his shoulder. 'C'mon. There's no one here.'

Twill circles the farmhouse, peering in the windows and pushing on doors until he's back where he started. He leans against a pile of neatly stacked logs next to a cutting stump with an axe buried in it, and rubs his leg.

'All clear,' Lucan says with a grin, emerging from an outhouse, doing up his trousers.

LoveSick appears from behind a rusting cultivator thick with moss, and gives a thumbs-up.

'One alarm box,' Twill says, backing away from the farm, shielding his eyes and looking up. 'SecureZone. Never heard of them.'

'See that flashing blue light?' Lucan is alongside him, pointing up. 'Means it's Wi-Fi connected.'

'So, we have to kill the Wi-Fi?'

'Not even that,' LoveSick says. 'Just kill the power. Cheap piece of shit.'

'Why even bother?'

'Means you're either confident no one knows you're here or you've got nothing worth protecting.'

Twill nods. 'Sometimes an expensive security system works the other way. Broadcasts you've got some—'

There's a smash behind him and he turns to see Lucan, coat wrapped around his hand, punching out the remaining fragments of glass from the window with the axe. He hauls himself through the frame, gives his feet a wriggle and disappears.

Twill looks down to his watch. The second hand doesn't even manage a half-revolution before Lucan appears at the window, grinning.

'Lesson number one, kids. Fuse box is always under the stairs.'

The lights go off on the alarm box and Twill exhales.

He gestures towards the window but Lucan shakes his head. 'Front door.'

Inside is musty and older than it looks from the outside. The floorboards are uneven and the doorways, small and leaning. Light floods in from tiny windows, creating shafts of dust motes hovering in the stale air. It reminds Twill of a crypt.

'I'll take upstairs,' Lucan says and begins to climb a low set of irregular steps.

'LoveSick, you take the kitchen,' Twill says. 'Take all the drawers out. Check the undersides. Cupboards, pans, the oven. Look for anything out of place.'

Twill ducks under a rhomboid doorway leading into a dark, crowded living room. A portable telly is perched on a rickety table facing a threadbare armchair, the stuffing bursting out of a split in the arm. A quick search yields nothing from the sideboard. He slashes the sides and back of the armchair with a pocketknife and horsehair spills out. Under the rug are shiny, worn flagstones. Lucan's boots thump across creaking floorboards above, releasing a cloud of dried ceiling plaster which dusts Twill's head and shoulders.

LoveSick appears in the doorway with a puzzled expression.

'Anything?' Twill asks.

'No. At least I don't think so.' He's holding a bunch of keys. 'Front door, back door, office…but I can't find a home for this one.' He singles out a long brass key.

Lucan trots down the stairs and out the front door, humming. He comes back with the axe. Twill and LoveSick follow him upstairs, across the landing and into one of the rooms. The wind whistles through a hole in the bedroom roof. A swallow swoops in and ducks into a mud nest in the corner of the room. The floor is streaked with bird shit and mouse droppings.

'What is it?' Twill asks.

Lucan motions for Twill to step back. He and LoveSick retreat to the doorway.

Lucan takes short, measured steps across the floor. A third of the way in and the wooden floor creaks and groans. He takes a half step back and does it again from a different angle. Same noise. Same place. He grins at Twill and LoveSick. 'Fuckin' bullseye.'

He hefts the axe into the air with a grunt and brings it down in a series of heavy blows.

'Okay, that's enough,' Twill shouts.

Lucan throws the axe to the floor and wipes his face on his sleeve.

They pull out a plastic sack wrapped around a bundle of files. Lucan opens the first one, labelled: *Animus*: *Washington, DC*. A cover page gives no clues. He flicks through it but none of the names or places mean anything to Twill.

'Looks like work files.'

'Why hide them then?' Twill asks.

'Dunno,' Lucan says, and stuffs the file back into the bag, and into his inside coat pocket. 'We can take a proper look when we get home. Soon as the police ID Max they're gonna be all over this place.'

'We good?' Twill says.

LoveSick nods but he's staring at the wall, tapping the key against his chin. 'Actually, no, not yet. I want to find a home for this.'

Fifteen minutes later, LoveSick calls them. He's standing in front of a small, windowless outbuilding of corrugated iron, little bigger than a single garage, almost reclaimed by thickets and trees. The door is thick oak—too substantial for a tool shed, Twill notes. LoveSick tries the key but the door is warped and stuck in place. He forces it with his shoulder and it scrapes open.

A shaft of light illuminates part of the room. The walls are thick, poured concrete, the corrugated iron nothing more than cladding. Twill lifts a kerosene lamp off a rusty hook and, with the help of LoveSick's lighter, the room is lit.

The walls are lined with egg boxes. It's empty apart from a work bench with a dented kettle covered in cobwebs, and a metal chair in the centre. Shackles secure the chair to the concrete floor. Twill's leg starts to throb. There's a dark stain at the base of the chair; a rust-coloured bloom.

They've found the killing room.

LoveSick crosses the floor, giving the chair a wide berth. 'There's something here.' He grunts as he pulls a solid metal trunk out from under the worktop. 'It's locked,' he says, fingering a heavy chain and padlock.

'I'll get the axe,' Lucan says.

'Hang on,' Twill says, crouching in front of the trunk.

He dials the padlock: 2-2-2-2, the lid clicks open and they crowd around.

Twill picks up an assault rifle and weighs it in his hands. 'Enfield SA80. SUSAT optical.'

He lays the rest of the guns and ammunition boxes out on the floor. Five rifles and four handguns.

Lucan picks up a Browning Hi-Power pistol, ejects the stock, blows the dust off and slams it back into the handle. 'Merry fuckin' Christmas, boys.'

LoveSick is rummaging around in the bottom of the trunk. He stands and holds up a folded and neatly ironed olive-green uniform. Twill thinks he's close to tears.

'Right. Get your arses in gear. Grab the trunk. I'll get the car.'

'Yeah,' Lucan says. 'Cos that sounds fair.'

113

14

They stow the guns at Lucan's, and LoveSick accepts an invitation to stay a few days. It's been good for him—he's stronger, more focused. Like the LoveSick Twill remembers. The rings around his eyes are fading and his speech is lucid. He hasn't drunk in two days and claims to be sleeping through the night without nightmares.

Twill is back home, trawling the internet but can't find anything new about JR—Barry O'Dowd—or his death. Some local paper led with the story but it's a puff-piece padded with glib tropes about a hero who sacrificed so much for his country.

Twill tries another approach and reaches a softly spoken woman from the SAS Regimental Association by phone. She promises to try and get next-of-kin details but stresses she'll need authority to pass them on, finishing up by consoling him—they get calls like this from all over the world, every day. The association sees itself as part of the global family and she'll do her best.

A cup of tea settles him and he's close to nodding off when the trill of his phone jerks him back to life. It's the woman with the kind voice, back already. She gives him the number for a Rachel O'Dowd, JR's widow.

The call is picked up on the second ring. Rachel is friendly and warm, and has been waiting for his call.

'Oh, I've heard all about you, Mr Twill.'

'Uh-oh,' Twill says.

Her laughter is like wind chimes.

'You're okay,' she says. 'Barry was very fond of you.'

It's odd to hear him called that.

'The feeling was mutual. I wanted to speak to you…I—I didn't make it to the funeral.'

'That's okay. There was a fair old turnout from the regiment. I assumed you hadn't heard.'

'It's not that. I…don't like funerals.'

Again, the laugh. 'They're not my favourite either.'

There's a pause. Twill can hear her breath on the handset.

'If it's not too upsetting, can I ask you some questions?'

'What sort of questions?' she asks.

'The sort some people find personal.'

She sniffs and there's another pause. 'Mr Twill…Owen, isn't it?'

'Yeah.'

'Owen, I loved my husband. We went through a lot together and we were very close because of it. There was a lot of resistance when we first got together. There's an age gap. I guess what Barry went through, what he saw in the regiment, made him more of a risk taker. He never wasted a day in all the time I knew him. Some people like a lie-in. Not Barry. Straight out of bed every morning, attacking the day. It was all about the adventure. That's why I loved him.'

'How was he, you know, in the head?'

'Absolutely fine. Listen, he never spoke about Northern Ireland but he used to say there's two ways of dealing with it: spend the rest of your life agonising over what happened or get on with it and grab life with both hands. That's what he did, just got on with it. I'm not saying it's right for everyone, and there's no judgement here, but he used his experience as a positive. I can't remember him ever turning down an opportunity. That's what getting shot did for him. It changed his outlook. Every day was a bonus.'

Twill clears his throat. 'I'm sorry to bring it up, but the newspaper said he took his own life.'

Rachel sighs. 'Not true. Absolutely not true.' A dog barks in the background. 'This is something they say when they don't understand what happened and they can't find answers. Or don't like the answers they *do* find.'

'How did it happen?'

'Excuse me.' She blows her nose. 'Barry left the house in the morning and drove to Farnham. He told me he was going to London.'

'What did he say he was doing there?'

'Meeting an old friend.'

'Did he say who?'

'If he did, I don't remember. It's funny. If I'd known it would be the last conversation we'd have, I'd have paid more attention. Held him a second longer. Given him a proper kiss.'

'Were there any clues? Did he seem unhappy?'

'On the contrary, he was excited and looking forward to it. Look, Barry was special…'

Special—that word again.

'People used to ask if he was okay, even hinting he was on the spectrum somewhere. I'd tell them he was just different to everyone else. He never cared too much about what other people thought. He just got on and did what he wanted. Selfish? Yeah, maybe sometimes. But that was his gift. He used to say he'd come so close to death, why waste time giving a shit what other people thought? When you ask if he was unhappy, you have to remember that he didn't always show his emotions like everyone else. He was special. My special Barry.'

There's a muffled sob, followed by another blast into a handkerchief.

'But he didn't go to London,' Twill says.

'No, no, he didn't. He went to Farnham and checked himself into the Holiday Inn. What they say happened next is that, sometime around midnight, he took the lift to the top floor, then the emergency staircase up to the roof and threw himself off.'

'Did he leave a note?'

'There was no note because he didn't kill himself, Owen. I don't know what happened that night, but I know what *didn't* happen. There's no way he killed himself. Not ever. We were happy together. I understood him like nobody else. They take one look at his military record, shake their head and reach for the suicide stamp.'

'What do you think happened?'

'Barry used to think he was invincible. They say it happens when you cheat death. Anyway, he smoked. A lot. Twenty, thirty a day. He'd laugh in your face if you said it was bad for him. I think he went up onto the roof for a fag, maybe stood too close to the edge, slipped and fell.'

'Had he been drinking?'

Another laugh, this time with an edge. 'Naturally.'

'Was there an autopsy?'

'Yeah, some alcohol in his blood. Not enough to impair his judgement. I mean, too much to drive—I assume that's why he booked the hotel. And there was food in his stomach. Pizza I think. That's not the way Barry would go out.'

'What do you mean?'

'My Barry was a curry fiend. If he could have chosen his last supper, it wouldn't have been a bloody Margherita. Prawn vindaloo, yes. And the hotter the better. Washed down with ten pints. Trust me on this.'

'I believe you. And you never found out who he was meeting?'

'I don't think he was meeting anyone. He'd tell me that so he could get away for a few hours. Not a conventional family man, our Barry. He'd say that, but sometimes he just needed some space. I didn't mind; the space was good for both of us. It made us work. The regiment asked around but no one owned up. And before you say it, there wasn't a girlfriend either. I know what you're thinking— mysterious rendezvous and hotel booked in the middle of nowhere. But that's not me sticking my head in the sand. He was on medication that made him impotent.'

'Medication?'

'Pills. Got them from some doctor the regiment put him in contact with.'

Twill sits up. 'Dr Walsh?'

'No idea.'

Twill changes direction. 'How are you coping?'

'I won't say it's easy but the support makes a difference.'

'Support?'

'You know, the regiment. I used to think all that talk of being a family was rubbish but it really is. A family, I mean. They swung into action, sent a financial adviser round, paid for the funeral, made all the arrangements. They still check in on me every week…probably shit scared of being sued.' Her laugh has gone from tinkling brook to low grumble. 'Ellis has been wonderful.'

'*Ellis*?'

'Sorry, Lieutenant Colonel Cromer. Wonderful man.' She sniffs. 'Why do you say it like that?'

'Sorry, I didn't recognise his first name. How so?'

'He was on the phone constantly after it happened. Checking in. Made such a difference. Plus, when we hit on some hard times, he helped Barry out with some work.'

'Wait.' Twill swaps his phone into the other hand and puts a finger in his ear. 'Cromer…Ellis was in contact with Barry before the accident?'

'Oh, yes. As I said, such a helpful man.'

'What kind of work?'

Rachel yawns. 'Sorry, I'm not sleeping so well.'

A knot tightens in Twill's guts. 'You said work. What kind of work?'

'Security, Barry said. He'd be gone for a few days. Sometimes a week or so but it paid well, and I think it did him the world of good. He'd always come back so alive. Like he was twenty years younger.'

'Does the name Animus mean anything to you?'

'Uh-uh.'

'Blaggard?'

'Nope.'

'Last question, promise. Did Barry ever get any calls that made him act strangely?'

The laugh is back to a mischievous chuckle. 'How would I tell the difference?'

'Any foreign callers? An American lady?'

'No and no. Not to my knowledge, anyway. Why all the questions?'

'Just wanted to catch up really. I believe you, you know. I hadn't spoken to JR for many years, but everyone said he was happy.'

'What do you think happened?'

'Like you say, probably just an accident.'

Twill wraps up the conversation with more platitudes and accepts an offer to stop by.

With the thought why lying comes so easy to him bouncing around his head, he hangs up and reaches for his laptop. And then his phone.

'Pizza Express, Farnham.'

He can hear coffee beans being ground, spoons clinking against the side of a cup and a background murmur of voices. The girl on the phone sounds harassed. Twill closes his eyes and visualises the scene—the phone and reservations book on the bar next to the coffee machine?

'Ah, yes. Hello. DS Stewart, Guildford CID. I've got a couple of questions I was hoping you can help me with.'

A sigh down the line. An order barked in the background.

'We're really busy. Can you call back or come in?'

'No. It won't take a sec.'

A pause, then, 'How do I know you're police?'

'If you don't believe me, call Guildford CID, ask for DS Stewart. It'll take ten minutes to get through.'

It's a gamble but a calculated one. She's rushed off her feet. No way she'll call.

'Or just answer my questions.'

There's a moment of silence in which Twill listens to the chuntering of a frothing machine.

'Okay. How can I help you, DS Stewart?'

'June twenty third, last year. A reservation in the name of O'Dowd.'

'We don't keep our reservation books I'm afraid.' When she says sorry, it doesn't tally with the relief in her voice. 'Is that all?'

'What about bills? Credit-card receipts?'

'Yes,' she says, breathing out heavily. There's a rustle and she shouts something he doesn't catch. 'Right, hold on.'

Twill checks his watch.

'Here we are. Yes, lunchtime session. O'Dowd. Got it.'

'What was the order?'

'Sec.' Some tapping. 'One Margherita, one Sloppy Joe, one bottle of Cabernet Sauvignon, four Peronis and two single malt whiskies. Doubles.'

Single malt. Twill thinks back to Cromer's office. A globe. The chink of ice on glass.

'Any CCTV?'

'Not going back that far…Look, I don't want to be rude, DS Stewart, but we're *really* busy.'

Twill hangs up and taps out a text with a single finger. Within seconds, his phone buzzes.

***

The Prettygate is always quiet at lunchtime. The usual faces prop up the bar, Joan Jett and The Blackhearts punch a tune through tinny speakers, and reruns of old football games play on wall-mounted screens. Twill gets himself a pint and finds LoveSick at the back of the pub, nursing a black coffee.

'Late one?' Twill asks.

'Ha. No. I'm back on the wagon.'

And he looks it. Clear-eyed and ruddy-cheeked.

'Any joy?' LoveSick says.

Twill raises his glass and takes a gulp. 'Where's Lucan?'

LoveSick waves him away. 'He's sulking. He'll come round. Did you speak to anyone about JR?'

'Yeah. I spoke to his missus. No way he killed himself.'

'Are you sure she's not just in denial? He tops himself and some of the blame's bound to fall on her.'

'Sure, as I can be. Life was good. Young wife. Seemed happy.'

'Why does she think he didn't do it?'

'Pizza.'

'Eh?'

'Long story. Basically, he didn't do it. And our good friend Cromer popped up again. JR did some work for him.'

'At the Houses of Parliament?'

'No…security work.'

'Fuck. Animus?'

'Got to be.'

'And we can now link Cromer to Animus.'

Twill folds his hands in lap. 'He's in this up to his arsehole. And JR was in therapy. Pills, the works.'

LoveSick raises his eyebrows and blows on his coffee. 'I spoke with Martin.'

'Martin?'

'Mincer's husband.'

'And?'

'Guess what? Reckons he didn't kill himself.'

'What does he think happened?'

LoveSick shrugs. 'The official version—icy morning, slipped on the platform. It does happen.'

'Does it bollocks. Not to us, it doesn't. We don't go round falling off roofs or in front of trains, for fuck's sake.'

'They'd just booked their dream holiday too. Who tops themselves *before* a two-week all-inclusive in the Maldives?'

Twill whistles. 'Sounds expensive.'

'Try seven thousand expensive.'

'Fuck.' Twill shakes his head. 'You had a look at those files yet?'

LoveSick laughs. 'I can't even get a full sentence out of Man-Baby. He's been locked away in his room with them. But this is good stuff. We can link Cromer to JR and Tumble, and show they didn't kill themselves. It's coming together. Lucan might not like it, but he's not stupid.'

Twill finishes his pint and gets up, wincing as he puts weight on his leg. 'Right, I'm off. You sticking around for a bit?'

'Yep.' He glances at his watch. 'I'm on babysitting duty.'

Twill rolls his eyes. 'Tell him to call me when he's got over himself.'

15

Charing Cross, London

Twill texts Cromer. A simple, two-word message: *Where? When?* The reply has a fawning tone, like Cromer's talking to a long-lost friend, but with the usual caveat—come alone. It sets Twill's teeth on edge.

They meet at a wine bar suggested by Cromer, a twenty-minute walk from the Houses of Parliament. Gordon's lies behind an easy-to-miss alley off Villiers Street. Twill limps down a short flight of steps into a dim and gloomy bar area. A heavyset male in an ill-fitting suit is studying the wine list even though he's nursing a bottle of water. Twill puts his hand to his jacket and feels the weight of his baton. If it comes to it, he'll have no qualms about using violence.

Cromer sits at the far end, in a grotto hewn from rock, framed in a corona of flickering candlelight. If Bond villain's the look he's aiming for, he's nailed it. He stands and beckons Twill over.

'Come on, sit…sit.'

Twill looks around. The air is cool but stale. A few metres away, two office workers whisper to each other. They're holding hands under the table and staring into each-other's eyes. Totally absorbed. He could open up Cromer's skull and they wouldn't notice. A lone figure enters the cavern and takes a seat near the exit. The gorilla in the suit glances over but looks away when he catches Twill's eye.

Cromer sips from a glass of red wine. 'I got you a water. You know, remove any temptation.' He follows it up with a nervous laugh.

'First things first, what news Croall?'

Cromer plants his palms on the table. 'Nothing new. He's gone to ground. He'll be back. And when he pokes his head above the parapet, we'll be waiting for him.'

Twill throws a thumb over his shoulder. 'I see you haven't come alone. Practise what you preach and all that.'

'Ah, yes, you noticed. Home Office rules, I'm afraid. Since Jo Cox, we're assigned protection twenty-four—'

'If I wanted to hurt you, you'd be on the floor before that clueless monkey could get to his feet. You do know that, don't you?'

Cromer shifts and fiddles with his tie knot. 'Is this what today is, then?'

Twill smiles viciously. 'Should it be?'

'Right.' Cromer sighs and shakes his head. 'Talk to me about Bridges.'

'Oh, you know, standard. I believe the expression is *he's taken an extended vacation.*'

Cromer raises his eyebrows. 'No problems? Nothing to come back on us?'

'Well, there was one small issue.'

'Which was?'

'Turns out he knew I was coming.'

Cromer's nostrils flare and he blinks twice. 'Impossible.'

'Not according to Bridges.'

'What are you saying, Twill?'

'You told Bridges I was coming and he was ready for me. The cards fall one of two ways—I die or he dies. Either way, it's one less problem for you.'

'Don't be ridiculous,' Cromer says, raising his glass. There's a tremor in his hand as he takes a drink.

'Unfortunately for you—and Bridges—I won that particular hand.'

Cromer leans forward. 'Let me guess. Bridge's last words were a plea for forgiveness. It wasn't him; it was *someone* else. *Anyone* else. A big boy did it and ran away.'

Twill shrugs. 'You tell me. And give me the truth. The stakes couldn't be higher…for you.' He pats his jacket.

A thin sheen of sweat glistens on Cromer's forehead. 'Come on, Twill. You know better than that. You've been witness to enough last words to know a desperate man will say anything.'

Twill shakes his head. 'I'm not buying what you're selling. Try harder.'

'Can't you see someone's trying to pitch us against each other? What possible reason could I have for wanting you dead?'

123

'Ah. Not just me. It was me or Bridges if you remember. You didn't care which. Turns out it was Bridges, so forgive me if I'm slightly cynical at this point.'

'Let me get this straight: I set you up? Have you any idea how fucking stupid that sounds?'

'Not stupid. And not the first trap you've set for me either.'

Cromer's eyes narrow. 'What *are* you talking about?'

'I know what happened, Cromer. I was fed misinformation and handed over to the Provos under the assumption I'd break and spill whatever horse-shit you wanted them to hear.'

'And I suppose Bridges told you this shortly before you killed him.'

'No. Actually, it was Max.'

Cromer freezes. 'You've spoken to Max?'

'Me and Max'—Twill looks up to the ceiling, searching for the right words, enjoying Cromer's discomfort—'had a full and frank exchange of views. It was…most enlightening.'

Twill can feel Cromer's knee bobbing up and down under the table.

'I think…we should meet Max together. Clear up this misunderstanding.'

'Oh, that's not possible.'

Cromer's mouth drops. 'Because?'

'Our dear friend Max has taken a rather long holiday…with Bridges. No idea when they'll be ba—'

'I'm not going to sit here and listen to this bullshit. Did you see me do any of these things? Have I ever given you reason to doubt me?'

'Now you mention it—'

'I'm serious, Twill,' Cromer shouts. 'I'm a Member of fucking Parliament and your commanding officer. You have no evidence to support this craziness, just hearsay and the final words of desperate, scared men.'

Twill lifts his glass. 'Thanks for the water, by the way. Most delicious.' He takes a sip, gargles it and smacks his lips. 'Spot of the old vino would've been nice though.'

'I thought you don't drink anymore.'

'Who told you that?'

'Y-You did.'

'No, I didn't. And you know why? Because it's not true. But you just proved that whatever I tell Walsh goes straight back to you.'

'Of course I take an interest in your health. Mental and physical. I have a duty of care—'

'Care schmare, Cromer. Whatever you're up to, it's over. Hear me?'

Cromer glances over his shoulder at the bodyguard then back at Twill. 'Are you off your fucking meds or something?'

'Now you mention it, yes, I am. And so's LoveSick. And we've both stopped having nightmares. Isn't that peculiar?'

'Okay, this is too much, really.' Cromer holds up his hands and laughs. 'You had me there for a minute.'

'It's a bit late for Mincer, JR and Tumble though, wouldn't you say?'

'You're becoming boring now.'

'Stop feeding me lies or I'll stuff them down your fucking throat. I know you met Tumble. And JR. Remind me now—what precisely was the nature of your relationship with Animus? Defence minister and a boutique security operation…you don't have to be Einstein to work it out.'

Cromer thumps the table. 'Listen—'

Twill pulls the baton out of his pocket and jams it into Cromer's groin. Cromer exhales, eyes bulging like hen eggs.

'No, you listen to me. It's over. You come near me, or anyone else in the two-two, and I'll come for you. You got that? Leave me alone. Leave the two-two alone. If you so much as touch a hair on anyone's head, you get the red card. And if I ever prove a link to you and all these *unfortunate accidents* I'll punch your fucking ticket. Got it?'

Cromer nods.

Twill grabs Cromer's lapel, pulls him close. 'You know what I'm capable of. I'll take you into deep water and drown you.' He shoves Cromer back in his seat and pushes himself up. 'Thanks for the drink.'

On his way out, he bangs into the bodyguard's table and grins. The man barely looks up from his phone.

***

The call comes the next evening. Twill's in the front room, turning his phone over in his hands. He's on his third whisky and his head is spinning. Two calls have gone into Lucan, and both went straight to voicemail. He's ignored another call-me text from Cromer, who's had twenty-four hours to come up with some bullshit story. *Fuck him.* Everyone who deals with Cromer ends up dead. The only question left is whether Cromer will let it be or accelerate events to the next level. In which case, Twill might be better served by a more proactive approach.

His phone buzzes and vibrates.

'Oh, at last. Finally got round to calling me back then?'

'We don't have fuckin' time for this now, mate. We have to meet.'

'Lunch tomorrow?'

'Now. The Prettygate, as soon as ya can make it.'

Twill sits up. 'What's wrong?' he asks, but the line's dead.

***

Twill walks around the Prettygate twice stopping in the car park to peer into the garden where a ragtag group of smokers are loitering. He goes in the back door and scans the room. Two punters at the bar have their backs to him and a man in a trilby is hunched over a pint in the far corner. Another man is shouting at a game on a wall-mounted TV. Lucan sits at their usual table, shoulders hunched, fiddling with a beer mat, two pints in front of him.

'Alright, Chuckles. What's so important?'

'Sit down,' Lucan says in a quiet voice.

'What is it?'

'It's Croall.'

Twill grips the edge of the table. 'Where is he?'

'He's here. In the UK. And he's got LoveSick.'

'*What?*'

'He's got LoveSick and he wants to meet.'

'Oh, I'll fucking meet him alright—'

Lucan places a hand on his arm. 'If we want to see LoveSick again, you've got to be calm, mate.'

'Don't fucking tell me to be calm. Have you forgotten what happened last time he got his hands on one of us? That cunt carved me up like a Christmas turkey.' Twill cocks his head. 'And where were you when that prick was snatching up our mate, eh? Sulking in your bedroom?'

'Now's not the time. We need to be cool. Okay?'

Twill exhales, nods once and leans back. 'Speak to me.'

126

'LoveSick went out to get some Chinese. The call came about half an hour later.'

'Croall?'

'No, LoveSick. Said he was with Croall.'

'How did he sound?'

'On the ball. Competent.'

'Has that fucker hurt him?'

'No.'

'Because he lays one finger—'

'Twill, calm. It's okay. We can handle this.'

'We? No.' Twill laughs. 'This is on me.'

'No. This is ours. All of us. The Eagles. The two-two.'

'Fuck that.'

Lucan looks over Twill's shoulder and dips his head. Twill turns to look. Trilby stands and removes his hat. Cilla. He raises a hand and smiles apologetically.

'What the fu—'

Lucan nods again over his shoulder. The two punters turn to face him. The one on the left is deathly pale. His friend is shovelling crisps into his mouth.

Ghost and Beast.

'We've got this' Lucan says. 'All of us. The two-two.'

Book II
October 2015

16

Englewood, Florida

The room is low ceilinged with thread bare carpets and outdated, mismatched furniture. The old man has drawn the curtains to block out the sun in an attempt to control the temperature. An air-conditioning unit rattles and drones over her shoulder but produces nothing more than a tepid whisper. It's hot. Florida hot. The thick kind of soupy humidity that wraps itself around you like an itchy blanket.

She undoes a button on her shirt and fans her face. The old man opposite is unblinking, as still as a statue. It's all she can do not to lean over and check he's still breathing. He shows no sign of being phased by the heat. Then again, she's yet to find anything that *does* phase him. With his dry, cracked skin and pink, urgent tongue he reminds her of a lizard. He's wearing a comically bad pelican-print shirt—complete with soup stains—and taupe flannel trousers pulled up above his waist. Florida chic. A clear plastic tube runs from an oxygen tank by his side to his nose; elastic straps around his ears hold it in place. If it weren't for an inscrutable glare, he'd look almost avuncular. She considers drinking from the glass of water he's set down on the table for her then remembers the yellowing tide mark and resists.

With an awkward smile and a nod, the interview begins.

'We was briefed, in what must have been February 1968, that the Viet Cong had retreated to Son My after the Tet Offensive.'

The journalist lifts a hand. 'Sorry, one second.' She takes a digital recorder no bigger than a packet of cigarettes from her bag, presses a button and places it on the table. A clock ticks loudly somewhere. She looks back up at the old man; he fixes her with rheumy eyes and she forces a smile. 'Go back. Please. To the very beginning. You were drafted?'

'Yes, in October 1967, I completed basic training north of here at Fort Benning in Columbus, Georgia, and was flown out in December to join my new division, Charlie Company, 1st Battalion, 20th Infantry Regiment, 11th Brigade, 23rd Infantry Division.' His chest puffs with pride, his first show of emotion.

'How did you find that? Was it your first time away from home?'

'I was eighteen. I'd never had much of what you'd call a home life. Leastways, not what passes for one these days. Not one you'd so much as miss. Never had no pa, and ma was plain leery-eyed mad, drowning at the bottom of a bottle. I'd say the army was just about the only family I ever had.'

'And how did you feel about that?'

He shrugs. There's a piercing, predatory look on his face that sends a wave of prickles down her back.

'I guess we was excited. You have to understand, this was early on. We'd been sold a yarn about this great big adventure. We was with buddies, we was unbeatable. We was…America.'

'And how was it when you first got there?'

He puffs air out of blue-tinged lips. 'Huh. The first couple of months was a cakewalk, no contact with the Viet Cong at all. We started to talk amongst ourselves, this was gonna be one long holiday.' He chuckles and shakes his head. 'Then the Tet Offensive reached us.'

He takes a glass of water with shaky, liver-spotted hands and lifts it to his mouth. Wets his lips with a small, pointed tongue. The journalist swallows her revulsion.

'And that was the start of it. And the end of the party. By mid-March, even though there still hadn't been any direct contact, we'd had twenty-eight casualties from mines or booby traps. There was a guy from back home, Billy Swayne his name was, went through basic training with him. Well, Billy walked straight onto a pipe bomb…ka-boom. There was a flash, and the explosion lagged half a second later. First off, there was a high-pitched ringing in my ears, but the smoke cleared and there was a new sound—one I'd heard before.'

The journalist tilts her head.

'See, summer nights, me and Billy used to go round Port Charlotte in his pa's pick-up. Someone would drive, usually Brandon—he didn't like to play on account of he had a dog hisself at home—and we'd sit up high in the back, taking shots at the local mutts with a twenty-two. Sometimes, you'd get them in the eye or the balls and they'd make this sound. Like a yowl. No way of reproducing it;

comes from here.' The old man pats his belly. 'It's the sound of agony…the sound of hell on earth.'

'What happened to Billy?'

'Didn't last all of five minutes. His legs was blown clear off. When we was clearing up later, we found one of his boots up a tree. Just hanging there on its laces, completely untouched, like a Christmas decoration. I searched for the other one…never hurt to have a spare pair of boots.'

'And Billy?'

The old man closes his eyes. Smoke and the smell of cordite rise above the coconut palms. Distant wails turn into a low sobbing.

'Oh, he yelled and hollered summat bad, but what you gonna do? Everything from the belly button down was gone. I stuck him with some morphine and he fell quiet. We used to do that you see, when it's a hopeless case. And you don't get much more hopeless than Billy Swayne, or what was left of him, flapping round like a fish out of water…making that goddamn racket. You'd hit them up with the full dose. Shuts them right up and sends them on their way. If you'd have heard the fuss he was making, you'd have done the same and been grateful for the peace that came with it.'

'And how did this make you feel? *Sending on* one of your friends?'

The old man gives her a stony glare. 'I'm not gonna bullshit you. It made us mad. Not because it was Billy Swayne or whichever poor mook's turn it was to take it in the ass but because it could be us next. We was all frustrated. We was taking hits daily and still hadn't seen one of these gook fuckers face to face. I'll tell you how we felt—we wanted blood. This wasn't the war we'd signed up for, the war we'd seen in the movies. We was like fish in a barrel, getting picked off. The top brass knew this and felt the same. After Tet wound down, the 48th retreated and melted into the countryside.'

'The 48th?'

'48th Local Force Battalion of the National Liberation Front. Viet Cong. Charlie. Gook fucking central.'

The journalist scribbles in her notebook and nods for the old man to continue.

'That's when they set up Task Force Barker. We was a battalion-sized unit formed from three rifle companies of the 11th Brigade, including Company C of the 20th Infantry. That was us. Company C.'

'Who was Barker?'

'Lieutenant Colonel Frank Barker.'

'And what was the specific role of Task Force Barker?'

'Search and destroy. Specifically, the 48th. Officially, it was the start of the fight back. Morale was low and we needed a tick in the win column. Unofficially, we all knew what was really happening. We was getting our asses kicked. Something had to change and this was a chance to take the gloves off and get down and dirty. We was hungry for blood.'

'Was this…unofficial line ever communicated to you or was this just your personal interpretation?'

The old man parts his lips. Dried saliva stretches across his smile. 'Personal interpretation? They was our goddamn orders. Henderson—'

'Henderson?'

'Colonel Oran K. Henderson, Commander, 11th Brigade, gave us the order, and these are *his* words: "Go in there aggressively, close with the enemy, and *wipe them out for good.*" Easy as that. Not a lot of room for misinterpretation, is there?'

The journalist looks up from her notebook and instantly regrets meeting the old man's gaze. His eyes are bright and wet. *He's enjoying himself,* she thinks.

'And this order was reinforced by the leadership?'

He chuckles. 'Barker himself—and bear in mind we was Task Force Barker—told us to go in, burn the houses, destroy food supplies, kill the livestock and destroy the wells.'

'But he didn't say anything about civilians?'

The old man raises his voice. '*Wipe them out for good.* What bit of that don't you get? Those was our orders.'

'The orders were to wipe out the enemy. How did you know who was the enemy and who were just farmers? Civilians?'

'There ain't no such thing as civilians in a war like that. You hide them fuckers, you *feed* them fuckers, you give them a roof over their head…then you *are* the enemy.'

'You said "go in" …where was this?'

'Intelligence suggested the VC was hiding in Son My.'

'Son My? Is that a village?'

'More like a *region* comprised of smaller settlements, like hamlets. My Lai was one of those hamlets. We called it Pinkville. Barker had already tried to take Pinkville in February, but things didn't work out too good that time.'

'You were ordered to go in, engage and destroy the hamlets?'

134

'Those was the orders right up until the night before, yes.'

The journalist stops writing. 'What do you mean, up until the night before?'

'We was given fresh orders. Same mission, but more detailed orders from Medina.' The old man's smile is so bleak that the journalist returns to her pad.

'Medina?'

He sighs, runs a finger around the collar of his shirt, which hangs loosely around his neck and billows out at the belt line. 'Captain Medina, Charlie Company. A good man.' A shadow crosses his face. 'It was a fucking disgrace the way he was thrown to the wolves.'

'What were *his* orders? How were they different from Barker and Henderson's?'

'He said all civilians would have left for the market by seven a.m. and anyone left would be NLF or NLF sympathisers.'

'And you took this to mean everyone in the hamlet after seven was the enemy?'

'Sometimes the officers have to be like politicians. Spell out the basics, and let you work it out for yourself.'

'So, this is where some of the confusion came in?'

'There was no confusion. Someone asked in the briefing, "Who is my enemy?"'

'And what was the answer?'

The old man closes his eyes. 'Anybody that was running from us, hiding from us or appeared to be the enemy. If a man was running, shoot him. If a woman with a rifle was running, shoot her.'

'But you shot women without rifles. And children.'

The stare she gets back burns. 'It all came out in court. Look it up if you don't believe me. Medina said, "They're all VC. Now go and get 'em." His orders were to destroy everything that was walking, crawling or growing. We was to give Charlie a bloody nose.'

'And you think what happened at My Lai was giving them a bloody nose?'

Again, the grim smile. 'Oh, they got a bloody nose alright.'

The journalist pauses, weighing up whether to drop the hammer so soon. 'And do *you* have any regrets about what happened that day?'

The old man leans on his elbows. 'Not. A. Single. One. See, I'm a soldier, Miss Clearwater. We was trained to follow orders and that's what I did. You might not like it but there's a reason we're sitting here today, speaking American and not Russian or Gook. And I'd do it all again tomorrow if I was asked to.'

There's anger in his voice. Time to move the conversation on.

'Tell me about your role in what happened at My Lai.'

He sighs and slumps back. 'The plan was to send in 1st Platoon with Bravo as backup, but not until we'd lit them yellow fuckers up like it was the fourth of July. We hit them hard with artillery and gunships. About eight a.m., we went in.'

'What was it like?'

The old man shrugs. 'Mud-hut settlements, rice paddies, irrigation ditches, dikes and dirt roads connecting the hamlets.'

'Did you come under fire?'

'No. See, the gooks love tunnelling—it's in their nature—and that's where we thought they were. Underground, or hidden away in the huts. As we approached we saw workers in the brush and rice fields. We fired at them so as they'd get the message.'

'Warning shots?'

'I'm sure *some* of them was warning shots.'

'What did the villagers do when you got there?'

'They was mostly getting ready for market day. Just milling around, no panic, no running away, like it was…interesting for them. We herded them into the hamlet's commons.'

'Then what?'

'This was the first time we'd come face to face with the enemy. We'd all lost friends and was hungry for revenge. The way they just casually hung around, staring at us, chatting away to themselves in that fucking language…it was like they knew we couldn't touch 'em.'

'And how did it start?'

'It was so damn weird. We was all just standing around; no one knew what we were supposed to be doing. Waiting for someone to take the lead. Some gook, tall, maybe in his thirties, laughed at something and that was that. One of our boys ran over and stuck him in the throat with his bayonet. One jab, boom. Just like that.' The old man mimes the action. 'Charlie looked stunned. He put his hand to his throat, then fell to his knees.'

'How did the villagers react?'

'One took a step forward and barked something.' The man chuckles.

'What happened to him?'

'Same trooper grabbed him by the scruff and pushed him down the well. Threw a grenade after him for good measure.'

The journalist is hit with a chill. 'What was everyone else's reaction?'

'No one *said* nothing. It was like someone had opened the gates to hell. Open season. We just let rip.'

'You fired on the villagers?'

'They was rounded up first. Once my lieutenant started, we took that as the green light.'

'Lieutenant Calley?'

The old man nods.

'How many villagers were there?'

'Fifteen…maybe twenty.'

'What then?'

'We set fire to the hootches and huts, waiting for the rest to come out. And when they did'—he raises his finger mimes pulling a trigger—'*pew pew pew*…we let them have it. This was our turn.'

'With rifles?'

'With machine guns, M16s. I saw one group rounded up…someone hit 'em with an M79.'

'M79?'

'Grenade launcher.'

Bile rises in the journalist's throat. She thinks she might vomit if she speaks so she nods for the man to continue.

'Once we'd finished in that village, we pushed on into the next. They were running away by now so we rounded them up and took care of them.'

'Were the villagers combat age?'

He shrugs. 'Some were.'

The journalist refers to her notes. 'According to the US Army Criminal Investigation Division Inquiry, they were mostly old women and children. Old papa-sans, women and kids.'

'Miss Clearwater, why do you ask if you already know the answer?' They lock eyes until the old man continues. 'What is combat age, now you ask? Huh? What age you gotta be to fire a gun? You think a woman can't pull a trigger? Now who's not being *politically co-rrect*? You don't think feeding and giving a bed to a soldier is any different to pulling the trigger or laying the mine yourself?'

'What did the women do when you started shooting them?'

Onyx eyes shine back at her. 'There's a strange thing that happens when people realise they're going to die...a look that comes across their faces. They beg, they howl for mercy. Those women threw themselves on top of the kids to protect them.'

'This saved the kids?'

He shakes his head. 'Some was alive...at first. The ones that was old enough to walk got up and that's when Calley started shooting them.'

Her breath catches in her chest. She puts her hands down by her side so the old man can't see them shaking. 'What happened when you'd...cleared the village?'

'Captain Medina came over the radio, calling for a lunch break. About eleven a.m., must have been. After that the helicopters landed. They wanted to evac our casualties but they weren't needed. There weren't any.'

'What about injured villagers?'

'Again, there weren't any...injured. The choppers left. They weren't needed.'

'But they came back, right?'

'They came back when they saw what was going on from the air.'

'And you didn't stop?'

'Why would we stop?' the old man yells, jabbing a gnarled finger in the air. 'We was following orders. Their job was to transport the injured out of the hot zone; ours was to secure it.'

'You say hot zone. Were you fired upon at any point?'

The old man shakes his head, but holds his jaw firm.

'And were any weapons found subsequently?'

Again, no.

'What happened to the rest of Task Force Barker?'

'When it became clear backup wasn't needed, Bravo Company was transported to a village a couple of miles away.'

'And what happened there?'

'Same as My Lai. Bravo secured the zone and mopped up resistance.'

The journalist half smiles. It's forced, pained, and she hates herself for it. She gathers her things and pretends to switch off the recorder. 'Thank you, Mr Thompson. I think that's all I need.'

The old man dips his head but doesn't move.

She turns back to him. 'May I ask why you did this? I mean, why you sat down with me today?'

He steeples his fingers under his nose. 'Miss Clearwater, there have been a million words written about that day. And not one of them from our point of view. You're all so quick to judge, to heap shame upon us and what we did. But you can't begin to understand what we do. What we was trained to do.' He leans forward and grips his knees with mottled, arthritic knuckles. 'There's a reason we're called a unit. We act as one. Independent thought is frowned upon. It presents a risk to your colleagues. And believe me, the last thing you want to do is let your colleagues down. *We follow orders without hesitation.* And you know what? It works. You and your shill friends in the media sit on the side-lines, puce with outrage, throwing accusations around like stones, but where are you when it really counts? When *men* are called upon to do *men's work* and defend our nation's borders, you all melt into the fucking background.'

The journalist clutches her bag in her lap and stares right back at the old man. 'Sorry to interrupt your stirring speech, Captain America, but I'm interested in how shooting a kid in the fucking face is defending our borders.'

He sniggers. 'I don't expect you to get it, Miss Clearwater. You've never sat up to your waist in mud and shit, with a pink rain that used to be your best friend falling around you.' He waves a skinny finger towards her bag. 'You just carry on writing your precious stories and feeling all warm and fuzzy about how righteous you are, until the next time *real men* are called upon to spill blood for your right to stand on a soapbox and let everyone know how fucking virtuous you are.'

She stands. 'One last question.'

He opens his hands, palms up, and angles his head. Like the Godfather granting an audience, she thinks. *The arrogance.*

'When you were fighting alongside Senator Vincent Kalcek, did you see him do any of the things you've described?'

The old man jumps up, eyes blazing coals, nostrils flared. He slams a fist on the table, knocking over the recorder. The journalist sweeps it into her bag and takes a step backwards. He bares his teeth and plants his legs wide.

'Is that what this is about?' he yells, shaking.

The nose tube pulls over the oxygen tank, and the elastic straps bend his ears forward cartoon-like. She darts out of the room, slams the door behind her and runs to the front door. Fumbles with the lock, hands sweating. A glass shatters against the frame.

She's at her car in three strides, fishtails down the road, clipping a garbage can on the way. In the rear-view mirror, the old man is standing in the doorway, thin lips stretched into a smirk.

***

She stops at a junction, glances in the mirror again, half expecting to see the old man chasing her, oxygen tank clattering along behind. Tiny shards of glass sparkle in her hair.

'Crazy motherfucker.'

She pulls into a parking lot making sure she's screened from the road by a truck. Turns the engine off but keeps the air-con running. How do people live in this heat? Doesn't it turn them mad? There's a moment of panic as she thinks she's left the recorder behind, but it's there at the bottom of her bag, LED blinking. Still recording.

The last thirty seconds of her tape: *Is that what this is about?* The smash of glass, the slamming door. And something she missed first time around. *CUNT!*

She turns the recorder off and her phone on. Two texts and a missed call.

How did you get on? You gonna make the two o'clock? Jack.

Call me x. Mom.

She sighs, lowers her head between her legs and brushes the glass from her hair.

The missed call is Mom. 'Darling, are you coming back tonight? Grace stole the show at the pageant. You should have seen it. Call her…It's not easy having a mum who's—'

She clicks the phone off and rubs her face. A guilt trip—just what she needs. It's nearly two. If she drives fast she might make the three-thirty shuttle from Sarasota. A quick calculation. Newark by six thirty, home by eight.

A text back to her mom: *Home by eight.* Another to Jack: *Good. See you tomorrow. Find out all you can about Task Force Barker and First Platoon, Charlie Company.*

She taps the steering wheel.

Fuck.

Another text to Mom: *Keep Grace up xx*

17

Manhattan

Kay parks in the basement, rides the elevator to the ground floor and crosses the hall to security. She greets the guard with a bored smile while her bag and coat are screened and takes another elevator to the third floor. The doors open and she's hit by a wall of noise—office and cell phones ringing, people chattering, and an old Reuters terminal puking an endless ream of paper. Journalists slouch in cubicles, jackets slung over the back of their chairs, hammering away at keyboards or squawking on phones. Some are eating breakfast, dead eyes trained on flat screens with twenty-four-hour scrolling headlines. Kay closes her eyes and breathes…body odour, coffee, second-hand air and heated-up food. Smells like home, and she loves it.

She heads to her office at the far end of the newsroom, cheerily acknowledging a tall man with a harassed face and tie undone to his chest. Chuckles when he scowls back at her.

'Soper's looking for you,' he yells as he fiddles with the water-cooler tap.

She doesn't stop, waves a hand over her shoulder.

She swipes the pass on the lanyard around her neck, and thick glass doors to her office click open. They shut behind her and it falls so quiet, her ears feel like they need to pop.

'Hey.' Her assistant points at her desk. 'I got you a skinny decaf.' He's got a face on him like a dog who's dropped a ball at her feet.

Kay nods. 'You want to shut the blinds?' It comes out sterner than she intended. 'Please. And good morning, Jack.'

He's quick to his feet. The room brightens and the headache that's nagged and gnawed at her all morning, recedes.

'You know they should be shut at all times, right?'

'Sorry. It's just…sometimes it feels like being on a space station or something.'

'That's kind of the point.'

The room has two desks, some filing cabinets and an outsized white board— a murder book with lists of names and places linked by a cobweb of lines.

'You may as well cross off Thompson,' she says, flapping a hand in the air.

'He didn't know Kalcek?'

'Oh, judging from his reaction I'd say he most definitely knew Kalcek.'

'So why rub him off?'

Kay pops off the lid of her coffee, takes a sip and grimaces. 'Decaf? Really? On a Wednesday?' Her monitor is framed by a wreath of Post-it notes. She looks at Jack and feels a twinge of regret. 'It's fine, but going forward you should know I'm almost exclusively powered by caffeine and red wine from northern Spain. Got it?' She gives him a smile. 'And seeing as it's nine a.m., I think caffeine's possibly more appropriate.'

He grins back. 'I thought you said the Thompson meet went well.'

'It did.' Another slurp, just to make him happy. 'It *went* well, but didn't *end* well. I'm not convinced our good friend Mr Thompson, the malicious old fuck that he is, will let us use anything.'

Jack pulls a face and plucks a Post-it from her monitor. 'That's odd. He rang. Said it was nice to meet you and that you could use whatever you want.'

Kay arches her eyebrows. 'How about that? I did *not* see that coming.'

'What did he say about Kalcek?'

'Nothing. But his reaction tells me we're on the right path. We can already prove he was there, plus we have a corroborating source. As nice as a third would've been, we mustn't get greedy.' She peels off the rest of the notes and sticks them on her desk. 'Soper…Soper…Soper…Soper.'

Jack nods and opens his mouth, but his phone interrupts. 'And here he is again.'

Kay sighs. 'Another reason the blinds stay shut, okay?'

'I'll get you a proper coffee. You might need it.'

Kay mouths *fuck-off* and lobs a screwed-up piece of paper at him. It bounces off his back. There's a blast of white noise as the doors open; then she's back in the vacuum.

She picks up the phone and clears her throat. 'Nick.'

'Kay.'

There's an awkward gap. 'How may I be of assistance?'

'Oh, I don't know. Perhaps you could stop harassing old men. Just an idea—one day you're going to put one of them in the ground.'

'Shit.'

'Yes, fucking shit indeed, Kay.'

She takes a carton of cigarettes from a drawer, telling herself that's not the real reason she wanted the blinds shut. 'What happened?'

'What happened? Fucking hell, Kay, were you not there?'

She draws the smoke deep into her lungs, holds it for a second and blows it towards the vent above her head.

'He's okay, since you're so desperate to know.'

'The turtle-faced shit threw a glass at me. I couldn't give a flying fuck—'

'Legal, however, take rather a dim view of it.'

Another drag on the cigarette and a glance at her watch. 'What's his beef? Cos he rang and said we could use the tape so he's not *that* pissed.'

'*He* hasn't said anything. The neighbours called the cops because they saw a car pull away like the start of the Indy 500.'

'And how was he?'

'Absolutely fine. Didn't want to make a complaint.'

'Wait—so exactly what *is* this all about?'

There's a groan down the line. 'Kay, he's an old man. With an old body and an old heart.'

'Uh-uh. He's also a sadistic asshole who can only get hard talking about shooting women and children.'

'That may be so, but you push one of these guys too far and you make him ill…or worse…then we've got a problem.' He pauses. 'And then *you've* got a problem.'

'Perhaps you can find me a fit, healthy thirty-year-old Vietnam vet, huh?'

'I mean it, Kay. Enough.'

'Okay, okay,' she says. 'Message received.'

There's a pause, then he says, 'Are you smoking?'

She takes one last drag and drops the butt into her coffee, stands on her chair and blows the smoke into the vent. 'Ha! Course not. It's called vaping, Grandpa. All the kids do it.'

'I've got editorial at nine tomorrow. Swing by at ten. You can give me an update then. Oh, and Kay, stop smoking in the office.'

***

Jack places the coffee and two files on her desk.

'What's this?'

'What you asked for. Task Force Barker and Charlie Platoon. Full register, charges, military records, history. Anything I could find.'

He stops speaking. Good job too; he's wasting his breath. Kay is already flicking through the first file.

'What are you looking for?'

'Anything that stands out, looks odd. A name or place that sounds familiar or contradicts what we already know…or what we *think* we already know.'

'How was Soper?'

'Mr Soper to you. Don't you worry about that. I can handle him.'

'I was thinking—'

'Do we pay you to do that?'

Jack laughs, but it sounds put on. 'At what point do we approach Kalcek?'

Kay lowers the papers. 'Not until the last minute. We're in the juice business, Jack. It's all about the squeeze. We go to Kalcek when, and only when, we know all the answers, and we've got enough to nail him to the cross. Whatever he says at that point, whatever he does to spin the story, is just fuel to the fire.'

'But we've got that already.'

'Aha.' Kay stabs the air with a finger. 'Maybe, but if we want to be anything more than a one-line header we need *juice*. Get it? Senator in war crimes is good. Front page for a day, maybe two. Senator hushes up war crimes is *very good.* Front page for a week. Expose and bring down a lying, cheating senator and you're on everyone's lips for a month. *Extremely* good. Pulitzer good.'

'Can't we speak to the military archivists? They won't lie.'

'They might not lie but they can only tell you what's in their records, and there's no way that oleaginous fuck hasn't already covered his tracks. Plus, they might tip him off. Or worse, go to the press themselves. And then, young Jack, we are up shit creek without a paddle. Four months' hard work down the john.'

'So, what do we do?'

'We carry on panning for gold.' Kay throws a file back at him and threads her arms into the sleeves of her jacket. 'If anyone asks, we're writing a book on My Lai. I suspect these'—she gestures towards the files—'have all been bleached. Any and all mention of Kalcek deleted. But there's got to be something…there's always something they've missed. And we have to find it. Look for names that sound familiar, dates that look out of sync with what we already know. You have that timeline of his bio?'

Jack rifles through his desk and holds up a folder.

'Right. When you've read the Task Force files, read them again. And again. If there's still nothing out of place, study his timeline until you know it like the back of your hand. Then stick it up on a board. Kalcek's public, white-washed résumé has to conflict with the "provably true" at some point. And that's what we're looking for. A tiny crack we can lever into and blow open. You have his version of events on one side, and all the information in the public domain on the other. I mean open-source documents, Google hits, newspaper archives, public statements, press releases, public and private gigs, digitised and non-digitised. All of it has to be cross-referenced with the bullshit they want us to believe. The microfiche is going to be your best friend. It's there, Jack.' She slaps a hand on the files. 'We just got to find it.'

'How will I know when I've found what we're looking for?' Jack says.

'Dentist.'

'Eh?'

'You know how a dentist pokes around in your mouth with a pointy little instrument?'

Jack puts a hand to his mouth. 'I have been to the dentist before.'

'Then you'll know they keep jabbing until you pull a face. That's how they know they've found what they're looking for. Look for ways to prove them wrong. Assume it's all bullshit. And look in their eyes when you're poking around in their mouth. Find the bruise. Then punch it.'

Jack crosses his arms over his chest. 'Meanwhile, you're off out.'

'Wow.' Kay holds her hands up. 'You're amazing. How *do* you do it?'

'I'm just wondering where the division of labour is in all this work *we're* doing?' Jack says, smiling.

She taps her nose. 'Executive privilege. I'll be back this afternoon…'

Jack pulls a face.

'What? What is it?'

'It's just…can you smell smoke?'

***

145

Although Kay has access to resources at the *Times*, the New York Public Library's Fredrick Lewis Allen Room has the dual benefit of being distraction-free—no Jack or Mom—and completely untraceable. They're entering the final, sensitive stages of the investigation. If a file is signed out at work, or her search history viewed, it could compromise the investigation and reveal the target. Paranoid? Maybe. But when the story breaks, it has to be on her terms. The tremors will be felt across America, all the way up to Capitol Hill. *If* she's allowed to do her job right.

Several hours' effort leaves her frustrated. Today, her dental skills have let her down so she trudges back to the office, thinking maybe what they have now is all they're going to get.

With a bit of luck—and given the number of enemies the senator has—his reaction and subsequent politicking will keep the story alive for a while and act as a catalyst for others to come forward.

Her headache returns with a vengeance. She needs to put some blue sky between her and work; it's becoming difficult to focus. An idea bubbles up to the front of her mind and she switches on her phone. Two messages from her mum.

Kay texts back: *I'll pick Grace up from school and take her out for dinner.*

The reply comes in seconds: *OK. I'm sure I'll find something in the cupboard. Mom x.*

Kay screws her eyes shut. She doesn't know if it's her mum's passive aggression or her own guilt, but they can't seem to have the simplest of conversations without anger or resentment taking a bite out of her.

The next text is to Jack, saying she won't be back. And to keep the blinds shut.

Then she's skipping through the underground car park, praying no one sees her. They don't. As soon as she emerges the other side of the Lincoln Tunnel, the traffic clears and so does her head, taking with it all thoughts of psychotic old men with flame throwers and replacing them with worries closer to home.

There's no point in sticking her head in the sand—it's all headed to shit, chez Kay. No matter how many times she keeps telling herself Grace will be okay, a big decision's looming. Children are durable. Or so the mantra she keeps repeating goes. They change, they adapt.

Who's she trying to kid? The last six months have been tough, balancing work and the new regime at home. Which is exactly how it feels at the moment.

Regime change might be in order. Grace seems fine, but Mom's constant chipping away is taking its toll on Kay; why wouldn't it affect Grace? And although Mom is supposed to be looking after Grace and taking pressure off her, why does it feel like she's got two kids now? She knows it's up to her to be more patient. If it wasn't for her mum she'd have to give up work. And if she was to give up work, she'd lose the house. It's an impossible situation. This new arrangement *has* to work.

She resigns herself to spoiling her daughter and being more gracious with Mom, but the idea withers and dies on the vine the second it's born. It's all on her. Everything. It's not about Mom's behaviour, it's about *her* reaction to Mom's behaviour. People get old, more cantankerous and forgetful. It's natural. *Gotta remember that.*

She pulls up at a set of lights and texts her daughter. A smiley face emoji pings back almost immediately and Kay's heart soars. Ten minutes later and she's parked outside the school, pulling fake smiles at the other mums, seeing pity in some faces and judgement in others.

She hears Grace before she sees her.

'*Mommmmmmyy!*'

The joy is pure and unadulterated. Her girl tears down the steps to the school, bag slung over one shoulder, the ever-present stuffed rabbit with floppy ears and button eyes tucked under her other arm.

Right then. Kay's body tingles with love, and she pledges to do whatever it takes to protect Grace for as long as possible. And if that means eating a steaming shit-sandwich at home, then pass the salt.

'I thought we agreed. Mr Flopsy stays home.'

Grace frowns as she gets in the car. 'No, Mommy. You agreed. Me and Mr Flopsy didn't agree to no such thing.'

Grace rattles off the minutiae of her day like a machine gun. Brandy has fallen out with Jackson and sat on another table at lunch. Jackson said Brandy smelled of milk and…Kay makes the appropriate cooing noises and nods, all the time resisting the urge to pick her up and squeeze her. There'll come a day when her angel becomes a surly, monosyllabic teenage grump. But it's not today.

They pull up outside the restaurant and Grace squeals and begins lobbying to order from the grown-ups' menu. Kay winks and says she'll take it under consideration. They park in the shade under a tall pine, and are led to a table away from the bar.

The waitress takes their order and Kay studies her daughter's small, perfect hands, porcelain skin and smooth cherub-like face. In ten years, she'll no doubt hate her upturned nose but at the moment it's just *too* cute.

'How's Meemaw?'

Grace shrugs. 'Okay, I suppose.'

'Just okay?'

'I had to wake her up this morning.'

Kay lays a hand on Grace's arm. 'Meemaw's getting old, sweetheart. You have to remember that.'

Grace pulls her rabbit into her chest. A six-year-old's face isn't built for hiding irritation. 'She put hand wipes in my lunchbox yesterday.'

'So? We've discussed this. It's good to be clean, right?'

'Instead of my sandwiches.'

'Oh. Did they not taste nice?'

Grace dissolves into giggles. 'I didn't *eat* them!'

Kay mutes her phone. No more mention of her mum. Nothing is going to ruin their time together.

***

It's almost dark and Kay is about to put the key in the front door when it's wrenched open.

'Oh, thank God.'

Her mom's face is etched with worry, eyes watery and rimmed in red. She launches past Kay and sweeps Grace into her arms. She turns to Kay, her face flushed, expression flinty. '*Where have you been?* I waited at the school for hours…I called the police…why didn't you answer your phone?'

'Ma! I told you I was picking her up.'

Her mom's eyes flicker for a moment, like she's being rebooted, then she disappears into the house, still cradling Grace. Kay remembers her promise to be more patient but is overrun by a sense of doom. Dress it up however you like— this is never going to work.

***

'I already got you coffee,' Jack says without looking up.

148

'You can never have too much coffee,' Kay says, relieved to see the blinds down.

Another whiteboard has appeared overnight, next to the first, but in portrait and with scribbles down, not across.

'Did you even go home last night?'

Jack smiles and jabs a pen in the direction of the board. 'Your wish is my command. Find anything interesting on your travels yesterday?'

'Only that I need a winning lotto ticket.'

'Amen to that.'

'Anything in the Task Force or Charlie Platoon files stand out?'

'No,' he says, tapping the pen against his teeth. 'Not in *those* files…'

Kay puts down her coffee. 'Where then?'

Jack holds up a thick folder. 'I was thinking about what you said yesterday.'

'Do we pay you—'

'You've done that one.'

Kay mimes zipping her lips and waves him on.

'The majority of our research to date has been online—internet and digital archives. I got to wondering about whether any original paperwork still existed.'

'Old school. And?'

'All physical archives are in the basement. Luckily, they're well indexed and I found this.' He holds the file up again.

'Go on.'

'It includes the same stuff we've already seen. Plus, plenty more. Dates, names, places. Mostly press releases, flagged newspaper articles, magazines. We've seen *some* of it before. Actually, whoever digitised these files did a half-arsed job—'

Kay's mobile buzzes.

'Jack, I could listen to your melliferous tones all day, but I'm going bare-knuckle with Soper at ten. Hop to it.'

'Right.' Jack pushes his glasses up his nose and waves a scrap of paper at her. 'Let's start with this.'

Kay holds out her hand. 'What is it?'

'It's an internal note. A memo. A slip for missed calls. It fell out when I got the folder from the crate. It didn't make the digital files…and before you say it, I know you're not supposed to remove paperwork from the archive but…'

She takes it from him and starts to read. Jack begins to speak but she holds up a hand. She inspects the reverse. Her phone buzzes again but she ignores it.

'It's from Anderson on the sport's desk.'

'Yes, but when he took the call'—Jack motions at the note—'Jan fourth, 2009, he was on domestic politics.'

Kay shrugs. 'Who's Camilia Lopez? And what's it doing in Kalcek's file?'

'Anderson took a call from a Thomas Elder.'

Kay looks blank.

'You don't know him. He's a nurse at Morristown ER. Says he admitted a Camilia Lopez on Jan third, 2009.'

'Back up a bit. Should I know this Lopez woman?'

'I wouldn't expect you to. I had to look it up.'

Kay snaps her fingers. 'Come on, get to it.'

'Camilia Lopez was long-time carer and nanny to Kalcek's three children from his second marriage. The woman who lived in the Kalcek household for over twelve years was admitted to Morristown ER with injuries consistent with aggravated assault.'

Kay's eyes widen. 'Did she file a complaint? Was there a police report?'

'No and no.'

'Did she carry on working for him?'

'Nope. I checked. She dropped out of all the family photos subsequent to her late-night trip to ER. I traced her.' He pushes some papers around on her desk. 'According to the electoral roll, she moved from Kalcek's in Ocean Port to Newark.'

'Was the lead followed up?'

Jack shakes his head.

Kay looks at her watch. 'Right, speak to Anderson. And this Thomas Elder. Find out what happened. I'll be back after Soper.'

Jack's shoulders slump. 'Not Lopez?'

'No,' Kay says, picking up her jacket. 'That's my job.'

***

Kay's first reaction to the two suited men in Soper's office is to treat them to an unambiguous hand-on-hips, hot-as-the-sun death ray.

Soper motions for her to sit down and mumbles a greeting.

She leans forward on her knuckles. 'Morning to you too, Nick. And Tweedle-Dee and Tweedle-Dumbfuck are who or what precisely?'

Soper takes off his glasses and pinches the bridge of his nose. 'Bamford and Haycock from legal.'

'And may I ask what Messrs Hayford and Bumcock or whatever the fuck they're called are doing at *my* meeting?'

'Kay, sit down—'

'No, Nick, I will not fucking sit down. In what parallel universe is it okay for you ambush me like this?'

The lawyers exchange glances, and the one on the left—pinstripes and a round, florid face—opens his mouth.

'No,' Soper snaps, pointing at him. Then to Kay. 'Sit down and I'll explain.'

She yanks out a chair and drops her bag on the table. Pushes up her sleeves and crosses her arms. 'This I'm looking forward to.'

'Kay, we have a responsibility to the board and the shareholders to report the news in a responsible fashion—'

'You know how investigative journalism works! We have a mandate to operate in absolute'—she glares at the suits—'ABSOLUTE independence. How are we supposed to retain our integrity if we don't have independence? These fucking guys get to choose what's news and what isn't? Is this how it works now? What's next? Team building barbeque and book burning?'

'Kay, you don't even know what they're doing here. Let me—'

'This is bullshit, Nick. Plain and simple. And you know it.' She stands and grabs her bag. 'We can continue this conversation without Laurel and Hardy whenever you want.'

Soper sighs and looks at the suits. 'Get out.'

Pinstripes looks at his colleague. 'I think it's most—'

'OUT.'

They shake their heads, gather their papers and leave the room. Kay waits until the door has closed. 'What the actual fuck, Nick?'

'Jesus, Kay. You're killing me with this shit.'

'You know the way I operate,' she says, sitting back down. 'Without absolute independence there is no integrity. I *need* to have that, and *you* need to give me that. Unless you can guarantee me one hundred per cent they won't leak or interfere, I'll have no part of it.' Her phone buzzes inside her bag. 'And if they won't interfere, I'd ask what the fuck they're even doing here in the first place.'

Soper puts his glasses back on and raises his hands. 'We always have the lawyers do due diligence. You *know* that.'

'Yeah, but always in the *final scrub*, just before we go live. *You* know *that*.'

'Whatever,' Soper says, turning to his computer. 'Just remember, I'm fond of you and we go way back, but I have a job to do. At some stage it will be my ass on the line, and you'll be on your own. And when it happens, don't expect to act all surprised. Got it?'

Kay smiles. 'Aye aye, Captain. Consider myself told.'

'Now gimme an update and leave me alone so I can get my blood pressure back under 140 over 90.'

'There's not a lot to add really. We're close. Beach-combing. Looking for something to ice the cake with.'

Soper peers over the top of his glasses. 'You got what you need?'

'Yep. We got the whistle-blower nailed down and a corroborating witness who was there in 'Nam. Both happy to go on the record. Old man Thompson would've been nice but we don't need him.'

'Tell me more about this whistle-blower.'

'What do you want to know?'

'Whether we're exposed on this. Who is it? What are they to Kalcek and what's their motivation?'

Kay shuffles in her seat. 'I don't feel comfortable sharing that right now.'

'Oh, I'm sorry. Maybe there's been some confusion. You see, what just happened was your executive editor just asked one of his reporters about a source on a story that leaves the paper legally exposed on a scale never seen before.'

'Uh-uh.'

Soper's face darkens. 'Listen to me. I'm your boss. Don't make me ask again.'

'It doesn't matter who or why, Nick. They came forward with the story, and it all checks out.' She leans forward, hoping he won't realise she doesn't know the whistle-blower's identity. 'Given the sensitive nature of the story, and the potential consequences, I'd say they had the right to a little privacy, right?'

Soper pauses, then looks away.

'We know Kalcek was at My Lai, and we can prove it from multiple sources. We know he lied and we know he covered it up. That's good enough for me, and it should be good enough for you. He was there, Nick.'

152

'In what capacity, though? You got to think how he's going to spin this and be ready to counter.'

'There's nowhere to hide this time. He was in Charlie Platoon, Task Force Barker. The epicentre of the biggest shit-storm in US military history.'

'Okay. What's the play?'

'We lead with the main story. I'm thinking the original whistle-blower, holding back some of the proof. Maybe one of my sources. If, make that when, Kalcek denies it, day two we come out swinging.'

'And you're happy it's watertight?'

Kay nods. 'We've got him, Nick. Trust me.'

'They'll carve those words on my gravestone.' Soper squares up some papers on his desk and glances at the clock on the wall. 'When do you think you'll be ready to go?'

'Couple of weeks. Maybe a month. There's a few last leads to follow up. You?'

'We've got primaries next week. Get those out the way and—barring any disasters, scandals or wars—we could be heading into a lull. This'll be perfect. Shall we say ten thousand words, three weeks?'

Kay's phone buzzes again. 'Let's call it a month.'

***

She slips back into her office. Jack puts the phone in its cradle and scribbles a note on the file.

'And?' she asks.

'Elder, the nurse who called in the Lopez injuries, no longer works Morristown ER.'

'Oh.'

'But switchboard tells me there is a Tom Elder in'—he looks down at his papers—'the Child Development Centre. Same hospital.'

'Great. You reach out to Anderson yet?'

'Kay, he's sports. The Yankees played last night.' Jack mimes tipping a glass. 'He won't be in till lunchtime.'

'Fine. I'll go see him.'

'What do you want me to do?'

'You're happy we've not missed anything on Task Force Barker?'

153

Jack nods.

'Okay. Build our own Kalcek timeline from news clippings, press releases and what we know. Use any new stuff you found too. Put it alongside the official timeline and compare the two. Cross-reference everything and see what stands out. Try looking outside our resources. The New York Public Library has digitised anything and everything. It's there, Jack. Go find it.'

Jack nods.

'I'll call Elder and pay Anderson a visit,' Kay says. 'Did you manage to get a number for Lopez?'

'No, but a Google search took me to Facebook. I think it's her. Or at least one of them is. I've sent you the link.'

'Right. Good work, Jack. Why don't you grab an early lunch? Don't rush back.'

He almost sprints out the door.

***

There are thirteen names in the link but only three spelled with one 'l'. Two are approximately the right age, and only one of those is in the United States. Kay scans her profile. She's a keen Facebooker. Kay sends her a short, friendly message without giving too much away. First contact has to have a soft landing. Now for Elder.

The phone is picked up on the fourth ring. 'Morristown Medical Centre.'

'Child Development Centre, please.' Kay sticks the phone under her chin and lights a cigarette.

A male voice answers.

'Hi. Can I speak to Tom Elder please?'

A giveaway pause.

'Who's calling?'

'Kay Clearwater. He doesn't know me.'

A longer pause. *It's him.*

'And can I tell him what it's regarding?'

'Mr Elder. Tom.' She taps her cigarette against her coffee cup. 'It's Kay Clearwater from the *New York Times*.'

'*Shit.*' Hissed. Too quick. 'What do you want Mrs Clearwater?'

'Ms. You treated a patient in 2009. A Camilia Lopez.'

154

'*Jesus Christ.* I was told I would never hear about this again. Are you trying to get me fired, *Ms* Clearwater?'

'It's fine, Tom. No one's looking to hurt anyone.' The nurse's breath is hard and heavy in her ear. 'If you can just run me through the bullet points, I'll leave you in peace.'

There's a rustle.

'I've already told you everything I know.'

'Please. Two minutes. Just a brief outline.'

A long exhale. 'Miss Lopez was admitted with a nasal fracture—'

'Broken nose?'

'Yes. Also, an indirect orbital floor fracture and fractured clavicle.'

'Tom, I'm from Brooklyn. English?'

'Miss Lopez had a broken nose, shattered eye socket and a fractured collar bone.'

'How did she say it happened?'

'I can't remember exactly, but I know it was bullshit. Something innocuous like walking into a door. You have to remember, in ER we've not only seen everything, we've also heard every excuse under the sun.'

'So, what was it? How did she get injured?'

'Definitely assault. I can't tell you who, but we see it most days and even more so on Saturdays and Sundays. And you can double that when the Yankees lose. That's all I know, Ms Clearwater. I really should be going.'

'And who did you tell this to?'

'Only the *New York Times*. As per our agreement.'

'Agreement?'

'Listen, I've told you all I know. Goodbye.'

The line goes dead. Kay taps the phone against her chin. Next up, Anderson.

***

The sports desk is on the second floor. Anderson is leaning back in his chair, staring at the ceiling. She approaches and he flops forward and nudges his mouse, but she's already seen the *Sports Illustrated* screensaver.

'Kay! What a pleasant surprise.'

'Brendan,' she coos.

The air is stale and a cloud of fumes cloak his desk. His face is a roadmap of broken blood vessels and he's gained at least fifty pounds since the last time they met.

He pulls out a chair and pats the seat. She smiles and taps her watch trying not to breathe through her mouth. The smell of liquor and body odour is overpowering. 'Just a quick one.'

'What brings you down here?' He stretches out a leg and pushes a drawer close with his foot.

'In 2009, you were domestic politics.'

'Yes.'

Kay digs in her bag and brings out the memo. 'You took a call from an ER nurse who admitted a Camilia Lopez. Injuries consistent with assault.'

Anderson shrugs. 'That was a long time ago. Burned through a lot of brain cells since then.' A coarse but friendly laugh turns into a hacking cough. He wipes his face on the back of his sleeve. 'Sorry, can't help.'

Kay believes him. 'No worries. Thought it was worth asking. Take care, Brendan.'

She walks to the door and is reaching for the handle.

'Wait.'

She stops and turns.

'At the bottom.' He scribbles in the air. 'I always put the initials of who I passed the lead on to. You know, like a paper trail.'

Kay looks at the bottom of the memo. In Anderson's handwriting, are two letters.

NS. Nick Soper.

***

Back in the airlock, as Jack has begun to call it, she checks her phone. Four messages from Mom, each more aggressive than the last, but all asking the same question: What's for dinner? Out of sight, out of mind, Kay thinks and places the phone screen-down on the desk. Long, sharp needles pierce her head. Another migraine threatening. She pops a pill and washes it down with a slug of cold coffee.

Soper's initials on the bottom of that memo. Should she confront him?

Undisputed: The *New York Times* had an agreement with Thomas Elder. They had a story, a big story, about an assault on a senator's live-in child-minder and they sat on it. Whatever the nature of the agreement with Elder, he was uncomfortable discussing it. If the *Times* had opted not to run it, he would have shopped it around and would have had no problem finding another home for it. And she or Jack would have found it.

Conclusion: Thomas Elder got paid by the *Times* but they stuck it in a locked drawer. Classic catch and kill. No, it makes no sense to confront Soper yet but maybe it explains the lawyers.

Pain slices between her eyes, sharp as a bread knife. The new daylight bulbs are way too bright. It's like working in a tanning salon. She considers calling facilities to get them changed but decides against it. The fewer people with access to the airlock, the better. At the moment it's just her and Jack; not even the cleaners get in. And that's the way she likes it.

Her phone buzzes and skitters across her desk. She checks her watch and rubs her temples. She needs fresh air. And now.

She takes a slow walk to the New York Public Library and logs onto Facebook. There's no reply from Lopez, but the message has been read. She flicks back to the profile. Lopez has location services enabled. Most of the posts are from Elizabeth, New Jersey, and her profile picture has her wearing an Avis car-rental shirt. Newark airport?

Her headache's getting worse and the recycled air isn't helping. The sun's up; the sky's bright. Central Park it is. She thinks of those poor schmoes at the office, including Jack and feels a twinge of guilt. It doesn't last long.

They might call it skiving; she prefers strategizing.

***

She returns to the office sometime after three, refreshed. She'd girded her loins and replied to her mom's texts, which bought some respite, albeit temporary. Jack is face down in some papers and she lets him get on with it. Google gives her the number for Avis Newark Airport, and she taps it into her phone with a pen, a familiar craving in her gut. She wishes Jack wasn't there.

There's a long, pre-recorded menu before she gets an opportunity to speak to a human.

She asks for a quote and rolls her eyes as she's put on hold. A few minutes later, a male voice greets her.

'I'm sorry,' Kay says. 'I have social anxiety. Please could I speak with a female operator?'

Another five minutes of middle-of-the-road rock and a new voice apologises for the wait.

Female. Forties or fifties.

'Hello. I'm flying in this afternoon and need a mid-size saloon for a couple of days.'

'Okay. It will absolutely be my pleasure to help you with that. Do you have a business or relay account with us?'

Latin inflections. The *z* sound in 'business' pronounced *th*. The *r* rolled.

'Personal.'

'That's great. My name's Camilia'—*Ca-me-ya*—'and I'll be helping you with your enquiry today. If you can give me a moment, I'll just check our inventory.'

Kay speaks quickly and evenly. 'Miss Lopez, my name is Kay Clearwater. I work for the *New York Times*.'

The line goes quiet for a moment. Then Lopez says in a small voice, 'Don't call again,' and cuts the connection.

'*Fuck.*'

Jack takes off his glasses and shrugs.

'I don't suppose you're having more luck,' Kay says.

'Maybe. I'm not sure.' He walks over to the tall whiteboard. 'Here'—he taps the column on the left—'is the public version of Kalcek's timeline. And here'—right-hand side—'is the timeline I've reconstructed using our research.'

Kay chews the end of her pen. 'So, on the left you got Kalcek stationed in the north, at Hanoi, '67 to '68.'

'And on the right—'

'My Lai, where we know he really was.'

'Exactly.'

'Right. Anything new?'

Jack writes '1971–73' on the board and circles it.

Kay leans in. Her phone buzzes and she grumbles.

'You want to get that?' Jack asks.

'Believe me when I say most definitely not. Go on…'

'In 1972, according to Wikipedia and cross-referenced with the bio on his own website, Kalcek was teaching asymmetric warfare at Fort Hamilton in Jefferson.'

He flicks through some papers and hands a sheet to Kay. She scans it and looks up.

Jack continues. 'The *Belfast Telegraph*, Monday 12th November, 1972. Colonel Vincent P. Kalcek, U.S. Marines, lays a wreath at the Cenotaph, outside City Hall.'

'So what? He was on a trip. Maybe a holiday.'

Jack grins and hands her another sheet of paper. '*Sunday Times*, March 31st, 1972. He was a guest at Sandhurst, presenting the new colours.'

'Isn't that some military school?'

'It's *the* UK military academy. Royal Military Academy Sandhurst to be precise.'

'What's presenting the colours?'

'That's not important. The point is he was in the UK.'

'Hardly breaking news, Jack. He visited the UK twice in one year—'

'Three times that I can prove. So far.' Again, he ferrets around on his desk. 'Here. *Tatler*. July 1972.' He throws the magazine to Kay. 'He was in Herefordshire in the summer 1972. So that's spring, summer and fall in the UK.'

Kay holds up the *Belfast Telegraph* next to the *Tatler*.

'Not conclusive proof,' Jack says, 'but certainly merits—'

'Hmmm.'

'What?'

'This look like the same guy to you?'

Jack leans over her shoulder and adjusts his glasses. Kalcek is beside a tall, slim officer in the olive fatigues of the British Army. Dark hair parted at the side. They're both saluting. The *Tatler* photograph shows the same man in a churchyard; the bridegroom is standing stiffly with several others, Kalcek amongst them. They're holding champagne flutes and grinning at the camera.

Jack snatches the magazine and begins reading. 'Colonel Vincent Kalcek, US Marines, attended the wedding today of Major Ellis Cromer, only son of Roger and Barbara Cromer to Mary Page, daughter of Anthony and Diane Page.'

Kay takes the magazine back and spends half a minute reading and rereading it. 'Okay. Get on this.'

Jack nods. 'It's probably nothing.'

'No. Whatever *it* is, it was important enough to airbrush out of his bio. Try the *Belfast Telegraph* and all the other locals. *Tatler* was a good find. If he was in the UK for an extended period of time, no way he could resist getting his face in the papers.'

'I'm on it,' Jack says.

'And Jack…'

He looks up, face open, eyes wide and probing.

'Well done.'

His reaction is unexpected.

'What's wrong?'

He brushes his shirt down and pulls on his sleeves. 'Are you happy with my work, Kay?'

'I literally just told you that I was.'

He looks away and his ears flush.

She plants herself on the edge of his desk. 'Jack, tell me what's wrong.'

'There's nothing wrong…it's just…you know I'm a little peculiar about the way I do things.'

'Peculiar? How so?'

'Maybe particular is a better word. I have obsessive compulsive disorder. Always have. Probably always will. When I was young I did the rounds, saw all the doctors. They tried to help, but…it's me. It's who I am.'

'Where are you going with this? I can't say I've noticed, but I can honestly say I don't give two hoots.'

He shakes his head and coughs. 'You're going to think I'm nuts.'

Kay grabs his shoulder and gives it a shake. 'Hey, I won't hold it against you.'

'I'm left-handed.'

'So?'

'My cup's always here. On my left. On a coaster.'

Where's this going?

'This morning, when I came in, my cup was on the right.' He slides it into position. 'Here.'

'So what? You're always digging around on your desk. You probably moved it.'

'No, my cup stays there.' He raps the table. 'That's where it goes.'

Kay goes back to her desk and spins in her chair. 'And you're positive about this?'

'Absolutely. I'm beyond sure. It bugs the crap out of me if anything's out of place. And it's why I'm perfect for this job. The smallest details leap off the page at me in neon. Trust me, my cup was out of place…Could just be the cleaners—'

'Cleaners can't get in.'

'Who can then? Me, you and who else?'

Obvious answer: Nick Soper.

Kay shoots him a smile. 'It was probably me.' Knows he won't believe her. 'You crack on with '71 to '73, and I'll see what I can find on this Ellis Cromer.'

'Maybe facial recognition will come up with something.'

Nick Soper. No one else has authority to enter the airlock. No one would think twice if they saw him coming or leaving. He's the only other person in the building who knows what they're working on. He shut down the Lopez story with a catch-and-kill. And he wants the lawyers in.

Conclusion: He's in the game. Somewhere, somehow.

'Kay?'

'Yes, good idea. Do that.' Her voice is too quick and too loud.

Jack returns to his work and Kay studies him. Folders on his desk, neatly squared and colour coded. Pens all lined up. Not a mark on the board that shouldn't be there. Hair a uniform length, neat parting. He looks up, moves his cup half an inch. How come she hadn't noticed before?

Her phone buzzes and she slips it into her bag without checking.

***

Kay takes the elevator to the top floor. She's known Soper for over a decade and thought they enjoyed a good working relationship. On occasion maybe even a friendship. Now's the time to find out. He might be the executive editor and all-round top dog, but she had his number. And for such an accomplished journalist, he's an astonishingly bad liar.

His secretary's phone is perched between her shoulder and chin, and she's holding her nails up to the light. Kay mouths, *He in there?* and gets a wink and a thumbs-up. She walks up to the door. Dark wood. Polished silver letters: *Nick Soper. Executive Editor*. She takes a deep breath.

'Moonlight Sonata' rings from the depths of her bag. The screen reads 'Mom' but falls dark before she can accept the call.

She backs away from the door and walks back to the elevator, lifting the phone to her ear.

'Mom? Okay, okay, relax. Where are you? I'll be right there.'

***

She's stuck in traffic at the Lincoln Tunnel and tries Avis again. Lopez is off shift. She leaves a message and regrets it before she's even ended the call. There's a fine line between probing and harassment, and she remembers something her first editor told her: you catch more flies with honey than vinegar. Maybe she should start applying this to her personal life.

She finds Mom's station wagon on the grass verge, rear sticking out into the road, forcing other cars to steer into the oncoming traffic. Grace is off to the side, knees drawn up to her chest, face buried in her hands. Mr Flopsy lying next to her. Mom is pacing a few metres away, jaw clenched and chin in the air. She sees Kay and launches into an impassioned rant, arguing she doesn't know what happened and pinning the blame on Japanese engineering. Kay agrees, trying to stop what's already a tinderbox from blowing up into a full-scale argument.

Kay slips down next to her daughter and asks what's wrong. Grace explains in a faltering stutter how she'd complained of being hungry. To which Meemaw had replied. 'Missing a meal won't hurt. I mean, look at you.'

Kay keeps her tone measured, says this is one of those occasions where Meemaw was wrong and didn't know what she was saying. Her daughter nuzzles into her and it takes every iota of self-restraint not to storm over and take a swing at Mom.

Flies and honey. Flies and honey.

Roadside assistance arrives. A couple of minutes of head-scratching and bonnet diving ensues. Turns out the Chevrolet is out of gas. Kay's anger drains away and is replaced by a crushing sadness. The guy takes a jerry can from the back of his truck and empties the contents into the tank, assuring them it will be enough to get them home. Mom tuts an objection and snatches the keys back. Kay puts Grace into her own car and says she'll see her mom back at the house, in a voice she only half hopes doesn't betray the extent of her anger.

Mom climbs into the Chevy and pulls out into the traffic, forcing a car to break and initiating a chorus of horns.

Back in Kay's car, Grace brightens at the offer of a trip to Dairy Queen.

They arrive home an hour later, the whole incident forgotten. The magic of ice cream, Kay thinks. Wouldn't it be nice if there was an adult remedy for forgetting your troubles?

And then she remembers the wine in the larder.

Kay's both pleased and relieved when Grace runs straight upstairs to her room. She finds Mom in the kitchen, her arms wrapped tightly around her chest, staring at the wall.

Kay opens her mouth to speak but Mom cuts her off.

'It's not easy…'

She puts a consoling arm on her shoulder. 'Ma, I know.'

'Was it really out of gas?'

'It's okay. It happens to all of us.'

She sniffs and wipes her face on the back of her hand. 'I think we both know it's not okay. I'm becoming more of a liability than a help.'

'No, Mom. Don't—'

'Oh, come on, Kay. You were always the pragmatic one.'

She looks exhausted. And something else. *That's it*—haunted.

'I don't know what we're going to do, Kay. I'm scared.'

They hold each other in silence.

'I know what we're going to do. Have a glass of wine and a good talk. I guarantee the world will seem a better place.'

Mom pulls back. 'We stopped talking, didn't we?'

'I suppose, but it's—'

'You're always so damned busy…I'm sorry. I don't mean to attack.'

'No, Ma. You're right.'

Kay leads her to the deck that overlooks the back yard and pours two glasses of Rioja.

'Cheers.'

Mom forces a smile and takes a sip. Pats her hair into place and looks out over the garden. 'I'm sorry you never knew your dad. All this is history repeating itself…I'm pleased to have had this time with Grace. I mean, I know it's difficult but I wouldn't swap it for anything. I'd hate for her to grow up resenting me.'

'Nonsense. She thinks the world of you.'

'Not this afternoon, she didn't.'

'You can't say things like that to a six-year-old, Mom.' Kay looks down at the clenched fists in her lap. 'It could have a serious effect on her mental health.'

'Say things like *what*?'

'You know…that she's overweight.'

'I've lost track of what I can or can't say these days.'

Kay squeezes her mom's hand. 'It's not easy but you've got to remember it's not easy for *any* of us.'

'You always were good with words, darling. But we're going to need more than words to help us out of this hole. For Grace. For you.' Her eyes fill with tears. 'For me.'

***

Jack gets up and scribbles on the whiteboard. Kay is still buried under a mountain of paperwork. She pushes her chair back, takes off her glasses and rubs her eyes. 'You should get some lunch.'

Jack looks at his watch and the corners of his mouth curl up. 'It's gone three.'

'Doesn't time fly when you're having fun!'

He takes a napkin from his top drawer and lays it on his desk, pulling on the corners until it's square. Next comes a Tupperware box, and a knife and fork. He pauses, then shifts the knife a quarter of an inch to the right.

'Left a bit,' she says, and grins.

His cheeks flush with embarrassment. 'Anything turn up this morning?'

Kay whistles and waves a hand in the air. 'Ellis J. Cromer. Anything you want to know, just ask. I'm now the world's leading authority.'

'Go on then. Let's have it.'

Kay picks up her notes. 'Ellis Jupiter Cromer. Born 6th September, 1943, Yeovil, Somerset—'

'Jupiter?'

'I know, right? Jupiter is the God of the sky and thunder and king of the gods. Why would you do that to a kid? Attended Milford Infants School, then boarded at King's College, Taunton. Yadda yadda yadda. A levels, whatever the fuck they are. Starts the Commissioning Course at the Royal Military Academy Sandhurst as a cadet officer in September 1961. Fast-tracked, passes out with flying colours, top of his class. 1963 to 1967 finds him in Aden.'

'Aden?'

Kay looks over the top of her glasses. 'Now the Yemen.'

'Oh.'

'1967 to 1970 Dhofar.'

'What was happening in Dhofar?'

'According to the *Sunday Times*, British troops were engaged in a secret war the sultan of Oman was fighting against guerrillas up in the mountains of Dhofar, to the south of the country…Citations for bravery. Back to Sandhurst, then goes dark for a bit. Then in 1972 he pops up in Northern Ireland. He gets married in '79, 1982 is the Falklands War, 1983 receives the Military Cross. Daughter, Tilly 1984. Son, Marcus 1986. Retires from the army 1988, elected as the Right Honourable Member of Parliament for Somerton and Frome in 1992, re-elected 1997 with a majority of 8,000, and serves to this day. Currently, the Parliamentary Private Secretary to the Secretary of State for Defence…'

'Christ, that's a lot of words. What the hell does it mean?'

'I have no idea.' Kay flicks back through her papers. 'The period we're interested in—early seventies—he was in Northern Ireland. I found one mention of him working with Special Forces. Given the lack of clarity regarding his role and the fact that he got married in Hereford, I think Major Cromer was doing something with the Special Air Service.'

'The 22nd Royal Rifles, it says here,' Jack says with a mouthful of salad. He wipes his mouth and swallows. 'I took his graduation pic from Sandhurst and got a few hits from a reverse-image search. That gave me more pics I could reference as he got older. He stayed in charge of the 22nd all the way through the Irish conflict. Funny thing is though…the 22nd Royal Rifles is a ghost regiment. Never officially existed. Beyond a couple of references that slipped through the cracks, there're no records. Nothing.'

'So, Cromer's in charge of a regiment that doesn't exist, maybe with some connection to the SAS?'

'Uh-huh, trained by or attached to, seems the most likely explanation. And I found this…'

Kay perches on the edge of his desk prompting Jack to slide his lunch away from her backside with a look of horror.

The screen shows two rows of men kneeling for the camera. Off to the side, Cromer stands rigid as a flagpole. And on his right, a young buzz-cut Kalcek looks on. The caption underneath reads *The Eagles. Hereford. 1972.*

'This is another one. Cromer and Kalcek.' Jack dabs at a smudge on the screen with his napkin. 'August 1972 edition, *Soldier* magazine. "Colonel Vincent Kalcek of the US Marine Corp, pictured here with Major Ellis Cromer, 22nd Royal Rifles, proudly announces a collaboration with Her Majesty's Armed Forces."'

'What was the nature of the collaboration?'

'Doesn't say.'

Kay flops back into her seat and spins a full circle. '1972, Kalcek was a veteran of the Vietnam war teaching asymmetric warfare, correct?'

'According to official records.'

'And Cromer, a veteran of the insurgency in Oman, was fighting a civil war on the doorstep of the British Empire.'

Jack nods.

'And they announce a collaboration.' Kay slams a hand on her desk. 'Kalcek was covertly helping the Brits in unconventional warfare. Has to be.'

'Why covertly?'

'It had to be under the radar. Remember, the official American position on "the Troubles" was one of indifference.'

'They really called a civil war "the Troubles"?'

'Yeah, I know. So British, right?'

Jack shakes his head and forks more food into his mouth.

'On one side, the US was keen not to meddle with or antagonise Britain, its main NATO ally, because they were in the middle of the Cold War. At the same time, we were juggling domestic calls by a politically active Irish-American population.'

'So, any co-operation had to be covert.'

'Precisely. We need to find out the extent of Kalcek's philanthropy.'

'If it's sensitive, what's it doing in *Soldier* magazine?'

'That, young padawan, is the official magazine of the British Army. It would make sense to play the audience, if you get my drift.'

'Got an answer for everything, haven't you?'

'I like to think so,' Kay says. 'It's why they pay me the big bucks!'

'What now?' Jack asks. 'Speak to Cromer?'

'Shit, no. He'll tell us nothing and might tip off Kalcek. No.' She taps the screen 'You find out everything you can about the 22nd Royal Rifles. Names, numbers. I'll keep working Lopez. Cromer comes right at the last minute, when we actually know what the hell we're talking about.'

Jack salutes. Kay returns to her desk and brings up Facebook.

'Son of a bitch. She's deleted her account.'

'Who?'

'Lopez. It's gone. *Fuck.* I pushed too hard.'

'You can still reach her at work, right?'

Her cell phone buzzes. She listens. Hangs up. Gets to her feet and snatches her jacket off her chair. 'Get onto the 22nd Rifles. I want to know everything.'

18

The Wollman Rink sits on the east side of Central Park, close to the zoo. A looping artery of honking cabs and looming skyscrapers surround it. Nervous kids hold on to low railings around the oblong perimeter like their life depends on it, while more seasoned skaters gouge contrails in the ice with sweeping turns.

Kay sits beneath a sprawling oak and checks her phone. Her visitor arrives, swift and silent, and with a lithe grace that belies his years. He slips onto the bench and pulls the brim of his fedora over his face. He's wearing a long grey trench coat, and string-backed gloves made of soft brown leather, incongruous with the warm evening. His chest rattles and air whistles between his teeth.

'Good afternoon, Ms Clearwater.'

'Is it?' she asks. 'That wasn't clear from your text.'

'When you reach my age, every morning you wake up is a good one.'

'You want an update?' Kay asks, lighting a cigarette.

'No, I care not *how* it is done, just that it *is* done. I want you to destroy that malignant fucker and heap such opprobrium and humiliation upon him that his kith and kin will wear the shame for a generation.'

Kay takes a deep draw, holds the smoke in her lungs until it burns, then blows it out. 'We're getting there.'

'Not good enough,' the old man says. 'I need you to pick up your pace.'

'It doesn't work like that. We have a process—'

'Forget your process. You're running out of time.'

'What does that mean?'

'It means, *he knows*, Ms Clearwater. About your investigation. You've been clumsy. Precisely what I warned you about at the very beginning.'

Kay shakes her head and laughs. 'No one's been clumsy. There's no way he knows.'

'He knows, and if you don't take this seriously, it will have a very ugly ending. For you. You see, you've put yourself into the crosshairs of a very bad man. This is no game. As of this moment on, you are swimming with sharks.'

'In that case,' she says, trying to keep the cynicism from her voice, 'what can we do?'

'Where are you up to?'

'We've got My Lai covered. We're just chasing a few more leads before we run with it.'

'What leads?'

'The child-minder.'

'She'll never speak to you.'

'I wouldn't—'

'You're wasting your time. What else have you got? What do you know about Belfast?'

Kay snaps her head back. 'You know about Belfast?'

'Yes. Animus, Ms Clearwater. That's the key. Find Animus and you'll have the link between Vietnam and Belfast.'

'Who's Animus?'

The old man ignores her. 'Now Kalcek knows what you're up to, you're vulnerable. He will never let you publish.'

'And how's he going to stop me? This isn't Russia, you know.'

'He'll find a way. Trust me on this. He's a very...capable man when motivated. You have to get it out there, into the public domain. It's the only way to guarantee your safety. The clock is ticking. If you stall, he'll come for you.'

Kay leans forward and squints. The sun is behind him—a dark shape with a golden corona. 'Who's Animus?'

'Not who. What.'

'Okay then, what's Animus?'

'You know what a dead man's switch is, Ms Clearwater? I suggest you not only put one in place, and sharpish, but also find a way to let Kalcek know it exists.'

Kay grinds the cigarette out with her heel. 'A question. And one I probably should have asked when you first approached me. What's all this to you?'

He heaves himself upright and walks away.

'Why are you doing this?' she calls out.

He turns, removes his hat and looks at her. His scorched pate is hairless and ridged with intersecting livid pink scars. The skin on his face is raw and grainy, streaked like a patchwork quilt of bacon. No nose, just a dark hole. The eyes are rheumy weeping slits in folds of melted purple flesh. His ears no more than angry red nubs.

'Good day. Happy hunting.' What would have once been lips tighten across his face. 'And stay safe.'

'*What's Animus?*' she shouts, but he doesn't even slow his pace.

19

By the time Kay's back in the airlock, she's talked herself off the ledge. The old man has a point. *If* Kalcek is as bad as the evidence suggests, and *if* he has been tipped off about what's going on, she might be in the firing line. But for what? He's a sitting senator, for fuck's sake, not some gangster. Worst case, Soper comes under pressure and pulls the story. That still wouldn't stop her from her pursuing her own book project.

'You okay?'

She looks over at a concerned Jack and smiles. 'Fine. I think.' Hangs her coat on the back of her chair. 'What you got for me?'

Jack stands and pushes a piece of paper towards her. 'I didn't find out much about the Royal Rifles but that shouldn't come as a huge surprise. Most of the Northern Ireland stuff is still locked under the Official Secrets Act and Special Forces don't generally go on the record.'

Kay groans.

'But...'

She peeks between her fingers. 'But what?'

'I tried the SAS Regimental Association, and they were very helpful. Got two names for you: Lewis Bridges and James Dwyer. Both left the army, but they're traceable. Bridges is on LinkedIn, and there's a James 'Jim' Dwyer, right age, on Facebook. Profile pic is the regimental insignia, a winged dagger and the words *Who Dares Wins*. Has to be him.'

'Excellent work, Jack,' she says, snatching the paper off her desk. 'Now then...'. She freezes.

'What?'

'Lewis Bridges, Director, Animus Security.'

Jack shrugs. 'So?'

'So, find me out everything you can about Animus Security. I'm going to call Dwyer and Bridges, see exactly what Kalcek was doing in Belfast in the seventies that was so important he lied to cover it up. Then we confront the Right Honourable Ellis Jupiter Cromer, MP.'

'What if he tips off Kalcek?'

'It's time to shit or get off the pot, Jack.' Kay fixes him with a sober stare. 'After Cromer, it's Kalcek's time in the barrel. Now'—she clicks her fingers—'Animus. Go.'

'Yes, siree.' Jack says, eyes already glued to the monitor.

***

The growing tempest behind her eyes is a beast. A run could be her last chance at shifting it. Like defragging a hard drive, getting rid of all the flotsam and jetsam. It might give her a sense of perspective too, line up her ducks, sort her problems into neat little boxes with solutions queuing around the block. It usually works.

Usually.

She heads out from home and pushes herself on, the hammering in her temples competing with the music in her ears. Her sweatshirt sticks to her skin. Each snatched gasp is alarmingly shallow like her lungs have shrunk to the size of walnuts. Lactic acid burns, every stride a battle of will over want. Her mouth feels like it's full of dust.

She glances at her watch. Not even two miles. Once-white trainers slap on the sidewalk. The pain will pass. It seems like an age. But it will pass.

Where's that second wind already?

She feels the buzz of her phone, ignores it, fumbles for the volume button. No matter how loud the music, it fails to drown out the voices crashing around her head. The genie's out of the bottle and she's in danger. Soper's playing games. The Lopez angle's going nowhere.

Then there's the two Brits. Bridges had been smooth, collected, with the charm of someone with something to sell. He'd laughed, as if a call from the *New York Times* was a daily occurrence. Animus is *his* firm, he'd said, and *he* has a policy of not speaking to the press. The whole conversation lasted no more than thirty seconds. There might have been an edge to his voice suggesting he wasn't as confident as he wanted her to believe but he was good. Very good. She's been lied to by the best and he was right up there. Maybe she's on the right track though.

The message to Dwyer on Facebook was deliberately oblique. He'd bitten and replied with his number. Different kettle of fish to Bridges, voice dripping with suspicion. A more obvious edge. Cold. Hard. His voice reminded her of time spent with African child-soldiers, electric with the threat of violence. A nervous, twitching energy. Not unusual in men trained to kill, let alone those that have been granted the opportunity to put their training into practice. She's met both in her time, and is keen to consign them to her past. Dwyer had listened patiently but was too quick to dismiss Animus. Not as polished as Bridges but maybe more dangerous. Definitely more feral, a frontline operator, not a corporate executive like Bridges and therefore less inclined to play the game. When he was tired of her questions, he'd sighed and told her to fuck off.

Here it comes. Her breath starts to flow more freely, her legs lighten. She opens her stride and pumps forward. Second wind.

Tomorrow, she'll speak to Soper and get the release brought forward. Perhaps one last push on Lopez, now she has nothing to lose. Then she'll call Cromer. Depending on how that goes, she'll decide whether to park Belfast for a later date. Then she'll ask Kalcek's office for a comment. It's a far from perfect end to the story, but the old man's words hang heavy: *The clock is ticking. If you stall, he'll come for you.*

A statement. Delivered as a matter of course, like instructions on how to bake a cake. But the stakes are too high to ignore. Her safety, and maybe her family's, is on the line. The old man might be straight out of a B-movie but there's been no indication he's prone to exaggeration. Everything he's given her since that first call has been measured, non-sensational. And it's all checked out. It would be easier if he were crazy or she knew his position in the game. He clearly has Kalcek's ear, knows the movements of Kalcek's inner circle.

She ducks between two cars, runs into the road and slams herself back as a van whistles past, missing her by inches. The horn cuts through the music in her headphones.

Shit.

She steps back onto the sidewalk and leans forward, hand on knees, until her breathing settles. Rips off the headphones. Hears the wail of a child.

Grace.

She barrels across the street and up the porch steps.

20

She bumps into Jack as he's leaving Starbucks.

'Ah, you genius,' she says, taking one of the two cups he's holding.

He smiles shyly but his eyes linger. 'You okay?'

Kay hooks an arm through his and leads him towards the office. 'Yeah, little domestic situation last night. Not a huge amount of sleep if I'm honest.'

'Oh dear,' Jack replies. 'Everyone good, I hope.'

'That's open for debate. Mr Flopsy's gone on the missing person's list.'

'Do I know him?'

'Sure. Might have had a different name and not been a rabbit, but we've all had a Mr Flopsy in our lives at some point. My Mr Flopsy was Charlie, the monkey.'

'Right.' Jack coughs. 'Good to know. Mine was a second-hand Barbie called Alice.'

Kay sniggers. 'Naturally.'

'So, do you want me to ring ahead and clear the front page? Alert Interpol?'

'Asshole,' Kay says, punching him on the arm. 'My daughter hears you making light of Mr Flopsy and your ass is grass.'

'Seriously, I hope it works out.'

'She'll be fine. Just part of growing up, I guess.' Kay shrugs. 'She took that rabbit everywhere. I'll make a few calls. It must be somewhere.'

Jack is silent the rest of the way, head down, embarrassed, Kay assumes, by the brief foray into her personal life.

They take their respective seats in the airlock and fire up their computers. A ping alerts her to a Facebook notification.

What the fuck?

***

174

She takes the M train to Penn Street and crosses over to the Tick Tock Diner, taking a table at the back, facing the entrance, with an unobstructed view. She orders an espresso, though she's already jittery with caffeine. Her phone buzzes.

Am I picking up dinner tonight? Do you think you'll make it home for once? Mom x

Kay rehearses several replies and starts to tap one out. A short, dark-skinned woman she recognises enters the diner, takes off her sunglasses and looks around. Kay stands and waves and the woman joins her.

Kay extends a hand.

The woman avoids eye contact and takes a seat, laying the sunglasses on the table between them. 'I won't be staying,' she says in a Spanish accent.

'But you're here!' Kay replies. 'Can I get you a drink? Coffee? Something to eat?'

'Ms Clearwater, the only reason I'm here is because my attempts to stop your harassment are clearly having no effect.'

'I think you have a story to tell, Ms Lopez,' she says. 'Can I call you Camilia?'

She shakes her head. 'No. You cannot. And I'm only going to say this once or I speak with my lawyers. Do not contact me, my family or anyone I know again. Okay? Is that clear enough for you?'

Kay looks at the sunglasses. 'Nice. Tom Ford. What do they run to? Five hundred bucks?'

'I don't see how—'

'How many child-minders begin a conversation with "I'll speak with my lawyers"? How many child-minders have one lawyer, let alone *lawyers*?'

Lopez blinks and looks over her shoulder at the entrance.

'Look, it's obvious you signed a non-disclosure agreement, but they don't apply if the law's been broken, Camilia.' Kay rests a hand on her arm. 'There's ways and means. No problem is too big.'

Lopez pulls her arm away. 'I don't know what you're talking about.'

'January 3rd, 2009. You were admitted to Morristown ER. Broken nose. Shattered eye socket. Fractured collar bone.'

Lopez's sigh is long and low. 'How do you know?'

'ER nurses work very long hours for very little money. There are ways to supplement their income.'

'I went through all this at the time,' Lopez says. 'It was an accident.'

175

'Puh-lease.' Kay swats at the air. 'If you're going to lie, load up and at least try and be original. Walked into the door? It's been done before, hun.'

'It was an accident. Senator Kalcek was very kind that day. He looked after me and drove me to the hospital.'

Kay's phone buzzes again.

Helllooo? Are you getting these? Mom x

Kay switches her phone off and puts it back in her bag. 'You worked for Kalcek for twelve years. You practically brought those kids up.'

'They didn't have a mother. What would you expect?'

'And when did you last see them?'

Lopez rubs her wrists. Her eyes are starting to moisten. She puts her glasses back on but makes no effort to leave.

An impasse. Kay leans back and looks her over. Dark eyes, nails bitten down to the quick, lips dry and cracked. A whiff of liquor hangs in the air. How do you talk around someone with nothing to lose? Answer: go all in; it doesn't matter.

'Let me remind you. Jan third, 2009. Why, Camilia? What happened that day?'

'I-I—'

'Don't you miss them? Don't you worry about leaving them behind?'

'Of course I miss them!' she snaps, colour rushing to her cheeks. 'I worry about leaving them with that fucking monster every minute of every day.'

Kay grabs her hand. 'Right, now's the time to do this. If not for yourself, for the kids.'

Camilia's head drops to her chest. Her voice is a whisper. 'I can't. Even if I wanted to.'

'Why not? It's all coming out, Camilia. With or without you. I'm giving you the opportunity to put yourself on the right side of history.'

'Because they watch my every move. Because they listen to me. On the phone. And probably at home. They know I'm here. It was their idea.'

What?

The chair scrapes as Lopez stands. 'I can't speak to you. You know that. Can't and won't. Any attempt to contact me again and I won't need those lawyers. And, yes, that is a threat.'

She swings her bag over her shoulder and walks out.

'Shit.'

Kay leaves a ten-dollar bill on the table and nods at a sharply dressed man who looks over the top of his paper as she walks past. And why not? He's a bright light in a world gone to shit.

***

The Post-it note reads *Call home*, souring her mood further. She rips it off the screen. Mom phoning the office now? This is a new and most unwelcome development.

Jack looks up but doesn't make eye contact or ask where she's been. Kay switches on her cell phone. Four missed calls and three texts.

Any news on the rabbit? Mom x

Grace won't stop crying. Do I send her in to school? Mom x

I've given her the day off. Mom x

'That from Mr Flopsy?' Jack asks, frowning at his screen. 'Send my love.'

'With the best will in the world, Jack, do fuck off.'

His reply is a grin.

Kay calls her mom. It seems to ring for an eternity and she's on the verge of putting the handset down when there's a hello at the other end.

'It's me,' Kay says.

'Who is this?'

Kay pinches the bridge of her nose and hopes her frustration doesn't travel down the line. 'Your daughter, Kay. Five eight. Black curly hair. Remember me?'

'No need to be snippy, dear. Hold on.'

She can hear her mom chatting with someone in the background but can't make out the words.

'Who you talking with?'

'Oh, a nice young man from AT&T. He's put in a new box or something. Needed access for an upgrade apparently. Not that I have the foggiest what one of those is, but those dungarees are really rather fetching,' she whispers.

'Nice, Mom. And you called the office to tell me this?'

'No, I–I…'

It's clear she either doesn't remember calling, or why she called.

'Listen, it's easy for you. I'd be going mad from isolation if it wasn't for…Sometimes, the only adult conversations I have are…'

Kay tries to stifle a groan, unsuccessfully.

'I…I called for an update on Mr Flopsy.'

Kay wedges the phone between her chin and shoulder and cracks her knuckles. 'Sorry, Ma. No news. The great stuffed-toy mystery of 2016 is lining up alongside Flight MH 370 and the Lindbergh kid.'

'Have you called the school?'

'Yes. No. Mom, I'll do it, but you really can't call me at work, okay?'

'Grace's fine by the way. I'm sure you were just about to ask.'

The line goes dead. Irritation turns to confusion. An uneasy doubt gnaws in the pit of her stomach, but she can't put a finger on it. Then it hits. A cold electricity passes through her.

'You okay?' Jack's on his feet.

'I switched cable two years ago. To Comcast. I don't have AT&T.'

Jack is on her in a second, grabbing her elbow and guiding her back to her seat. She lays her forehead on the desk and takes in long, slow breaths. The room stops spinning and he hands her a glass of water. She takes a sip, then a cooling gulp.

'What is it?' Jack asks.

'It's everything, Jack. It's slipping out of reach. I've got to s-speak to Mom.'

'Unless you need me, I'll give you some room,' Jack says, backing away.

She taps speed dial. 'No. Stay. I want you to take copies of everything. Got it? Stick it all in a box and put it under my desk. And tomorrow, load it into my car. Then scan everything we've got and…I don't know…stick it on the cloud or something.'

'On the cloud?'

'Just do it. But don't use your work computer.'

Jack leans back against his desk and crosses his arms. 'What aren't you telling me?'

'And use the copier on the fourth floor; you won't need to log in. There'll be plenty of time to explain, I…*Mom!* Are you okay? Where's Grace?'

***

By the time she clears the tunnel, the fear has been replaced with a slow, creeping embarrassment. Odds are it wasn't even AT&T who'd called around. After all, her mum's hardly reliable. Probably the Comcast guy and Mom just went giddy over a young man in tight denim. And she'd sounded fine when Kay called back—playing hide and seek in the garden with Grace. Even told her to stop worrying.

Christ. This job.

Maybe Mom's right. There are too many creepy old men crowding her days at the moment. It's getting to her. She could really do with a break. She'll see Soper in the morning and get his blessing to pull the trigger. It'll be good to get it over and out into the open. Get on with her life. Maybe, when the storm's blown over and the shit's dripping from the fan, she can take a week, visit her aunt in Vermont. It would be nice to—

Her bleeping phone shocks her and she swerves into the oncoming lane. *Fuck's sake*. She's a nervous wreck. She rights the car with one hand and fumbles in her bag with the other. Finds the phone and answers.

'Mom, I'm nearly there…ten minutes tops.'

'Do you know the Waffle House on Colbert, Ms Clearwater?' The voice is almost effeminate. English accent.

'I…who is this?'

The caller sighs. 'It was a rhetorical question. An ice breaker, if you will. I'll see you there in fifteen minutes.'

21

The Waffle House sits between a hardware store and a Goodwill shop. Single storey, stucco-fronted building with large bay windows and a near empty lot at the rear. Kay snaps a picture of the parked cars.

A sign above the door reads *Sweet, tasty goodness on a plate since 1953!* She doubts a tin of paint has been popped in anger since. A bell tinkles as she pushes on the door. She takes a red-leather booth by a smudged window overlooking the street. The waitress swaggers over with a bored expression, like she's performing a personal favour. Kay orders a coffee and checks her phone. The caller's number is unidentified. What did she expect?

There's a rumble and she looks out the window but it's just a passing truck. Jesus, her nerves.

A suited man, mid-thirties, with brushed-back blonde hair and iceberg-blue eyes lowers himself into the seat opposite. *Him*. The man from the Tick Tock. He takes a paper towel from the napkin holder and places it underneath him, lips curled with disdain.

'You smell that, Ms Clearwater? The grease, the oil. That's the odour of cheap, fried carbohydrates. The aroma of poverty and a lifetime of bad decisions. These people, they shovel trans fats into their bodies, craving endorphins like addicts. And even if it's for just a few seconds, they achieve respite from purgatory.'

He speaks with the crisp, tutored cadence of the English upper classes.

Kay looks at his folded hands on the table. Soft and pink. Perfectly manicured nails shimmer like glass.

'Safety in numbers, you see,' he says, then adds in a Southern drawl, 'Mama did it. Papa did it. Cousin Joe did it. All their friends do it. Eat, drink, sleep— and if you're lucky, a little bit of fucking somewhere along the line—then all aboard the good ship Diabetes.'

Kay's coffee arrives.

'As fascinating as your little socio-political commentary is,' she hisses as the waitress turns away, 'you want to tell me who the *fuck* you are, and what the *fuck* you want?'

He fixes her with a glacial stare that penetrates all the way to the pit of her stomach and pulls the coffee towards him. He picks up the cup, sniffs, pulls a face and slides it back.

Kay takes the coffee just so she has something to do with her hands. She takes a sip. He's right about one thing—the coffee is disgusting. 'You're going to tell me—'

The man raises an elegant finger to thin, ruby lips and shushes her. Kay is stunned into silence. There's something strangely mesmerising about him.

'That's not how this is going to work, Ms Clearwater. This is not a debate nor a frank exchange of views. You are going to listen to what I have to say. And then you're going to do it, okay?'

He treats her to a smile of unspeakable bleakness. Kay swallows and nods.

'Excellent. Please bear in mind that this is *not* the first time I've danced this tango, so you're advised to put aside any notions of begging or pleading. I've heard it all before. You would, quite literally, be wasting my time and yours.'

'What do you want?' she croaks.

'Ah, progress!' He beams. 'You've been sniffing around the business end of some friends of mine, and it displeases them. Which displeases me. As you can imagine, this is not an acceptable state of affairs.'

'Who?'

The man frowns. 'Let's go not backwards, Ms Clearwater. We were doing so well. You know who. And so do I. Remember how we agreed not to waste each other's time?'

Kay nods.

'Forthwith, you are going to forget all about what Senator Kalcek did or didn't do during his lengthy and glittering service for his country. You are to desist immediately from all further investigations and there will be no more ungainly transatlantic phone calls about Animus, Belfast or the Right Honourable Ellis Cromer.' The man crosses his arms and raises an eyebrow. 'Are we on the same page?'

Kay stares at him. Counts to ten. Shakes her head. 'This is some bullshit you're trying to pull here. *You* might want to consider this is the *New York* Fucking *Times* you're dealing with. Do you honestly think we haven't been shaken down before? Did you not consider the possibility that your little tough-guy-in-a-tailored-suit routine hasn't been seen like, a hundred times? And, if we're being completely honest…quite frankly, I've seen better.'

The man leans back and chuckles. 'You would be well served by remembering who you are dealing with, Ms Clearwater. It would be a grave mistake to take us lightly.'

The smile on his lips dies. He places a black leather briefcase on the table and clicks it open.

Kay pushes back from the table.

'I guess what I'm saying is stay in your fucking lane.' He studies his nails. 'Now, I'm no wordsmith like you, but please take a moment to remember what it was that killed the cat.'

He reaches into the case, places the object on the table in front of her, and leaves.

Big black button eyes.

Long ears worn threadbare with hugs.

And Mr Flopsy's head twisted through a hundred and eighty degrees.

22

'Morning!' Jack says.

Kay weaves her way through drifts of files, head held low.

'Which one's the copies?' she asks.

Jack hesitates, then slaps one.

Kay throws him her keys; he fumbles but catches them.

'Put them in the trunk of my car.' She sits at her desk and rubs her face. 'Wait…put your coat over the box.'

'Right, and why would I—'

'Just do it, Jack.' There's a hardness to her voice that shocks her, like some out-of-body experience.

She'd slept fitfully but had woken with a fresh focus. What she had to do seemed clearer. Yes, what was supposed to be an exciting but essentially normal job had taken her to a bad place with some very bad people but once she'd conceded that, the solution became blindingly obvious. Do what the very bad people want and get the fuck out of Dodge City. All notion of fighting the good fight and courageous journalism went out of the window the second she saw Grace's toy. Pick your battles. This isn't about cowardice either; it's about self-preservation. No. Even that's not true. She might put herself on the line, for a Pulitzer. But Grace? Nuh-uh. Not in a month of Sundays.

She fires up her computer. Grace's face pops up on her screensaver, hardening her resolve. It's a few minutes short of nine. She'll ring Soper on the hour. He'll fob her off or the secretary will say he's not available but she won't take no for an answer. Not this morning. She'll be vague, but firm. Announce she's closing the investigation into Kalcek. Apologise for wasting the paper's time and money and take the hit on the chin. Maybe she'll say the whistle-blower didn't check out…

Christ. She doesn't know what she's going to say. Only that she's doing it, regardless of the fallout. She's sick of the crazies and the morally bankrupt, with

183

their dead eyes, cynical smiles and half-loaded threats. Madness begets madness. And she's all madnessed out. If she's right about Soper, he won't put up too much of a fight.

It's nine. She reaches for the phone—

Jack bursts back into the room, puts a sweaty hand on top of hers, and pulls the keyboard towards him.

'You're going to want to see this…'

Her phone rings. She picks up. 'Nick, I was about to—'

'My office. Now. And bring John.'

'Jack.'

'Jack, John, fucking Jill. Bring him. Now.'

***

Soper sits at the end of a long, polished mahogany desk, flicking through papers, glasses perched on the end of his nose, face screwed tight with concentration. A twenty-four-hour news channel plays on a flat screen on the facing wall, set on mute. Kay and Jack are ushered in by his secretary, who's refused to meet their eyes.

Soper motions for them to sit without looking up. There are two places set, each with notepaper, pen, glasses and a pitcher of water. The only noise is the gentle blow of the air conditioning and the squeak of the leather chairs when they sit.

Jack's forehead is shiny with sweat and his left eye is twitching. He shoots sidelong glances at Kay and pulls on his cuffs. She reaches under the desk and pats his knee.

'Right.' Soper removes his glasses and looks down his nose at them. 'You should know that Senator Vincent Kalcek's office released the following statement this morning.' He holds up a piece of paper, slips his glasses back on and coughs into his fist. '"Late last summer, Senator Kalcek discovered a lump under his armpit. Further tests revealed a malignant tumour in his lymph nodes. The senator was diagnosed with adenocarcinoma, an aggressive form of cancer of the pancreas. The senator wishes to pursue his treatment with the full focus and energy with which he has become synonymous his entire career. Therefore, he is reluctantly vacating his seat in the upper chamber of the United States Congress and requests that he and his family be granted privacy at this time. This is just another battle Senator Kalcek has to fight. There will be no further statement until the position on his health becomes clearer." And that, wouldn't you say, leaves us a tincey-wincey little bit fucked?'

This just made my life a whole load easier, Kay thinks.

Jack makes a noise like a squeaky toy.

Soper squints. 'Is he okay?'

Kay nods.

'That's it? I'm shutting you down and you…nod?'

She shrugs.

Soper leans forward on his elbows. 'Can the real Kay Clearwater please stand up?'

Kay summons some steel she isn't feeling. 'Would it make any difference what I say at this point?'

'No. No it wouldn't. If we go after Kalcek now, it looks like we're hounding a sick old man who's served his country for seven decades. Have you seen the papers? He's the all-American hero, Kay. We'd look like bullies. Maybe if he returns to health we can revisit but'—he checks the paper again—'a-de-no-car-cin-oma…sounds like a little bit of a bastard to be honest.'

'When he dies?'

'Good God, no. If it looks like we've been sitting on this, we're fucked. Either way, this is the point at which I say thank you for your tireless efforts, but it's over. Take a week and we'll see if we can find you something new to get your teeth into, okay?'

The onscreen news switches to long-range footage of Kalcek emerging from a church, in a wheelchair, a blanket on his lap, being pushed by a stooped figure in fawn leather gloves and a fedora pulled low over his face.

The whistle-blower.

Kay takes a sharp breath.

Soper's voice is soft. 'You okay?'

'Sure,' Kay stands and nudges Jack on the arm.

***

They wait for the elevator, Jack shifting his weight from one leg to the other. 'So, is that it then?'

'Is it fuck.'

'Eh?'

She turns back to the lift. 'Are those files in my car?'

'Yep.'

'Good. Fuck Kalcek. There's nothing wrong with him. Fuck Animus. Fuck Ellis Jupiter Cromer and fuck Nick Soper of the *New York* fucking *Times*.'

Book III
October 2016

23

Greenhithe, England

The central atrium of the Bluewater shopping centre is split over two levels. A pedestrian footbridge spans the top-floor mezzanine with up-and-down escalators running off it. Inside, it's bright as daylight. Glass shopfronts with polished chrome pillars reflect multi-coloured signs. Twill is on a bench outside a shoe store assessing the state-of-the-art CCTV rig suspended above him from a sky light. Close behind, someone calls out to a friend and he spins around. Two boys, early teens, laugh and slap each other on the back. He turns back to the escalators and emergency fire exit. Across the walkway, Cilla is garbed in a raincoat, cap and thick glasses. Twill nods; Cilla scratches his ear in response.

The greasy tang of barbecued meat wafts down from the food court and combines with the heady aroma from a beauty counter. A wave of nausea hits him. His guts are already dodgy but it's not nerves. It's expectation. A sense of impending closure. Regardless of how the next few minutes play out, there will be answers. Whether they're soaked in blood has yet to be seen. But whatever lies ahead, he's ready.

He spots Beast halfway across the footbridge, pushing Ghost in a wheelchair. Ghost's head lolls on his shoulder and his face is frozen in a grimace. But his eyes are busy. His hands lie vice-like on a blanket on his lap.

'Jesus Christ,' Twill mutters.

Still, under the blanket is an Enfield SA80 assault rifle, capable of one hundred and eighty rounds a minute. Cilla has a Browning Hi-Power pistol tucked into his belt, the same as the one weighing down Twill's jacket pocket. Between them, they have the firepower of a small army.

Lucan, after a protest that had nearly spilled over into violence, is in Twill's car in the loading bay on the other side of the fire exit, Enfield tucked under his seat. The engine's running and he's listening through Twill's open phone-line on the stereo's Bluetooth. An emergency medical kit awaits LoveSick on the back seat, should he need it.

Twill checks his watch and rubs his leg. Two minutes past three. Everyone's in place. The only thing missing is Croall.

Another glance over to Cilla, who's scanning the crowd over the top of a newspaper. Twill reaches into his pocket and flicks the safety off. A gawky teen in a trench coat slumps next to him and begins texting with both thumbs. Twill slides along the bench until their hips touch. 'Seat's taken.'

The teen leaves, shaking his head but still texting.

A stocky figure stops by the bin and straightens.

'C'mon. Coffee.'

Londonderry accent.

Croall nods over his shoulder to a Starbucks.

Twill tries to hide his pain as he stands. They lock eyes. 'You're buying.'

Croall heads towards a closed-off booth with a limited view but Twill shakes his head and walks to a high bar, its stools overlooking the atrium. Better position and easier to slip on and off without betraying his lameness. Cilla sits a table away.

Croall returns with two hot drinks and takes a seat. He brings the cup to his lips and blows the steam away. A glance from Twill to Cilla and his lips curl.

A calm descends upon Twill. The past forty years have all been leading up to this point. There's a hunger in his heart and mercury in his veins. He won't be denied.

'If you've laid a finger on LoveSick, I'll gut you like a fish.'

'See, this way you're feeling, ya gotta let it go. It's not good for yer long-term mental health.'

Twill rears up, elbows wide. Cilla scrapes his chair back and takes a step towards them.

Croall breaks eye contact first, returning his attention to his coffee. 'If ya were to act on yer baser impulses right now, one of us'd be dead within half a minute. But which one?' He taps a finger on his top lip. 'Meh. I'd say seventy–thirty in my favour.'

Twill lowers himself back down.

'What? You don't agree? But...the leg. Oops. Don't mention the leg. Awkward.'

'Where's LoveSick, you cunt?'

'Calm down. I'm only pulling yer leg. Aw, shite. There I go again.'

His voice is higher than Twill remembers and his face is lined and craggy. Still the same cold, grey eyes that once stared at him through the slit of a balaclava.

'And ya can tell yer boys to stand down,' Croall says. 'This isn't going to be some gunfight at the OK Corral. But I should warn ya, if ya do feel inclined to be stupid you'll never see yer man LoveSick again.'

'Where is he?' Twill says again, pushing his anger down.

Croall shrugs. 'He's fine. We had a good chat.'

Twill shifts forward. 'Where is he?'

'Nearby.'

'I want to see him before we talk.'

'I'm not a fuckin' idiot, Twill, so don't treat me like one. You'll have to take my word.'

Twill folds his arms. 'Your word? Don't treat *me* like a fucking idiot. Word has no place at this table.'

'Bollix. We're both professional soldiers who just happened to be on different sides of the same war.' Croall cracks a biscuit in half and throws it into his mouth. Winks at Cilla. 'Ya might not like sitting down with me, but at this moment in time, we need each other. Besides, ya shouldn't take things so personally.'

'Call me old fashioned but it's difficult not to take what you did personally.'

Croall yawns. 'I don't want yer life story, Twill. I have no regrets. I don't care what happened in Belfast, ya hear me? I don't care about the past. I'm even prepared to let yer little one-man crusade slide.'

Twills digs nails into his palms.

'Someone has been targeting members of yer regiment,' Croall says. 'And if it's youse, I want ya to know that whatever's done is done. But it ends here, today.'

'Or what?'

Croall lowers his head so close to Twill's that he can feel hot breath on his face.

'I'll wipe every single last one of ya off the face of the planet.'

They hold glares, then Croall slumps back into his seat and sips from his cup.

'It's not me,' Twill says.

'Then who is it?'

191

Twill arches his eyebrows.

Croall hisses, 'It's not me either.'

'And you'd say if it was?'

Croall pops a sugar cube into his mouth and crunches. 'I think we're all played out, don't you? We've got nothing to gain by lying, and nothing to lose by telling the truth. It's cards-on-the-table time.'

They pause, looking each other up and down.

'See, we're not so different, you and me.'

Twill huffs.

'It's true. What we did back then. I took down one of yours; you took down two of mine. Next week, same but the other way round. It's not fuckin' rocket science. Just a game of chess.'

'Bullshit. You're a fucking animal.'

Croall chuckles. 'We're both fuckin' animals, Twill. We were'—he lifts a palm up—'butchers. Only with different bosses. Ya know it's true; ya just don't like hearing it from me.'

'We know what we were,' Twill says.

Croall yawns again. 'Yes, and isn't it liberating? Never having to second guess yer actions or lie awake at night thinking about what an awful person ya are.' He leans closer, eyes shining. 'We, me, youse, the two-two, or what's left of them, even fuckin' Cromer in his ivory tower. We're all cut from the same cloth. Men of war.'

Twill rubs the back of his neck. 'Get to the point.'

'Yer colleagues are dropping like flies, and if you're not responsible—and as I hold all the cards right now, I'm inclined to believe ya—I want to know who is. We're on the same side this time round. It makes sense to share intelligence.'

'What do you care if someone's taking us down?'

Croall's eyes widen. 'Ya have no idea, do ya?'

'About what?'

'Me. Cromer. The two-two.'

Twill stops breathing. 'What about you?'

Croall takes his cap off and runs a hand through his hair. 'After the Good Friday Agreement was signed most of us thought life would return to normal. Most, but not me. To me, the old life was the new normal. How do ya go from what we did to being a teacher or a bus conductor? A few of my former colleagues began having, shall we say, mysterious, unexplained accidents. I came close myself a couple of times. I was pretty sure I was being followed; my phone clicked every time I made calls. Strange cars would park in my street all night; the same cars would follow me round. And this was *after* we were supposed to be such good buddies again. Now, I'm not a great believer in coincidences so I paid yer man Cromer a little visit at his house in Hereford one night. Wanted to remind him that the most common place for an accident is right there in the home. Anyways, we got to talking, one thing led to another and we ended up coming to an arrangement.'

'What kind of arrangement?'

'A commercial arrangement.'

'Animus. You started Animus?'

A smile flirts at the corners of Croall's lips. 'Animus is way bigger than just me, and it was around a long time before Belfast. When I spoke to Cromer, a few of yer old mates were able to put aside...previous differences, and come on board. It was a natural progression.'

'What mates?'

'I think you already know. JR, Mincer, Tumble, Max...we were the muscle and Bridges was the brains. Cromer brought us together and supplied the contracts.'

Twill's insides twist. 'Who's Blaggard?'

Croall narrows his eyes. 'Are ya fuckin' kidding me?'

Twill repeats the question, spitting the words.

'It's youse, ya daft cunt. You're Blaggard.'

Twill stiffens and sits upright. 'And the American woman?'

'American woman?'

'No matter.'

Croall takes a gulp from his cup, smacks his lips and slaps a business card on the table. No name. Just a number. 'Here. If ya find anything out, let me know. I won't answer. Leave a message. If I want to get back to ya, I will. Remember, Twill, we're all grown-ups now. Cards on the table. Same side. And if ya persist in following me about like a little lost duckling, I'll fuckin' end ya. No more warnings.'

Twill gives a small nod. 'Did you tell Cromer you were coming here today?'

'Did I fuck. I wouldn't trust that lick-arse as far as I could throw him.'

In his pocket, under the table, Twill powers down his phone. The next bit isn't for Lucan's ears. 'Didn't you ever wonder how I kept on finding you?'

'What're ya saying?'

'Your precious mate Cromer was feeding me intel. Where you were. When you'd be there.'

Croall presses his lips into a thin line and looks down. 'Cunt.' There's a wait before he looks back up. 'And he was tipping me off too. Where ya was, when you'd be there.'

'I'd say Cromer knows more than both of us put together.'

'I'd say you're about right on that one, pal.' Croall throws a set of car keys on the table. 'White Focus, alpha papa five five, alpha papa victor. John Lewis car park, south-eastern corner. Yer man's in the boot. Unharmed.'

Twill scoops up the keys, sees movement—Cilla launching himself towards the fire escape. He swivels; Lucan's pushing towards them through a throng of shoppers on the footbridge.

When he turns back, Croall is gone.

**

They walk towards John Lewis, Twill and Lucan bickering like an old married couple.

'I didn't scare him off. He was leaving anyways.'

Twill rolls his eyes. 'You were supposed to stay put.'

'Yer fuckin' phone went dead? What was I supposed to think?'

'Think? That would be a new direction for you.'

'Wait!' Beast cries, and they turn around. 'What am I still pushing this prick for?' He up-ends the wheelchair and Ghost pitches forward, laughing. He spreads his arms, takes a tentative step and turns to his friends. 'It's a miracle!'

The tension drops a notch.

Lucan slaps Twill on the back. 'C'mon. Let's get LoveSick.'

**

The white Focus is exactly where Croall said it would be. They watch from a distance, then split up. Twill approaches from the south while Ghost, Beast and Cilla move to an adjacent car park separated by a tall hedge. As Twill nears the Focus, a Mercedes two rows up roars into life. Twill rears back, hand flying to his jacket. The brake lights go out and it glides away.

Twill exhales and approaches from the rear. He circles the car twice, glancing around and up to make sure he's not being watched. It's what he suspected—what he'd have done—the car's been left in a CCTV blind spot. He makes a show of fumbling with the keys and dropping them, wincing as he bends. For a moment, he wishes he still had his pills, but it passes.

He lies flat on the ground, checking the underside of the car with the torch on his phone. Repeats the exercise on the other side. No hidden surprises. He goes to the rear and runs a finger along the edge of the boot, feeling for wires. 'It's always fucking me…' Pulls the keys from his pocket, and shuts his eyes. 'Here goes nothing.'

The car chirps and the indicator lights flash twice. He opens his eyes and nods towards the hedge where his mates are cowering. Another button on the fob opens the boot.

'Oi. Sleeping Beauty. Time to wake up.'

LoveSick doesn't move.

'*Fuck.*' He grabs LoveSick's head and presses two fingers to his neck. '*Shit. LoveSick!*'

LoveSick opens one eye and winks.

'Twat' Twill say, dropping his head with a bang.

LoveSick shields his face from the daylight and rubs the back of his head. 'Fuck's sake, Twill. I was having a dead good dream then.'

'You okay?' Twill asks, extending a hand.

He sits upright and stretches. 'Yeah…fucking ace.'

Twill twirls a finger in the air—the signal—and his Rover appears from around the corner. It slows alongside them and Lucan lowers the window. 'Taxi for Twill? Men's sauna?'

'Budge over,' Twill says. 'I'm driving.'

***

'What you're saying is, Croall knows even less than us?'

'Yeah,' LoveSick says to Lucan. 'Once he figured out it wasn't us, he kind of settled down, you know?'

Twill glances into his rear-view mirror. 'Did he hurt you?'

'No. It wasn't like that. I mean, I knew he was armed so no point in kicking off but it's not like he ever got heavy. He knows where you live though. You might want to remember that. We went for a drink.' All eyes in the car turn on him. 'Coffee. We went for a coffee. Said he was feeling exposed, that it was like that kid's song, nine green bottles sitting on the wall and he was the last bottle standing. He told me he'd worked with JR, Mincer, Bridges, Max and Tumble at Animus. Said that was all over now. Said there was no one left.'

Twill looks back at the road ahead. 'Same as he told me.'

'You believe him?' Cilla asks.

'Yeah,' LoveSick says. 'I do.'

'And you, Twill?'

Twill shrugs. 'Guess so.'

'I'm so proud of my little boy. He's growing up so fast.' Lucan messes Twill's hair and the car swerves.

'Fuck off.'

'Think about it,' Lucan says. 'It's all the Animus lot that's getting wasted. This is nothing to do with us. Croall knows he's next. There's no reason for him to hide anything.'

'He's going underground. Retiring. That's what he told me,' LoveSick says, unscrewing the cap of a bottle of water.

Twill flexes his hands on the wheel. 'That only leaves Cromer.'

Lucan groans. 'You're on yer own there, pal.'

LoveSick takes a swig. 'No, he's not.'

'You too?' Lucan squawks.

Cilla takes off his hat. 'We know Cromer's been playing us off against each other. I can't think of a single reason to give him the benefit of the doubt.'

Lucan twists in his seat. '*Really?*'

'Well, in that case, what do we do next?' Ghost says.

'We confront him,' LoveSick says.

'Done that,' Twill says. 'He sat across the table, looked me in the eyes and denied everything.'

'Maybe we need to show him a bit of muscle,' Ghost says. 'Let him know we're not fucking about.'

Lucan reaches behind, snatches the bottle from LoveSick and sniffs it. 'Fuck it. In for a penny and all that.'

Twill smiles. 'I dug his balls on the end of my baton.'

'Well, let's see how he fuckin' reacts with a gun in his mouth.' A minute passes and he turns back to Twill. 'Fuck, man. His ball bag? That's cooold. How'd it feel?'

Twill looks over and his face splits into a grin. 'Fucking magic.'

24

Frome, eastern Somerset

Balesbury Grove is a Georgian country house built in the classical style from golden Bath stone, set in twelve acres of parkland with landscaped gardens at the front split by an oak-lined driveway. Horses graze in a fenced-off paddock to the east, and to the west is a pond the size of a boating lake. The rear of the house backs onto the River Frome and has its own boathouse and pontoon.

One way in, one way out. Unless you want to get wet.

A morning mist rolls in from the river, enveloping the house in a swirling fog. Not heavy enough to obscure Twill's view, but enough to resemble the opening scene in a horror film. He's parked in a yellow transit, high up the kerb of a road that loops around the hill overlooking the house and its grounds. There's a small gatehouse with mirrored windows and a security barrier in the upright position. CCTV cameras mounted onto the side of the house cover the grounds. Cromer clearly feels the need to protect himself above and beyond burglary concerns. Which answers one of Twill's questions. Although the gatehouse probably has room for one, maybe two security guards, the barrier is insubstantial. Nothing that would stop someone from getting in if they really wanted to.

Twill doesn't want to get in. This time, Cromer will come to him.

The transit is facing the oncoming traffic, nose-to-nose with his Rover. Both vehicles have their bonnets up, jump cables strung between them. To any passing traffic, it will appear to be just another emergency call-out, though they've been there forty minutes and have yet to see another car.

Twill's in the cabin. Lucan's complaining in the back, crouched among boxes of tools and piles of rags. LoveSick's in the Rover. Cilla, Beast and Ghost are in a silver Honda half a mile down the road in a layby hidden by trees, just before the narrow track that links the drive to the road.

At seven thirty on the dot, a grey Jaguar with blacked-out windows starts down the gravel drive, slowing at the gatehouse.

Twill calls Cilla. 'It's on.'

He starts up the van. The Jag pulls over the hill. When it's twenty metres out Twill stamps on the accelerator and lurches forward blocking the road. The Jag skids sideways to a halt and its reverse lights come on. The Honda slides in behind the Jag trapping it. Cilla gets out. Ghost and Beast are already swarming around the Jag waving their Enfields in the air and shouting at the driver.

Twill walks to the driver side and lifts up his jacket to show the Browning tucked into his belt. Inside is the bodyguard from the wine bar. The guy looks from side to side, face milk-white, eyes like saucers. A glimmer of recognition lights up his face but collapses at the sight of the gun.

Twill makes a winding motion. The blacked-out glass lowers.

'Open up,' Twill says. 'And keep your hands where I can see them.'

'I-It's just me,' the driver says, putting his hands on the wheel.

Twill reads the panic on his face. Could be trouble. He looks at Lucan standing cross-armed in front of the Jag then back to the car. Pulls the Browning from his belt and points it at the terrified driver. A little injection of reality is required.

'Open the fucking doors.'

The driver scrabbles with buttons on the centre console, and the rear doors click. Twill nods to Ghost, who edges forward, hooks the door open and swings in front of it, arms out straight. Shakes his head. 'He's not here.'

Twill sighs and turns back to the driver. 'Get out.'

The driver pauses and Twill bellows the instruction.

The guy fumbles with the door handle, stands and presses his back against the car.

Twill tucks the Browning into his belt and clicks his fingers. 'Wallet.' Flicks through the cards. 'Alwyn Harris…That Welsh?'

The driver nods.

'Royal Welsh?'

'Two Para.'

'Northern Ireland?'

Harris straightens. 'Before my time. Iraq and Afghanistan.'

Twill nods. 'Good. Then you know the rules. Here's what's going to happen, Alwyn. I'm going to ask you some questions, then we're going to let you on your way. You are not to speak to anyone until you've spoken to Cromer, okay?'

The driver looks around and nods.

LoveSick jumps into the passenger seat and rifles through the glove box.

'I don't think your boss is going to want to make a fuss out of this and it's very much in your best interest to keep him onside. Understood?' Twill pulls out the driver's licence and a photo of two young kids, holds them under Harris's nose, then tucks them into his back pocket and passes the wallet back.

The driver stiffens and holds Twill's eye.

'Where's Cromer?'

'He stayed in London last night. Didn't come home.'

'Bullshit, Alwyn. Let's try again.'

The driver looks down at his feet, then back up at Twill. 'He did but he told me to do the commute as usual.'

'Oh, he did, did he? And why do you think that was?'

A bead of sweat pop trickles down the side of Harris's face.

'Has he ever done this before?'

The driver shakes his head.

'I've got a message for your boss. And I was kind of keen to be in a position to pass this on to him personally, face to face, like.'

LoveSick emerges from the car and shakes his head.

'Tell him he's all out of moves. It's over. Animus is dead.'

Harris nods vigorously.

Twill cups his hand behind his ear. 'Sorry?'

'It's over. He's out of moves. Animus is dead.'

'Very good. And remember, Alwyn, we can find you if we need to. Speak to Cromer. Do not call this in. Got it?'

The driver opens his mouth to speak but Twill beats him to it. 'Right, fuck off.'

Twill climbs back into the van and reverses onto the grass verge. Lucan moves out the way and the Jag shoots forward and zig-zags down the road.

Twill walks over to Lucan. 'Double back to Bath using the side roads, then come in via the M4. LoveSick, follow me while I dump the van. We'll meet at the McDonald's at Cobham services.'

Beast's face brightens at the mention of food. Cilla slings the Enfield over his shoulder and nods. 'Roger.'

Lucan is still standing in the road, staring after the Jag.

Twill calls out to him but he doesn't move. '*LUCAN.*'

'Eh?' He scratches his neck and shakes his head. 'Sorry. Fuckin' hate the Welsh.'

***

By the time Ghost, Beast and Cilla join them, Lucan's on his second breakfast.

'So then. What's next?'

Everyone looks at Twill, except Beast, who's staring anxiously over his shoulder. 'Where's *my* fucking breakfast? Thought this was s'posed to be fast food.'

Twill takes a sip from his cup. 'Thoughts?'

Cilla shrugs. Ghost sticks out his bottom lip and lifts his hands up. Beast stands and shouts at a girl in uniform, scanning the restaurant. 'Over here, love.'

A booth to her left catches her eye and she walks over to it.

'Fuck's sake.'

LoveSick chuckles. 'Beast, focus.'

Beast shakes his head. 'I'm fucking hank.'

Cilla lays a hand on his arm. 'You know what, I think he's going to cry.'

Beast shakes him off and looks over his shoulder.

Twill to Beast: 'What do you think?'

'I think someone cut my throat and forgot to tell my stomach.'

'Beast…'

The big man tuts. 'Cromer's in this up to his scrawny little neck. Croall's in the wind. We won't hear from or see him again now he's cut links to Cromer. I also think we sent Cromer a message this morning. We're united. Take on one of us, take on all of us…I don't see—'

'Forty-seven,' the waitress shouts.

Beast is up and out of his seat, waving his arms.

'I'm with Beast,' Twill says. 'Croall's a pro. When he says he's gone, he's gone. That only leaves Cromer. Does he really have the stomach for a fight?'

Cilla nods.

'We're all in this now. The next move has to be a joint decision. Do we go after Cromer, or let it all die down?'

'I vote no,' LoveSick says. 'Let's leave it. Keep in touch, keep our eyes open, keep speaking. But it's over. Cromer's game is up. There's no way he's going to keep going now he's been rumbled.'

Twill scratches an eyebrow with his thumb. 'So, you're happy to let him win?'

'This ain't about winning no more. If he's behind it, he's never going to own up. But now he knows that if it continues—whatever *it* is—he's fucking toast. Hounding him might only back him into a corner and force his hand. And if he escalates, it's not good for anyone.' He lays his hands flat on the table. 'We're all sitting on the same grenade. Us, Cromer. Croall. We can let it off but we all go with it. It's time to put the pin back in.'

Cilla grunts. 'He's right. I don't like it any more than you, but it's over.'

Beast returns to the table with a paper bag.

'Ghost?'

'You know what they say about revenge, Twill. Dig two graves.'

Lucan stops chewing and speaks out the corner of his mouth. 'What he said.'

Twill throws his hands in the air. 'I think you're making a mistake, but okay. It's over.' He looks at each man in turn. 'Until it isn't.'

25

Colchester

Twill is reclining in his armchair, Graham fussing around his ankles, when the call comes in. He doesn't need to check the caller ID.

'Sorry to have missed you this morning.'

'Ah, how sweet,' Cromer says. 'But it does make me wonder if you've got any more tricks up your sleeve.'

'That very much depends on you.'

'And how would that be?'

Twill sighs and shifts his legs. 'You could stop being such a thundering piss-pipe and get the fuck out of our lives. That would be a good start.'

'Huh. I'm not in your shitty little life, Twill. In fact, I can't think of anything worse. Listen to me carefully. I want you to say the words. No more fucking games.'

'You think this is a game?'

'I think a bunch of silly old men have got themselves in a muddle and are lashing out at the wrong people.'

'Silly old men with guns, mind, so there's that. And ones who'd seriously enjoy stringing you up by the balls, so I suggest you take us very fucking seriously.' Twill waits to let the words sink in. 'It's simple. What happens next is up to you. If we never hear from you again, it's too soon. You don't turn up to any regiment parties. You don't contact another fucking soul. You don't speak another word about the two-two. And then, maybe, it's done. But anything happens to the unit and you better run for the fucking hills. I mean it. You should pray every day you have left in your miserable fucking life that no accidents befall us. You get it? One of us even so much as catches a head cold and we're coming for you. Are we clear?'

'Us? We're?'

'I speak for the unit. We're all on the same page. Ask your driver.'

There's a pause and Cromer says in a quiet voice, 'Okay. We're clear.'

'Good. Now fuck off.'

He drops the phone on the floor and scoops Graham onto his lap. The cat turns several times, flicks its tail in his face and settles into a ball, purring like an idle motor. Twill leans back, closes his eyes. How Cromer reacted to the ultimatum is one thing, but Twill can't shake off how he knew they'd be waiting for him.

***

The morning light starts to shine through the curtains. Graham gets bored and wanders off and Twill stands stiffly and stretches. A darker unease has infected him. The multiple scenarios that rattled through his brain all night have landed at a single point.

Fact: Cromer was tipped off about the ambush.

Fact: Only LoveSick, Beast, Ghost, Lucan, Cilla and himself had known about it.

Fact: Cromer's always one step ahead.

Fact: Whoever led JR, Tumble and Mincer to their deaths was known to them. They were never going to be easy marks.

Conclusion: Someone in the two-two is still working with Cromer.

But who?

Fact: Only one person has consistently resisted the idea that Cromer has anything to do with it.

Lucan.

His oldest friend.

A couple of weeks ago Twill would have laughed at the idea, but now?

Occam's razor: The simplest solution to a problem often turns out to be the correct one.

Twill drags himself upstairs, using the banister for support. He's lightheaded and there's a dull thump in his chest. He pauses on the landing and sways. Instead of turning into his bedroom, he unlocks the door at the far end of the corridor with a key taped behind the radiator.

Heavy curtains nailed into place keep the room dark. He flicks the light switch. A single bulb casts a spotlight on a thick carpet covered in plastic sheeting. The room is bare apart from a metal-framed chair in the middle and a small side table laid with a ball-pein hammer, cable ties, and row of chef's knives. He weighs the hammer in his hand, then puts it down. Picks up a knife and slashes at the air. The plan had always been to get Croall in here one day. But plans have a habit of changing.

He lets out a long sigh and squares the knife with the others.

He leaves the room and goes to bed. A jumble of names, faces and a creeping voice churn through his mind as he falls into a deep and untroubled sleep.

***

He's woken by his phone. He sits up and rubs the sleep from his eyes.

'Yeah.' He sounds rough, like a bag of nails.

'Mr Owen Twill?' The voice is female and bright.

'Not interested,' he says and throws the phone on the bed.

He's drinking from a water glass when it rings again.

'I said I'm not fucking interested.'

'Mr Twill, wait, please. It's Diane Poulter from the Regimental Association. We need to speak to you.'

'Do you now?' He glances at his bedside clock. It's nearly midday.

'We've been sending you letters but get no replies.'

'I don't get your mail.'

'Ah, I see. That's the problem. We have you as 32, The Cannons—'

'No.'

'Oh…Can we update our records?'

'No.'

There's a pause. 'You haven't been attending your therapy, Mr Twill. It appears you've missed the last three sessions.'

'Did you call to tell me what I already know?'

'I'm not sure you've grasped the—'

Twill yawns loudly. 'They're done. I'm done. With them.'

'They're for your own good. It's not quite as easy as you deciding you're not going to attend your sessions. They're mandated by—'

'I'm not going and if you have a problem with that, speak to Ellis Cromer. He signed me off.'

'Right, okay.'

Twill detects the first notes of irritation in her voice.

'I guess I'll speak to Mr Cromer and get back to you.'

'No need.'

There's a sharp inhalation down the line. 'One more thing, I need your authorisation for an ECD.'

Now he's curious. 'What's an ECD?

'Exchange of Contact Details. We've had a request. *Someone*'—she draws out the word, thick with sarcasm—'*wants* to speak with you.'

'And who would that be?'

'Hold on.'

Twill can hear her tapping on a keyboard. 'Request logged yesterday afternoon. Dah-di-dah.' Then louder. 'Right, a Miss Kay Clearwater is trying to reach you.'

'Who's she when she's at home?'

'I don't know,' the woman replies, sounding bored. 'Do I give her your number or not?'

Twill grips his bad leg and bends it at the knee. It's starting to throb and his bladder is burning.

'No.'

'Fine. I'll pass on the good news.'

The line goes dead and Twill flops back onto his bed.

Kay Clearwater? Never heard of her.

***

Twill showers, dresses, attacks a tower of washing up and half-heartedly mops the floor. Gives up midway throwing the mop to the ground. He checks his watch—not even one p.m.—and clucks. Bored stiff. He considers calling Lucan but changes his mind as his fingers hover over the button. He tries reading but can't concentrate on the words. The TV's no better. He flicks through the channels, scowls at a panel of self-described 'Loose Women'.

His phone buzzes. Lucan. He lets it ring out. Ten minutes later, he's regretting his decision.

One of the women makes a comment about her husband's penis and laughs like a chainsaw. The others cackle along.

'Jesus Christ.'

He clicks the TV off and he's playing with his phone, the desire for a pint close to trumping his suspicion when it rings again.

'Mr Twill? Owen?' A female voice.

Twill sighs. 'The Association had no right to give you my number—'

'You gave me your number. It's Terri Dwyer.'

He sits up. 'Right, yes. I'm sorry.'

'Still sorry then?'

Twill smiles. 'No. No, I'm not sorry.'

'That's more like it. I've got someone here who wants to speak to you.'

A hole opens in the pit of his stomach. 'Are you okay, Terri?'

'I'm fine. Here…'

Twill hears her suck on a cigarette.

'Mr Twill?'

American, female. He steadies himself against the arm of his chair.

'You there?' she says.

Bridges: *She'll find you.*

'Yeah,' he croaks. 'And you are?'

'Kay Clearwater.'

'You've been talking to my friends, Mrs Clearwater.'

'*Ms* Clearwater. Yes, I have and I'd like to speak to you, too.'

'You see, *Mizz* Clearwater,'—he crosses the room and pulls the curtain aside with a hooked finger—'people have an unfortunate habit of dropping dead after talking to you, so forgive me if the idea doesn't fill me with enthusiasm.'

The road outside is clear.

'I've literally just found that out…Wait. *People*? More than one?'

'And why would that be, do you think?'

'I'm not sure. What's going on? Who else? You said more than one.'

'You're not sure, or you don't know?'

There's a pause. He tries again. 'Who are you, Ms Clearwater?'

'I'm a journalist.'

'And even if I could help, what makes you think I'd want to?'

'I've come a long way to speak to someone who's dead so I'm prepared to take that risk.'

'Who sent you?'

'No one sent me. I'm working a solo project.'

'You've got three questions. Shoot.'

'Who's Vincent Kalcek and what does he mean to you?'

'Never heard of him. Next.'

'What's your relationship with Ellis Cromer?'

'Non-existent.'

'Really?'

'Is that your last question?'

'Err, no. What can you tell me about Animus?'

Twill tries to keep the surprise out of his voice. 'What do you know about Animus?'

'Let's just say every time I ask, people get upset. So, I keep asking.'

'In that case, we should meet.' Twill gives her the address for the Prettygate. 'Who knows what you're doing?'

'No one,' she answers.

'Good. Keep it that way. Five o'clock.'

***

Twill arrives early and takes his usual seat facing the door. He's two sips into his first pint when a tall woman, early forties with a mop of corkscrew hair, pushes through a group of men surrounding the fruit machine. Twill lowers his head and holds his breath.

Caitlyn.

She circles the bar, scanning the room. She's attractive, but not in the conventional sense. Her unmade face is pale as moonlight, her eyes dark and fiercely intelligent. Thick tortoise-shell glasses balance on a nose approaching Roman. She carves through a cluster at the bar, wheeling an upright suitcase behind, tugging at a canvas bag over her shoulder.

Twill sits upright and waits for her to see him. She smiles, lifts her free hand and makes her way over.

'Mr Twill.' She's flushed and sweating by the time she reaches him. 'It's great to meet with you.'

Twill holds the table for support and lowers himself back with an old-man gasp. 'We'll see about that.'

'Can I get you a drink?'

Twill lifts his glass and downs it in three long gulps. 'How kind.'

'Impressive.'

'I'm here all week,' he replies, and burps.

Twill drags a chair from another table for her while she gets the drinks. Then she's back with his pint and a glass of wine.

She takes a seat opposite him and raises her glass. 'Cheers.' Sips and grimaces. 'Wow.'

'Cheers.'

'I've got something for you.' Kay digs around in her bag and passes him a gift-wrapped package the size of a book.

'Really,' Twill says, 'you shouldn't have.'

'I didn't. It's from Terri Dwyer.'

Twill lifts it to his ear and gives it a shake. Shrugs and rips off the paper. It's the framed photo from Tumble's mantelpiece.

'What is it?' Kay asks.

Twill looks up. 'It's the two-two.'

'Your regiment, right?'

Twill looks back down at the picture. 'Yeah.'

'You're all in jeans…and crazy long hair. Not traditional army style.'

'So we are,' Twill mumbles.

She places a Dictaphone on the table and presses a button. A red light flashes. 'Do you mind if I record this?'

Twill switches it off. 'Yes, I do.' He puts the frame to one side and coughs into his hand. 'This is to see what you know and what you want. If I think we can help each other, I'll tell you everything.'

'Fine,' Kay says, and flicks her hair back off her face. 'Are you sure you don't know Vincent Kalcek?'

'You think I should?'

'It seems he worked with your old boss Cromer in the seventies.'

Twill's chest tightens. 'Tell me more.'

'Kalcek was a career soldier—Vietnam and a bunch of other theatres—until he moved into politics in 1984. Being America, the land of the brave and all that, his military background didn't hurt one bit, and he's now or was until recently, Senator Kalcek.'

Twill scoffs. 'Same shit, different country.'

'Yes. Cromer's an MP, right?'

'If your Kalcek is *anything* like Ellis Cromer, then I'm beginning to see why you might think there's a story here.'

'Oh, there's a story here,' Kay says, leaning in. 'Kalcek is a violent, manipulative war criminal and all-round bastard. Amongst other things.'

'War criminal?'

'You heard of the massacre in My Lai?'

Twill nods.

'That little episode is on Kalcek's résumé.'

'And what does this have to do with me?'

'A source tells me the answer I'm looking for can be found in Belfast in 1972.'

'Answer? To what question?'

'What connects war crimes in Vietnam to civil war in the United Kingdom to a senior British government minister to a sitting US senator? I have the feeling the answer's Animus.'

Twill looks around the room and wets his lips. 'And what do *you* think Animus is?'

'I don't know.' Kay says, throwing her hands in the air. 'That's the million-dollar question…Mr Twill, I have been threatened with violence, my *family* has been the target of death threats, and I've been followed, chased and harassed. All because I've gone looking under stones and asked questions about Kalcek. I lost my job; I lost my house and I'm living with my daughter in my aunt's box room in Vermont.'

Twill lifts his pint to his lips. 'Some might say the intelligent thing would be to walk away.'

'Yeah, but I'm not always known for my intelligence. Besides, when I publish my book, I get to—*Jesus*, this stuff is like battery acid.'

'What do you want from me?'

'There's a connection, a link, somewhere. I think Kalcek was giving covert support to the British Army in Northern Ireland…maybe training, I'm not sure. He was some kind of asymmetric warfare specialist after Vietnam. I dunno. I was hoping you'd be able to tell me.'

'And why's 1972 so important?'

'Because whatever he was up to in 1972 was important enough to bleach out of his bio and pull favours to get me shut down. He even faked cancer and stepped down from the House of Representatives. So, whatever it is, it certainly ain't nothing.'

Twill pulls back, chewing his lip. 'Describe him, this Kalcek.'

'Old. Bald. Wrinkly.'

'No, I mean as he would have been in '72.'

'About the same height as Cromer, bit shorter maybe. Slightly wider, marine buzz cut...wait.' Kay slings her bag on the table and sticks her face in it, drops a folder of loose papers in front of him. She flicks through the pages and hands him a copy of a newspaper cutting.

Twill squints at it for nearly a minute and hands it back. Picks up the picture frame, flips it over and eases off the back cover. He spreads the photo out on the table, revealing the part that had been bent back on itself.

'Oh my God. This'—she points at Cromer—'is your man. And this'—she taps the other part of the image—'is Kalcek.'

'We never knew his name.'

'What did he do?'

'I need a drink.' Twill stands and points at Kay's glass, still full.

'Oh, something different. A New World, maybe. Something with less tannin.'

Twill laughs. 'Good luck with that. Red or white?'

Kay pulls a face. 'Get me one of those then.'

Lucan rings while Twill's at the bar. He clicks off the phone and returns it to his jacket, glancing back at Kay, who's putting on lipstick.

Lucan. Even if he has been working for Cromer, so what? He hasn't let any harm come Twill's way. Everyone that's died was Animus. And haven't they decided it's over?

He steps outside, makes a call, then returns to the bar and adds to the order. He made a promise to the guys—they'll act together, as a unit. Besides, Lucan is his oldest friend. The past few weeks have muddied the waters and there's a chance he isn't thinking straight. As improbable as it sounds that Lucan would turn on him, the only way to find is to test his loyalty. Make him own the decision about whether to expose Cromer.

Twill carries three pints back to the table. Kay's more relaxed and with the barest application of make-up, younger and prettier. He feels the heat in his cheeks and an unfamiliar lightness. What could be happiness? It's been a long time.

'Three pints? Double stacking. Nice.'

Twill grunts, takes his seat and slips back into grumpy. 'I'm expecting company.'

Kay's hands drop below the table and her face turns ashen.

'It's okay,' Twill says. 'He's one of the good guys.'

'So, *you're* the good guys?' she asks with an impish mischief. 'I was wondering.'

'That's a good question. I always thought I was.'

'Then, who's Mr Third Pint?'

Twill slides the framed picture across the table and taps on Lucan. 'I won't make a unilateral decision about talking to you.'

Kay nods. 'That's fair enough.'

Twill's eyes move to her empty wine glass. 'It wasn't *that* bad then.'

'I spilled it.' She holds his gaze and smiles. 'I kind of did it on purpose to be honest, in case you made me drink it.'

'Waste not want not.'

'*Yes!*' Her laugh is like a cool breeze. 'Actually, I think it's taken some of the varnish off the table.'

Twill sits back and stretches his legs out. 'What have you got so far.'

'I've had enough to nail Kalcek for some time but he reached out to my employers. There was some cooked-up story about cancer and they shut me down. Next thing I know, I'm packing my stuff into a crate and being thanked for my service. Kind of don't let the door hit your ass on the way out.'

'They say why?'

'Digital media, cost cutting…whatever. It's all bullshit. I was the only one in a "wave" of cut backs. Ha! A one-person wave…How about that?' She takes a deep gulp of her beer. 'This isn't bad, you know? Anyways, I've got a source who told me Animus connects the dots.'

'Who's your source?'

'Can't say.'

'British or American?'

'Don't worry—American, one of Kalcek's inner circle. You don't know him. I'd already found a link to Belfast and made a few calls. My source said I was *making waves* over here in the UK. Then the paper dropped the bomb on me so I took some time out. But it never left me, you know?' She taps her temple. 'It was always there, the little voice. Eventually I decided I couldn't walk away so here I am.'

'Thought you'd lost your job?'

'I did, but now I've got the time to write the book. This way I don't have to answer to anyone and I get to control what goes in. And what stays in.'

'Isn't that dangerous?'

Kay shrugs. 'That's what I told myself when I got laid off but I kept asking myself why I'd become a journalist in the first place. I guess that kind of answered it. The deeper I dug, the more shit I uncovered. These are not nice people I've been dealing with. In fact, I'm not even sure I believed in evil until I started this. I kinda want to stop these motherfuckers from winning, if that makes sense.'

'And how do you know I'm not the same?'

Kay pauses. 'You seem okay, and Terri Dwyer vouched for you. Plus, you bought me beer, so…friend for life.'

Something stirs. She's right. *They* are winning. Not him, Lucan or anyone else in the two-two. Not Kay, Terri Dwyer or even Croall.

Cromer.

Kalcek.

A fist tightens in Twill's gut. He takes another draw on his pint and makes the decision to help the journalist regardless of Lucan.

'So, was I?'

He turns back to Kay. 'Were you what?'

'Making waves. Here in the UK?'

He leans in, one hand on his leg, and lowers his voice. 'When did you start calling around?'

'Must be…about twelve, thirteen months ago. Why?'

He puts the picture between them. 'In the past year.' His finger hovers over Max. 'Dead.'

He points to Bridges. 'Dead.'

Tumble. 'Dead.'

JR. 'Dead.'

Mincer. 'Dead.'

Kay's hand flies to her face mouth. 'Holy shit. I had no idea.'

'Making waves is certainly one way of putting it.'

'I'm dreadfully sorry. Am I interrupting?'

Lucan towers over them, cradling three pints, a wide grin splashed across his face. Twill experiences a rare twinge of pleasure.

'Sit down, you scruffy bastard,' he says. 'You're making the place look untidy.'

'I come bearing gifts!'

Kay smiles awkwardly. 'I'm fine. Thanks.'

Lucan frowns. 'Ah. The septic.' A few seconds later he's beaming again. 'Lucan,' he says, holding out his hand. 'Pleasure to meet ya.'

She reaches out and he bends to kiss her hand, but she yanks it away and wraps it around her drink. She turns to Twill and cocks her head. 'What's a septic?'

'Septic tank.'

'Are you even speaking English?'

'Septic tank. Yank. 'Cockney rhyming slang, innit?' Lucan grabs a chair from the next table and slips in next to Twill. 'I got summat for you, too.'

'If it's a kiss, you can keep it.'

Lucan slaps a folded plastic bag on the table.

Twill peers inside. The files from Max's farm.

'Who's yer friend?' Lucan elbows Twill in the ribs and scans the room. 'Not speed dating, are ya?'

'Ms Kay Clearwater. Journo from the US of A,' Twill replies, stuffing the bag into his coat.

'The same one Bridges talked about?'

'Yes,' Kay says, clearing her throat. 'I spoke with Lewis Bridges. And Jim Dwyer.'

'I see,' Lucan says, 'And what are you doing here?' His voice is cold.

Kay starts to speak but Twill shushes her. 'She's been working on a story that links into Belfast and Cromer.'

'His fuckin' name keeps popping up all over the place, doesn't it now?'

Kay leans forward. 'It's not just Cromer, it's Animus.'

Lucan scratches his cheek. 'Animus, eh? What do ya know about that, then?'

'Zero. You asked why I'm here. To find out.'

Lucan looks over at Twill. The silence becomes awkward.

Kay stands. 'I'll get some drinks.'

Lucan waits until she's out of earshot. 'Are ya sure talking to a fuckin' hack is the right thing to do?'

Twill shrugs. 'That's why you're here. I won't do it without you.'

'Won't it just stir things up again?'

214

'Not the way I see it.'

Lucan drains his glass and crosses his hands in his lap. 'And how would that be, then?'

Twill looks around and lowers his voice. 'If you think about it, it's perfect. It *protects* us. What's your biggest concern right now?'

Lucan sticks out his bottom lip. 'Dunno. Guess getting fuckin' whacked has gotta be up there somewhere.'

'Exactly. If this goes public, we're untouchable. Cromer is fucked, *and* no one dares come near us.' Twill holds a hand in the air. 'We're completely insulated. It's a win–win.'

Lucan's face tightens. 'But what we did…The only-following-orders line didn't work so well for the Nazis.'

'Forget about it. Those Provo pricks got away with everything. Full amnesty. No court in England is going to prosecute a bunch of old men who fought for their country when the Provos are running around scot-free.'

Lucan pulls a face. 'Old men, you say? Fuckin' rude, that is. Speak for yerself.'

Kay returns with three pints.

'Good girl,' Lucan says, grabbing the nearest glass.

'So, how we going to do this?' Kay says.

Twill eyes her, then turns to Lucan and taps the photo on the table. 'Who's this?'

Lucan picks up the picture and holds it at arm's length. 'It's, er, that American bloke. Don't think he ever said his name. If he did, I've forgotten it.'

'What did he do?' Kay asks.

Lucan responds. 'He was the first one to approach me. For the two-two.'

'And so you weren't originally in Northern Ireland with the two-two?'

'No. Royal Engineers in Chatham.'

Kay removes her recorder looks at Twill. Lucan shrugs. Kay switches the machine on and puts it on the table. 'How did you get from Chatham to Belfast?'

Lucan leans back and knits his fingers behind his head. 'The American.'

'Kalcek?'

'Whatever. Him. Can't remember his name. The American.'

'And when did you first meet him?'

'Must have been '69 to '70. He came to see me at the barracks. I proper shit meself. There'd been a few'—he glances sideways at Twill—'scrapes I got caught up in. I was plucked out of roll call to the CO's office. Thought I was for the brig. But, instead, there he was.'

'On his own?'

'No. Cromer was there too. But he did all the talking.'

'What did he say?'

'Said he was putting a team together. A specialist team of like-minded people. Wanted to know if I was interested.'

'And you said yes?'

'Fuckin' right I did.' He drinks deeply and wipes his mouth on the back of his hand. 'Every fucker wanted to get involved. At that time, the Provos were bombing us on the mainland, and picking our boys off left, right and centre.'

'And the specialist team was the two-two?'

Lucan reaches over and laces his fingers with Twill's. Squeezes gently. Says in a soft voice, 'It's where we first met.'

'Fuck off,' Twill snaps, shaking his hand away.

'And you were straight into the squad?'

'No. Not straightaway. There was a week of interviews and tests. They had…specific needs. They needed to check I was a suitable candidate, they said.'

'What kind of tests?'

Lucan waves her away. 'I dunno. All kinds of crazy shit. Lots of sit-down interviews. Multiple-choice tests. What would you do if this, that and the other happened? How would you feel about etcetera etcetera? They showed me lots of photos. War zones. Airplane crashes. Bombed schools. Some proper nasty shit. All the while I was wired up to some machine. And those ink-blot things. They did that a few times.'

'Rorschach?'

'Say what now?'

'It's a test. Profiling. These interviews, were they with a team of people?'

'No. Just the one.' He spins the photo around, narrows his eyes and stabs a finger at the pic. 'Him. Doctor Doolittle.'

Kay takes the photo and takes a closer look. 'Doolittle?'

'A little joke. Ya know, he talks to the animals. Us.'

'And you met whatever requirements were expected for this new unit?'

Lucan takes another drink. 'Yes. Proudest time of my fuckin' life.'

'And what was the role of the two-two, this specialist squad?'

Lucan dips forward, resting his elbows on his knees. 'We were Uber before Uber even fuckin' existed—'

'That's enough,' Twill says. 'If we decide to take it further, we'll answer your questions.'

Kay nods. 'Okay. Can I ask when you first met Kalcek?'

'Same as Lucan,' he replies.

'You were in the Royal Engineers?'

'No, same sort of thing. I was Two Para, already in Belfast.'

'And you were approached by Kalcek and Cromer?'

'There was…' Twill picks up his drink and Lucan looks down at his feet. 'I was caught up in something. Bought me some time out. Kalcek and Cromer offered me a way back in.'

'You want to tell me about it?'

Twill coughs and gets up. 'Not now. Bog.'

When he returns, Lucan's got a face like a slapped arse. Whatever had happened in his absence, Lucan looks like he came off second best. Twill puts down three fresh pints, and Kay groans.

'Don't you ever eat?'

'Abso-fuckin-lutely.' Lucan's smiling again. 'What do ya want? Salt and vinegar or pork scratchings?'

'I don't even want to know what they are. It's like a different language.' She studies Twill. 'I noticed your limp.'

'Yeah, me too,' Lucan says. 'New shoes?'

Twill sighs. 'Fuck off.' Then to Kay: 'Long story.'

'I'm all about the stories. I was just saying to Lucan, all this is great but are you actually going to let me in or just watch me drown in warm beer?'

'Don't fuckin' rush us. We like to be romanced.'

Kay turns to Twill and raises her eyebrows.

'What do you think?' he says to Lucan.

'Fuck it. If it gets me on Jeremy Kyle, I'm in.'

'Jeremy Kyle?' Kay says, looking down at the photo. 'Was he in your unit?'

Lucan shoots a glance at Twill. 'Yes. Yes he was.'

'Which one is he?' she asks, pushing the photo across the table.

Lucan snatches it up and pulls a face. 'He's not in this one.' He leans over and taps the side of his nose. 'Probably covert ops.'

She takes a notebook from her bag and flicks it open. 'You mind if I?'

'Go ahead,' Lucan says. 'K-Y-L-E.'

'Got it,' she says, scribbling it down. 'Can we talk about who *is* in the photo?'

'That handsome chap there is me,' Lucan says, stabbing at the pic.

Kay takes a closer look, then makes a note. 'Lucan. That a first or last name?'

'Neither. It's a rather cruel and undeserving nickname.'

Twill scoffs. 'Bollocks. Fucking spot on is what it is.'

Lucan shakes his head. 'You can be very hurtful sometimes. You know, the Nepalese have a word for people like you.'

'And what's that then?'

'I dunno. Whatever the Nepalese for cunt is.'

Twill rolls his eyes and says to Kay, 'So, you heard of Lord Lucan?'

Kay looks blank.

'Killed his kid's nanny and went on the run.'

'What, you kill nannies?'

'No. Nothing quite so interesting,' Twill says. 'He fucks off. Disappears. Could be pint five, pint eight or last orders. But by the end of the night, he's missing.'

'In the States, we call that French Leaving.'

'In the UK we call it fucking rude.'

Lucan salutes. 'Richard Puller, at your service.'

Kay scribbles in her notebook and shakes her head.

'I know, right? My name's Dick Puller and Lucan is the best these fuckin' eejits come up with?'

Kay looks across at Twill. 'Right…Now, Owen Twill. What am I missing?'

Twill shrugs. 'Nothing. That's my name.'

'Hmm. Okay then. Let's start here,' she says, pointing at the top left row in the picture. 'Bridges, right?'

Lucan nods.

Twill grabs his glass with both hands. 'Lewis Bridges. Surveillance, intelligence gathering, used to keep the files up to date. Generally, didn't get his hands dirty.'

'Real name?'

Twill nods.

'And he's dead?'

Lucan kicks Twill under the table. 'We don't know that. We do know he's missing. And, in light of what's going on, we put two and two together.'

'I see.' Kay makes a further note. 'Okay, now who's this?'

'That's JR,' Twill says.

'Junior?'

'No. JR. Like the TV show.'

'*Dallas*?'

'Yeah. JR got shot, like on the programme. Same week as the episode came out. Hence the name. Straightforward through and through. No lasting damage.'

Kay chews on her pen. 'Real name?'

'No fuckin' idea,' Lucan says, laughing.

'Okay. Him?'

'That's Cilla,' Lucan says.

'Because?'

'Cilla Black,' Twill says.

'Of course,' Kay replies. 'Silly me. And is Cilla still with us? And what did he do?'

'Yeah, he's fine. Driver. He used to wring the bloody neck out of those cars. No one quicker.'

'Real name?'

Twill and Lucan look blankly at each other.

Kay flips the page on her notebook and scratches some more. Glances at her nearly full glass and takes a big gulp. 'And this?'

Twill looks over. 'That's Max.'

Kay looks up and giggles. 'He's actually quite cute. So, you and Max didn't have nicknames?'

Lucan looks at Twill and smiles. 'This is awkward.'

'Max *was* his nickname,' Twill says.

'Cos he's big?'

Lucan stifles a giggle. 'You're getting warmer.'

'What am I missing here?'

'It's short for maximum penetration.'

Lucan holds up his hands a foot apart. 'Honestly, it was a fuckin' monster. Like a horse's. It was so big he had to kick it dry—'

Kay's neck flushes. 'Is he…single?'

'Well, he's not seeing anyone. He's dead.'

'Just my luck.' She puts down her pen and drains the last third of her pint in one. 'You boys not drinking?'

Lucan roars with laughter.

'Right, next. Ah. I know this one. Jim Dwyer right?'

Twill leans forward. 'Yeah. Tumble.'

'Tumble?'

'Tumble Dwyer,' Lucan says.

Kay takes off her glasses. 'What are you, five years old?'

'Aw, c'mon. It's *funny*!'

'And they gave you people guns?'

Lucan replies, leaning in. 'And bullets and everything.'

Kay perches her glasses back on the end of her nose. Twill's chest thumps—it could be Caitlyn sitting across the table from him.

'I spoke with Terri, Jim's daughter. How do *you* think he died?'

'They say he jumped off a cliff,' Lucan says.

'And what do you say?'

Twill lowers his voice, keeps it steady. 'He was killed.'

'How do you know?'

'I saw CCTV. He wasn't alone the day he died.'

Lucan leans back and crosses his arms. 'You kept that fuckin' quiet.'

'Who was he with?' Kay says.

Twill shrugs. 'Dunno. Couldn't see.'

'But that's enough to make you think he was murdered? He was with someone else?'

'*Not just that.*' Twill slams his glass down. 'That's not what we do. Not who we are.'

'But Terri said Jim was seeing a therapist—'

'So, fucking what? We all were. It was mandatory. And it fucking stinks.'

'How so?'

'That's not for today. Later, maybe. Just believe me when I say Tumble didn't top himself. Neither did JR or Mincer.'

'Okay. Which one's Mincer?'

Lucan spins the photo around and points him out. 'There.'

'Right. And Mincer because?'

Lucan whistles and flops his hand over. 'C'mon. You know. 'Ello sailor. A poof. Fairy. A fag.'

Another shake of the head from Kay.

'Listen,' Twill says, 'it doesn't mean anything. It's just words. He was a brother to us, gay or not. You won't find a more loyal friend or harder soldier.'

'I get it. Real name?'

Twill shrugs.

'And how did Mincer die?'

'Looked like suicide,' Lucan says.

'But not. *Made* to look like it,' Twill says. 'Fell in front of a train. Two weeks before the holiday of a lifetime.'

Kay scribbles some more. 'Him?' She points at the pic.

'LoveSick.'

Kay's crosses her arms. 'Can't wait to hear this one'

'He got lovesick in Belfast.'

'How so? A tangled tale of unrequited love?'

'No, chlamydia.'

Kay wrinkles her nose. 'Eww. He still alive?'

'Yeah. And kicking,' Twill says.

'And what did LoveSick do?'

'Comms, mostly. Bugging. That sort of thing. A bit of interception, too. Wasn't afraid to get his hands dirty. A good man.'

Kay asks his real name. Twill and Lucan shrug. She points at Ghost.

'Alive,' Twill says. 'Don't know his real name.'

Lucan shakes his head too.

Kay bends forward. 'On account of his complexion?'

'Not just that. Reconnaissance, scouting. Breaking and entering. He could get into your house, take your wallet from your bedside table and comb your hair while you slept and you'd wake up in the morning thinking how smart you looked.'

'Right. So that just leaves the big guy.'

'Beast. Still with us.'

'Guess that's self-explanatory. What did Beast—'

'Munitions and all-purpose muscle.' Lucan upends his glass on the table.

'Name?'

'Fletcher. Maybe.'

'Listen, we can get you all that stuff later. But nothing goes in your book if they don't sign up, okay?' Twill says.

'Okay,' Kay replies, putting her notebook back in her bag.

'That's enough about us,' Lucan says. 'Let's talk about you. Kay. That short for something? Kathy? Katherine? Kaylee?'

A flush creeps across her cheeks and she turns the recorder off. 'My round.'

'Whoa. C'mon. What's your name?'

'It's K. The initial K. Not K-a-y. Not Kathy, not Curly or whatever you just said. Somebody just called me Kay and I never corrected them, so it's Kay. Okay?'

'We ain't saying zip till you tell us yer fuckin' name,' Lucan says with a grin. Twill nods.

'Oh, for fuck's sake. What does it matter? It's Kennedy.'

Lucan explodes and slaps his knee.

'Mom was a fan. Anyways, it's just a name,' Kay says, and gets up. 'Nothing funny about it.'

She walks to the bar, although Twill notes, not in a straight line.

Lucan calls after her, 'Kennedy, get some pork scratchings while you're there, will ya?'

"The Stranglers" come on the jukebox. Kay returns with the drinks and snacks. Lucan rips open the foil packet and spills the contents onto the table.

Kay sniffs. 'Looks like an old man's toenail. What even is this?'

'Deep-fried pig skin.' Lucan crunches down hard. 'Fuckin' lush.'

'I'll pass…So, will you tell me what you did in the two-two?'

'I'm like ya international man o' mystery, ya know? Good with guns. Good long range. Good with covert ops. Fuckin' *great* with the ladies…'

Kay winks a glassy eye. 'Oh yeah. I can see that, tiger.' She turns to Twill. 'What's your superpower?'

Lucan rubs his hands together. 'You're gonna love this.'

Twill groans and covers his eyes with his hands.

'Right, Kennedy,' Lucan says.

'Kay.'

'As I said, Kay. Choose someone in the pub. Anyone. Don't describe them. Just say where they are.'

'Okay. One, two, three…third back from the bar, on the right. Closest the door.'

'Man or woman?' Twill asks.

'Eh?'

'There's a man talking to a woman. And it's not his wife.'

222

'*What?* How do you know that?'

Twill holds out his hand and clicks his fingers. Feels the cold pint glass against his palm. 'He's wearing a wedding ring. She isn't.' Takes a drink. 'And, I mean, just look at them. Laughing. Happy. Flirting. No fucking way they're married.'

'Okay then. What's he wearing?'

'Blue jeans. White trainers. White button-down shirt, untucked. Gold-framed round glasses.'

'That's *crazy*,' Kay says.

Twill helps himself to a pork scratching and Lucan elbows him in the ribs.

'Fuck, Twill. Look. It's Gary.' Lucan cups his hands around his mouth. '*GARY!*'

Half the pub turns around. Gary's England shirt is like a second skin but it's flab not muscle that's causing the squeeze. He's standing on the spot, staring at their table, jaw slung low.

Lucan waves and Gary runs out the door. Lucan chuckles and shakes his head. 'Aw. Classic Gary.'

'I'm going to the ladies.' Kay rises and stumbles against the table.

Lucan flies from his chair and catches her. 'See. I told ya. Women just throw themselves at me. It's a gift.'

'Nice try, cowboy,' Kay rights herself and wiggles a finger in his face. 'And don't go pulling your disappearing act, Seamus McFuckFace or whatever your name is. It's your round.'

***

Kay shoots bolt upright in bed, hair stuck to her face with sweat. A wave of nausea hits and she flops back and squeezes her eyes shut. Even in the dark, it feels like she's on a teacup ride at the fair. She opens one eye, lets it adjust to the darkness. The spinning sensation recedes and she pushes herself up on her elbows, wincing as a scalpel slices into her frontal lobe.

She switches on the bedside lamp. Clothes folded at the end of her bed, case and bag next to them. She lifts up the blanket—still wearing underwear. *Thank fuck.* Powers on her phone. The screen says three a.m. She necks a glass of water with shaky hands and fumbles with the Ibuprofen packet she finds at the bottom of her bag.

223

The room is decked in washed-out pastel tones. Not a man's taste, and definitely *not* Twill's handiwork. The curtains and bedsheets are lace-edged, the wallpaper floral and thirty years out of fashion. On the wall opposite is a scrappy collage of sepia photos on a cork board. In the centre, a young Twill in full uniform. Various snaps of him as a fat baby, a fat boy, a slimmer teen and a proud soldier. He's wearing the same blank, almost detached expression in all of them.

She switches off the light and dives back under the covers with her phone. 3.17 a.m. 10.17 p.m. Eastern Standard Time. Grace should be asleep. *Should.* She calls anyway but it goes straight to voicemail. The confident little voice makes her heart ache. She doesn't want the message to end so she dials again.

What happened last night? She can't remember coming back from the pub. Snippets…being told Lucan had gone, bright strip lighting, the smell of chips, and sitting in a kitchen pulling at some kind of grey, stringy meat. A doner, whatever that is. Her stomach lurches, and she throws back the sheets and edges out the bedroom door.

The landing light is on. The first door along is locked, but the key's in it. Can't be Twill's room. She twists the key and pushes the door open. The light from the hall casts a yellow rectangle into the bare room. There's plastic sheeting on the floor and a single chair in the centre. A table to the side though it's cast in shadow. He must be decorating. She pulls the door shut and locks it.

She finds the bathroom on the other side of the landing, pulls the door shut and sits on the toilet, head in hands. When she feels steady enough, she splashes her face with water and pulls her hair back. Looks in the mirror. Wishes she hadn't. Her eyes are red like a bloodhound's, the flesh beneath saggy. Like a corpse that's been fished out the canal, she thinks. What a mess.

The medicine cabinet holds a spare toothbrush, still in its plastic wrapping, and a tub of prescription pills. Thorazine. No painkillers. Maybe sleep it off.

She leaves the bathroom and turns off the light in the hall.

A low groan freezes her to the spot. There it is again. Like someone's in pain. She tiptoes along the landing, almost knocking a picture off the wall, and stops at what she assumes is Twill's bedroom. Hears words. Unintelligible. A guttural sob.

She presses her ear against the door and holds her breath, heartbeat thrashing in her ears. There's a scream and she jumps back against the banister. Next, a whimper. She scuttles back to her room, cringing as the door slams behind her, and throws herself onto the bed and under the duvet. Her breath is hot and heavy against the fabric.

Click—a door opening. She peeks out. *Not mine.* An irregular tread down the hall. Light spills from the gap under her door, and a shadow pauses there. It passes on and she hears the click again.

Kay wraps her arms around her belly, sucks in air, and falls asleep listening for sounds of movement.

***

She wakes in daylight, feeling almost human, crosses the landing and hears the chink of plates from downstairs. A quick, scalding shower energises her. She pulls on a fresh jumper and jeans and finds Twill at the kitchen table nursing a coffee amid a pile of paperwork.

She watches from the doorway for a few seconds.

'Coffee?' he asks without looking up.

'I'd love one,' she says, and joins him at the table. 'The stronger the better.'

Twill points towards a gurgling machine on the counter. 'It's strong alright.'

She waits for him to move. He doesn't. 'It's okay. I'll get it…want one?'

Twill lifts his mug and wiggles it.

Kay fills their mugs and sits opposite him. Now he looks up. His face is grey and strained. The wire-framed glasses make him look scholarly, but old. He gives a curt nod.

She takes a sip. 'Ahh. That's the best coffee I've had since I've been on this wretched island.'

'That's the first lesson in surveillance. The value of good coffee.' Twill takes off his glasses and scrubs his face. 'How're you feeling?'

'Fine.'

'No, really. How do you feel?'

She sticks out her tongue. 'Like the devil shat in my mouth.'

Twill looks back down, and tidies the pile of papers.

'What's that?' Kay asks.

There's a pause. 'Animus. In some shape or form, anyway.'

'May I?'

'Not yet.'

Kay rolls her eyes. 'When, then?'

Twill stretches out his leg. 'To understand Animus, you have to understand what the two-two was.' He fixes her with a stare. 'What its mission was, and what it became.'

'Can I get my Dictaphone?'

Twill shrugs. 'Whatever.'

When Kay returns with her bag, there's a rack of toast on the table and a selection of spreads. She feels his eyes on her as she butters a slice.

'Tell me what you *think* your story is,' he says.

'It's how a war criminal wound up being a United States senator.'

'So, what are you doing here?'

'You know what. We've discussed this.'

'No,' Twill snaps. 'I'm trying to get *you* to think this through. You're about to feed the gremlin after midnight. That's fine. But see it for what it is. There will be consequences. And once you start, there's no way back.'

Kay puts down her toast. 'What are you saying?'

'I'm saying you don't know *anything*.'

She reaches into her bag and puts the recorder on the table. 'What do you mean, I don't know anything?'

'Kalcek. The American. He's not your story.'

'How's that?'

Twill refills his cup and leans back against the worktop. 'I can't tell you what Animus is because I don't fully know myself. I know what it *was*, up until recently. But I was told it goes back years. Decades even.'

Kay switches on the recorder and pulls out a pen and notepad. 'Why don't we start with what you *do* know?'

'For that we have to talk about the two-two.'

'Let's do that, then.'

He comes back to the table. 'In the early seventies, there was a feeling in Whitehall that we were losing control in Northern Ireland, and they were right. Simply put, we were playing to the rules, and the IRA wasn't. We were an occupying force with one hand tied behind our back and I don't have to tell an American how that plays out. We had the street presence, strutting about with guns, nothing more than scared kids playing at soldiers. But they were picking us off and the headlines back on the mainland were having political repercussions.'

'How so?'

'Politicians only give a fuck about themselves—you know that. They won't act until it affects them. It was a slow burner but eventually they realised they had to do something.'

'I'm not sure that first bit's exclusively true, but go on.'

'All the while there was a steady supply of sacrificial lambs, but it was going nowhere. There was no plan for winning and no appetite for war. Just a steady drip feed of bad news. The public were restless, and the politicians wouldn't do anything until it was their arses on the line. And the decision was made, at the highest level, to take back control.'

'How did—'

'The mandate they gave us…they called it *victory at any cost*.'

'Us? The two-two?'

Twill nods.

'So, the two-two was put together to turn things round. I get that. But what does "at any cost" mean?'

'It means go in hard, burn these fuckers to the ground and salt the earth so nothing grows back. Aim—decapitate the leadership of the Provisional IRA. Start local. Start with the hardest guy in the street. *Poof.* He disappears. Next, you take the hardest guy in the town. Soon enough, you end up with the guy making the decisions. The boss. Take him out. At every step of the way, these guys are replaced with someone who's less experienced—and this is critical—someone who knows what happened to his predecessor. Someone who thinks, *This could happen to me.* It's only a matter of time before your hand is raised.'

'So, a minute ago, you said the reason you were losing was because the British state was playing by the rules, and the IRA wasn't. What are you suggesting? That the two-two stopped playing by the rules?'

Twill shrugs and looks away. 'Call it what you want. Rip up the rulebook, level the playing field. Blah blah blah. They're just words. Politicians *talk*. We *do*. And what we *did* was take the gloves off.'

'What did you mean by *disappears*?'

'Take a fucking guess, Sherlock.'

Twill's voice chills her. Empty. Cold.

'Why did Lucan say you were the first Uber?'

'We used to pick 'em up off the street. Intel told us where and when most of the time. Sometimes…we just drove around. Looking.'

'And these were your orders?'

'Yes.'

His eyes drill into her. Challenging. 'It was the elimination of IRA ringleaders, without prejudice. No questions asked.'

'You were an assassination squad.'

'Call it that if you like but we knew what we had to do. Destabilise the Provisional IRA. Attack, subvert, undermine, deter. That's how it started at least. Then things got fucked up. Fresh orders came in. Start hitting the UVF and UDA as well.'

'Wait.' Kay scribbles down in her pad. 'Who?'

'Ulster Volunteer Force and Ulster Defence Association. Loyalist paramilitary groups.'

'Loyalist? They're on your side?'

Twill shrugs. 'The orders were to stir things up. Get them at each other's throats. Motivate them to do our dirty work for us.'

Kay stiffens. 'You do realise what you're saying? You glibly talk about tearing up the rules but when those rules are international human rights established under the Geneva Convention, that's something else altogether. You're talking war crimes.'

Twill looks away, takes a bit of dry toast and chews slowly. 'I know what we were and what we did. And what it looks like. It's too easy to take it out of context. There was a problem, and we were the solution.'

'And you were okay with this?'

'Absolutely fine. Why do you think they finally negotiated? Our job was to keep them off balance, keep punching them *hard* until they lost the will to fight. And *that's* what brought them to the table.'

Kay folds her hands in her lap and whispers, 'Asymmetric warfare. That's it. That's the connection.'

'To what?'

'Kalcek and the two-two. Kalcek was lecturing on asymmetric warfare before he came to Northern Ireland. He was drafted in to train a team of specialists for the British government.'

Twill gives a bitter chuckle and shakes his head. 'I think you're missing the point.'

'The point? This *is* the point, surely.'

Twill rises to his feet and puts his plate in the sink. 'No. The point is Kalcek's experience in Vietnam. *Alternative means of quelling insurgencies.*'

'Yes, that's what I mean, with asymmetric warfare—'

'No. What we did wasn't new or innovative. We identified targets and took them out. We just did it...better. More efficiently, and with an unrestricted mandate. And we were able to do that because of *who* we were. His only input was recruitment. It was *who* he got to do it. Kalcek had first-hand experience of what happens when you let the right people off the leash. What was needed was a hammer. And he helped Cromer get one.'

'You think Kalcek just helped Cromer find the right people?'

'I know he did.'

'What, your specialist skills? Why would Cromer need Kalcek for that? Surely the British armed forces has drivers or surveillance or covert operatives?'

Twill sits back down and holds his chin high. 'In the First World War, only twenty per cent of infantry fired their guns. Twenty per cent. And of those, nearly half aimed above the enemy's heads. That's why wars drag on for so long. Most people aren't hardwired to kill. Kalcek saw first-hand what happens when you get people who don't fire above heads. You get real killers. Actual soldiers. Triggermen. I keep on getting told we were special. And, fucking hell, we were.'

'You're saying Kalcek was trying to reproduce My Lai in Belfast?'

'No. I'm saying Kalcek *did* reproduce My Lai in Belfast.'

Kay underlines her last paragraph and turns a page. 'And you think what you did accelerated the peace process and ultimately brought the IRA to the peace table?'

'Yeah, I'm sure it did.'

'But the war went on for years afterwards.'

Twill hustles forward and levels his face with Kay's. 'What you have to realise is when you up the ante, the other side reacts one of two ways. They either fold like a deckchair or ratchet things up. And that's what they did. We didn't have a monopoly on killers.'

'But you said your actions speeded up the end of the war. Now you're saying you systematically and intentionally inflamed the situation and made things worse?'

'I did and it did. Listen, it's only when things get really bad that anyone actively looks for peace. We had to create hell on earth to make that happen. The way it was, if we hadn't come along, it would still be going on now.'

'You really believe that?'

'That week of interviews. With Kalcek. You had that too?'

229

'They all did. Except me.'

Kay looks up. 'Why not you?'

Twill's hand moves to his leg and a shadow crosses his face. 'We'll get to that.'

'But this profiling week, you know all the others did it?'

'Yeah.'

'Psychological profiling?'

Twill shrugs again. 'So they say.'

'What *exactly* were they looking for?'

Twill picks some lint from his trousers like he couldn't be less interested. 'Someone special. Someone from the ten per cent that fires their rifle with the intention of taking a life.'

'He weaponised spectrum thinking.'

'He did *what*?'

'You, your unit. You keep getting told you're special, right? Different.'

'Had to be to get the job done.'

'*This*. This is my story.'

Twill wrinkles his brow. 'How so?'

'The autism advantage.'

'Fuck off. Who said anything about autism?'

'I'm not saying all of you are—'

'*All?*'

'Hear me out. The autism advantage—it's a thing. Companies employ people with'—she looks across at Twill's darkening face. *Keep digging*, she thinks— 'people who exhibit spectrum thinking.'

Twill dismisses her with a wave and sits back. 'Bollocks. Why would they do that?'

'Tech companies do it. Google. Microsoft. Give them safe spaces to work, quiet places. People on the spectrum, with their attention to detail and their intolerance for errors, have very good pattern-recognition skills. Perfect for IT. They can detect the smallest of discrepancies that neurotypical people miss and their loyalty is beyond that of other employees. The structured environment suits them.'

'That rules me out. It took two years to work out how to use my phone.'

'It doesn't have to be autism. Spectrum thinking covers a whole range of characteristics. Listen, you've got a difficult job to do; use someone who's unshackled by the conventional moral or psychological constraints.'

Twill purses his lips. 'Profiling week.'

'Exactly. We need to speak to the doctor. What's his name?'

'Doolittle.'

'Real name?'

'I can probably get that.' He pulls his phone from his pocket and stabs out a text.

'Good,' she says. 'Now, how does all this tie into Animus?'

'We're going to need more coffee.'

He fills the machine with water and spoons more grounds into the top.

'Did you hurt your leg over there?'

Twill flops back into his seat, holds her gaze for a moment then looks down. 'Yeah.'

'How?'

'I got a taste of my own medicine.'

'How come?'

'I was betrayed. Sold down the river.'

'Who by?'

'Ellis fucking Cromer, that's who.'

'And to what end?'

'They spoon fed me a load of old shite and threw me to the dogs.'

'They planted disinformation?'

'Yeah. And it would have worked if I'd talked.'

Kay rubs the back of her neck. 'This gets worse. You were tortured?'

'It marked the end of my ballroom-dancing career, for sure.'

'And who knew about this? Just Cromer?'

'Maybe Bridges. Max knew but was spun some yarn about me being in on it.'

She squints at him. 'I want to be clear about this. Your commanding officer was prepared to let you be captured and tortured in order to place disinformation in the enemy's hands?'

Twill snorts. 'Torture was the least of my worries. Cromer signed my death warrant when he set me up. And he knew it. He *wanted* it.'

'Fucking psycho…then how did you get away?'

'Some prisoner exchange. Cromer didn't see that coming. The story was on the front page for a week. They bowed to public pressure. He'd lost control of the narrative.'

'And you re-joined the regiment?'

'Briefly. Cromer was always going to get rid of me, one way or the other. Claimed I was damaged goods and got me pensioned off.'

'And were you?'

Twill looks up at the ceiling. 'No. All I wanted was to hurt the person who'd hurt me, which isn't unreasonable given the circumstances.'

'And did you?'

'I spent many years and a lot of money trying to do just that.'

'Did you ever…get the opportunity?' Kay asks.

'Actually, I had coffee with him last week.'

'I'm going to want to know all about that.' She scribbles in her notebook. 'So, you thought you were fine, but you still went along with the therapy.'

The coffee machine beeps and Twill fills their cups. 'We all did.'

'Although you thought you didn't need it.'

'It was mandatory.'

'And you also said it was bullshit or something.'

'Yeah, stinks. Just another way of fucking with us. Controlling us. Keeping tabs. Get us on the couch, get us to open up, find out what we were thinking. What a crock of shit. Anything and everything we said went straight back to Cromer.'

'Were you given medication?'

Twill waves a hand in the air. 'Pills. Fuck with your head. Rather have a dead leg than a dead brain.'

'What about nightmares?'

Twill sits up pencil straight. 'Sometimes.'

'Last night?'

'As it happens.'

'Often?'

'Was worse on the pills.'

'And what happens in these dreams?'

Twill looks down at his feet. 'Is this relevant?'

'Maybe.'

'It's bullshit. But it's the same bullshit every time. I'm stuck in the mud and attacked.'

'By who?'

'Not who. What.'

'What, then?'

'A swan.'

Kay writes it down and looks back up at him. 'Why a swan?'

'Fuck knows.'

'Were you attacked by a swan when you were young?'

Twills reddens and snaps his head away.

'That's okay,' she says, laying a hand on his arm. 'Talk to me about Animus.'

'After I left, when it all died down and the Good Friday Agreement was signed, there was obviously a massive de-escalation. It all felt...rushed. There was plenty of unfinished business and it felt like we'd given away too much. The guys we'd been fighting all got off the hook. Just melted away. Took up normal jobs. And us? We were expected to do what? Security guards at Boots? Chase snotty-nosed kids through a shopping centre for nicking sweets?' His voice rises. 'With my leg? How do you go from being a killer to a fucking painter and decorator?'

'You did those things?'

Twill grunts and shakes his head. 'Fucking Boots.'

'You think it was difficult to assimilate back into society?'

Twill leans in. 'I want *you* to think about it. It's impossible. One minute you're fighting a war, the next you're stacking shelves in a nine to five.'

'What did you do then?'

'Me? Nothing. I was out of favour, remember. Out in the cold. I didn't feature in any of Cromer's plans. As far as he was concerned, I died the night I was snatched up. I tried a few jobs but Civvy Street's not for me. I've got the army in my veins. If I can't do that, I'd rather do nothing.'

'How do you live then?'

'Day to day.'

'What about your plans? *Is* there a plan?'

'Same as it ever was. Always have a plan to kill everyone in the room.'

Kay laughs but it's no joke; she knows it.

'What about the others?'

Twill slides the pile of paper towards her. 'The work continued. Different targets, but this time for money. Not all of them. Bridges was the brains. Max, JR, Mincer and Croall the muscle.'

'What work?'

'Same work.'

Kay glances at her Dictaphone. 'Can you be explicit, please?'

Twill takes off his glasses and pinches the bridge of his nose. 'Hits. Wet work.'

'Who for?'

'Guess.'

'Cromer? By now he was in the government—'

'Yes. Customer numero uno.' Twill pats the pile of paper. 'And it wasn't only the *British* government...'

Kay snaps her fingers. 'Kalcek!'

Twill nods. 'Ten points for the blue team.'

Kay scribbles furiously. 'So, a team of killers was formed from the aftermath of Northern Ireland and hired out to the highest bidder?'

'Yep. And from what I've seen here, it's almost exclusively US or British government contracts. Below-the-radar solutions to their problems with little chance of being traced back to them. Kalcek and Cromer carried their model through to the private sector.'

'First they weaponised, then they monetised.'

'If you say so.'

'Wait. Go back a bit.' She flicks through her notes. 'You mentioned a Croall. Who's that?'

Twill's face freezes. He glances down and pats his leg. 'The animal that did this.'

'Croall's IRA?'

'Cromer doesn't discriminate. Carving me up was probably Croall's first interview.'

Twill's phone beeps. He looks at the screen. 'It's Lucan.'

'What's he got?'

'George Leeson-Vaughn. That's the doctor.'

Kay brushes her hair off her face. 'I think we need to have a chat with Dr Leeson-Vaughn.'

26

It doesn't take Kay long to find a Dr G. Leeson-Vaughn on the Register, practising in Tenterden, Kent. They leave the house after an early lunch. The drive takes a couple of hours. Twill might be a highly trained professional but he's an appalling driver. On more than one occasion, Kay slams her foot on imaginary pedals and grips the dash. Every time, Twill gives the same breathy huff.

There's a brief argument about whether to use the map or the satnav on Kay's phone, then another over which exit to take on the M25. By the time Kay checks her phone, she's missed her window to call Grace. Still, the mood's thawed by the time they reach the village of St Michaels and Kay is buzzing at the prospect of getting some answers.

They turn into the narrow high street and Twill pulls around the back of a red-brick pub called The Crown.

Twill to Kay. 'Is it far?'

'Only a two-minute walk. Feel up to it?'

He switches off the engine.

The surgery is in on the second floor of a bowed Tudor building held up by a Subway on one side and a glass-fronted charity shop on the other.

Kay nods towards the lift but Twill rolls his eyes and starts up the stairs. They're greeted at the top by a brightly lit waiting room with two rows of plastic chairs separated by a coffee table covered with dog-eared magazines. The walls are lined with posters screaming stark warnings.

Twill pushes past Kay, leans on the counter and stares at the receptionist until she looks up from her computer. 'How can I help?'

'I want to speak to Doctor Leeson-Vaughn.'

The receptionist takes her glasses off and shakes her head. 'I'm sorry, he's not in today.'

Kay squeezes alongside him.

'Hi. We don't need an appointment. My dad is an old friend of the doctor's and we're just trying to catch up.'

Twill shoots the receptionist a plastic grin that lasts all of two seconds.

'There's nothing I can do, I'm afraid. He's off all week.'

'The thing is,' Kay says, 'we're flying back to the States tomorrow. This is kind of our last chance.' She pats Twill's shoulder.

The receptionist scribbles an address on a piece of paper and slides it across to them. 'Here. He'll be pleased of the company,' she says in a voice that doesn't quite match sincere.

Twill reaches for it but she pulls it out of reach, 'And you didn't get it from me.'

On the way back Twill insists they stop at The Crown. He sits a table in the corner of a dark saloon bar with low ceilings and the air of stale beer while she gets the drinks.

'At last,' Kay says returning, 'my beloved Cabernet Sauvignon. How I've missed you.'

Twill takes a pull on his pint. 'Dad? Are you fucking sure?'

Kay laughs. 'C'mon, Dad. Drink up. You know what you get like if you haven't had your pint.'

'What's that all about?' she asks, pointing at his wrist. You wear your watch with the face on the inside.'

'Old habit.'

'Old army habit?'

'Yeah. So, it doesn't catch the light, Brains.'

'Luckily I'm getting accustomed to your particular type of charm. Tell me, if you didn't undergo profile week, how well do you know the doc?'

Twill shrugs.

'You do know him, right?'

'Sure,' he says over the top of his glass. 'We had monthly sit-downs.'

'Just you?'

'No. Everyone. That is, everyone who'd'—Twill scratches his ear—'been active that month.'

'What happened in the meetings?'

'He'd ask questions. You know, usual stuff. Blood pressure. That kind of thing. Few times there were tests.'

'Tests?'

236

'Yeah. The sort I guess the others went through in profiling week.'

'How old were you?'

'1972? Twenty-six.'

'And how old would he have been?'

Twill looks blankly at her. 'Dunno. Mid-thirties, forty maybe.'

'Which would make him upwards of eighty something now. We have to prepare ourselves for the possibility we've got the wrong person.'

'Wrong Leeson-Vaughn? *Pah*, no chance. Not with a name like that. These old country doctors work till they drop.'

'We'll see,' Kay says, brushing her hair out of her eyes. 'What's the address?'

Twill removes a piece of crumpled paper from his pocket and throws it on the table. 'Wittersham.'

Kay checks her phone. 'Fifteen-minute drive.' Looks up at Twill. 'With you at the wheel, maybe five, tops.'

'Har de har,' he says, smacking his lips. 'Drink up. I've got a doctor's appointment.'

***

Black Horse Lodge. The name seems grandiose for what is a modest, clapboard cottage with a drooping willow over a small pond. Behind the cottage there's a leaning stable, its doors open. A short gravel drive, blocked by a painted five-bar gate, leads to the front door.

'Should we go straight in?' Kay says.

Twill nudges the gate with the nose of the car and it snaps open. 'Yes.'

They pull up beside the pond in front of the stable. 'Do you know what you're going to say?'

Twill grunts as he gets out and leans on the roof. 'When he sees it's me, he'll talk. Don't worry about that.'

Limp wisteria on the porch conceals a doorbell that doesn't work. Kay peers through a small window in the door. Twill bangs his fist three times, making her jump and setting the ducks off into a frenzy of honking.

She pulls her jacket open, undoes the top two buttons of her blouse and scrunches up her hair.

Twill looks down at her cleavage and back to her face. 'Now *that's* asymmetric warfare.'

'Don't knock it. You'd be surprised how often—'

There's a click and the door opens. A middle-aged man in carpet slippers, cardigan and half-moon glasses holds a pen and a newspaper with a half-finished crossword. 'Hello?'

Twill tuts and looks away.

Kay steps forward, hand outstretched. 'Hello!'

The man's eyes flicker over her and he straightens his back. He takes her hand and Kay offers him her most dazzling smile.

She pulls away from his clammy grip. 'We were wondering if we could speak with Doctor Leeson-Vaughn.'

He smiles proudly, clasps his hands behind his back and rocks on his heels. ''Tis I.'

'Oh. Sorry. I think we've got the wrong man.'

The doctor laughs, an odd seal-like bark, and pushes his glasses up his nose. 'You thought I'd be older, am I right?'

Twill is tapping his watch, his expression pained.

'Umm…Yes?'

The doctor grins. 'It's okay. You're looking for Father.'

'George?' Kay asks.

'Yes. That's him. And me.' More seal noises.

Kay forces a polite laugh and lays a hand on her chest. 'And is he in?'

'What, Father? God no. Father's been gone over twenty years.'

Damn. 'Oh. I'm sorry.'

The doctor looks left, right and leans in. 'Don't be. He was an appalling human being.'

Twill sighs loudly and puts his hands on his hips.

'Sorry to have wasted your time,' Kay says.

Twill grabs her by the arm and spins her around. 'Wasted *his* time? What about—'

'Do you want the files? I assume that's why you're here.' The doctor's eyebrows squish together and he scratches at his cheek. 'That *was* you that called last week, wasn't it?'

'Yes,' Twill says, halting in his tracks. 'Yes. Sorry. That was us. The files.'

Kay hits him on the arm. 'Yeah, you dope. The files.'

The doctor leads them to the stable and flicks a wall switch. Tube lighting flickers on. 'When you called, it gave me the excuse for a good clear out,' he says over his shoulder. 'I know Father wasn't supposed to keep copies but'—he turns and pulls a sneer, exposing a row of small, menacing teeth—'he wasn't what you might call a rule-follower.' He strafes Kay with his eyes and a small, pink tongue dampens his lips.

'So, the files…' Kay says, doing up her jacket.

He drags a cardboard box from under a work bench and stands back triumphantly. Written in neat cursive in a blue marker pen is a single word. *ANIMUS*.

Twill lifts the box and marches towards the car.

'Won't you stay for a coffee?' the doctor says.

'No,' Twill barks over his shoulder.

Kay shrugs and runs to join him.

'You didn't call about the files, did you?'

'Course not. Get in the fucking car.'

Kay does up her seatbelt, trying to ignore the forlorn figure waving from the doorstep. His face drops as Twill sprays gravel and noses the car through the gate.

'Then who did?'

Twill swears under his breath. 'It's not over.'

27

The files cover most of the living-room floor. The armchair has been dragged over to the corner, and Kay's cross-legged in the middle, like a yogi, taking files from a central stack and dropping them into piles. There's some kind of system in play, though how it works isn't obvious to Twill from his position in the doorway. Graham has made himself comfortable on a smaller pile close to Kay.

Twill starts to speak but she interrupts him.

'Sorry, but...this is my thing. What I do. Let me break the back of it, then I'll walk you through it.'

Twill makes a snuffling noise and backs out of the room. He returns an hour later and she hasn't moved. Her face is screwed up with concentration and her hair is pegged up with a pen.

'Are you okay with me reading your medical records?'

Twill nods.

'Good. I'm making progress. At least I know everyone's name now.'

Twill lowers himself into the armchair. 'There's something you should know.'

Kay raises her eyebrows. 'What's that?'

'What I meant when I said it's not over. There's a leak. A rat. Somewhere, in one of those files. Someone tipped Cromer off we were coming for him and that explains why he's been ahead, every step of the way. He's got a man on the inside. Probably the same person who called your boyfriend looking for the files. Probably the same person who drove Tumble to Eastbourne and had pizza with JR. I thought it was one of the others—Max or Bridges maybe. But they're dead and it's still going on. He's still out there.'

'That CCTV footage—Tumble's last journey. You said in the pub you couldn't make out who was driving.'

'No. Only Tumble in the passenger seat.'

'Then why not get CCTV from the other side of the road?'

Anger flutters in his chest.

Kay pulls herself onto her knees. 'Soldier, who do you think it is?'

'No fucking idea.'

Kay purses her lips. 'Do you think it could be Lucan?'

'I did for a while. I don't…shit. I don't know anymore.'

'Croall?'

'No. He's too selfish. There would have to be a pay-off. Besides, he's unlikely to want to do Cromer's dirty work anymore—that cat is firmly out of the bag. Croall's gone. Forget him.'

Kay picks up a file and flicks through the pages. 'That means it's one of the two-two.'

'I'll put the coffee on,' Twill says, thoughts of betrayal hanging heavy.

Kay checks her watch and pulls a cheeky grin. 'Something stronger might give me the will to live.'

***

It's nearly nine and Twill is dozing in his chair. He hears a long, heavy sigh and opens one eye. Kay stands and pushes her sleeves up her arms.

'So, what you got?'

'I've barely scratched the surface.'

'What are they then?'

'Personnel records of the two-two. Test results, psychological profiles, interview notes, mission reports. Memos between the doctor and Cromer. Comms from Kalcek.'

'Kalcek?'

'Recruitment guidelines. An outline of what Cromer was to look for, initially.'

Twill folds his arms. 'Which was?'

She shakes her head. 'I'm not sure. Kalcek told Cromer to look for a certain pattern of behaviour. I'm going to need more time. I want to get this right.'

'Fine,' he grunts.

He fixes them a sandwich and watches her work for a bit. She scans pages and jots notes in the margins and in her notebook. He sees *Caitlyn* underlined at the top of the page and a pit opens up in his stomach. He leaves the room.

***

Twill wakes, sensing he's being watched. He switches on the bedside lamp. Kay is in the doorway, ashen-faced. She's wearing his mum's old dressing gown, crossed arms hug her waist.

'What is it?' His throat is rough and dry.

She doesn't answer, just stares him down.

Twill kneads his eyes and sits up. 'Fuck's sake, what?'

'I—I need to ask you some questions.'

Twill glances at the clock. 'At 4 o'clock in the fucking morning?'

She nods. 'And if you don't come downstairs right now and answer my questions, it's off. All of it. And I'm off too.'

Her face tells him she means it.

Neat piles of papers cover every surface of the kitchen, each tagged with a yellow Post-it. Two steaming mugs sit on the table and the coffee machine is gurgling. Kay squares a tower of papers and flinches as Twill plonks himself down.

He takes a deep swig from his mug. 'So, you gonna tell me what this is all about?'

Her eyes are dark rings and her lips are pressed into a thin line. 'I want you to answer some questions. Truthfully. And then we'll see where we are.'

'You want to shine a light in my face? You know, do it properly?'

'I'm not fucking joking,' Kay says.

Her breathing is short and shallow. Twill tells her it's okay, reaches out for her, but she pulls back. Her other arm is flexing, hand hidden beneath the table.

'I. Am. Not. Fucking. Joking.'

Twill blows out. 'Fine. Do your fucking test.'

Kay pops the button on the end of her pen. 'Okay. Some of these I've answered for you.'

'What are you talking about? Who's taking the test, me or you? What the fuck is this?'

'It's the profiling test Leeson-Vaughn used. All your colleagues did it.'

'But not me.'

'But not you.'

'Go on then, shoot. It's been forty years but it clearly can't wait till morning.'

242

Kay looks down at her papers and puts her glasses on. 'Do you have a grandiose sense of self-worth?'

Twill looks down at his stained T-shirt.

'Please. Yes or no answers. Or an explanation if the answer's somewhere in-between.'

'No,' he says with a sigh.

She writes in the margin. 'Do you have an excess need for stimulation or proneness to boredom?'

'I get bored. So what? Who doesn't?'

'Are you a pathological liar?'

'I don't lie. Lying is to make other people happy, and for that you have to care what other people think. I couldn't give a rat's arse.'

'Do you lack remorse or guilt?'

'Nothing really bothers me. Don't see the point. Most of the time it's just to show other people you're sorry. Doesn't change anything.'

'Do you have a parasitic lifestyle?'

'What the fuck does that mean?'

'Do you manipulate others to fund your lifestyle?'

'Fuck off.'

'I'll take that as a no. Do you have a history of promiscuous sexual behaviour?'

Twill grunts. 'Chance would be a fine thing.'

She glares across the table at him.

'No.'

'Do you have a history of early behavioural problems?'

Twill looks away.

'I've got that one. Now, do you lack realistic long-term goals?'

'You mean, what do I want to do when I grow up?'

More scribbling. She even manages a smile. 'Only a couple more. Do you fail to accept responsibility for your own actions?'

'No. I do something, I own it…I mean, what the fuck is this?'

'Okay. Last one. Have you had many short-term marital relations?'

'Never been married.'

'That's not what I asked. The relationships you've had, would you characterise them as long term or short term.'

'Only been a couple. Long term, I guess.'

'Fine,' Kay says. She takes her phone and taps in the numbers she scribbled in the margins, flicks to a new page in the notepad and does more sums. Flops back in her chair with a shaky smile.

'That it?'

'Yeeeess.'

'Then you can put down whatever it is you've got in your other hand.'

She places a breadknife on the table.

Twill looks from the knife to her. 'I'd have that off you before you could even *think* about using it.'

She rises, puts the knife back in the drawer, and tops up their mugs.

'And? How'd I do?'

She exhales heavily. 'You did good.'

'In that case, seeing as it's quarter past stupid o'clock and you've dragged me out of bed to depress me about my non-existent sex life, you fancy telling me what the fuck this is all about?'

Kay sits opposite and crosses her hands on the table top. 'This test was devised by Doctor Robert Hare in 1970. It was considered pioneering work at the time and, in fact, still is. Twenty questions, each answer ranked on a three-point scale. You score zero if the question doesn't apply. One point means the question applies somewhat and two points means it definitely applies.'

'So, how'd I do?'

Kay bunches her fists, stretches and yawns. 'You scored low. Very low actually.'

'Never did well at tests.'

'You don't get it. A low score is good. The lowest score possible is naturally a big fat zero. The highest is forty.'

'What did I get?'

'Eighteen.'

'That's low?'

Kay opens a file, flicks through a few pages to a handwritten note. 'Lucan got thirty; he was next lowest. Bridges thirty-two. The highest was Barry O'Dowd—JR. He got thirty-four. And so, it goes on. Every member of your unit scored thirty or above. Which is the pass mark.'

'For what?'

There's an unnatural stillness.

'This test, the Robert Hare test, has another name.'

244

Twill leans forward.

Kay takes a deep breath. 'It's also known as The Psychopath Test.'

'*Piss off*. What are you fucking talking about? Psychopath? Fucking nonsense.'

Kay's voice sinks to a murmur. 'No.' She lays a hand on the pile of papers. 'It's all here. Cromer was looking to recruit clinical sociopaths. Monsters who would follow orders unflinchingly. Do the unthinkable with no questions asked. And Kalcek told him what to look for. *This* was Project Animus. How it all began. The only people capable of delivering their aim—carnage.'

'I'm not buying it.'

'Listen to me. It makes sense,' Kay says. 'You've already told me the two-two was special. They were handpicked to do a job no one else could. You told me that yourself but it wasn't the ten percenters you were recruited from; it was the one per cent of the population with'—she ticks off her fingers—'impaired empathy and remorse, boldness, lack of inhibition, egoism, callousness, manipulative tendencies…all psychopathic traits.'

'Okay, even if that's true, how were they going to control a bunch of psychopaths?'

'Medication. They doped you all up between jobs and changed the medication when they needed you to…you know, perform.'

'Different meds?'

Kay refers back to her notes. 'What do you think you were given?'

'Thorazine. For my leg.'

'Thorazine is a brand name. The generic drug is chlorpromazine. It's used to treat mood disorders including bipolar disorder and schizophrenia. And psychosis. It was administered in your food and drink without your knowledge. And when you were discharged they continued prescribing it, with an embedded pain killer for your leg. The extended therapy was a way of keeping tabs on you.' Kay pats the files. 'It's all in here.'

'What about when we were on duty?'

'The drugs were changed. From chlorpromazine to what the US Air Force calls "go pills."'

'Which are?'

'The technical name is dextroamphetamines. Speed.'

Twill stares into his coffee. 'And you don't think…I'm a psycho?'

'No, I don't,' Kay says gently. 'Although you've got a cat called Graham, and that's fairly fucking weird.' Her face softens. 'But, no. You're not.'

'And you can tell from twenty questions?'

'No. Not solely. But when it's completed as a semi-structured interview in the context of collateral information, it remains the best indicator of a psychopathic personality.'

'But you didn't do that, so you might be wrong.'

'But I know you. And'—Kay stabs her pen at Twill—'I'm not on my own. I just confirmed Leeson-Vaughn's assessment.'

'Hold on—*they* didn't think I was a psycho?'

'At first they did. After Caitlin. But when they realised you weren't, it sealed your fate.' Kay opens another file to a bookmarked page. 'Fifteenth October, 1972. You refused an assignment. This was a first for them. Must have set off all kinds of alarms. You were then admitted for testing by Leeson-Vaughn.' She looks over the top of her glasses. 'Do you remember?'

'I wouldn't do it.'

'Do what?'

'The job. They wanted to send a message. But this time it was different. It wasn't just the target they wanted eliminated. It was the whole family—aunts, uncles, grandparents. It would've been a massacre. They said it would broadcast loud and clear that the old rules no longer applied. Everyone was fair game. Join the IRA, you're no longer putting just yourself at risk; it's your family and friends too.'

'What happened?'

Twill looks up to the ceiling. 'It was a christening. All set up. We were waiting for them as they came out of church. Three of us. Me, Lucan and LoveSick. They were waiting for my order. I couldn't do it. There were kids, for fuck's sake. Young kids.' A pause. 'I pulled the operation.'

'What happened when you got back?'

'Cromer was seriously pissed off. They took me off active duty while I sat interviews with Leeson-Vaughn. For a week at least.'

'And after that week?'

Twill shrugs. 'Back on duty.'

Kay shakes her head. 'Bastards.'

She turns the file towards him. There's a big red stamp at the bottom of the page: UNFIT FOR DUTY, then the date—24th October, 1972—and Leeson-Vaughn's signature.

'Nine days after you refused the job.'

'Those fuckers.' He closes his eyes, breathes in, then out. 'They wanted me gone. Out the way.'

'Your abduction?'

'Two days later.'

Kay writes something down. 'So, you refuse a mission, and they discover you're not quite the swivel-eyed loon they had you down as. It was easier to sacrifice you strategically then have you continue.'

'Or let me go. They couldn't take the risk I'd spill the beans on their little set up.'

Kay arches her back and yawns.

'And you can fucking stop doing that,' Twill snaps.

'I've been up all night—'

'Don't bullshit me. You're doing that thing…to see if I yawn back. It doesn't fucking work, okay? I'm not a fucking psycho so you can cut out the amateur detective shit.'

Kay raises her hands. 'Okay, okay. I'm sorry.' She closes the folder and puts it on top of the pile.

'Something you said when we first met,' Twill says. 'It stayed with me.'

A crease appears across Kay's forehead.

'You asked whether we were the good guys. It made me think.'

'And you said you thought you were.'

'I still do but…I dunno. It's not that simple. I was convinced I was doing the right thing. I've always been different. A lot of what comes naturally to most people just…isn't there. The please's and thank you's. The niceties. I never cared about all that shit. That doesn't mean I don't know the difference between right and wrong but all the other stuff just left me…numb. I know I've done bad things. But does that make me a bad person? I've never done anything I didn't want to. Not once. I'm not ducking responsibility, just saying there was a reason for it. And, however my brain's wired, I was comfortable with it. I'm not the worst man to ever walk the earth. I just understand how the world works. How *men* think.'

Kay picks up her pen. 'You know, it could be something else.'

'Like what?'

'I don't know. Asperger's. Maybe with a little OCD mixed in.'

'Asperger's? Don't know what that is.'

Kay takes his arm. 'It's a developmental disorder.'

'Like autism?'

'It's a milder spectrum disorder. Look, I'm not an expert but from what I've seen, you present some of the characteristics. Difficulties in social interaction, one-sided verbosity—'

'Eh?'

'You don't talk unless you have to. And you use the minimum of words.'

Another grunt.

'But I've also seen loyalty, friendship, kindness and a strong moral compass.'

'Oh, yeah.' Twill says. 'That's me all over. I'm the third chuckle brother.'

Kay releases his arm and leans back. 'What I don't understand is why you were recruited in the first place, how you got dragged into all this. Why would they think you're a psycho? How did they find you? You clearly took a different route to everyone else. And you passed go and skipped profile week.'

Twill sits still as a statue.

'Tell me about Caitlyn. Was she how they got to you?'

Twill jumps up so fast that the coffee cups spin off the table.

'Or maybe you don't want to,' she whispers.

Twill recovers his composure and sits back down. Kay picks up the mug.

'It's okay. You don't have to.'

'No,' Twill says. 'I want to. It's part of my story.'

Kay nods for him to continue.

'Caitlyn was the only person I ever had a connection with. Apart from mum. I could be myself around her. Never had to put on an act. She loved me for who I was. Warts 'n' all.'

'Where did you meet her?'

Twill sniffs and rubs his nose. 'Belfast. When I was in Two Para. She worked in the pub we used to go to. The Five Points.'

'You were allowed to socialise?'

'It was encouraged. Team building. Obviously there were pubs that were off limits, but a couple of times a month we were allowed out to blow off steam. We could never follow any kind of pattern…weren't supposed to go back to the same place twice.'

'But…'

'But it was a nice boozer. And I couldn't stop thinking about her.'

Kay tilts her head and speaks softly. 'What did you like about her?'

'She was kind. Don't get me wrong, she was fierce. Wouldn't take shit off nobody. Maybe I liked that too.'

'So, what happened?'

'We started going back. Regular, like.'

'Like you were told not to.'

Twill nods. 'Like we were told not to.'

'Were you not worried about disobeying orders?'

Twill laughs bitterly. 'We didn't give a shit. We were young and thought we were invincible. We could have walked into any pub in Belfast and held our own.'

'What happened?'

'Turned out she liked me too. A couple of times a month turned into once a week. And always back to The Five Points.' His voice drops. 'Fucking stupid.'

He takes a moment.

'What next?'

'One night, we hit the drink hard. Got a proper load on. I refused to return to the barracks with the others.' Twill sighs. 'It got late and it was just me in the pub.'

'You couldn't go back?'

Twill shakes his head. 'Nah. If you come back in a big group you might get away with it. But sneaking back on your own? No chance. You'd end up target practice. Besides. I had other things on my mind.'

'Go on.'

'Caitlyn lived in a room above the pub, along with another barmaid and her boyfriend. She was worried about me leaving in the state I was in, and I wasn't in a rush to go.'

'You stayed the night?'

Twill sniffs. 'Yeah.'

'And what happened?'

'Someone tipped off the Provos.'

Kay takes off her glasses. 'We can stop if you want.'

249

'No. About two in the morning I heard a door being kicked in and two gunshots.'

'The other barmaid and her boyfriend?'

'Yeah. Shot in their bed.'

Kay puts a hand to her throat.

'And if they'd turned right at the top of the stairs, and not left, that would have been me.'

'What did you do?'

'By the time they got to us, I was ready. The first one stuck the barrel of his shotgun through the open door. I slammed it shut in his face and grabbed the gun off him. Caved his fucking head in.'

'First? There was more than one?'

'The second was on the landing. He fired at me and missed. Took a chunk out of the doorframe. I got one shot off. Missed.' Twill closes his eyes. 'All I could hear was Caitlyn screaming. Next thing I knew, she was by my side. There was a flash and a bang. Then the screaming stopped.'

'She was hit?'

Twill puts a hand over his mouth and nods. Clears his throat. 'Threw her up in the air like a rag doll. I knew by the way she landed she was dead.'

'*Jesus H,*' Kay says. 'What did you do?'

'I jumped out the window.'

'Was it open?'

Twill runs his fingertips over his scars. 'No. Didn't realise that till later.'

'How do you just jump out of a window from the top floor?'

Twill shrugs. 'I was lucky. Landed on the garage.'

'Were you hurt?'

'Just winded. I looked up. The shooter was at the window. He aimed and I rolled. I was lucky. Again. Landed on my feet.'

'Did he come after you?'

'He had no chance. This was before the leg, remember. I was off into the night. Took all the side streets, avoided the main roads. I hid behind walls, bins, in front gardens. I got back to the barracks around dawn.'

'What happened next?'

'They were pissed off. Said it wouldn't have happened if I'd followed orders.'

'Did they discipline you?'

'I got the usual hair dryer but it was half-hearted. For fuck's sake, I still had Caitlyn's brains on my shirt.'

Kay fetches him a glass of water. 'Do you want to take a minute?'

Twill shakes his head.

She sits back down and steeples her fingertips. 'So, what happened next?'

'I was sent for decompression. About a week in, I was told I had visitors.'

'Cromer and Kalcek?'

'Yeah.' Twill closes his eyes and visualises the scene. 'I was taken to a room. Cromer was behind the desk. Kalcek was perched on the corner. I remember the look in his eyes. Hungry.'

'What did they say?'

'The usual muttered condolences. Meant nothing. Just words. And then they dropped the bomb.'

'The bomb?'

'Cromer asked me if I wanted an opportunity to right wrongs. Stupid fucking question. Kalcek must have liked what he saw.'

Kay folds her arms across her chest. 'Fuck's sake, you must have still been in shock. Probably PTSD.'

'Whatever, we didn't know what that was back then. Anyway, Kalcek nodded and Cromer told me to stand to attention, and forced some keys into my hand. Motorbike keys. Said the bike was outside, fully fuelled, waiting for me. Said there was a PAP M92, ammo and map in the top box. Then he tucked a piece of paper in my top pocket.'

'What was on the paper?'

'Two names. The gunmen from The Five Points. And an address—an IRA safe house, a farm in Jonesborough, South Armagh.'

'And?'

'I took the keys and did what any man would have done.'

'On your own?'

'No, I had my M92.'

'And it…went smoothly?'

'For me, yeah. Put an end to those fuckers, then spent the night in a barn. When I got back the next day, Kalcek had gone but Cromer was waiting for me.'

'And then?'

'Then…was the two-two.'

Kay puts her pen down and closes her notebook. 'Listen, it's been a long night. Why don't we call it?'

'Fine with me…' Twill pushes himself up. 'Are we okay?'

'There's a lot to process and I can't imagine what it must have been like for you, but yes, we're good.'

Twill hears her feet on the stairs and looks at the files. There's two things he needs: The manila folder with his name and *Blaggard* on the front. And the A4 sheet listing the names of the two-two.

***

He trudges up the stairs, paperwork tucked under his arm. Each step feels like Croall's shuck is sliding into his leg again. Everything Kay said fits. He doesn't like it but that doesn't stop it being true.

What a fucking mess.

The bed feels bigger and emptier than usual. Either that or he's shrunk. He lies down, leg propped up on a pillow, arms by his side, staring straight ahead. Like he's in a coffin. The only picture on the wall is a black-and-white portrait of his mum. She's staring down at him with what could be a suppressed smile. Or not. There's times he's seen love in those eyes. Tonight, there's only reproach.

She'd known from the start that he was different and tried to protect him from it. From himself. Thought the discipline and structure of the army would be good for him. And look how that ended up.

He can't get comfortable. An unfamiliar heat tingles under the skin of his face. Sleep won't come, not least under his mother's glare. He gives up and clicks on the bedside lamp, puts on his glasses and pops a pill. Damn things are no good for him but he needs a few hours of calm or he'll lose his mind.

He opens his file and reads down the list of names. Halfway down, a chill hits the core of his belly.

The rat.

Cromer's rat.

He's got him.

He turns his attention to the Blaggard folder. It's stuffed with typed reports and handwritten memos. Some originals, some carbon copies. Fitness and psychological tests. A different time, a life lived over four decades ago. He

252

spreads them out on the bed and arranges them in chronological order. The pain in his leg begins to numb as the pills kick in.

Twill reads. The oldest reports are interviews from his time in Two Para, attesting to his toughness and loyalty but all making the same point—that he's somehow *different*. A couple express doubts that he has any kind of limits, they don't want to see what he's capable of. One CO likens him to a new gun—one you hope you'll never have to use but still want to fire to see how much damage it can do.

At the back of the report is a tattered, ragged sheet bearing the letterhead of his old school. It's addressed to his mum. He rubs his eyes, smooths the page and reads.

The Colchester Royal Grammar School
Cc: The board of governors
Dear Mrs Twill,

I regret to inform you that Owen is to be excluded from CRGS with immediate effect. His behaviour has fallen beneath the expected level on a number of occasions. Given the previous spoken and written warnings, this news should not come as a surprise to either of you.

Earlier today, Owen was involved in a fight in the playground which exceeded the threshold for high-jinks and crossed into what can only be described as a sustained and clinically administered beating. It resulted in the hospitalisation of two fifth-form students, Daniel Alexander and Charles Firth.

Here at CRGS, we pride ourselves on our ability to manage situations such as these. This is not the first time Owen has launched such an attack on his classmates. However, the severity of today's assault means it is the first time we have felt a responsibility to report his actions to the police.

I appreciate it can't be easy bringing up a child on your own, especially one like Owen, but please understand that we have a duty of care to ALL our pupils and can no longer justify the risks that accommodating Owen in our school entails.

Yours sincerely,

Twill looks up at his mum with a thickness in his throat. The letter's signed by the headmaster, a tweed-wearing stuffed-shirt called Meckiff. Under his signature is a single, handwritten line.

A well-aimed brick, in ink.

Meckiff's parting shot.

Your son has a black heart.

Twill reads it out loud. Repeats the last two words.

'Black heart.'

Blaggard.

28

Twill wakes late with pins and needles in his leg. His head pounding and an odd feeling he's been shouting. The memory of the letter washes over him with a ferocity that raises the hairs on his neck. He pulls on clothes with a renewed sense of purpose. Wherever this is headed, at least it's headed *somewhere.*

Kay's door is closed and there's no sign of her downstairs. Graham shoots him a withering look, then turns back to his bowl with a flick of his tail.

'Furry prick.'

Whale song from his gut reminds him it's twelve hours since he's eaten. The cupboard is bare apart from a tin of parsnip soup that further examination reveals a best by date which makes him wince. He grabs his coat from the banister and texts Lucan.

An overnight rain has cleared the sky, leaving a wide, bright morning with high, fibrous clouds and a bracing nip—winter lifting its skirt to flash its ankles. He scans the road. The usual cars line the street but there's an Audi he doesn't recognise by the junction with The Commons. He crosses the road and sits at the bus stop, studying the car in the reflection of the bay window opposite.

Five minutes pass and there's no sign of the owner. He limps towards the Co-Op, dismissing a nagging voice in his head.

It's just the tablets. They always make him paranoid.

He's blocked in the doorway by a cheery, plum-jowled shopkeeper. Twill avoids her eye, sidestepping her significant girth and grabbing a basket. Bacon, sausages, beans. A full English. That's what's needed. Treat Kay to some British haute cuisine.

The voice gate-crashes again, whispering up dark conspiracies and foul theories. Why is the Audi parked outside *that* house? He knows the old man who lives there—he's got no children and doesn't drive. He shakes the thought from his head. Probably a visitor. Jesus, he's become exactly what he hates most—a tittle-tattle curtain-twitcher. But if it *is* a visitor, why not park on the drive? And if the driver's visiting next door, why not park *next door*?

Twill lowers his head and joins the queue behind an old woman who's placing each item from her trolley on the conveyor belt one at a time. He coughs and forces down his irritation.

The shopkeeper comes around a pyramid of tins and waddles behind the counter, muttering apologies and chuckling. The old lady cups a mottled hand around her ear and leans forward, craning her neck. The shopkeeper says something and beams. Twill looks around the shop, trying to ignore the tightness in his chest, but the voice won't leave him alone, like a crow pecking in his ear.

He closes his eyes, pictures the Audi. Remembers.

The windows were steamed up. Someone was *in* the car.

Twill shifts his weight from one foot to the other and checks his watch. The old woman's still talking and the shopkeeper points to the pyramid and starts off about the merits of a new brand of tinned soup.

NEW.

The Audi is a new model but has 2008 plates.

Shit.

Twill drops his basket and blasts through the door and around the corner into his road.

The Audi is gone.

His heart rate steadies. He slows, clutches his thigh but as he gets closer…

His gate is open. Front door ajar.

He strides forward, ignoring the spiny twinge. Hits the top step and throws himself into the hall. Empty.

'*KAY!*'

There's a flash of movement from the kitchen and Twill brings his arms up to his head and braces for impact. Graham shoots between his legs and skittles out of the front door and into the street.

'*KAY!*'

No reply. He flicks the baton from his pocket and snaps it to its full length. It won't stop a bullet but it's all he's got until he gets upstairs.

The front room is clear. Kitchen too.

He's on the stairs and hears a creak. Thinks about a terraced house in Belfast.

'*KAY!*'

He reaches the landing. A body's slumped against the airing cupboard, head resting on its chest in an expanding pool of blood.

Twill takes a deep breath and shakes his head clear. He straddles the body and presses two fingers against Lucan's neck. A pulse. Faint, but it's there.

He runs into the bedroom and pulls the Browning from behind the headboard, then snatches two towels from the radiator.

Lucan moans—a low, guttural noise from deep in his chest. Twill pulls up his jumper and presses a towel to his stomach.

'S'okay, mate. Just a scratch.'

Lucan's eyes roll back. Twill calls his name and his friend focuses. His complexion is sallow and waxy. A bubble of blood-flecked foam oozes through thin, grey lips onto his cheek. Lucan reaches up and grabs Twill's hand, squeezes. Twill puts his ear close to Lucan's mouth but there's nothing but ragged breath on his face.

His friend's throat floods with blood. Eyes glaze and stare past him at the ceiling. A sharp whistle of breath escapes through his teeth. His grip loosens.

Twill lowers his head back gently and rocks back on his haunches. He leans forward to close Lucan's eyelids and his friend's hand spills from his lap and hits the floor.

And that's when Twill sees it.

By the fingers, drawn on the carpet in blood, are letters.

A knot of rage, roiling and churning, rises from his stomach. He pulls himself up and tucks the gun into his belt.

All this, everything, is a result of his passivity. His fault.

It ends. Today.

He hears a bump and freezes. Holds the breath. Listens.

A muffled whimper from the airing cupboard.

Twill drags Lucan's body to the side, levels the gun and flings the door open.

Kay pushes herself back. Her hand is over her mouth and she's hyperventilating. Twill tucks the gun into his trousers and reaches for her. She takes his hand and he pulls her to her feet but she crumples to the floor. He hooks his arms behind her back and squeezes her close, letting her sob for a moment.

She starts jabbering but he hushes her.

'Get your bag and passport. We leave in two minutes.'

***

'Tell me what happened.'

The north Essex countryside streaks past, a blur of grey and brown. Empty fields, red-brick estates and hedgerows with plastic bags stuck in their branches.

Twill nods at the bottle of amber liquid in Kay's hands. 'Drink. It'll help with the shock.'

She drinks deeply. When she speaks it's so softly, Twill has to ask her to repeat herself.

'I was getting in the shower. I thought it was you—forgotten your wallet or something.'

Twill tightens his grip on the steering wheel. 'Who?'

'I don't know. He was wearing a hood over his face.'

'Did you let him in?'

Kay shakes her head. 'No. Although I would have if they'd have knocked.' She lifts the bottle and takes another gulp. 'The door just opened...it wasn't forced.'

'He waited for me to leave.'

'I was on the landing. He had...' She sniffs and wipes her nose on her sleeve. 'He had a gun. He was holding it out in front of him.'

'What happened next?'

'I ducked down behind the banister. He was going from room to room. I can't get over how quiet he was. It was creepy like watching a horror movie. If I hadn't seen him enter...He had one foot on the stairs and then the door opened...That could have been you.'

He pats her hand. 'It wasn't. Go on.'

'He leapt behind the door and Lucan bowled in. He shouted out...I didn't know what to do. I should have warned him.'

'It was you he was after. If you'd warned Lucan, you'd be lying there next to him right now.'

Kay exhales heavily. 'He saw me. Crouched down. Lucan, I mean. Through the rails of the banister. He realised. And then the man stepped forward and pointed a gun at his head. And Lucan was telling me to hide, with his eyes, you know?'

Twill nods. 'And what did you do?'

'Lucan put his hands up and circled around the gunman, really slowly, so the gunman had his back to me. He was giving me time. And that's when I hid in the cupboard.'

258

'And you never saw his face?'

'No. I heard him speak, though didn't recognise the voice. Lucan said something like, "I can't believe it. Not fucking you," or "it's you." And the gunman just kept saying, "Where is she?" And then I heard footsteps on the stairs. Quick ones. And there was a bang and a thump and breathing. And then more footsteps but softer this time. And a minute later you turned up.'

Kay breaks down and sobs. 'It's all my fault.'

'No. I texted him when I left, told him to come round. He must have already left to get there that quickly.'

'Who was it? The man in the hoodie?' Kay says.

Twill takes a moment to think how best to answer. 'At this stage, the less you know, the safer you are.'

'So, what do I do now?'

'You do as you're told,' Twill says. 'You're going to get on the first available flight.'

Kay nods.

'You have to go via a hub from Stansted, so Paris, Frankfurt, whatever. Then get on a plane to the States. *Not* New York. Take a bus, a train. Use cash. Take some dollars out at the airport but don't use your card. Find a motel outside a small town and sit tight. Wait for my call. If you haven't heard from me in a week, go home. It'll be safe by then.'

Kay's brow is furrowed with worry but her lips are set in a defiant scowl. 'I'll be fine. What are you going to do?'

'I'm going to finish this.'

The next ten minutes of the journey are spent in silence. Twill sets her down at the terminal and gets her case from the boot.

'I'm going to keep the car. Report it stolen if you like, but not until tomorrow.'

Kay takes his hand, whispers, 'Are you going to be okay?'

Twill looks away. 'I will or I won't. But that doesn't matter. It needs to be done. I promise you'll be okay. If you haven't heard from me in a week, write it up. Everything.'

Kay squeezes his hand. 'Come with me.'

'No.'

She embraces him. He stiffens then loops an arm around her waist.

'Be careful, Owen. And take this.'

259

Kay presses something into his hand. He puts it in his pocket. And then she's off. When she's in the terminal he digs around in his pocket for his mobile. The call goes through to answerphone. He waits for the beep and leaves a message.

29

Frome

Dusk turns to dark. Twill stumbles down the hill through long, wet grass and bracken. Branches scrape his face. For once, there's no pain.

He pushes through a perimeter fence and pulls his coat where it's caught on barbed wire. A tall oak offers cover. His breath gathers around him like so many ghosts.

Balesbury Grove looms black and hostile on the horizon against a star-pricked sky.

Twill waits.

Lights flicker on at the back of the house and the drive lights up like a runway. Spotlights illuminate the ivy-clad front of the building.

He keeps low and jogs parallel to the road, not in a straight line but following the natural cover of the garden and staying in the shadows. At the security hut, he waits for two minutes. There's no activity and he enters. The cabin is empty; the barriers are raised.

Cromer knows he's coming.

Twill moves on, hits the river, creeping as close to the house as he dare. On the ground floor at the back, the lights are on in a book-lined room, the curtains open. Motion-activated floodlights line the soffits. If he gets too close, the garden will light up like Old Trafford and he'll be a sitting duck.

A noise from behind startles him. He spins around. A swan launch into the river. He flinches and stumbles backwards, swallowing a howl, and retreats to a flower bed. Drops to his knees and selects a heavy flint. He regulates his breathing and hefts the rock high over the orangery, ducks and sprints towards the front of the house. The front door's the last place they'll expect.

On the other side of the house, floodlights come on and bathe the landscaped lawn and the sides of the building in dazzling light. Twill throws himself flush to the wall and waits.

Nothing.

The garden plunges into darkness.

He inches along the wall to the edge of the gravel drive, lowers himself to the ground and pokes his head around the corner. Cromer's Jaguar sits in front of two double-height doors, one of which is wide open.

Twill steps into the light. There's no screaming alarms, angry shouting or rush to arms. Just the crunch of gravel underfoot. The door leads into a softly lit, wood-panelled reception hall with an ornate, teak staircase twisting off to the right, and double doors straight ahead. High, vaulted ceilings are decorated with plump cherubs in pastel shades. He pauses, listens, and leans an ear against the doors. Again, nothing.

He readies the Browning, counts to three, pushes the door. It swings open soundlessly, revealing a long, low-lit passageway with doors on both sides. His trainers squeak against the hardwood floor as he jogs the length of the corridor, gun arm in front, coat flapping behind.

At the end, he leans against the wall and shuts his eyes. Furniture polish and floor wax. Another, more pervasive scent: firewood smoke. And then, a familiar metallic odour.

The door opens with a low groan, and he pokes his head through. Beyond is another wood-panelled ante-room draped with antique rugs with a suit of armour in the corner. He pushes the door. It sticks and he stops. A quick glance—it's blocked by a body.

Twill slides in, gun trained and breath held in his lungs. A man. Face down in a pool of congealing blood. One arm reaches out, fingers jammed under the door. The back of his head is matted with gore, hair parted around an angry hole. Gobs of glistening tissue spatter the floor around him. Twill bends and place fingers against the man's neck. The flesh is as cold and hard as marble. The hair around the wound is singed, the scalp scorched black. Shot at close range, from behind. The smell of cordite is heavy but it's the sickly, ferrous odour of blood that turns his stomach. He stands and rolls the body over with his foot.

Alwyn Harris. Cromer's monkey.

Harris's eyes are milky, unseeing, his mouth stuck wide in a silent scream.

A darkening cloak of anger gathers around Twill as he remembers the photo of Harris and his kids, still in his back pocket. He didn't deserve to die like that. Just a man doing a job. There's a flash in the recesses of his mind and he's back in a clearing in the woods, shovelling clumps of dirt into a hole. The earth falls into a corpse's open mouth and screaming eyes. Then the face is covered but an arm is still poking out of the ground…

Twill bangs his head with the heel of his palm, steps over the body and strides across the room, no longer bothering to hide his approach. The smell of burning firewood is stronger by the door. He kicks it with his good leg and steps inside.

The dry heat hits him like a hammer. The room's musty, lined with books, with a seating area and a mahogany captain's desk. Thick velvet drapes bunch at the sides of tall French windows. The ceilings are high and set with crown moulding. Wood spits and crackles from a roaring inglenook to his right. It smells of fire and leather.

Twin high-backed chesterfields with worn armrests sit in front of the fireplace.

Cromer pushes himself out of the nearest one, straightens his trousers and smiles warmly. 'Ah, Twill. I've been expecting you.'

Twill widens his stance and lowers his gun. 'You've been watching too many Bond films.'

Irritation flickers across Cromer's face. 'A drink?' He starts towards the desk and turns with a smirk. 'After all, we're not savages.'

'I didn't come for a drink.'

Cromer crosses his arms. 'Well, what did you come for?'

'To kill you.'

Cromer throws back his head and laughs. 'Of course, you did. But first, a drink.'

Twill scans the room. There's something not quite right with the bookcase opposite. The spines are too regular and there's the smallest of gaps between the top shelf and the ceiling.

Cromer holds out a glass. Twill doesn't move and Cromer rolls his eyes, takes a sip and holds the glass back out. Twill takes it and follows Cromer to the fire.

Cromer goes to sit but Twill says no and takes the seat for himself, not wanting his back to the bookcase.

Cromer's smirk has turned to contempt. 'Looks like you've finally grown a pair of bollocks, Corporal Twill. About forty years too late, mind, but at least I'm finally seeing a return on all that expensive therapy.'

'Why kill Harris?'

'I didn't. You did. At least, that's what I'll tell them. And I'll be backed up by the psych report Dr Walsh was kind enough to write.' He sticks out his bottom lip. 'Poor little Twill. Failed by the system. Unbalanced, grudge-bearing, psychotic old man, unable to let go of the past.'

Twill tightens his grip on the Browning. 'Where is he?'

Cromer scratches his cheek. 'Where is *who*?'

'Fuck off, Cromer. LoveSick. Where's LoveSick?'

Twill's eyes flit to the bookcase and Cromer chuckles.

'He said you'd spot the hidden door.' And then in a raised voice, 'C'mon out and say hello to our guest.'

There's movement behind and Twill spins. LoveSick steps out from behind the curtain, gun aimed squarely at Twill.

'Didn't you play hide and seek growing up, Blaggard?' Cromer says. 'Maybe *you* should watch more Bond films.'

'Why?' Twill says to LoveSick.

'Put the gun on the table.' His voice is as flat as his expression.

Twill puts down the Browning. LoveSick crosses the room and pulls a chair from under the desk, eyes and gun aim trained on Twill as he sits.

'Why?'

'You're wasting your time,' Cromer says. 'You wouldn't ask a shark why it kills the seal, or a lion why it mauls the zebra. They just do. It's their nature. Natural-born killers.'

'How did you know it was me?' LoveSick says.

'Tumble's daughter said he'd been talking to a Mason. I didn't realise that was your name until I saw your file.'

LoveSick fans his free hand and nibbles on a hangnail. 'Oh.'

'And Lucan confirmed it.'

'Lucan weren't telling no one nothing when I left him.'

Twill draws *LS* in the air. 'On the carpet. In his blood.'

LoveSick nods. 'Fair play.'

'And the others? JR? Mincer?'

A twitch of a shrug.

Cromer sits in the chesterfield and the leather squeaks. He glares at Twill. 'You could have been part of something remarkable, Twill. You could have helped shape history. But, no. You had to go and fuck it all up.'

'History? Don't flatter yourself.'

'I changed—'

'You changed nothing, Cromer. It amounted to nothing more than a failed project. You herded up a bunch of freaks and gave them guns. Big fucking deal. That's your legacy.'

Cromer smiles but there's irritation behind it. 'There's a proud history of freaks with guns, as you so charmingly put it.' He nods towards a painting of Churchill above the fireplace. 'You think we were the first to realise the value in...*decisive leadership*?'

Twill shuffles in his seat and LoveSick's gun follows him.

'Churchill ordered the destruction of the French navy to stop the Nazis getting their hands on it. Thirteen hundred sailors dead.' Cromer holds out his glass towards another painting, this one of a soft-faced, white-haired man in uniform. 'General Patton issued orders to kill German POWs so their progress wouldn't be slowed—'

'You really going to put yourself up there with Patton and Churchill?'

Cromer leans forward and wets his lips. 'The order that saw five hundred German guards rounded up and shot at Dachau because of stretched supply lines. Real leadership. Real men.' Cromer jabs a finger into his chest. '*My inspiration.*'

'Bollocks. Ancient history.'

'Oh, it's everywhere you look, Twill. The highway of death. Thousands of *retreating* conscripted Iraqi troops incinerated on the road to Basra. Farmers. Students. Stuck in a uniform and turned to ash less than thirty years ago. You won't learn about *that* at school because it was done by us. But of course, you've heard of Rwanda, Serbia, Armenia, Nanjing. History is written by the victor, Twill.' Cromer sips from his glass. 'Let's call it winner's amnesia.'

'You forgot My Lai.'

'Don't get pissy,' Cromer says. 'Men have been making tough decisions for thousands of years. Real men. Men like me. Men like LoveSick. And, once upon a time, men like you. Men with a real talent for violence. And although rare, it's entirely natural. Just another personality trait, like a good sense of humour or a bent for mathematics. The ability to see through the fog of human emotion and make decisive calls for long-term good. It might suit you to sit in judgement, but you're no better than the rest of us. How many did you put in the ground, Blaggard? Twenty? Twenty-five? No. I refuse to be lectured by you. *We* were fully committed. *You* were the failed project.'

'Churchill, Patton, they were men of honour. They never turned on their own.' Twill stabs a finger at Cromer. '*You* served me up to the Provos.'

Cromer waves him away. 'Oh, stop crying. You sound like a little girl. It's embarrassing. Our model wasn't perfect but it worked. We selected from a pool of…neurological diversity, and it was really rather something to behold.' Cromer smiles blackly, closes his eyes and recites from memory. 'Cold logic and an absence of morality make the psychopathological ideal candidates for the arena of covert operations. The subjects can be, by turns, charming and superficially sociable yet fiercely intelligent and goal driven. Untethered by moral qualms, they are incredibly effective in achieving political and military objectives.' He grins. 'Really, it was too perfect. An easy sell, too.'

'Did your little sales pitch include handing your own men to the enemy?'

Cromer shrugs. 'Collateral damage. And a model that's been repeated all over now. I'm sorry you feel betrayed but your chum Croall only came on board after the Good Friday Agreement. Our little … synergistic alliance has worked well for both of us.' Cromer rolls liquor around his mouth. 'Look at you. You're a fucking disgrace. Still having bad dreams, you fucking bed-wetter?'

Twill casts his eyes down.

'You have no idea, do you?'

'Fuck you. We're not doing this.'

'Oh, this is too beautiful. The big, scary swan. You don't know *why*, do you?'

Twill flinches.

'You don't remember Adventureland? Our designated … landfill?'

Twill's shakes his head to clear Cromer's voice.

'Children's play park, a few miles north of Warren Point. The landlord was…sympathetic to our cause.'

Each word lands like a punch.

'Leave the van in the car park and take your *customer* across the crazy golf to the boating lake. Use one of the swan pedalos to reach the island…and come back alone.'

Bile rises in Twill's throat and spots of light dance in the corner of his vision. He sees the swan's flaming eyes and lashing neck; its human screams ring in his ears. Dizziness washes over him.

'I've got no regrets,' he croaks, glancing up at LoveSick and letting his eyes linger.

'But you're haunted,' Cromer says, his tone mocking, expression loathing. 'Pathetic.'

LoveSick looks from Cromer to Twill and waves his gun in the air. 'It ain't personal, mate.'

'What happened to you?' Cromer says. 'Doesn't seem that long ago you were a real soldier.' He shuffles forward, face rosy, eyes shining with a missionary's zeal. 'Now look at you, sitting there, clutching your pearls, all righteous and offended. A pathetic, mere quisling of a man. Not even angry.'

'What's to get angry about?' Twill snaps. 'I know what we were and I don't need some pencil-dick pen-pusher to tell me. You might want to turn that forensic focus onto yourself. You're nothing special, Cromer. Just another suit starting to believe his own bullshit, dishing out orders from a safe distance.'

Cromer bolts up, spittle flying from his mouth. 'Bullshit? Sixty million people look to me to keep them safe so don't tell me it's bullshit. Sixty million souls rely on me. *They* don't understand our world; it scares the shit out of them. They don't know what it takes to be kept safe. And you know the best thing? They don't care.'

'They don't fucking know so how could they care?'

'The world is a dark and rudderless place, Twill. You see, it's like sausages,' Cromer says. '*Everybody* loves sausages. *Nobody* wants to know how they're made. They just want to be coddled and told it's all going to be alright. And it's my job to do just that.' He slams a hand against his chest. '*We* are the guardians. *We* protect them from the monsters that live in the dark corners of the house. What we did back then was one hundred per cent necessary. The solution was so blindingly obvious, there was almost a beauty to it. We faced an enemy that didn't think twice about shooting, bombing and murdering men, women and children. Soldiers or civilians. They didn't care. How do you beat an enemy like that? I'll tell you how you *don't* win. You don't win by throwing your hands up and running home to mummy because they bent the rules. You win by writing your own fucking rules. You feel squeamish about what we did?' He waves a hand in Twill's face. 'Then fuck off and join the Women's Institute. You want victory? You have to *take* it. You win by being *better* than them, and you win by being *worse* than them. My people need strong, clear-eyed leadership. And I won't apologise to anyone for giving it to them.' Cromer settles briefly. 'Look at the scoreboard, Twill. I'm a decorated Member of Parliament and you live alone with a cat. You lose.'

Twill drains his glass and smacks his lips. 'That's quite some speech. I suppose that's why you started winding things up. Got your eyes on a promotion?'

Cromer sits back down and pulls on his cuffs. 'Yes, as it happens. It's my time. People are scared. Immigration, globalisation, the internet—everything's changing and I've got a shot at the top seat. And I'm not going to let you, that American bitch or anyone else fuck it up for me.' He taps the side of his head. 'The most strategic terrain today is the six inches between your ears. I know that, and *knowing* that is the difference. I *get* it. There's no doubt in my mind I'm the right man for the job.'

Twill clucks and shakes his head and says to LoveSick, 'Did you fall for all this? Did he say you were making history?'

LoveSick doesn't twitch.

'Do you have one of them there, *synergistic alliances* too? And what's the finer detail of that one, eh? Cromer shits and you wipe?'

Cromer swings one leg over the other. 'You're wasting your time.' He cups his hands around his mouth and whispers, 'He's not a people person.'

'LoveSick, once I'm gone, you're next. You know that, right? You're the last link. You honestly think he's going to let you just walk away?'

LoveSick's eyes dart from Twill to Cromer and back again. 'I didn't mean to kill Lucan. I always liked him. I only wanted the files. And the American.'

Twill puts his glass down and glares at Cromer. 'For all the noise you make, you actually did fuck all. You just sat in an office, stroking your chin and pulling your cock. *We*'—he points at LoveSick—'did the heavy lifting.' He hawks phlegm onto the floor. 'You think you're some kind of Superman, but you're really just the fat kid on the subs bench, looking down at his feet while everyone gets picked in front of him.'

Cromer smiles. 'Fuck Superman. You know what I am?' He rolls up his sleeve to reveal the regimental tattoo. 'An eagle. The only predator that that never looks behind him. Why? Because it doesn't *care* what's behind because there's *nothing* meaner. It's the biggest bully in the playground. The ultimate killing machine. I found these assets, I cultivated them, and I put them to good use…I don't even know why I'm bothering. Fuck you, Twill. You're boring me.

If you're close to God, now's the time to talk to him. LoveSick,'—he clicks his fingers—'kill him.'

Twill taps his chest. 'Yeah, do it. Right here. So, I don't have to listen to this mad cunt anymore. And while you're at it, put one in your own head. No way he's going to let you walk away from this.'

LoveSick looks from Twill to Cromer. Then his gun arm falls to his side.

'Just fucking shoot him,' Cromer shouts.

LoveSick shrugs, brings his gun back up. His face hardens.

Beyond, through the window, there's a blaze. A garden light has come on, bright as daylight. LoveSick spins around, arm raised. Light floods the grounds.

'*Shit.*' Cromer spits.

The lights inside and out click off, one by one, and the room is plunged into darkness save the glow from the fireplace. Twill launches from his chair, snatches the Browning, half-rolls and loses off a couple of shots in LoveSick's direction. A loud crack in return. LoveSick's face is lit by muzzle flash— screwed up with hate, teeth bared like a dog.

There's a whistle by Twill's ear and a bullet smashes into the wood panelling behind him. Cromer throws himself to the ground and covers his head. Twill pulls himself along the floor behind Cromer's seat. Hears cursing and heavy breathing. More orange flashes lance the dark. To his right, the crack of splintering wood. He lifts his gun and fires over the top of the chair in the direction of the gunshots.

'Just fucking kill him,' Cromer screams.

Twill pushes up into a crouch and runs along the far wall, around to the door. More shots. Books shred behind him, filling the air with confetti, but LoveSick's aiming at sound and he's a half pace behind.

Twill fires twice more, trips on a rug and crashes down. The gun skitters across the hardwood floor. He crawls towards it but is stopped by a foot planted on his chest. He looks up. LoveSick is silhouetted against the fire.

'It's over.'

Twill flops back, closes his eyes and tries to picture Caitlyn.

'Sorry, mate,' LoveSick says in an even voice.

Twill hears a scrape, opens his eyes.

'Do it, Mason. *Now!*'

LoveSick turns to Cromer. 'Shut the fuck up.' Looks down at Twill. 'Fuck me, he's so annoying.'

'Hurry up, Mason,' Cromer squeals. 'There's others. We need to—'

'*I SAID SHUT THE FUCK UP.*'

Twill's Browning lies in a square of moonlight maybe three, four feet away. Impossible to reach before LoveSick pulls the trigger.

'Mason—' Cromer says in a quiet voice.

'*DID YOU NOT FUCKING HEAR ME?* One more word and I'll put one in you—'

Cromer raises an arm and points.

LoveSick looks down. A red dot tracks up his body and settles above his heart. He jerks his head towards the window.

'Fuck,' he says quietly.

There's whip-like crack, an explosion of shattered glass and he freezes. Blood, black as treacle, blows from a single, spluttering cough.

LoveSick's head hits the floor with a dull thump, landing next to Twill's.

The red dot dances across furniture, up Cromer's torso. It nestles between his eyes.

'*Make them stop, Twill. Make them stop!*'

Twill stands and brushes glass from his clothes. 'Enough,' he shouts.

His words echo around the room. He picks up his gun and gestures for Cromer to raise his arms. The dot disappears.

Cromer's breathing is heavy and snatched. Beads of sweat glisten in the moonlight on his top lip. Stripped of his swagger, he looks wan and thin. Like a scared old man.

'Are…you going to kill me?'

'Me?' Twill says. 'What, do you think I'm some kind of psycho?'

Cromer takes a step forward. 'I can save the girl. I can call them off. I can do it; one call and your girlfriend lives.'

Twill laughs. 'You already saved her.' He takes Kay's voice recorder from his inside pocket. The LED is flashing. 'And once your confession hits the front pages, no one will dare touch a hair on her head. It's going to land on you. All of it.' He clicks a button. The light glows solid then goes off. 'Probably best to stop recording now, don't you think? What happens next might get a bit…you know…icky.'

A cool wind blows through the broken window, ruffling the drapes, gusting around the two men and cowering the flames in the fireplace. Cromer straightens his back and drops his hands to his sides. 'There's nothing you can do to hurt me, Twill.'

Twill motions with the gun for him to sit. 'I've done all I'm going to do. Your legacy is fucked. You're fucked. Check the scoreboard, Cromer. *I* win.'

Cromer leans forward. 'It's not too late.'

Footsteps echo in the hall. Strong, confident strides. Walking to their destiny.

Cromer looks at the door and back to Twill. His voice is a whisper. 'It's not too late.'

'Shhh.' Twill lifts the gun barrel to his lips. 'Oh, and stop crying. You sound like a little girl. It's embarrassing.'

A stocky figure enters the room, rifle slung over one shoulder, bag in hand, and casts a long shadow across the pair of them.

'Glad you could finally join us,' Twill says, standing.

The figure steps forward into the moonlight and takes his cap off, revealing a tumble of red hair.

'Fuckin' ingrate.'

'Croall?' Cromer gasps. 'Wait...'

'Shut yer mouth,' Croall says, and turns to Twill. 'His whining is going to get old, real quick.'

'You're telling me. Anyway, your problem now,' Twill says, doing up his coat. Then to Cromer, 'See ya.'

Cromer rushes forward and Croall puts a hand on his chest.

'Please, Twill. Don't leave me with him.'

Croall shoves him back into his seat and puts his bag on the table. Even in the dim light, Twill can see a roll of duct tape and a bunch of plastic cable ties.

'Before ya go,' Croall says to Twill, 'whatever we had between us. It's finished, right? We're even. After tonight, I'm off. Ya'll never see or hear from me again. Do us both a favour and don't come looking.'

Twill holds the man's stare and nods once. 'I won't.'

***

On the way back to his car, Twill hears a screech like a howling prairie-dog. Maybe it's the night breeze whistling through the tree tops.

Or maybe it isn't.

30

Walton, Essex

18 months later

Twill angles his head towards the sun, embracing its healing caress. The surf crashes and fizzes onto the sand, soothing him with its rhythmic familiarity. Thinks back to a freezing wet Glenmachen Street. Lets it go. The briny spray is crisp on his skin. Warmth spreads from his toes up to tingling fingertips.

He allows himself a full smile and sets off down the boardwalk. In one hand is a bone-handled walking stick; a plastic bag swings from the other.

He stops at the café at the end of the pier and chooses a south-facing table, sticky with vinegar and ketchup. This far down, a quarter of a mile out to sea, the chaos of whooping children is replaced with squawking gulls, dive-bombing for chips.

A young waitress with a pitted face, dark roots and blonde ponytail approaches with a smile as wide as the sky.

'Morning! What can I get ya?'

'Tea, please,' Twill says. The bag goes on the table, the stick against his chair.

'Been shopping?'

He feels no irritation and that pleases him. 'Yep.'

'Can I?' she asks, glancing down at the bag.

'Go ahead.'

She tucks her notepad into the belt of her apron and pins the pen behind an ear. 'Ooh.' She removes a shiny hardback from the bag. '*Animus. The Anatomy of Violence.*' She flips the book over and scans the back. 'Bit of light reading, eh?'

Twill nods.

'I'll get ya that tea,' she says.

272

Twill turns the hardback over and opens the cover. There's a black-and-white photo of Kay and a short bio. She looks ten years younger.

'Huh. I s'pose that's a recent pic, then?' He skips the front matter and reads the dedication.

For Lucan
Named for his disappearing act, but there when I needed him.
Rest in Peace

A lump grows in Twill's throat and he sniffs. The next page is the regimental photograph. He runs a finger across the faces of his friends. So many memories. Good and bad. Each person is numbered. Below the photo is a key identifying them by name. Familiar faces, so young. JR, Mincer, Beast, Cilla, Bridges, Ghost, Max, LoveSick, Lucan. Him. The last name is asterisked and sets off a giggle in his belly.

Jeremy Kyle*.

He follows the asterisk to the bottom of the page.

*Jeremy Kyle is not shown here. It is believed he was on covert operations when the photograph was taken. Research has not revealed any further information, so his role and the extent of his participation in Project Animus remain unknown.

The giggle turns into a snort, and then a low, rumbling chuckle. By the time the waitress returns with his tea, it's a runaway train, shaking his body. People on nearby tables look over.

'You okay?' the waitress asks.

'Yes,' he replies, wiping tears on the back of his hand. 'I'm bloody perfect.'